Something pin took a step toward his car, and a puff of gravel flew up at his feet. He stopped. Cassidy swung around toward the house and saw a curtain flutter. She screamed, "Run!" Instead Jasper fell flat on his face, his arms covering his head. "I said, run, Jasper!"

Holding a finger to his lips, he scrabbled like a lizard around the trunk of the Lamborghini. He rose on his knees, hoisted himself up to a crouch, and took off after her. They sprinted down the lane till they were out of sight of the house. "Hold on, Cass." Jasper panted. "We're out of range now. Let's walk back to Fort George. Maybe Flint's still there. We need to call the police."

The caretaker was nowhere to be seen. Cassidy slumped down on a rock. Jasper bent over, hands on knees, catching his breath. She indicated his pocket. "Why don't you just call 9-1-1 on your cell?"

"Left it in the car. Where's yours?"

"Left it in my purse. In the car."

"Well, Ollie, here's another fine mess you've gotten us into."

Praise for M. S. Spencer

The Penhallow Train Incident: "I suggest carving out some time before you start reading. Stockpile food, tell the family they're on their own, and lock the door."

~*Rochelle Weber, author and editor*

~*~

Flotsam and Jetsam: the Amelia Island Affair: "This book has it all. A smidgen of romance. A murder or two or more. Entertaining, amusing, and page turning."

~*Barbara Tobey, Netgalley reviewer*

~*~

Lapses of Memory: "Mark my words, you will laugh, grumble, and then laugh some more. This book was memorable."

~*Romance Authors at Large*

~*~

Artful Dodging: the Torpedo Factory Murders: "Spencer's characters are so real, it's easy to get drawn into their lives. About the time you think you've figured things out, she throws in a curve or two."

~*Mark Love, best-selling author*

~*~

The Pit and the Passion: Murder at the Ghost Hotel: "Interesting, creative plot and well-written dialog. Several twists…and plenty of tension."

~*Cindy M., NetGalley reviewer*

~*~

Orion's Foot: Myth, Mystery, & Romance in the Amazon: "[A] unique, compelling, fast-paced read. Petra and Emory are great, relatable characters, and the sizzle between them leaps off the page."

~*Alicia Dean, award-winning author*

Mrs. Spinney's Secret

by

M. S. Spencer

Mrs. Spinney's Secret

COPYRIGHT © 2021 by Meredith Ellsworth

Cover Art by *Tina Lynn Stout*

The Wild Rose Press, Inc.
PO Box 708
Adams Basin, NY 14410-0708
Visit us at www.thewildrosepress.com

Publishing History
First Crimson Rose Edition, 2021
Trade Paperback ISBN 978-1-5092-3448-6
Digital ISBN 978-1-5092-3445-5

Published in the United States of America

Dedication

To Polly
A Great Friend and a Wicked Good Egg

Chapter One

Nemo's, Camden, Maine, Saturday, June 17

The man shoved through the huddle of late night patrons, bellied up to the bar, and plunked down a credit card. "Martini, two olives. Keep 'em comin'."

The bartender, a pretty, if slightly faded, brunette in her early thirties, wiped her forehead. Her tired brown eyes searched the man's face. "You okay, sir?"

He loosened his tie and opened the collar button of his shirt. "Yeah. It's just that I've been on the road all day. Stiff. Bored." He looked up at her and attempted a sly grin. "At least I've got somethin' nice to look at while I get plowed. What's your name, hon?"

She dropped her eyes to a framed picture set below the bar, in which a pair of faces smiled up at her. The figure on the right, a slim, balding man of about forty wearing a plaid shirt, had an arm draped around a little boy. She took a deep breath. "Pauline. Yours?"

"Ahearn. Rick Ahearn. Travelin' salesman."

She glanced quickly at the photo and attempted a giggle. "They all say that."

"Well, it's *kinda* true. I freelance out of Boston." He hitched his belt up and grinned. "Up here scoutin' for Hollywood."

"Hollywood!" Pauline pulled a few strands out of her ponytail and curled them around her finger. She leaned over the counter. Shimmying her shoulders, she whispered in a husky voice, "You lookin' for the next Marilyn Monroe?"

He pinched her cheek. "I wish. No. I'm a location scout. Scopin' out good spots to make a movie. Ya know, like towns and houses that fit the profile. Hollywood loves Maine."

" 'Cause it's so beautiful?"

"No, 'cause it's cheap." He pushed his empty glass toward her. As he did, a beefy hand came down on his arm.

"Rick? Is that you? Rick Ahearn?"

He turned around and searched for his accoster. The pack parted slightly to reveal a man of medium height with a brush of dun-colored hair. "Yeah. Who's askin'?"

"It's me. Izzy. From Gloucester."

Ahearn's eyes widened. "As I live and breathe. It's been, what, twenty years! How are you?"

"Still alive." The man didn't grin.

"Siddown! Siddown." Ahearn waved a gracious hand. "Buy you a drink?"

"Sure. Mind if my buddy Bill joins us?" He gestured at a huge man standing nearby, his brawny arms bursting from the sleeves of his T-shirt like Hulk Hogan flexing his biceps.

"No problem."

The crowd surged, flowing around the little group. The next stool freed up, and Izzy lowered himself onto it, Bill filling in the space behind him. In contrast to Ahearn's thickening belly and sparse hair, the two men appeared muscular and trim. Bill sported a gray ponytail, while a neat beard covered Izzy's square chin and inched up his jaw to his ears. He held a finger up to catch Pauline's eye. "Beer, please. Whatever's on draft."

Bill held up a finger as well. "Same here."

Pauline filled two mugs and passed them across. Her eyes sought out Ahearn, but he had turned his attention to his friend.

"So…What've you been doin' since high school, Izzy?"

"I go by Bill now. Dumped the nickname when I left school."

"Good move. I'm guessin' you got sick of kids callin' you 'Dizzy Izzy.' " He scrunched up his eyes. "And 'Sissy Izzy.' Am I right?"

"Got it in one." Bill took a long pull at his drink.

Ahearn chuckled. "So…Bill…" He glanced from one man to the other. "People ever confuse you two?"

The two men looked blank. "No."

The big man muttered, "Lotta Bills out there. We ain't the only ones."

"Oh…er…Well. You still in Massachusetts, Izz…I mean, Bill?"

The man shook his head. "After graduation, I worked on Dad's boat out of Rockport for a while, but when they set the new fishing limits, he had to sell his business. So I decided to hitchhike out to California—try my luck there."

Ahearn checked out his friend's frayed jeans and worn polo shirt. "Looks like it didn't work out for you."

Bill's eyes narrowed. "You'd be wrong then. Just because I was voted biggest loser at Fernwood High doesn't mean I haven't made it."

Ahearn held up his hands in apology. "Hey, sorry!

I had nothin' to do with that. That bitch Marcia O'Henry? She had it in for you after you dumped her. Used her position as editor of the yearbook to rig the results of the poll."

"Really?" He seemed surprised. "I never knew that."

Ahearn accepted a second martini. "Yeah. A woman scorned, that sorta thing. No one ever told you?"

"No." The man's lips set in a thin line.

Ahearn studied his friend. "It's all water under the bridge now, right? Right? I mean, people do dumb things in high school." His eyes canted away, as though he had just recalled a few ill-advised stunts of his own.

Bill didn't say anything. He set his and the other Bill's empty mugs on the bar. Pauline refilled them and set out a bowl of peanuts, then took a tray of drinks to a table. Ponytail Bill reached over his friend's shoulder and grabbed a handful of nuts. He stood cracking them open and tossing them into his mouth. Ahearn eyed him, then turned to his friend and ventured cautiously, "So, whatcha doin' now?"

He put his mug down. "Ended up in LA. Got a nice gig with a studio there—Black Brothers. Worked crew on a buncha big movies—*Spynet*, *Mission to Pluto*, like that. Me and Bill here met up on the set of *Spynet*." Behind him, the other Bill nodded silently.

"That's neat. Wait—did you say Black Brothers?"

"Yeah, why?"

"I'm working for them too. Well, I have a contract with them. That's why I'm here in Camden. Location scout for their new disaster flick *American Waterloo*."

"Really? Small world. We just signed on for that

one."

Ahearn frowned. "Does that mean they're ratcheting up their schedule? I've still got some towns to check out."

"No, no. Bill has family here. Me, I decided to come out a few days early to do a little sightseeing."

Pauline returned and refilled the bowl. "Did I hear you say disaster movie, Rick? Like *Titanic*? Or *The Towering Inferno*?"

"Yeah, like them. Shipwrecks—lots of fireworks." He pumped a fist in the air. "*Pyoo pyoo! Boom! Wham!*" He lowered his arm. "According to the one-sheet, it's about this whole armada of ships sinking right here in Penobscot Bay. Horrific loss of life— except for the hero of course." He finished his martini.

Ponytail Bill opened his mouth, but Pauline interrupted. "Shipwrecks in Maine, huh. A sequel to *The Perfect Storm* maybe?"

Ahearn pinched his lips. "Nah—I think this one's historical. You know, one of those docu-dramas." He looked to the others for help, but neither responded.

"You must mean the Penobscot Expedition then. It wasn't like *Titanic* at all." She scooped up the peanut shells that littered the bar and dumped them in the trash. "It was a naval battle. If I remember my sixth-grade history right, it was the worst American defeat of the Revolutionary War. Or at least the most embarrassing."

"Oh, yeah?" Bill yawned. "Luckily, I don't have to worry about that. I just do my job—and it's not reading no history." The other Bill agreed.

Ahearn took the opportunity to lure the bartender's interest back around to himself. He leaned over the rail, unaware of the speck of green olive stuck to his lower lip. "*I'd* like to know more, Pauline."

She gave him a speculative look. "O…kay. See, it was right in the middle of the war. The redcoats snuck across the Canadian border and established an outpost at Castine." She waved vaguely toward the back of the bar. "That's a town over on Blue Hill. The idea was to settle loyalists—"

"You mean Tories?"

She nodded. "Yeah. The poor slobs were being persecuted by the patriots, and the English wanted a safe haven for them. They also needed to block the privateers who were marauding in the area. So they waltzed into American territory, bold as a burglar with his own key. It really pissed off the revolutionary leaders in Boston. See, Maine was part of Massachusetts then—"

The two men from Gloucester growled simultaneously, "We know."

Pauline made a face. "*So*…They decided to put together an armada to oust the interlopers."

"Armada," Ahearn repeated, his voice glimmering with satisfaction. "See? I was right."

Ponytail Bill picked a shell out of his teeth. "What happened then?"

She put her elbows on the bar. "The dumbass Americans screwed it up big time and ended up burning their ships and running away. They abandoned all their weapons and supplies." She paused, and her eyes twinkled. "They also left behind—at least according to local legend—a million dollars in gold."

Her last words seemed to have struck a chord, for other patrons drew near. An older woman in an Oscar de la Renta sheath and rope of perfectly matched pearls, who had been listening intently, pressed even closer to the men. Ahearn spluttered, "Gold! What was all the money for?"

Pauline shrugged. "No one knows for sure, but my teacher said one of the ships was secretly headed to Canada to bribe the Indians."

"To do what?"

"To come in on the side of the rebels against the British."

Ahearn snorted. "Why not just give 'em whiskey? Indians'd probably prefer firewater. Waste of good gold, I say." Oblivious to the disgusted reactions from the other customers, he wiped his mouth with a napkin, finally dislodging the olive.

The well-dressed woman carefully set her wine glass down next to him. Pauline picked it up. "That was a Pouilly-Fuissé, right?" The woman nodded, her eyes not leaving Ahearn's face.

Pauline handed her the refilled glass and then raised her voice. "Of course"—her mouth twitched— "the gold might not have been British at all. It might have belonged to the Baron."

Everyone's attention snapped back. "Huh? Baron who?"

"The Baron de Saint-Castin. He established a trading post at Castine and made a fortune. When everybody began squabbling over the land, he split. Rumor has it he took several chests of money with him, but he was forced to bury them somewhere before he could escape."

"Where did he go?"

"Back to France eventually." She split open a peanut with her nail and popped it into her mouth. "A hundred years later, some loggers found French coins in a field near the town. Could've been his."

"Huh. Okay, so maybe it's not a disaster movie—or even a war movie. Maybe it's a treasure-hunt movie." Rick winked.

Ponytail Bill mused, "Could be somethin' in it. Might ask the folks if they've heard the story."

Rick's friend rolled his eyes. "No skin off my nose *what* they make, as long as we get paid."

"You got my vote." Ahearn put down his glass and swatted his friend's shoulder. "Hey, while I'm up here in Maine, I'd like to see what you all do. Never been to a Black Brothers movie set. Can you get me in?"

Bill shook himself. "I can try, but they have to decide on the locations first. Can't build the sets until they do."

"Oh, right. About that. I found a great site." He patted his pocket. "Got to remember to leave a message for that PR gal."

"Sally Crook?"

"Yeah, that's her. Only one at the studio I've talked to."

"You haven't met her?"

"Nope. I do most of my work by email—more efficient than traipsing back and forth to their office in California. Why?" He ogled Pauline. "Is she hot?"

Ponytail Bill guffawed. "Let's just say, you might wanna keep your contacts online."

Ahearn patted Pauline's arm. "So I guess it's you and me, kid." She didn't pull away.

His friend handed his glass back to Pauline for a refill. "So, what's the site?"

"It's a little village called Amity Landing, just

south of the town of Penhallow."

The woman in pearls paused, her wine glass halfway to her mouth. She gently placed it back on the bar and made the universal sign for the bill. Pauline handed her the tab and took her credit card. She signed and disappeared back into the scrum.

Pauline stuck the receipt on the spindle. "Did you say Amity Landing? I live there—or rather, just about a mile away."

"Oh, yeah?" Ahearn smirked. "Bet you got a nice place."

Ponytail Bill interrupted, a little too loudly. "So you found a village. That's great, but we need an actual house to film in. One we can take over."

"I know. In fact, I've found the perfect one right in Amity. Place owned by a Mrs. Grace Spinney. It's right on the water and sooo New England. It would work for the captain's house or maybe even for the Canadian scenes—"

Just then Ponytail Bill's elbow jerked, knocking the other Bill's mug out of his hands. Beer spilled over the bar. He watched as Pauline mopped it up, making no move to help. At one point, he seemed to notice her glare and said absently, "Sorry." He checked his watch. "Oops. We gotta go. You said you'd drop me off at the hotel."

"Oh, yeah. I forgot." Bill turned to Ahearn. "It's been great seeing you, Rick. Thanks for the beer."

The scout caught his arm. "Where are you staying? Maybe we could get together for another drink."

He shook himself free. "Up the coast at a town called Penhallow, but I think when the rest of the crew gets here, the studio's going to put us up in RVs somewhere." He hopped off the stool and disappeared down the stairs. Ponytail Bill grabbed a last handful of peanuts and followed him.

Ahearn turned back to Pauline. "Sheesh. Not much for genteel conversation, are they? Sorry about that, dearie." He put his glass down. "I didn't want to tell Izzy the truth, but Marcia didn't fix the poll. We all voted him Biggest Loser. You know, the kid who always got a flat tire on the way to the prom, and never caught the fly ball." He smiled at Pauline. "Forget about them. So, when do you get off?"

"About ten." She checked the picture under the bar. Her face crumpled.

"Whassa matter?"

"Nothing."

"Come on." He leered at her, but in a friendly way.

"It's…oh…I feel so alone now." She angrily wiped a tear away.

Ahearn bent toward her, his face sympathetic, his words a bit slurred. "Tell me about it."

"It's just…it's just losing them both. It's so unfair."

"Who?"

"My son, and then my husband." She told him about the diagnosis, about the slow march to death that began when Noah was five and ended when he was nine. She described the mounting medical bills. "We had no way to pay for them on Jerry's sales commissions, so we skipped out and came up here. Things started to improve—we both got jobs. Jerry worked as a carpenter's assistant, and the pay was decent. We even talked about paying off some of the debts…but then he got hurt and was laid off. When I lost my job too, we were back to square one."

"Who'd you work for?"

"A video production company over in Augusta. I do—did—public relations. Loved the work. They sent me all around the state. Even met a few local celebrities." She gazed damply at Ahearn. "I guess in your line of work you meet lotsa A-listers, huh?"

"Nah. Like I said, I just communicate with the PR person by email or phone." He looked Pauline up and down. "Say, maybe she could use an assistant. I can ask her if she needs help."

"Really? That would be swell."

He grew expansive. "No problem. Just give me your phone number." He blinked. "Er…you did say you lost your husband too?"

Pauline's face, which had brightened at his suggestion, reverted to its customary gloom. "Yes. What with all the bad luck, Jerry went downhill fast." She glanced at Ahearn's glass. "Started drinking. Then one day he packed his stuff and lit out. I haven't heard from him since."

"Think he's dead?"

Pauline gave him a curious look. "No idea."

He must have realized how callous he sounded, for he set down his drink and focused on her. "I'm sorry. I'll bet it was awful tough. What happened after that?"

After a minute, she told him. How she'd gone from a nice bungalow in Penhallow to a basement apartment in a cottage south of Amity Landing. "I had nowhere else to turn. Mrs. Roybal was my mother's best friend. She took me in and, bless her heart, only charges me for utilities. The money I make bartending is keeping me above water, but"—her voice broke—"I don't know why I want to. Now that they're gone."

Ahearn, his eyes half shut, managed a groggy, "There, there." He shook himself. "I'll check with Sally. I have to call her about the Amity house tonight anyway. Maybe we can work something out." He gave her a smile. "Say, even if she doesn't need someone in the PR department, I can ask her to put in a good word for you—maybe get you a bit part in the movie. You're pretty enough."

She simpered. "That's sweet of you. Actually, I *have* dabbled in theatre. After my acclaimed portrayal of Margaret Thatcher"—she struck a melodramatic pose—"they asked me to stick with building scenery."

"Ha-ha."

She grew thoughtful. "Now, my husband Jerry—he was real active in his high school musicals. He even had a role in an off-Broadway show once. When we moved back to Penhallow, he joined the Water Street Maskers." Her eyes filmed with tears. "His last show was one of those English operettas—Gilbert and Sullivan, I think."

Ahearn perked up. "Oh, yeah? I love their stuff. Lessee—was it *The Yeomen of the Guard*? *The Mikado*?"

She shrugged. "I don't remember. He was in the chorus—danced too. He looked so handsome in his costume." She lapsed back into despondency.

The conversation seemed to give Ahearn a second wind. "Listen, Pauline, I'm happy to see what I can do. There are all sorts of positions on a movie set." He waved behind him. "Bill—the man who was just here? My high school friend? We could ask him too—I'll bet he can find you something. What do you say?"

Just then a buxom woman, her unnaturally red hair cascading down her back in equally unnatural curls, bustled in. "Pauline, your shift is over. What are you hanging around for? You better keep to the terms of your probation, or I'll have to let you go." She surveyed Ahearn with an experienced eye. "You ready for your check, mister?"

He gave Pauline a sidelong look. "Yeah." He signed it, then remarked casually, "Say, you want I should escort you home? We could talk over ideas about a job. Happy to."

Assorted emotions passed over Pauline's face. She seemed to come to a decision. "Sure." She took off her apron, and they walked out of the bar into the night.

The manager stared after them. After a moment's thought, she picked up the phone.

Chapter Two

Maude's cottage, Penhallow, Wednesday, June 21

"I tell you, my dear, Penhallow is a *very* small town." Maude took a noisy slug of her coffee and set the mug on the porch railing. She settled back in the old green Adirondack chair and patted her companion's knee.

"You mean insular? Close-minded? Inbred?"

The older woman, her bright brown eyes as sharp as a squirrel's, contrived to look affronted. "Now, Cassidy Jane, Griffin Tate—being from away—can say that. You can't." She ran a hand through her short, iron-gray hair. "You have to stand with the rest of us Mainers. It's statutory."

Cassidy shrugged. "Griffin may think he can call us names because he's not a local, but it's the other way around. If you're from away, you *have* to be polite. I'm allowed to malign my home state if I want to. So, yeah, Penhallow is a small town. What's your point?"

"Well…it's like those Agatha Christie stories. You know, the ones with the little old lady who knits."

"Miss Marple?"

"That's the one. She was always on about how everything that happens in the big city happens in a village as well."

"Meaning human nature is the same everywhere?"

Maude sang in an atrocious Cockney accent, "It's the sayme the ol' world over, it's the poor, what gets the blayme."

Cassidy cut her off. "I knew I was going to regret inviting you to perform 'Songs that Killed Vaudeville' at last summer's talent show." She lowered her brows at her friend. "I'll bite. Why bring Miss Marple up now?"

The older woman allowed her gaze to dwell on the hummingbird sipping from her hanging geranium. "Are you ready for a juicy slice of gossip? There's been another death in Amity Landing."

Cassidy took a deliberate sip from her cup. "Ah."

Maude raised a brow. "You don't seem surprised. Either you're not interested, or you've already heard about it."

Cassidy shot her an amused glance. "Not interested? Me?"

"Okay. So what have you heard that I haven't?"

Her companion picked up a piece of canvas on which a nativity scene was outlined in blue. She pushed a needle up and through, drawing the yarn with it, and said darkly, "It happened at Black Rock."

Maude let out a horse laugh. "Black Rock? You been reading Toby's Zane Grey paperbacks again? No, it happened on Maple Street."

"Yes, that's right." Cassidy deepened her voice in a fair imitation of Vincent Price. "Rose Dingle was found dead in her kitchen. It was a grisly scene."

"She died from a heart attack."

"Aha! So they would have you believe." Cassidy put down her needlepoint and spoke confidentially. "Did you know they found bare footprints on the back porch?"

"If you mean Harold's prints, yes. So what?"

"Eunice Merithew has been gunning for him."

"Eunice Merithew doesn't own a gun. And anyway, she's a pacifist."

"Figure of speech. She asked Sam the rent-a-cop to hunt him down."

"Good." Maude gave her head a gratified shake. "Nasty fellow."

"Just because Harold raided Rose's store of old Halloween candy doesn't mean he killed her." Cassidy raised her eyes to the clouds. "He's really rather sweet, you know. I was taking the trash out one night, and there he was, mooning at me."

"Showing you his butt?"

Cassidy cast a gimlet eye at her friend. "Excuse me?"

"He dropped his trou?"

"Don't be silly, Maude. Raccoons don't wear trousers. He gave me this pleading look that said, 'Can't we just be friends?' "

"I see. And the fact that his tiny, human-like hands were covered in last night's spaghetti didn't give you pause?"

Cassidy finished her coffee. "At any rate, poor Eunice's plans for his demise have run into a rather chunky snag. Deirdre McGilvery is trying to start a PETA chapter in Penhallow. I believe the first order of business is to denounce anyone who disparages our friends and neighbors, the raccoons."

"Huh." Maude popped a piece of cruller in her mouth. "Typical Red Hat Society shenanigans. Deirdre is getting loonier by the day."

"So is Eunice. But you digress. We were talking

about the latest unfortunate demise."

"At Black Rock—wherever that is. You really ought to write your stories down, Cass. You could have a display and sell them in your bookstore. Let's see…we'll call this one 'Gunfight at the Green Store Corral.' " Maude chortled.

"Actually, the corpse was wearing a sailor suit—you know, blue, with bell bottoms. And one of those corny white hats…" Cassidy knit her brows. "What are they called? Dixie caps, I think."

Maude gaped at her. "I thought Rose Dingle was the one who expired."

"She did. Of a heart attack. Like you said. When Harold snuck up behind her and nipped her ankle."

"So he *is* the culprit."

"In his defense, she had discovered his stash of M&Ms and was in the process of stuffing them down the disposal."

"Don't tell that to Deirdre." Maude clucked her tongue. "If not Rose, then who are you talking about?"

Cassidy let the anticipation build before answering. "Toby Quimby told me Newt Slugwater found a dead man down near Kelly's Cove last Monday. He's hoping the sheriff's office can take the lead on the case, but the state police are making noises."

Maude set down her mug with extreme caution. "A dead man. Kelly's Cove. Shit."

"Maude!"

"I'm sorry, dear, but I don't think I want to go through another murder fest."

"What? Oh, you mean the train incident in Penhallow. But that really had nothing to do with Amity Landing. Or Kelly's Cove."

"What are you talking about? Of course it did. John and Mary Pinckney were from Amity Landing. I taught Mary math. Come to think of it, I taught John as well."

Cassidy picked up her needlepoint again. "You know, I always believed that Mary only went along for the ride."

"Well, you should have said something." Maude examined the canvas in Cassidy's hands. "What's that you're working on?"

"Another Christmas stocking. This one's for Toby's new granddaughter."

"I notice you're not embroidering a name on it."

"Not yet. Jury's still out. Edna Mae assumed the child would be called Clementine after her mother, but apparently Rodney's wife has a spine."

"Yes, I gathered that at the christening, when she loudly interrupted Reverend Peavey mid-sentence and announced her daughter would be named Ursuline, after her French ancestor."

Cassidy grinned. "What a glorious melee that was—right there in First Congregational Church! Kept Penhallow busy for weeks."

With an effort, Maude wrangled her expression into one of disapproval. "Edna Mae says the worst part is that the ancestor—Ursuline d'Abbadie—came from Castine."

"Not Penhallow? Oh, my."

The two women fell silent, mulling over the stigma attached to any kinship connection with the next peninsula over, the oft-vilified (by Penhallowans, anyway) Blue Hill region. After a suitable interlude, Maude mumbled, "Well, to give her her due, Ursuline *was* the daughter of the founder of Castine."

"The Baron?"

"Yes. One of twelve children born to Jean Vincent d'Abbadie, Baron de Saint-Castin, and his two Indian…wives." She peeked at Cassidy.

Her friend presumed Maude had stopped short of saying "squaws" in deference to Cassidy's lineage. Everyone in the county knew she'd inherited her café au lait skin, as well as the shimmering ebony hair that fell to her waist, from her Passamaquoddy forbears. She said mildly, "I believe they were Abenaki princesses. The first wife was the daughter of the chief, the sachem. So…native nobility."

"Yes, there is that." Maude finished off the last cruller. "Now where were we? Oh, yes. A dead sailor was found in the bay. What else have you heard?"

"Not in the bay. On the floating mussel barge. That's all I know. Toby has been very tight-lipped—"

"Which means he knows nothing."

Cassidy sighed. She knew Maude was right, but it was so frustrating. *I mean, a man dressed like the figure on a box of Cracker Jack and the sheriff can't find out who he is?* "Couldn't get a thing out of his deputies either. We need Rachel here. And Griffin. They'd solve the mystery."

Maude sniffed. "It's not like they're detectives. They really only solved the train mystery by default."

"That's not fair. Rachel figured out everything but the first murder." She began to roll up her needlework. "Speaking of our amateur sleuths, have you heard from them?"

Maude gazed out at her front yard, where her neighbor was stealthily raking his leaves into her garden. She got up and leaned over the porch railing.

"Godfrey, I'm only warning you once."

The man shaded his eyes and pretended not to see her. He waited a face-saving minute, then quietly raked the leaves back into his yard.

"Maude? Rachel and Griffin?"

Maude's brow furrowed. Cassidy knew she missed her friends. Griffin and Rachel Tate's adventure with long-lost tombs and hidden treasure had whetted their appetite for more. Once they solved last year's murders in Penhallow, they left for a protracted trek around the globe. "Just the one text as they left the airport in N'Djamena."

"Huh?"

"Capital of Chad. Rachel said something about H. Rider Haggard being wrong. That's the last missive I've gotten from them."

Cassidy pressed her lips together. "It's hardly what I'd call a honeymoon. Wandering around the Sahara with only one extra pair of underwear, in a totally dry country—by which I mean no booze—just to find some stupid priceless artifact."

Maude's eyes glazed over. "So romantic." She sat up. "Why in hell can't they ever search for buried treasure somewhere within driving distance?"

"You forget—they did." Cassidy stood. "Speaking of treasures, I've got to get back to the store. Leon is dropping off a box of donations from the Freedom library. I always find something interesting. Freedom folk read a lot."

"The summer season means an influx of used books, doesn't it?"

"Yes, and Mindful Books needs some new fuel to see us through the winter."

****

Mindful Books, Wednesday, June 21

Maude waved her off the porch of her tiny yellow cottage on Elm Street, and Cassidy drove into the commercial district of Penhallow to her used bookstore. Felicitously situated at the principal intersection of the town, it sat across from the police station. She found the sheriff's wife, Edna Mae Quimby, sitting on the little bench by the store entrance.

"There you are, Cassidy Jane Beauvoir. You were supposed to open at two." She would have looked more imposing if her hat hadn't taken that moment to drop down her forehead, obscuring her left eye. She squinted at Cassidy. "Well?"

"Sorry, Mrs. Quimby."

"I'm not my mother-in-law, Cassidy Jane. As I've told you myriad times, you may call me Edna Mae." She patted a gray ringlet that had escaped from her old-fashioned bun. "Makes me feel younger."

"All right, Edna Mae it is." Cassidy smiled to herself. The formal address followed by the gracious invitation to use her given name was a ritual Edna Mae insisted upon. "Was there something I can help you find?"

The old lady stood up and straightened her voluminous skirt. "No, no. I had merely stopped to take a breath here and noticed your sign." She pointed at it, rather unnecessarily in Cassidy's view. "See? Tuesdays, Wednesdays, Thursdays, Open 2 p.m. to 5 p.m." She glared at Cassidy. "It's very clearly marked."

"Why, yes it is." She decided to change the subject. "Were you going to see the sheriff?"

Edna Mae's chin quivered petulantly. "It's about

that dead man who bobbed up in Kelly's Cove. The sailor. Quite unacceptable. Poor Audrey Carver. She was taking little Maisie for a walk down by the water when Newt Slugwater brought him ashore. She was the first to see the corpse—aside from Slugwater, of course."

"Oh my God, how awful!" Cassidy had to make sure she'd registered the requisite shock before asking her questions. The local ladies of the Red Hat Society were sticklers for proper etiquette. "What did he look like?"

"Slugwater? I swear, next to him Bert Weems could be Mr. Clean. Deirdre says she saw him stealing clothes from the Goodwill dumpster. Eunice says—"

"I meant the dead man."

Edna Mae shook her umbrella at Cassidy. "What do you think he looked like? He was dead. Had been for some time." She said it with some relish. "All wizened and pruny. Must have been in the water for *days*."

"In the water? I heard he was found on the mussel barge."

"What? Oh, yes. His throat slit, I hear."

"Throat slit! So he was murdered?" When Edna Mae didn't answer, she promised herself she'd reinvigorate her efforts to get the real scoop from Edna Mae's husband. *Wait a minute…how did she describe him?* "You said he was 'pruny.' If he was on the barge, and not in the water, how did he get pruny?"

Edna Mae was not the sort to admit she lacked a complete grasp of the facts. Instead, she bowed with ill grace to Cassidy and marched across the street to the police station, narrowly avoiding a passing pickup truck. Cassidy unlocked the door to her store and went inside.

Leon, the Freedom volunteer librarian, had left two large boxes by the back door, and she spent a happy couple of hours sifting through the literary detritus left behind by vacationers. She noticed a marked increase in hardbacks, which seemed odd. *Tough to lug one of these five-pounders around in your purse.* Plus, the authors tended to be those that always topped the best-seller charts. She sighed. *I wouldn't mind if they wrote well, but it's so painful to slog through the repetitive phrases and mutilated syntax. Not to mention the head hopping.* She longed to find a Jane Austen or even a Tom Wolfe hidden under the stacks of mysteries by lady writers whose heroines always seemed to run bakeries.

The bell rang as a customer entered. "Hello?"

"I'm in the back." She dusted off her knees and headed to the front of the store. "Can I help you?"

A man about her own age stood uncertainly on the threshold. "I…uh."

She took a minute to look him over. His gray eyes sparkled behind rimless glasses. As she drew closer, she realized he was much taller than she originally thought. *He's hunching his shoulders. Is he shy? Or embarrassed about his height?* Being a short person who was forced to look up to so many people she didn't look up to, she had trouble sympathizing. His large hands dangled from lightly muscled arms almost like an afterthought. Someone—a girlfriend?—had cut his fawn-colored hair rather haphazardly, making it stick out at uninhibited angles. *Probably an ex-girlfriend now.* One tendril trickled down his temple, lending him a slightly roguish air. "Are you looking for something in particular?"

"I…uh…yes." He took a step forward. "Do you have anything on Maine history?"

At last. Thank you, Lord. "Yes, indeed. We have a whole section on it. Right this way." She led him to a corner in the back of the shop, where, in an excess of optimism ridiculed by her friends, Cassidy had amassed a fairly significant collection of works on Maine. Someday—she would remark when in her cups—her prince would come, demanding the rare copy of B. F. Decosta's 1871 *Rambles in Mount Desert* she had found in Bert Weems's hay loft. She started to speak, but the man was staring with almost carnal avidity at the shelves. "I'll leave you to it then, shall I?"

She retreated to her desk and watched him from under her lashes. He perused the shelves with great deliberation, his eyes inches from the book spines. *Near-sighted?* Still, they were an awfully nice shade. *Soft gray, like the gentle ashes left from a romantic campfire.* She shook herself. *Of course, the milky color could be due to his myopia.*

He pulled a leather-bound book out and opened it at random, then turned to the title page. His slim fingers handled the elegant vellum with a kind of awestruck affection. He dropped it on the table next to him and continued down the shelf. At one point, he stopped, cast a stealthy glance in her direction, then slipped a book out. Turning his back to her, he stood holding it a minute, his back rigid. *What caught his eye?* He straightened and lifted his heels as though about to sprint out of the store. She half rose to forestall his exit. When instead he reverently placed the book on his pile, she relaxed, feeling foolish. *Still, I intend to find out which book made him go all skittery like that.*

Chapter Three

Mindful Books, Wednesday, June 21

An hour later, the young man lugged an armload of books to the counter. "How much do I owe you?"

"Let's see…" Cassidy checked the flyleaf of each book for the price, glancing at him periodically in case he gave any hint of which one had been so interesting, but his eyes never left her face. She looked at the total and sucked in a breath. "A hundred and eighty-six dollars." She added quickly, "That includes tax of course."

He handed her a card without flinching. Cassidy flinched though. Incomes were pretty low in this part of the country, and Mainers tended toward parsimony. Two hundred dollars would pay for a half cord of firewood. Spending it on books was too extravagant even for Cassidy. She began to plan her winter vacation. *Maybe I could even spring for Florida this year.* As she ran the card through the machine, she asked casually, "You're from away, aren't you?"

He stared at her, bemused. "I beg your pardon?"

"I mean, you're not from Maine?"

"No. I'm from California."

Her eyes widened. The West Coast! Maine didn't have many visitors from the other side of the continent, at least on the midcoast. Maude used to say

Californians didn't even know there *were* other states in the union. "Cleveland, Ohio, is like another planet to someone from Malibu." *Of course, she's never actually been to Malibu.* She inspected the young man while piling the books into a box. "So…what brings you to the Pine Tree State?"

His glance darted once around the store, then he leaned toward her and whispered, "I'm making a movie."

"What?"

"A movie." He started to put a finger to his lips, but dropped it.

"Why are you whispering?"

The question seemed to surprise him. "I'm told people don't like it when a movie production crew descends on their town."

"Really? Why not?"

He just smiled. "You'll see." He picked up his box, nodded to her, and left. Cassidy checked the time. *Five o'clock.* She closed up and drove the four miles down Route 1 to Amity Landing. As she made the right turn onto Center Street, she noticed a line of black Land Rovers parked along Broadway in front of the inn and down Maple to Chick and Sissy Ketchum's house, which doubled as the real estate office and gathering place for the village. Little clumps of people milled around, sneaking peeks into the cars. She pulled her Subaru, its rusty old chassis squealing in protest, into her carport at the top of the hill, and walked back down.

Chick stood on his front stoop, nose in the air and jaws grinding like a furious baby hippo. Sissy had stepped down to the street and was talking to three men in identical black suits. Cassidy looked them over. *The*

27

Men in Black? Feds? Gumshoes? Thank God Chick had sent out the attack team: Sissy—maybe five feet tall, close-cropped red hair, and a nose like a tater tot. At her side yipped Thor, a tiny, nasty terrier, known in Amity as the Scourge of Maine. She approached warily from behind. "Sissy? What's going on?"

The little woman forgot to alter her expression when she whirled around, and Cassidy caught the full force of classic Mainer distrust. The grimace dissipated at the sight of her. "Oh, Cassidy, I didn't know you were there." She jerked her head at the three men and whispered loudly, "Weirdos."

Cassidy wondered if she knew—or cared—that they could hear her. Up close, each was quite different from the other. One—tall, aristocratic, and tanned—stood a little apart. The other two resembled no one so much as Oliver Hardy and Stan Laurel. Laurel scratched under his collar, and Hardy patted his bald head nervously. She held out a hand to the tall one. "How do you do? I'm Cassidy Jane Beauvoir, chairman of the Board of Overseers for Amity Landing. And you are?"

"Philip MacEwan. I was given Mrs. Ketchum's name. As I was explaining to her, we have chosen this town as the site for our next movie. We shall be shooting *American Waterloo: The Rout of the Penobscot Expedition*, in Amity Landing. We're here to go over the ground rules."

Now there's a good way to start a relationship. "Oh?"

He hesitated only a moment before indicating the fat man, who was wringing out a sopping handkerchief and reapplying it to his forehead. "This is my producer,

Oliver Hadley." He crooked a finger. "And this is our line manager, Stan Lowry." The third man stepped forward, his eyes blinking rapidly. MacEwan looked around vaguely. "I don't know where Sally Crook has got to. She's our location manager and publicist. She should have been in contact with you."

"And you are?"

"I told you, Philip MacEwan."

Does he assume I know the name? Should I be hyperventilating? Gushing? Asking for his autograph? Jackass. She waited, a bland smile plastered on her face. *Eventually he'll have to tell me.*

He must have gotten the point, for he barked, "I'm a general partner in Black Brothers Studios." He looked down his nose at her. "Perhaps you've heard of us."

"Er…" She pretended to think. "You're from Hollywood?"

MacEwan's mouth snapped shut. Oliver Hardy's doppelgänger took up the slack. "Yes, ma'am. Black Brothers has produced seven Academy Award winners. *Beethoven's Paramour*? *Pirates of the Spanish Main*? You ever hear of *them*?"

"*Hmm.* Yes, I think so." She toyed with the idea of continuing the charade that she wasn't familiar with the hottest movie production company in America. *But…wow…*Pirates of the Spanish Main*!*

MacEwan added, "My son, Jasper, will be the director." For the first time he exhibited some uneasiness. "It's his first film."

Cassidy pounced. "Well, Mr. MacEwan, before we give you permission to work here, we'll need to know a lot more about you and what this whole thing entails."

"And about the film," interjected Sissy with only

slightly less disdain.

"Certainly. We're staying at the Penhallow Harbor Inn." He handed Cassidy a card. "Come by at ten tomorrow." He dismissed her with a nod and turned to his companions. "Find Sally Crook *now*. I'm heading back to the hotel." He walked away from an audience struck dumb by what Cassidy later pronounced as his Olympian insolence. Even Thor was speechless.

The caravan of Land Rovers had rolled out of the village when Chick remarked heavily, "What the hell?"

****

Amity Landing, Wednesday, June 21

Moments later, a gaggle of older women of various sizes and shapes pulled up in an ancient, turquoise Cadillac. One massive female heaved herself out of the back seat and stood holding her chest and panting. "Cassidy Jane Beauvoir! What's this we hear about movie people invading Amity Landing?"

"Hi, Deirdre. We don't have many details yet." Cassidy gestured down the road. "A Mr. MacEwan wants to do a film here. We're supposed to meet tomorrow to iron out the details." *Might as well at least try to sound in charge.*

Another woman, this one matchstick thin, slid out from behind the wheel. She towered over Cassidy, her hawk-like nose flaring. "Well, I think it's frightfully exciting! A Hollywood movie! Katie down at Durkee's says they're asking around for extras. I do hope it's a horror movie!" Her eyes sparkled.

This from the woman who took to her bed after seeing Slugwater's corpse?

"Control yourself, Audrey." Deirdre was stern. "I doubt whether they expect the Red Hat Society to stand in the background waving flags. We'd be much too conspicuous."

"*Hmmph.*"

A battered yellow Volkswagen hatchback, spewing exhaust, pulled in behind the Cadillac, and a tall woman in a tight knit dress got out. Cassidy was struck by her most obvious attribute—those items of a woman's anatomy known in less rarified circles as "sweater monkeys." It took a serious effort to raise her eyes to the woman's face. Though not what would normally be called pretty, it nonetheless projected intelligence and a certain competence. She retrieved a briefcase and a large, flowered tote bag from the rear seat, checked something on her phone, then directed her gaze to the group of women. "I'm looking for a Cassidy Jane Beauvoir?"

Cassidy stepped away from the Red Hats. "I am she."

"Ah. Hi. I'm Sally Crook, publicist and general factotum for Black Brothers Studios. They said at that little store out by Route 1 that I'd find you here. This *is* Amity Landing, right?" She paused to survey her surroundings.

Tiny cottages lined the lanes surrounding a large green. Behind her rose the nineteenth-century inn—a three-story pile, now converted into apartments. An old lady rocked on one of the balconies, keeping an eye on her domain.

Cassidy waved at her. "Good afternoon, Mrs. Puddleby!"

The woman stared coldly down at her. *Whew, if looks could kill.* Cassidy guessed the doyenne of Amity Landing hadn't forgiven her for officiating at the late

Commodore Puddleby's ignominious loss to the Drinkwater elementary school sailing team.

Down the hill, a mother and her toddler fished off a large floating dock, while a sailboat luffed its sails as it gently pulled into its mooring. A man in fishing waders trudged up the hill past a couple of boys, who paused in their basketball game to gawk at Sally.

"Yes, you have arrived at the village of Amity Landing." With an eye on Mrs. Puddleby, Cassidy raised her voice. "And this is Puddleby Park."

A wave of whispers spread across the grass and up onto the porches.

"Black Brothers Studios. That's the big movie company!"

"She's from Hollywood? Neato."

One of the basketball players said loudly, "Maybe she's recruiting!"

"Yeah, right. Like you have a chance to be a child star, Lucas."

As the boys fell to wrestling, Sally beckoned to Cassidy. "May I talk to you?"

Cassidy did not move. She could feel Sissy beside her rolling her hands into fists. "Sure. What can I do for you?"

"I understand you spoke with Mr. MacEwan. He'll fill you in tomorrow morning, but meanwhile, could you help me? We sent an advance man to identify possible sites for the production. We'd received a text from him a couple of days ago with directions to…" She checked her phone again. "Number 2 Bay Street. Place belonging to a Grace Spinney. Can you show me where it is?"

"Mrs. Spinney's house? Sure, but she's not here."

Cassidy pointed down the street. Just where the paved road veered right and a park began sat a beautiful New England house nestled into the bank. "See? No flag."

Sally seemed confused. "Huh?"

Sissy spat out impatiently, "You got a flea in your ear? The lady said 'no flag.' "

Cassidy explained. "When Mrs. Spinney's in residence, both the Canadian and the American flags are displayed."

"Canadian?" Sally stared at her. "Why?"

"She's from Nova Scotia." Cassidy hesitated. "I think she—her family, that is—never quite got over Canada losing Maine to the upstart Americans." She waited for the customary laugh, but none came.

Instead, the publicity agent pulled a clipboard from her tote bag and consulted it. "Right. Says here she's back home in Canada. My people have been in touch with her. She's given permission to Black Brothers to use her house if I decide it's suitable." She looked up. "But I can't seem to find the advance man who did the initial legwork."

"What does he look like?"

She shook her head. "No clue. He's a subcontractor from Boston. Somebody in the HR office in Burbank hired him to come up here and find good sites. He found this one and was headed to some town called"—she checked the clipboard again—"Castine. That's the last I heard from him." She crossed an item off. "Typical of these freelancers. Can't trust 'em to follow through. So, can you take me to the house?"

Cassidy turned to Sissy. "Do you have a key?"

"I'll get it." She ran inside the office and came out with a skeleton key. "No one's been in there since last

September. It might need airing."

"Oh, we'll only occupy the ground floor."

"Huh?"

Leaving a sputtering Sissy behind, Cassidy led Sally to the house. The traditional white clapboard with green trim, it sat on a small promontory overlooking the bay and a rocky beach. A tall flagpole stood proudly at the edge of a stone retaining wall. Wooden shutters enclosed the second-story windows, while two dormers were tucked under the eaves. A thick vine exploding with red trumpet flowers snaked up the rain spout.

They walked down a flight of stone steps and around to a small porch. The key let them into a tiny kitchen. A refrigerator the size of an old-fashioned icebox buzzed quietly in a corner next to a deep enameled sink. Taking up the opposite wall was a battered wooden table. Curtains covered in appliquéd apples and hens let little light in. Sally gazed with concern at the appliances. She finally said, "I guess they eat out a lot."

Cassidy didn't tell her that Mrs. Spinney was happier with a kitchen her own age—ninety-three come August. "She doesn't really cook much anymore. Did you require a modern kitchen?"

"No, no. We bring in a fully equipped canteen for the actors and stage hands. I'll have to find a spot for that too." She wandered down the hall to a spacious living room. Three-quarters of it was glassed in, overlooking Penobscot Bay. She whistled. "Jeepers, this is perfect!"

Cassidy agreed. Grace Spinney's was her favorite house in Amity Landing. Sure, she loved her own cottage, but it would be nice to have a place where you didn't have to sit in a corner of the porch and cock your head just so in order to get a clear view of the water.

Sally stepped to the front and marked something on her pad. "Okay. That's done. Now, do you have any open space—a park or whatever—where we can set up the editing area and the canteen?"

An hour later, Cassidy dragged herself up her steps. They had walked all over Amity, a spot famous for its steep hills, while Sally made numerous notes in a mysterious code on her pad. Cassidy wasn't sure what the owners of the cottages on Beacham or Nobby parks would say when they found tents and wires filling their front yards, but she didn't expect it to be positive. Sally hadn't satisfactorily explained how all this was supposed to work.

It occurred to her that she should talk to the chief of police. *Oh, no, I forgot. Chief Nichols just retired.* Sheriff Quimby was temporarily in charge of both the police and the sheriff's office. *Well, I should at least let the other overseers in on it.* She booted up her laptop and sent a collective email to the board. By bedtime, she'd received exactly one reply. Bobby B. Goode (he insisted on the middle initial to torment his wife) would be happy to escort Cassidy to meet the movie folks. "Boat's in the yard getting debarnacled, so I've time on my hands and Mary Jo wants me out from underfoot." Should he wear a tie?

Just as she turned out the light, the phone rang. Edna Mae Quimby's stentorian tones filled the room. "Cassidy Jane Beauvoir, is that you?"

Who did you expect? "Yes, Edna Mae. What can I do for you?"

"I hear you're going to confront those Hollywood

dissolutes tomorrow. I'm going with you."

"*Hmm.* I think, Edna Mae, that this is really a job for the Amity Landing overseers. It doesn't concern Penhallow."

The old lady tut-tutted. "In that regard you are misinformed. Those people have taken over all the hotel rooms in Penhallow and even up Route 1. They're driving massive trucks down our quiet streets and scaring the children. Why, I even saw one young man with a pornographic tattoo on his stomach!" She paused for breath.

"How did you know he had a tattoo on his stomach?"

"How? How?" Her voice rose to a level of high dudgeon. "Because he wasn't wearing a shirt, that's how! There he was, waltzing down Front Street *bare naked*! Audrey Carver called me from her cellular phone and I rushed over."

"Surely he wasn't totally naked. He had trousers on, didn't he?"

She gruffly acceded the point. "Still, it gave us quite a turn. I immediately took our concerns to my husband."

Cassidy could just see the rotund, jolly sheriff listening to his wife rant. "What did Toby say?"

"He…uh…said we should keep an eye on the fellow. If he did anything suspicious, we were to report to him."

The sheriff is a very smart man. "Good idea. Now I can sleep well, knowing you're on neighborhood watch."

This remark blew past the good woman like a stiff breeze. "Yes, indeed. In fact, that's what I'm calling about. You're meeting with the ringleaders tomorrow at the Penhallow Harbor Inn, correct? I intend to accompany you. I want to see if the rest of the mob is as disreputable as that…that Zouave."

Sigh. Cassidy knew from experience that Edna Mae would not be deterred. Like Toby, she had learned to acquiesce while gently steering the old lady into calmer waters. "Fine. Meet me at the store at nine thirty."

Edna Mae didn't bother to thank her, instead mumbling about illustrated men and carnival freaks as she hung up.

Chapter Four

Penhallow Harbor Inn, Thursday, June 22

The next day Cassidy drove to East Penhallow, trailed by Bobby B. in his truck and Edna Mae Quimby in her Buick. They parked at the Penhallow Harbor Inn and walked into the lobby. Cassidy dinged the bell. "We're here to see Mr. MacEwan, Jesse."

The sixteen-year-old sang in a jarring falsetto, "Oh, hello, Miss Beauvoir! Mr. MacEwan is waiting for you in the business center." She lowered her voice, but not much. "They're from *Hollywood*."

Cassidy led the others into a small room down the hall. MacEwan stood at a sloping ship captain's desk. He bowed. Two men sprawled on a chintz-covered settee. MacEwan indicated them. "You remember Stan Lowry, our line manager?" The emaciated fellow did not get up but doffed an imaginary hat. "And Oliver Hadley, our producer." The fat man wheezed and flicked an idle hand. Cassidy nodded at them, the names "Laurel" and "Hardy" running amok in her brain. Another person stood with his back to them. He held the heavy curtain to one side and stared out the window.

Cassidy introduced Bobby B. and Edna Mae. MacEwan made no effort to acknowledge them. The two continued to stand in the middle of the room,

Bobby gawking at the strangers and Edna Mae fidgeting. MacEwan raised his voice. "Jasper? Come here and give Miss Beauvoir a rundown on the film and the production process. Then we'll go over our requirements."

Cassidy had stiffened, ready to counter with her own stipulations, when the man at the window turned around. Her jaw dropped.

He started at seeing her. "You're the bookstore lady."

"Yes. Cassidy Beauvoir." She smiled at him. "Are you ready for more Maine history?"

The question seemed to puzzle him. "Not really. But thanks."

MacEwan had been tapping his foot. "I see you two have met. Jasper, Miss Beauvoir is a town councilman—"

"Overseer." Cassidy pushed her companions forward. She may not have wanted Edna Mae to come, but she refused to let MacEwan marginalize her. "Mr. Goode is an overseer as well. And Mrs. Quimby is…is…" Her mind went blank.

"Whatever." He dismissed them. Edna Mae sat down abruptly. Bobby backed out of the room, slamming the door as he left. Philip resumed. "Miss Beauvoir should have already received the paperwork for our permits as well as support specs for shooting in Amity Landing. She claims to know nothing about it. What's your excuse, Jasper?"

Ignorant of normal procedures in movie-making, Cassidy wasn't sure if this was fair criticism or not, although she noticed that Lowry stirred and frowned. In a voice distinctly unlike Stan Laurel's, he growled,

"Enough, Philip. We don't have time for blame. Just give her the papers and be done with it." He glanced at Jasper. "All the information they need is in there. We've got to get over to Castine to scope out the other location."

MacEwan's eyes closed to slits, but he said nothing. He snapped his fingers. Jasper handed him a thick manila envelope, which he gave to Cassidy.

"There, that wasn't so hard." Lowry playfully punched MacEwan on the arm. Cassidy saw the tall man wince, but again, he said nothing. The manager stood and picked up a briefcase. "I want to start construction as soon as the crew gets here. Come on, Ollie." The producer followed him. Edna Mae launched herself off the chair with a bit of a wobble and announced to the rapidly emptying room, "I am leaving."

It didn't cause much of a ripple. The galling indifference emboldened Cassidy. It was time to put her foot down. "No."

The men paused. Jasper said, "What was that?"

"I said, no. You can't start construction—or anything else—until you have the consent of the overseers."

Hadley shrugged and pointed at Jasper. "You explain it to her." He headed to the parking lot, MacEwan and Lowry behind him.

Cassidy turned a burning face to Jasper. "Well?"

He gave her a lopsided grin. "Have you ever heard of the Mafia?"

"Excuse me?" She took a step back. "The Mafia?"

Jasper grinned. "Figure of speech. No, we're not...er...affiliated with the mob, but I had a feeling

40

you were wondering about us by now—the black suits, the entitled attitude, the bulging pocket."

Cassidy was still too angry to laugh. "Well, what *are* you then?"

"Hollywood's version of an exclusive club, like Boodle's or the Cosmos. The black suits are Ermenegildo Zegna—it's the signature look of the Black Brothers Studios. The entitled attitude is an unfortunate side effect of living in the California bubble."

"And the bulging pocket?"

"That would be Oliver's. He's the Wimpy of our little cabal." She seemed clueless, so he explained, "He always carries a spare sandwich." When the lost stare persisted, he added, "Popeye's friend. You know: 'I'll gladly pay you Tuesday for a hamburger today.' " He looked at her askance. "Don't tell me you're unacquainted with the classics?"

"Oh…yeah. Popeye the sailor man. Got it." Cassidy's irritation began to dissipate. *He really is kind of sweet—for someone from away, especially that far away.* "So, what do *you* do, Mr. MacEwan?"

"Call me Jasper. Whatever Philip MacEwan tells me to." He nodded toward the entrance. "He's not only a partner in Black Brothers, he's my father."

The Mainer in Cassidy bridled at his submissive attitude. She said frostily, "Oh, really? You never question your lord and master?"

He gave her an odd look. "I'm not really in a position to. I work for him. I'm directing the movie."

"Oh. I'd forgotten." Deflated, she cast about for a comeback. "Er…have you done many movies?"

He rubbed his chin ruefully. "No, this is my first.

At least my first major motion picture. I've done several documentaries—the one on the Big Year won an International Documentary Association award."

"Big year?"

"Yes, that's the term for the famous competition among birdwatchers. The goal is to rack up the highest number of species identifications in one year. I followed two archrivals through every African country that wasn't actually waging war. An incomparable experience." He grinned. "I do believe birders are the platypuses—platypi?—of the animal kingdom. Eccentrically put together."

Cassidy was tempted to put him in his place. *Birders? Eccentric? Tell that to Bobby B. Then watch your back.*

Jasper had gone on talking despite her preoccupation. "This one started out as a documentary too."

"This film? It's about Maine birders?"

"No, no." He got up and filled his mug from the urn. "Coffee? No?" He sat down on the sofa next to her. "See, I did my master's thesis on the Revolutionary War, with a special emphasis on the use of privateers to beef up the Continental navy. You probably know that most of the so-called 'soldiers' in the militias were farmers and other citizens—armed with their own rifles and lacking even basic training. Well, the same was true of the navy. Ship's crews were mainly made up of young boys and old men...or able-bodied seamen shanghaied into service." He grew animated. The shock of sandy hair fell over his eyes. He brushed it back impatiently. "The best—or rather, worst—instance of their inexperience affecting the war effort was the

Penobscot Expedition."

Cassidy searched her memory and came up empty. "Penobscot? As in our bay?"

"Yup. By some lights, the most devastating naval disaster in American history. And the most avoidable."

"Oh, wait. I did learn about it in school." She wracked her brain but couldn't come up with anything beyond the name. Unwilling to admit a foreigner knew more about her own history than she did, she said haughtily, "Let's see what you can tell me about it."

He eyed her, a sardonic twist to his lip. "Happy to. In 1779, at the height of the Revolutionary War, the British snuck into Maine and captured Castine, then called Bagaduce." He correctly pronounced it "bag-a-doos," which greatly impressed her. "At the time, Maine was still part of Massachusetts, and the boys in Boston took offense at the blatant theft of their territory. So they organized a flotilla to sail up the coast and remove said Brits. Trouble was, the fledgling Continental navy consisted of a total of some thirty ships and very few seasoned captains. So they pressed several privateers and commercial craft into service to make up an armada of forty vessels and nearly three thousand men. Sounds impressive, right?"

He seemed to expect a response, so Cassidy said perkily, "Right!"

"Wrong. Their leaders—including the revered Paul Revere—were dumb as tree stumps and couldn't decide how to attack the city—a city that sticks out like a sore thumb on the Blue Hill peninsula. A simple three-pronged approach would have done the trick in a matter of hours. For their part, the redcoats—a mere four hundred men, with an array of heavily armed ships before them, no cannon, and fort walls that were all of five feet high to protect them—were prepared to surrender. General McLean had his white flag out and everything. Instead, the Americans dithered offshore for almost three weeks, which it turns out was just enough time for English reinforcements to arrive and surround the hapless armada."

"What happened then?"

"Most of the transports were sunk or burned. Then, in a totally irrational attempt to save the rest from the English, the Americans sailed *upriver*." He rolled his eyes. "The remaining seventeen vessels, bristling with cannons, were chased off with their sterns between their legs by four—count 'em, *four*—ships."

Cassidy's brow creased. "But the Penobscot River is only navigable for a few more miles. They would have been boxed in."

"Nobody ever accused Saltonstall—he was in command of the fleet—of foresight. When faced with disaster, he ordered his captains to burn or scuttle the ships. The expedition lost some seven hundred men and all but one ship."

"You said there were three thousand men. What happened to the rest of them?"

"Most escaped to the mainland and made their way back to Boston. At least one that we know of went east into Canada."

"But their ships were at the bottom of the river! How did they get home?"

Jasper shook his head and smirked. "They walked."

"They *walked*?"

"Uh-huh. All two hundred and fifty miles. My guess is they were in no hurry to face their superiors."

Cassidy heard something rumble. She checked her watch. "Oh, look at the time. I have to get back to the store." Her stomach growled again.

A corner of his mouth turned up. "You sound hungry." He stood. "Mindful Books doesn't open until two, right? Would you like to catch a bite to eat first, Miss Beauvoir?"

"No, no. I don't have time. I…" Her throat closed up. *Oh, dear. Lunch…with a movie producer. He's probably one of those seduction experts who'll lure me onto his couch with his silken words and smoldering eyes.* She was surprised to find the thought not entirely displeasing.

"I can finish the story."

He looked so eager she relented. "That would be acceptable, Mr. MacEwan."

"Jasper."

"Jasper. And I'm Cassidy." She held out her hand, and he gravely shook it. "Do you know Durkee's?"

"That little restaurant perched above the marina? I think I passed it on my first perambulation through the town."

"I'll meet you there."

As she foraged for the keys to her Subaru, he passed her in a low-slung, lime-green sports car and turned left on Route 1. She gulped. *Is that a Lamborghini?*

Chapter Five

Durkee's, Thursday, June 22

Durkee's was empty of customers. Cassidy walked down past the bar to look for a hostess, Jasper on her heels. She waved at a short, dark-haired woman with a bustling, efficient air and pointed at a booth. "Katie? Can we sit here?"

"Hi, Cassidy. Sure. Be right with you."

They settled on the hard benches, an awkward silence filling the space between them. Cassidy, a few minutes earlier perfectly comfortable—in fact, enthralled by Jasper's narrative—now felt a little queasy. *I mean, I hardly know the man, and here I am eating lunch with him. A Californian.* She remembered the Lamborghini. *A super-rich Californian. Maude will kill me.*

The waitress came over. "Long time no see, Cass. What'll it be?"

"The usual for me, please, Katie."

Katie cast a critical eye over the young man sitting across from Cassidy. "And for you, sir?"

Jasper eyeballed the menu. "I…uh…"

Cassidy took pity. "He'll have the lobster roll with drawn butter, too. And a Geary's."

Jasper looked up. "Wait. Aren't lobster rolls made with mayonnaise? And celery?"

"Not the good ones. No, sir. It should consist of fresh lobster chunks, gently folded into melted butter and placed lovingly in a square bun." She added dreamily, "The kind of bun that's so soft you can make little pills of it and pop them in your mouth."

"Huh. And what's a Geary's?"

"You'll like it."

"Okay."

Cassidy checked out his heavy gold cuff links. "I suppose you're more used to champagne and caviar." *And restaurants with tablecloths.*

"Who, me?"

She gestured at his sports car in the parking lot outside. "You're obviously one of those Hollywood millionaire types who's never seen the inside of a pickup truck."

"Oh, really?" His voice dripped sarcasm. "I—"

"I'm not finished. You're a vegan, except for fish." She rolled her eyes. "You've never met a Republican. You think Iowa is in Canada and Nebraskans are Oompa-Loompas. You despise anyone who questions the global-warming gospel—" Here, she had to stop for breath, which unfortunately took long enough to allow him to interrupt the flow.

"Whoa, there. Stereotyping isn't nice." He lifted his chin. "For your information, I was driving a tractor before you were born."

I'll bet it was a Rolls Royce. And you had a chauffeur. "Yes, but—"

His voice drowned her out. "Yes, we have money. Yes, I was pampered and spoiled as a child, but don't hold it against me."

She had the nasty retort ready when she noticed his

47

lip twitching.

"However, I can be redeemed."

"All right. I'll give you the benefit of the doubt…for now."

"Thank you. Meanwhile, may I depend upon you to brief me on Maine lore and customs?"

"I've already told you about lobster rolls—what more do you want?"

He reached out and touched her glistening sable hair, the thick braid tumbling like the rapids of a rock-strewn river down her back. "I understand there are still native American tribes right here in Maine. You had quite a collection at the bookstore about the Penobscot Indians and the….Passa something."

"Passamaquoddy. Yes, one of the tribes of the Wabenaki confederacy. There are still bands in Canada and New England. My mother is part Passamaquoddy." That iron-spined woman wore her native lineage proudly, tracing her roots back to a famous chief. Just the thought of her made Cassidy sit up straighter.

"Is that where you get your coppery skin and the high cheekbones?"

"Yes." She reddened under his scrutiny.

"What about your father? Did he give you those aquamarine eyes?"

She blinked the aforementioned eyes. "Uh-huh. Father came originally from the County."

"The County?"

"Aroostook County—the northernmost county in Maine. It's surrounded by Canada—New Brunswick to the east and Quebec to the west. Most County folk speak both French and English. Pop was a descendant of French trappers who settled in Nova Scotia in the seventeenth century but were forced by the British to leave Canada."

"He was an Acadian then?"

"Yes."

"Ah, the great deportation. I was reading about that. The British expelled the French from Nova Scotia in the late eighteenth century, right before the American revolution broke out." He smiled at her. "You have a, shall we say, *textured* background."

The blush quickly became painful. "It's not unusual for Mainers."

"Or for any Americans, for that matter." He grew serious. "Actually, what I'm most interested in is Maine's role in the war. I've been going through the books I bought—"

"We do have a library you know—you don't have to buy all the books." She swallowed hard. *What am I saying? He's the angel who's going to put me into the black for the first time ever.* "Unless you…er…want to."

He hadn't appeared to hear her. "Since the movie is about the Penobscot Expedition, I want it to be as authentic as possible, but there seem to be a lot of conflicting stories about what happened."

Katie placed plates piled with fries, coleslaw, and New England split-top rolls stuffed with steaming lobster on the table. "Another Geary's?"

They both nodded. "You were right, Miss Beauvoir. I do like it."

Cassidy smiled. "I told you to call me Cassidy."

"And so I shall. As for you, you may call me Jasper."

"I know." She chewed on a french fry. "You said

you originally wanted to make a documentary. What happened to that project?"

"Dad." He frowned. "As usual, he appropriates my ideas and stupendifies them—his word, not mine. He's like P. T. Barnum—everything has to be splashier and bigger—and more expensive than it needs to be."

Cassidy thought of the tall, austere man she'd crossed swords with that morning, and begged to differ. "He doesn't strike me as a splashy kind of guy."

"He saves it for the celluloid."

"I see. So he insisted on turning your documentary into a fictional movie?"

"But based on true events." His eyes crinkled. "I was telling him about the battle and made the mistake of mentioning the legend of the ghost. After that, he was hooked."

"Ghost?" When he didn't answer, Cassidy looked up to find Jasper staring at his plate. "What's the problem?"

"Where do I begin?"

"Oh, for God's sake, are you going to start whining about the ozone layer or exploiting animals? You ought to know that lobsters have no brain. They—"

"Um…Cassidy? All I wanted to know was which end to begin on."

Cassidy shut her mouth with a snap. *One, two, three...* "Begin at the end nearest you. Duh."

He gingerly picked up the roll. All the meat immediately oozed out the other end onto his plate. He dropped the whole mess and threw up his hands.

"Here." She passed him a spoon.

Katie dropped two more beers on the table and handed Jasper a roll of paper towels. "Figured you'd need this by now."

When he had finally managed to scoop some lobster back into the bread, Cassidy asked, "So what was that you were saying about a ghost?" She thought she'd heard every fable about her home, but this was new.

He finished the bite. "The ghost in the fort."

"Fort?"

Jasper put down his fork. "Well, you know about the treasure."

"Treasure?"

"He sighs. Look, I've booked a room at the Waldo Bed and Breakfast right up the street and—"

"You aren't staying at the Penhallow Harbor Inn with the others?"

He shook his head. "I want to be closer to the set. Plus I can think better without my father constantly chittering in my ear."

Are we talking about the same man? "Sorry, but I can't imagine Mr. MacEwan chittering any more than being splashy."

"Believe me, in private he's a total chitterer. I maintain my mother went deaf on purpose so she wouldn't have to listen to him." He puckered his mouth and clicked his teeth together.

Cassidy giggled, then stopped. "What were we talking about?"

"The hotel," he said promptly. "I dropped those books there. If you like, I can show you the sections that talk about the drummer boy."

"Drummer boy?"

"Ghost. Drummer boy. Treasure. Yes. It's too long a tale to go into here. Come back to the hotel with me."

At her look of horror, he added, "I'll bring the books down to the lobby. Lord knows I wouldn't want to fit the *stereotype*." He grinned. Katie handed him the bill. He laid a credit card on top.

Cassidy noticed it was a platinum American Express card. She whipped out her wallet, shagged her credit union debit card, and laid it on top of his. "Dutch, please."

He drew back surprised. "Oh, okay, but it's no problem. I—"

"Thanks, but no." She handed the folder to Katie. "I'm perfectly capable of paying for my own lunch." *Take that, Richie Rich.*

His eyes flickered. "It's not my fault, you know."

"What's not your fault?"

"That I have skads of money."

"Why waste it then? Why not spend it on a good cause?"

His smoky eyes burned into hers. "I thought I was."

Cassidy felt suddenly ashamed. *I am being ungracious, aren't I?* But something about him got under her skin. Was it the way he flaunted his wealth? *The Lamborghini? Puleese. It's gotta be a rental anyway.* Unless he paid someone to drive it across country for him. She mentally shook herself. *What does bother me about him?* It surely couldn't be the way the corner of his mouth curled when he was trying not to laugh, or the way his fingers danced on the table when he talked. No. *He's just a rich jerk from the wacko West Coast, and I hate those people.* She noticed the hank of sandy hair that straggled across his forehead and down into his eyes and found herself longing to brush it away.

"Um…"

"Tell you what. You buy next time." He rose. "My offer stands, but perhaps you have to open the shop."

"What? Oh…uh…yes. Yes, I do." She checked her watch. *Oh, dear, it's almost two o'clock. I'll be late opening again.* "Well, see you." She walked out ahead of him, breaking into a trot when she reached the sidewalk.

Chapter Six

Mindful Books, Thursday, June 22

"Well?"

"Well what, Nellie?"

"Who are they, and what do they want?"

"They're from Hollywood, and they want to shoot a film in Amity Landing."

"Cool!"

Her best friend's enthusiasm had the effect of aggravating Cassidy even further. "Not cool! They waltzed into town demanding this and that, assuming we'd go all gaga at the glamorous, rich, movie people, with their fancy sports cars and designer jeans and fat wallets. Well, I'm going to show them they can't push us around."

Nellie picked up a pile of books from the table and set them on the mantelpiece. "Sports cars?"

Cassidy set the books upright, spines showing. "He drives a Lamborghini, okay?"

"Cool!"

"Would you stop saying that? I'm serious. You know how I despise that kind of person—"

"You mean Californian, right? Just because your cousin went out there and decided to become a witch...or is it a warlock? You never know nowadays with all this gender switching or modification or whatever it is. Did you know you're not allowed to say actress anymore? They're all actors. I mean, you get some girl with a name like Sydney, and unless you see her, you're going to assume she's a man. It's enough to put you off movies altogether. So—" She lifted a book from another pile and leafed through it. Without looking up, she said, "I take it you like the guy? Is he the star?"

"No, he's the director. And I don't like him. He's rolling in money."

"And this is a bad thing?"

"I guess it's the Scot in me—I'm offended by ostentation."

"Which is why you've been wearing the same ratty sweater all week. And last I checked, you're half Passamaquoddy, half Acadian. Not even a smidgen of Scottish blood."

Cassidy took the book from her friend and carried it to a shelf in the back of the store. "Why are you here anyway, Nellie? Shouldn't you be knocking down your booth at the farmer's market?"

"Hank's doing it. I wanted to show you this." The young woman pulled a clipping out of the pocket of her dungarees. "They identified the dead guy."

"Our very own Horatio Hornblower? That didn't take long. Who is it?"

Nellie skimmed the article. "Says his name is— was—Richard Ahearn. From Boston."

"How did they dig up the name? I heard his wallet was missing."

"Since he obviously wasn't local, they made inquiries at the hotels around here. A man answering to the corpse's description was registered at the Duke of

York in Camden. Went missing five days ago. They had his address in Boston, and the police got hold of a landlord who confirmed his identity."

"Did they find out what he was doing here?"

"Dunno." Nellie gestured toward the port. "Maybe he fell off a freighter going up to Searsport."

"Are you kidding? Did you see his picture? He looked like something out of *Mutiny on the Bounty*. I don't think merchant marine sailors wear bell bottoms and those wide collars. At least not anymore." Cassidy opened a box and began removing packing paper. She dug out a set of Mickey Spillane paperbacks. "Ah, Melvin's order has arrived." She set them by the register. "Edna Mae said his throat was slit."

"Really? I thought he drowned."

"It hardly matters." Cassidy got up and turned the sign on the door to CLOSED. "I don't have time now. I've got to get to the overseers' meeting so we can figure out how to get rid of the Hollywood mafia."

"Mafia? Isn't that a little harsh?"

"That's what they call themselves." *Sort of.*

Nellie followed her out. "Have fun. Say—what are you going to do if everyone else wants them to stay?"

****

Amity Landing, Thursday, June 22

Cassidy marched up the stairs to her bedroom and flung herself face down on the bed. She lay there for a minute before pounding both fists into the mattress. "Shit, shit, shit. How could they? I can't believe it. They're all nuts."

She'd given an impassioned speech to the four people in the room (only three overseers had made it, plus Merle Crosby, the village maintenance man).

She'd laid out all the points against having their town taken over by a movie production crew. Holding up a sheet of paper from the envelope Jasper had left with her, she proclaimed, "Says here everyone has to stop what they're doing when the cameras roll. That means you, Merle. You won't be allowed to work on Mrs. Connally's shed for months. And Water Street will be closed to traffic so the *celebrities*"—she had pronounced the word with a really magnificent sneer— "can walk to and from the outdoor canteen they're going to set up in Eunice Merithew's garden. I ask you, do you want foreigners"—there was a noticeable snort from Merle at that point—"ordering us around, treating us like second-class citizens in our own community? It's outrageous!"

Reaction? Nothing. Nada. Faces as impassive as a Mt. Rushmore president. She spoke to her pillow. "It was like talking to Edna Mae's cat."

And then came the vote.

She pushed off the bed and went down in search of diversion. She was opening her second beer when someone knocked on the front door. Most people in Amity Landing knew to come up the back stairs to the deck and sliding glass doors, so Cassidy assumed it was the UPS man or someone asking directions. She checked the time. Eight o'clock. *Awfully late for someone to drop by.* She peeped around the corner. Jasper stood on the front stoop, his nose stuck to the glass.

The last person on earth she wanted to see. *If he's come to gloat, I'll spit on his shoe. Which, with any luck, is a five-hundred-dollar tassel loafer made from the pelt of a baby rabbit.* She was still muttering when she opened the door. "What do *you* want?"

"Er…hi. Sorry to come by so late, but I just heard about the overseers' vote." He must have noticed her fist lifting, for he said hastily, "Mrs. Ketchum said it was unanimous, so I'm hoping you're on board with it. If it helps, we promise to be as unobtrusive as possible." He continued to stand on the stoop. She continued to stare at him. Finally she unfurled the fist and crooked a finger. He followed her back to the kitchen.

He trained his eyes on the bottle in her hand until she broke down and offered him a beer. "Thanks, but I brought a peace offering." He held up a bottle of wine.

Cassidy read the label. Those hours spent poring over *Alexis Lichine's Encyclopedia of Wines and Spirits* for her first job at a fancy restaurant in Portland bore fruit. She recognized a premier cru French burgundy that was so expensive the Penhallow Co-op kept it in a locked case. For an instant, her reluctance to have his income thrown in her face vied with her longing to taste it. Desire won out. "Um…okay." She retrieved her corkscrew and two glasses from the cabinet, thanking her stars Grandmother Soctomah had bequeathed her the delicate leaded crystal globes.

Jasper opened the wine with an expert twist of his wrist and poured. They sat down at the dining room table. Cassidy couldn't think of anything nice to say and didn't think being surly was in order, so she took a sip. She closed her eyes. "Oh my Lord, it's sublime!"

He grinned. "So…am I forgiven?"

"Only temporarily." She couldn't help but smile at him. "All right, how do you plan to make a major motion picture production invisible?"

"I'll talk to Stan about limiting the hours of actual filming so you don't have to stop what you're doing every two minutes. When we're working inside the house, you'll be free to move about—we'll put darkening curtains on all the windows." He poured more wine. "The only obstacle to a convivial time being had by all will be Digby."

"Digby?"

"Digby Toff-Smythe. Perhaps you've heard of him?"

Even Cassidy, who had to be dragooned into going to the Roxie theater in town, had heard of the current box office rage. Chiseled looks, swimmer's build, long blond hair that he tossed at least fifty times in every movie. Piercing green eyes that most men assumed were artificially enhanced. Women didn't care. "Yeah, I think so. What about him?"

"He was hired to play Nathaniel West, the captain of the *Black Prince*, although Father thinks he's more suited to the role of the British commandant. Much more dignified and heroic, if somewhat disloyal."

"Was the *Black Prince* the flagship of the armada?"

"No. It was one of the privateers the Americans scuttled in the river after the rout."

"*Hmm*. Does the ship have some significance then? Are you basing the script on historical records?"

"As far as possible. The Massachusetts military archives produced records on the naval vessels, but I wanted to focus on the commercial ships."

"Because that's your specialty."

"Right. More important, we wanted to emphasize the civilian angle. The regular Joe's experience, that sort of thing. I could find useful information for only one ship: the *Black Prince*. We have a listing of its voyages, plus I found several government files on its cabin boy. One document is a petition for a pension, in which he details his escape from the battle and his subsequent trials. Remember, I told you we knew of one sailor who went north—or rather east—to Canada instead of south to Boston? It was this fellow. He claims he got lost while trying to escape. Eventually, a Canadian fisherman picked him up and took him across the bay to a town called Westport. It's on the south-westernmost tip of Nova Scotia."

"Westport! That's where Mrs. Spinney is from."

"Spinney? You mean the lady who owns the house we're renting?"

"The very same."

"Interesting. Perhaps that's why the scout thought it would be perfect for the Canadian scenes."

"So…the cabin boy. Did he ever get back to America?"

"Yes—it's detailed in the petition. I did come across a mention of another document…a diary…" He paused and screwed up his eyes. "As I recall, it's disappeared. The petition is a bit dry, but it does give us enough to weave his narrative into the Penobscot battle. It'll provide a human element to the story line."

"Tug at the movie-going public's heartstrings?"

"Yeah. Dad is perfectly happy to embellish a story if it adds pathos. And the awards committees love it."

"I can see why he rejected the documentary idea."

For answer, Jasper swigged his wine.

Cassidy went back to the original topic. "You were explaining how you'd be quiet like little mice while shooting?"

"Even quieter than mice. Mice squeak." He put a hand to his mouth in a show of dismay. "Oops, except for the Toff. He may not squeak, but he does *intone*."

"You mean Digby Toff-Smythe. So he's a prima donna?"

"He is the mascot of the prima donna guild." He massaged his temples. "It's going to be a bitch keeping him under control and tantrum-free."

"Is that your job?"

"No, thank God—although he'll try to make it so. I shall hand it off to Sally Crook, our PR person." He poured the last of the wine into her glass and rose. "Well, it's late. I'd better get out of your way."

Cassidy's mood dropped precipitously. It suddenly occurred to her that she'd been enjoying the conversation. She liked watching his mobile face as he talked, liked the way his eyes lit up when he got into a discussion. She pinched her arm. *Remember? He's a rich jerk.* "Oh. Uh. Of course. I usually go to bed at…nine fifteen." *Huh?*

"You probably have to open the shop early." He sighed. "What I wouldn't give to own a bookstore."

"It's hardly glamorous—my profits don't generally rise to the Rodeo Drive level." *Unless* you *happen to be in town.*

He said earnestly, "You don't understand, Cassidy. I know you think so, but really, I'm not like those Beverly Hills types. I'm not Digby Toff-Smythe. I love, love, *love* books."

"Do you hate movies then?"

"Are you mad? Movies are great. Where I come from, no gathering is complete without a picture show.

And it's definitely considered impolite to read a book in public." He caught sight of her mulish expression. "But you can escape censure as long as you confine your reading to certain designated areas. Like they have for smoking."

Cassidy, prepared to be annoyed, was surprised into silence. Jasper took his glass to the counter. "So…good night."

She stood. "Good night. Thanks for the wine."

They stared at each other. Finally he mumbled, "I'll see you tomorrow."

"Yes….Yes."

Still they stood. Finally Jasper leaned toward her. "Do you mind?" He kissed her cheek. Before she could react, he sauntered out the door.

Chapter Seven

Mindful Books, Friday, June 23

"Thanks for filling in, Maude. I'll be back in a couple of hours. Leon's coming with another load of books from Freedom, and I don't want him to find the store closed."

"No problem. My tai chi class was canceled anyway. So what's in Camden?"

"You know Connie Fuller, the owner of Food for Thought? She bought the entire library from the Pardoe estate sale. Half of the collection is works on Maine. She doesn't stock much and wants to unload them on me. I got a great price."

"You know that stuff never sells, Cassidy. Mainers like to stick to the history they learned at their granddad's knee. That's good enough for them without all that nuance."

"I'll have you know I just sold almost two hundred dollars' worth of it last week."

"Really? To whom?"

Cassidy shut her mouth with a snap. *Do I want to attract the old cat's eye to my new mouse?* Maude was almost as bad a gossip as the Red Hat ladies. "Some guy from away."

"*Hmm.* Well, have fun."

She drove down Route 1, through Knightston to

Camden. As usual, the traffic was backed up for five miles before the left turn onto Main Street. As she inched along, she thought about Jasper. The kiss still tickled. *He's really not* so *bad. Maybe I've been a teensy bit unfair.* Of course, the *other* movie people were just as condescending and rude as she expected. *Will the eminent thespian Toff-Smythe be a model of humility? Or a heel?* She thought she could guess.

When she finally got to the blinking light, she hung a right, following the back streets that took her around the mobbed center of town. A parking spot opened up as she neared the bookstore on Pearl Street. She snagged it and walked the few yards to Food for Thought. Connie's shop was even more cluttered than Mindful Books—cases stuffed with leather-bound, dusty volumes, stacks of old Life magazines on the floor, rolled up circus posters from the 1920s in tall bins. An antique crank cash register stood guard at the front door. The place appeared to be empty. She called out, "Connie?"

"That you, Cassidy? I'm with a customer. Go on to the back room. The books are on the green table."

She was sorting through the titles and filling a box when Connie came in. "Sorry to keep you waiting. The fellow was rather demanding. I would have left him to his own devices, except he's already bought four hundred dollars' worth of books."

"What's he looking for?"

"Mainly stuff on Maine—bless him. I'm clearing my shelves out nicely." She looked down at the various piles of books. "He seemed quite taken with the first-edition Oz books as well."

"Huh. That tells me he's not looking for bargains

then. You mark them up way too high—especially the Ruth Plumley Thomson ones. And most of them aren't even first printings."

Connie shrugged. "I got the impression that money was no object for this guy. Really expensive shoes. And I'm pretty sure it's a Rolex on his wrist, although I've only seen them in TV commercials."

Cassidy looked up. "Oh? What does he look like?"

"Go see for yourself—he's still browsing."

Couldn't be Jasper. Camden literally teems with millionaires…but how many of them buy truckloads of books? She put the biography of N. C. Wyeth down and wandered through the narrow aisles. In a dark corner, Jasper stood on a stool, holding a thick volume. "Mr. MacEwan? Jasper?"

"What? Who?" When he saw her he dropped the book. It crashed to the floor, landing on its spine.

She picked it up. "*Tik-Tok of Oz*. One of my favorites." She checked the flyleaf. "Two hundred dollars, my Aunt Fanny. Connie should be arrested for gouging."

"Oh, gosh, I hope I didn't damage it."

She examined the book. "No."

Jasper stepped off the stool and took it from her hands. "It *is* a little steep—even for me—but it's one of the few Oz books I haven't acquired." He patted the cover. "And it's a first edition."

She opened it to the copyright page. "Third printing. Plus, the foxing on some of the pages—see? Here and here—it cuts the value by a third."

He didn't seem concerned. "I buy them to read, not to sell."

She looked at him shyly. "How come you collect

Oz books?"

"It's my grandmother's fault. My grandparents lived in a Colonial-era house in New Jersey with all kinds of secret passageways and hidey holes." He smiled reminiscently. "It was the perfect house for a curious little boy. The living room contained a row of cupboards built under the windows that Grandmother had filled with children's books. Extraordinary books. *The Queen's Museum*—that was by Frank Stockton. And all the Mary Poppins books. Doctor Doolittle. And of course many of the Oz books. When I visited her as a child, I'd head straight for those cabinets and read for hours." His gaze grew distant. "She had this wooden rocking chair with a writing shelf attached. I'd read and rock and read and rock."

Cassidy was mesmerized by the lilting rhythm in his voice. *Sing-song—like an itinerant troubadour.* She hadn't quite realized how handsome he was until now. His pearly eyes were thoughtful and warm, and his hair reminded her of soft doeskin—lustrous and thick. A straight nose added dignity to an otherwise winsome face. She liked him. *But only because he loves books.* "Sounds like a wonderful house. Does she still live there?"

"What? No. The house actually belonged to the university. My grandfather was a dean, and they lived on the campus. When he retired, they had to move." He sighed. "How I wish I'd been able to take those books with me. I've spent the last five years trying to locate as many as possible." He hefted the Oz book. "So, in answer to your unspoken question, yes, I'm going to buy this. Of course"—he chucked her under the chin—"that'll use up this month's allowance, and I'll have to touch you for a drink."

"I'm sorry…What?" Cassidy resisted the urge to check her ear for wax.

"I thought, since we'd run into each other, and—as my uncle used to say—the sun is almost over the yardarm, I could talk you into sharing a nosh and an ale with me. Your treat."

Connie came in. "Do you want the books or not, Cassidy? I'm about to close up."

"Oh…oh, yes. Sorry, Connie." She turned to Jasper. "I have to take these to my car." She hesitated. "I can meet you somewhere."

"Perfect. Can you recommend an establishment?"

"How about Nemo's? It's down on Commercial Street. It has a nice view of the harbor." She hesitated. "It's kind of a dive, so not so many tourists."

"Does this mean I've been accepted into the tribe?" When she didn't respond, he said, "Nemo's it is. In ten?"

She nodded.

A few minutes later, she climbed the stairs to a place crammed full of nautical memorabilia. She spotted Jasper at the bar in spirited conversation with a woman sitting on the stool next to him. She looked familiar, but it wasn't until Cassidy reached the couple that she recognized the Black Brothers press person. This time the sweater monkeys were encased in a tight spandex blouse that rose and fell with her breaths. Jasper turned his head and saw Cassidy. "Oh, there you are. Do you know Sally Crook? She's in charge of pretty much everything on the set."

"Yes, we've met."

"I totally forgot that I had promised to help Sally

pick up supplies for the imminent arrival of His Majesty. She had to shoulder the burden herself, for which she should be amply recompensed. I thought maybe a teddy bear."

"His Majesty?"

Sally grinned at Cassidy's puzzled face. "He means the Toff. Besides the imported satin sheets and the non-GMO-cotton pillow, we must have on hand a certain kind of yogurt, gluten-free müesli, and a ready supply of sushi and sashimi." She wrinkled her nose. "Can't stand the stuff myself."

"Don't forget the cognac. He only drinks Courvoisier—"

"With Evian. Not Fiji. Not Pellegrino. Evian." She laughed.

Jasper moved over and helped Cassidy onto the stool next to Sally. Before she could speak, he said, "I understand from Mrs. Ketchum that you appreciate a gin and tonic now and then, so I took the liberty of ordering one for you. Pauline here"—he nodded at the bartender—"tells me we're just under the wire for happy hour. Bar drinks are half price."

Cassidy noticed that he had a mug of beer and Sally a glass of seltzer. *Thank you, and my budget thanks you.* "Sounds good."

Pauline pushed a wooden model of a peapod lobster boat aside and handed Cassidy a highball glass. "Here you go." She rested her elbows on the bar. "I …uh…hear you guys are part of the movie crew."

Cassidy saw Jasper hesitate. *He's probably worried that she's the groupie type.*

"Yes, we are. How did you hear about it? We've been trying to stay under the radar."

She started to say something, but suddenly stopped. "Oh…a customer mentioned it, I think. News travels fast in a small town." A haunted expression flitted across her face.

The other two fell to discussing logistics. Jasper groused, "Dad's making a fuss about the caterers. They're already bellyaching to him about the distance from suppliers to the site."

Sally clucked her tongue. "Penhallow is only four miles away from Amity Landing. What's the big deal?"

He scowled. "They do this at every off-campus site he sends them to. They whine and complain and finally accept the job—with a suitable increase in their remuneration of course."

"Speaking of, I think I deserve a raise for hazardous duty. Guess how I spent yesterday?"

"Has to be with the Red Hat ladies. Bunch of old coots in purple dresses who rampage through town harassing the inhabitants like a modern-day James gang. The one in charge accosted me the other day. Ripped me up and down for crossing against the light." He shivered. "She's terrifying."

"That would be Edna Mae Quimby." Cassidy suppressed a smile.

Sally turned to her. "Quimby, you say? It must be her husband I had to deal with then. The sheriff."

Cassidy started. "Sheriff Quimby? What did he want with you?"

"He was asking about Rick Ahearn—the subcontractor who found the Spinney house for me. Evidently he's dead."

Cassidy thought of the news article Nellie had brought in. "That's right. They found him a mile from

Amity Landing. He was dressed in a sailor suit."

"Yeah—pretty queer, huh? I didn't have to ID him, thank God. Wouldn't have been able to anyway—we only spoke on the phone. The hotel found my card in his room and gave it to Quimby. He wanted to know what my connection was to him. I told him I'd hired him to find sites for the filming, but that I hadn't heard from him in days." She blew her cheeks out. "Bit of a jolt to hear what happened to him."

Jasper drained his beer. "Sailor suit, huh. So they think he fell off a boat and drowned?"

"That's what they thought at first, but no."

"No?"

"No. Sheriff told me he was found on this floating barge out in the middle of the cove." Sally jumped off her stool and plopped some bills on the bar. "Gotta go. You coming, Jasper?"

"Might stay for dinner." He regarded Cassidy tentatively. "Fancy a bite to eat?"

She nodded, afraid to speak, afraid he'd see her pleasure at his invitation. She followed him out, but at the top of the stairs remembered her purse. She ran back. Pauline was standing behind the bar, a singular expression on her face. It might have been panic, but the fear was mixed with a hefty dose of sheer bafflement.

Chapter Eight

Amity Landing, Saturday, June 24

"Will *someone* get this sound cart out of my way? Where's that key grip? Lyle! Lyle Korn! Dammit." The man's voice was loud enough to carry up to Cassidy's deck, where she sat with her morning coffee. She got up and leaned over the railing. Down the hill, a figure stood in the middle of Broadway, his golden locks glinting in the sun. He waved his arms. Behind him, steam rose from a glossy, pumpkin-colored convertible, a McLaren by the looks of it. In front of him, a cart bristling with microphones and boom poles sat in the middle of the intersection. She watched, amused, as a jeans-clad man with the shoulders of a linebacker came running up. The blond crooked a finger at him. "You a grip? Hurry up, would you?"

It's gotta be the Toff. She decided to mosey down the hill and take a gander at the great man. She grabbed her mug and arrived just as the grip rolled the cart off to one side. Up close, the actor appeared older than the purportedly candid shots in the magazines. Fine lines and dark spots littered his face. *Candid, my eye. He's at least in his fifties.*

"Took you long enough, man. What's your name? I've a mind to report you to Lyle. I don't like to be kept waiting."

The man tipped his hat and muttered, "Name's Trent, sir. Sorry to inconvenience you. I would never have left this here. The sound mixer did."

"Huh." Apparently Toff-Smythe was not one to be troubled by pesky facts. "No excuse anyway." He got in the McLaren and roared off at twenty miles an hour above the speed limit. They heard a screech of tires and a horn honking. Cassidy didn't need to look to guess he'd nearly run over someone. Amity Landing was a walking town, with very little room for cars. Water Street—the lane Toff-Smythe had just raced down—was usually more a parking lot than a road, and pedestrians had full rights-of-way down the middle of it.

She smiled at Trent. "So that's the inimitable Digby Toff-Smythe?"

The man gazed at the dust settling. "The great man himself, yes." He looked her over. "You a denizen?"

"You mean, do I live here? Yes. Cassidy Jane Beauvoir. And you are?"

"Trent. Bill Trent." He turned his back on her and went toward the dolly.

I guess that's the end of the conversation. Cassidy was headed back uphill when a car beeped behind her. She turned to see the Lamborghini stopped in the spot the McLaren had just vacated. *What is this? Hundred-Thousand-Dollar Car Day?*

"Hey, Cassidy!"

She took a last sip of cold coffee and walked back down. "Hi, Jasper. So do you guys keep a car in every port, or do you pay coolies to bear your precious automobile on their backs across country?"

He didn't miss a beat. "Don't be silly. It travels in a

specially made railroad car. No? Actually, I have a custom-built sledge for it, drawn by ten matched stallions, who canter from city to city in my wake, driven by my personal coachman."

Cassidy decided she could safely ignore the sarcasm. "I think I just encountered the Toff."

"You *think*? The man gives 'demigod' a whole new definition."

"Okay. Greek hero with Samson's locks and Julius Caesar's nose?"

"That's the chap. I've been ordered to introduce him to the Spinney house. Want to come along?"

She checked her watch. She didn't have to open up the store for another couple of hours. "Sure."

"Hop in." They proceeded at a more sober pace past the row of tiny houses perched on the cliff above the bay and pulled in next to the green-shuttered Spinney house behind the McLaren. They walked down the steps and entered the kitchen. It looked the same as when Cassidy showed it to Sally, but the rest of the house had been transformed into Prospero's cave. Black curtains covered all the windows—even the great bay ones looking out to sea. Equipment and captain's chairs were strewn about, the original furniture pushed against the walls. Cassidy sucked in a breath. "Why did you need a real house if you were going to turn it into a studio?"

"Oh, we'll move stuff around as needed. There's Digby." He led her over to the current heartthrob of dozens of middle-aged women. The actor was standing in the middle of the room, eyes shut, with a hand over his heart.

"Digby?"

He started. "Who disturbs me in my cogitation?" His round BBC tones resonated in the room. He opened his eyes. "Oh, it's you, MacEwan. What do you want?"

"I would like you to meet Miss Cassidy Beauvoir." He made it sound as if he were doing Toff-Smythe a favor of the highest order. "Cassidy? This is Digby Toff-Smythe, star of our little project."

"Little? My dear boy, this will be the toast of Sundance, of Cannes, of Venice. It has all the makings of my best effort yet." He smiled graciously at Cassidy. "Are you with the crew, Miss Beauvoir?"

Jasper jumped in. "No, she's the president—"

"Chairman."

"Chairman of the board of overseers of this town."

"I see." He shook her hand. "It's always gratifying to connect with the local establishment. Are you here to present me with the keys to your municipality?"

This question met with astonished silence. Finally, Jasper—his voice rather desperate—added, "And she owns Mindful Books. It's a bookstore in Penhallow. I'm pumping her for recommendations for nearby watering holes. I know you prefer to avoid the canteen—all those fawning stagehands."

The Toff gave him a sharp look. "Yes. Well." He waved a hand around the room. "This will do nicely. I've been communing with the spirit of the house. I want to be one with it."

Cassidy couldn't help herself. "Why?"

"Why? This, my dear, was the home of Captain Nathaniel West, scion of the distinguished Wests of York, England, and Rockport, Massachusetts."

"But Digby—"

His voice swept over Jasper's. "I must inhale the

74

atmosphere of centuries of sailing tradition if I'm to understand the man."

Cassidy stifled the giggle. "You do know this wasn't actually his house, right? Although there are several real captain's houses in Penhallow, number two Bay Street has been in the Spinney family for several generations. As far as I know, they're grocers from Nova Scotia."

He gestured grandly. "No matter. In a couple of days, it will become the refuge of a wandering privateer, the place from which he launches his expeditions, and to which he bears his booty." He paused to sip from a bottle of water. Cassidy noticed the label. *Evian*.

"But Digby—"

"I propose to sleep here."

Jasper gasped. "I don't think that's possible. It's not in our contract."

"Well, make it so. Where's Crook? She can handle that. Or your father. Just fix it." He sailed out the side door. They watched him stalk down the steps to the rocky beach. Cassidy was sure he planned to pace the shore, like a sailor waiting for his ship to come in. *Or a sailor's wife.*

"Damn."

"I'm sure Mrs. Spinney wouldn't mind if he stays here, Jasper. After all, she's renting the whole house to you. Do you want me to call her?"

"Would you? I have to go find Sally and have her get his things from the hotel. And figure out how to tell him that we're using this house for the Canadian scenes with Mercy Spinney. Oh, and that Dad wants him to play the British general." He went out to the car and started it up. "See you later."

****

Amity Landing, Saturday, June 24

Mrs. Spinney was perfectly happy to have a lodger in the house. "I spoke with that young public relations girl—a Sally Crook I believe. Such an odd name, don't you think, Cassidy Jane? Anyway, I told her she was free to use the house however she sees fit, but that I expect it to be returned to its original condition before I arrive."

"And when will that be?"

"What? Just a minute, let me check…Here it is. August the first. Oh, that reminds me. I had some items shipped to Amity Landing from here. I'm trying to clear the Westport house out before I move in with my sister in Winnipeg. Can you make sure they are put on the top floor? There are a couple of rooms under the eaves. Either one will do."

"No problem. What kind of items should I be looking for?"

"Well, let's see…There are some boxes of books and paintings. That portrait of Patience Spinney as a child. Then there's an old chest and a few lamps. That's it. Come to think of it, that's a lot for you to contend with. Just tell Chick. He can direct the movers."

"Of course. Any idea when they'll arrive?"

"Any day now. Oh, dear, I hope it won't interfere with the movie people."

"I'm sure it won't." She hung up and called Chick.

"Mrs. Spinney's stuff? She told me about it last week. It was delivered yesterday. Took care of it."

"Great. I'm afraid Mrs. S. may be getting a bit vague. It's probably a good thing she's giving up the

Westport house. Thanks, Chick."
****

Cassidy's house, Saturday, June 24

With Digby happily ensconced in the upstairs front bedroom of Mrs. Spinney's house, Cassidy and Jasper sat on her deck nursing beers as the twilight thickened into night.

"I told you he was something else, didn't I?"

"Almost a caricature, I'd say."

"Almost?"

"Do you suppose he's cavorting with the cobwebs?"

"I—" Whatever Jasper was going to say was punctured by a screech. He leapt out of his chair. "Where the hell did that come from?"

She pointed. "Over there. Probably raccoons scuffling."

Another screech—this time definitely human—brought Cassidy out of her chair too. Jasper muttered grimly, "Digby." He tripped down the back stairs and loped down the hill, Cassidy hot on his heels.

They found the Toff standing in the gravel road, barefoot, wearing an old-fashioned long, white, ruffled nightshirt. Jasper—who'd had the presence of mind to grab a flashlight—shone it in the fellow's face. His eyes were wild. He grabbed Jasper's sleeve and babbled, "Lights, action, roll 'em. Cut…cut. Lights…lights."

Jasper gently peeled him off. "We're not filming, Digby. Did you have a bad dream? What's the matter?"

By this time, the cottages around them had emptied of people and a crowd had formed around the trio. Voices rose above one another. "What's happening?"

"Who's caterwauling? It scared my cat!"

"This is *not* proper Amity behavior. Will you look at the time! It's almost nine o'clock." Cassidy recognized the voice of Velma Puddleby, the matriarch of Amity Landing.

Ooh, Digby's in trouble now!

Digby had barely recovered his composure when he became aware of his audience. He straightened, and his tone grew less shrill and more strident. At a decibel level more suitable for the Broadway stage, he declared: "I have been visited by an unearthly phenomenon. Strange lights. Loud noises"—he pointed a trembling finger at the Spinney roof—"coming from above me. I felt a *presence*."

A low hum rippled through the pack. "A presence, you say? Was it freezing cold?"

"Did it moan?"

Digby maintained his dignity. "Laugh if you will, but I was first awakened by a knocking sound—"

"Acorns on the roof."

"And then a whitish light flashed on and off several times."

The man who lived across the street stepped between Cassidy and Jasper. "That was me."

Cassidy introduced him. "This is Graham Rutter."

Rutter's bathrobe fell open and he tied it, but not before everyone glimpsed his Captain America pajamas. "I thought I heard a skunk in the garbage and went to investigate. What you probably saw was my flashlight."

Digby was beginning to falter. "And…and steps on the stairs."

This finally had an effect. "*Hmm*."

"*Hmm*."

In the speculative silence, Velma Puddleby chuckled. "Ah, I see you've met Snookie then."

Chapter Nine

Amity Landing, Saturday, June 24

"Snookie? Who's Snookie?"

"She's our resident ghost. Every Maine village has one. State law."

"Ghost? Was she murdered? Did she fall from the rafters and die, impaled on the flagpole?" He whirled around to face the shore. "Was she hurled against the rocks in a storm and broken to pieces? Does she…does she haunt anyone with the temerity to stay in her house? Oh my God, was she burned as a *witch*?" Digby began to wail, all traces of affectation gone. "I…I *really* don't like ghosts." He turned to Jasper and grabbed his shirt again. "I'm not doing this, MacEwan. I'm out of here." He started to stride down the road, his nightshirt flapping against his ankles, when Cassidy coughed.

"Mr. Toff-Smythe?"

He spun around. "What?"

"Don't you want to know what kind of ghost Snookie is?"

"No!" He must have finally registered the smirking faces around him, for he paused. "Okay, what is it?"

Mrs. Puddleby responded. "She's about seven. Her hair is a rich chestnut brown. She has lovely long floppy ears and wags her tail a lot."

"Huh?"

"She's a cocker spaniel. Belonged to Grace Spinney's grandmother Patience. She was run over by the milk wagon in 1888. Very sad. Patience was still a child, and she was so grief-stricken she set up a little memorial to the dog." She indicated a small cairn in the park. "It's over there. You'll be able to see it better in the morning."

"So…" added Cassidy, "it's hardly a bloodthirsty ghoul out to gnaw on your bones."

Someone chirped, "She might try to bury them though."

The audience began to disperse. Soon Cassidy, Digby, and Jasper were left alone in the faint light from the streetlamp. Jasper asked, "Are you going to be okay, Digby?"

The actor was quiet. "I shall cope for now, but I want to move back to the hotel tomorrow morning. Make the arrangements, would you? And I think…yes…I shall agree to take on the role of the British commandant instead of West. His scenes will be shot in Castine, I believe. The American doesn't have the…er…gravitas that what's-his-name does."

"Brigadier General Francis McLean. Who was also, by the way, the governor of Nova Scotia."

At this, the Toff brightened considerably. "Then it's settled."

"Sure, sure. We'll square it with my father. Here, I'll walk you back inside."

"I'm coming too." Suddenly Cassidy didn't want to be left alone. *It may be a dog, but it's still a ghost.*

They walked slowly down the steps and into the kitchen. Digby flipped on every light switch as he went through the house. He checked the living room. "Look!

Part of the blackout curtain has been detached."

Jasper snapped it back into place. "Probably just the wind. I'll come by in the morning to get your stuff."

Cassidy knew it took an effort, but Toff-Smythe managed a weak smile. "Thanks. Appreciate it." He saw them out. The lights in the house were still on when they turned the corner to Cassidy's house.

"Whew. That worked out well. I hadn't yet come up with a plan to wheedle him into taking the new part."

"The British general?"

"Yup. Also, I won't have to deal with Digby underfoot here in Amity, at least until the last scenes." Jasper stopped at his car. "Well, it's been a long night."

On impulse, Cassidy stood on her toes and kissed him. "You were kinder to that ham sandwich than I would have been."

In response, he pulled her into his arms. A fierce kiss later, he stumbled back. "I…I'm sorry, Cassidy. I don't know what came over me. You already think I'm one of those Hollywood reprobates with a casting couch and a stable of starlets. I'll leave you alone. I promise." He jumped in the car before she could reply.

She watched him out of sight down the street. When she was sure he was gone, she whispered, "You idiot."

****

Amity Landing, Sunday, June 25

The rumbling of big trucks and shouts snapped her awake. She started to rise and fell off the couch. A beer bottle rolled out of the way. The television was playing a muted episode of *The A Team*. She stood up and tripped over the book on Maine history she'd been reading, in a probably futile attempt to catch up to Jasper. Cassidy's mouth felt sticky, as did her hands. *Why didn't I just go to bed last night after Jasper left?* That's right. She was ruminating on her prejudices. And on a pair of intense gray eyes. *And a kiss. Don't forget the kiss.* She touched her tongue to her teeth. *Ick.* The doorbell rang. She peered out the window. A familiar sports car was parked on the verge.

"Oh, shit." She ran upstairs, shedding her clothes as she climbed, and jumped in the shower. Toweling off with one hand and brushing her teeth with the other, she bounded back down the stairs wearing only a shift, just in time to see the Lamborghini disappear down the hill. "Damn, damn, damn."

Oh, well, might as well finish my toilette. Her stomach made its emptiness felt. *And get some food.* What with all the commotion, she never did eat the previous night. She fixed her makeup first—*just in case*—then cooked breakfast. The smell of bacon frying reminded her of her father. He'd been a farmer out in Unity until his knees gave out. At the age of fifty, he opened what became the most popular restaurant in Penhallow and presided over it for fifteen years. He let his daughters do the farming, and Mainers came from as far away as Greenville and Lewiston to eat his potato pie. Late in life, he'd taken up beer brewing and traveled all over the state exhibiting his wares.

Cassidy smiled at the memory. *He was so proud of his Penhallow stout. He always said it beat Old Haley's brew by a full keg.* Ichabod Haley, his arch rival in all things, had finally acknowledged the superiority of her dad's beer and gone back to making blueberry wine. *And moonshine.* She cracked an egg into the pan and popped a piece of Mrs. Scoggins' homemade rye bread into the toaster.

She stared at her reflection in the shiny aluminum, her thoughts inevitably veering onto the old question. *Why...how did Pop die, Lord?* They never found out. Her sister Jennika had taken the call from the police. *Has it been five years now?* He'd been discovered in the tasting room, his skull bashed in. A steel keg was found by his body, and the police assumed it had fallen from the shelf above the bar. The coroner pronounced cause of death to be accidental. At the funeral, Cassidy had glimpsed the exultant expression on Haley's face just before he switched it off. Jennika and Gaby refused to believe there was anything suspicious about Pop's death, but Cassidy had never been satisfied. *One of these days I'm going to force Sheriff Quimby to reopen the case.*

She readied herself to go to work. The store wouldn't be open, but she had inventory and some numbers to record. *I've gotten way behind in the last few days.* As she took the stairs down to the carport, she saw the Lamborghini fly by in hot pursuit of the McLaren heading north. Oblivious to the twenty-five-mile-per-hour speed limit, they roared out of Amity. She followed sedately, parked behind the store, and walked around the corner to upper Main Street. Sure enough, the two sports cars were both double-parked in front of the Waldo Bed and Breakfast where Jasper was staying. *So the Toff is leaving Mrs. Spinney's to the dogs.*

She was shelving a set of the works of Henry Wadsworth Longfellow when the bell rang. She unlocked the door, and Jasper came in.

"Er, hi." He kept his eyes on the floor.

She spoke cheerfully. "Good morning! What can I do for you? Technically, I'm not open until Tuesday, but I just found a new book on the Father Le Loutre War, if you're interested."

"Who?"

"He was a priest and leader of the Acadians, French settlers in Nova Scotia and parts of Maine. They battled the British before the French and Indian War broke out and eventually were forcibly removed. Very sad."

"Oh, so he was part of the diaspora?" He smiled into her eyes. "It's lucky a few of them stayed around. Lucky for me, anyway." Before she could think of a response, he said, "Wait, I just thought of something. Aren't the Cajuns descendants of the Acadians?"

"Good for you. Yes. When the British governor expelled them, some were sent back to France, but many more went south."

"Not so sad then. We wouldn't have andouille, and shrimp étouffée, and…what's their music called?"

"Zydeco. Don't ask me where the word originated." He seemed to be warming up to list more Cajun specialities, so she quickly interjected, "You didn't say why you were here."

"Oh!" He blushed purple. "What with all the brouhaha last night, I…uh…I forgot my sweater at your house. Do you mind if I come by and pick it up this evening?"

"The royal blue cashmere with the little designer insignia? That one?"

"Oh, come on, Cassidy. I can't help it if I was born with a silver spoon in my mouth."

"That explains why you talk so funny." She decided to let him down easy. "I was making a joke. It's very soft. As a matter of fact, I slept on it last night." *On the couch.* She grinned at him. "Did you get the Toff settled at the B&B?"

"Yes. Unfortunately, he had to take my room. They're booked solid." He gestured outside. "I've got my stuff in the car. I've been assigned ghost duty in Mrs. Spinney's house."

"Do you have to stay there?" Cassidy wasn't sure she liked that idea. Snookie might decide to be ornery and bite him.

"It's all right. I've got a military grade flashlight. And a penknife." It was his turn to grin.

"You might want to stock some dog biscuits, too."

****

Amity Landing, Sunday, June 25

When Cassidy got home, she showered and changed into an old cotton dress the color of seafoam. Her sister Jennika always complimented it because, she said, it matched Cassidy's light blue-green eyes, the one feature she'd inherited from her father. The rest of the family sported his fair skin and blond hair, but Cassidy's coloring was a throwback to the raven tresses and olive skin of her mother's Passamaquoddy ancestors. As for her, she liked the dress because it had pockets.

She picked up Jasper's sweater and walked down the hill to Mrs. Spinney's house. Jasper had a bag of groceries on the kitchen table and was attempting to find space in the tiny refrigerator. He looked up. "Oh! You didn't have to do that, Cassidy."

"I figured you were busy unpacking." She eyed the

open refrigerator door. "Where were you planning to put the case of beer?"

He pulled a couple of cans from the carton and handed one to her. "How thirsty are you?"

They went out on the little side porch. In the mist of early evening, the moored boats seemed to float inches above the flat water. Jasper heaved a sigh. "It's so nice and quiet here."

"Um. So when does the shooting start?"

"In a few days. We're still scouting places in Castine. A lot of the heavy equipment has yet to arrive. Lowry and Hadley are in charge of that."

Lowry and Hadley? "Oh, you mean Laurel and Hardy."

He stared. "Huh?"

"Well? You don't see it?"

A slow grin formed. "Thanks a lot. I am *never* going to get that image out of my head."

Cassidy took a sip of beer. "So what are *you* in charge of?"

"I'm supposed to be going over the script with the Toff. Also, working on stage directions and finalizing the shooting schedule."

"You'll be very busy then." *Why am I suddenly depressed? What happened to that buoyant feeling of just a minute ago?*

"Yes." He glanced at her. "I'll be out of your hair most of the time."

She so wanted to say he could get stuck in her hair any time he wanted but guessed that would sound peculiar. *Besides, he's from another planet. He isn't interested in a small-town girl like me.* She looked down at her dress. *With no fashion sense.*

"Cassidy? Do you mind if I kiss you?"

"What?"

"Oh, well, never mind." He took a big gulp of beer and began to cough. Drops flew out his nose, and he grabbed for the first thing handy, which turned out to be a lace mat that Cassidy happened to know was a Spinney family heirloom. She snatched it from him and gave him a tissue from her pocket.

"Jasper?"

"I'b all right. Just by node iz stuffed ub." He blew it vigorously.

"Jasper? I don't mind."

"You don't mind what?…Oh." He looked at her, his eyes streaming. "Give me a minute, will you?"

Well, at least I can kiss the chance *goodbye.*

Cassidy took a step toward the kitchen, but Jasper grasped her elbow and turned her to face him. He ran his hands up and down her arms and scrutinized her face. After a minute, he said, "Ready?"

The kiss left her wobbly.

She stumbled to the door. "Gotta go. See you. Night." She ran up to the street and all the way to Chick's before slowing. She heard him call, but she walked home as fast as she could. *I have to think about this.*

But she didn't. She floated around in a haze of happy dreams on top of a pillow of cotton candy and finally took herself to bed.

It was after midnight when she awoke to screams.

Chapter Ten

Amity Landing, Monday, June 26

"*Again*?" She threw on a robe and went downstairs. *At least it can't be Digby this time.* Down the hill, lights were flashing and moving. Voices shouted. *If it's that damned ghost dog...Wait...if it's that damned dog, she's bothering Jasper.* She took off running.

By the time she reached Mrs. Spinney's house, the usual mob had gathered. In the midst of it, the red light atop Sam the rent-a-cop's patrol car twirled. She forced her way through and poked her head into the driver's seat side. "What's going on?"

Sam held up a hand and spoke into his phone. "Yeah, Sam Spade here. Amity Landing security." He listened. "Right, we need a hook and ladder stat. Spinney house, number two Bay Street. Hurry." A siren started up in the distance.

Just then, a husky man appeared, pushing a large rolling ladder. "Out of the way, folks! I'll get him down." He set the ladder in place by the wall and proceeded to jack it up.

For the first time, Cassidy turned to look at the house. A body was hanging half in, half out of a dormer window. "Oh my God. Jasper!" *He can't be...oh, please God, don't let him be dead.*

Graham Rutter came up beside her. "Skunk was

making a ruckus again. I came outside to chase it off, but then I heard this cracking sound and looked up. Fellow came flying out the window." He played his flashlight over the house. "He must have caught his feet on the sill. I hope he's all right."

The fire engine came to a stop at the end of the street and turned its headlights on high. One fireman shouted at the would-be rescuer, who ignored him. He caught Jasper under his arms and slowly pulled him from the window, seating him on the work platform. Then, using a lever handle, he gradually lowered the platform to the ground. Two responders rushed to the slumped form and began to check his vitals. The man stood to one side, hands on hips.

Cassidy went over to him. "Is he…is he…alive?"

He nodded. "Yeah, and damned lucky to be. Would've fallen if we'd waited for the fire truck." He spat.

She looked at him curiously. "Do you work for Black Brothers?"

"Yeah. Name's Phalen."

"How did you know he was up there?"

Graham offered, "He probably heard me shout."

"No, I didn't hear anything." He waved toward the street. "I was coming down the lane. Saw someone standing in the window, swinging at something. Maybe a bat. Probably lost his balance."

"Where did you find the ladder?"

He gazed over her shoulder. "I…uh…"

"Never mind." The medics were helping Jasper to his feet. Cassidy ran down to him. "Jasper! Are you all right?"

He nodded, then winced and put a hand to his head.

One of the medics said, "Looks like he hit his head on something. He'd better be evaluated for concussion." He signaled for a gurney. "We'll take him up to the hospital and have them check him out."

She frowned. "What would he hit his head on? He fell out of the window."

The grip leaned in. "Likely whacked himself on the window frame trying to shoo the bat. Got a close look at the siding. That house is a death trap. Nobody should be staying overnight in it."

The EMT shrugged. "Tell it to the judge." He and his partner rolled the gurney up the bank and into a waiting ambulance.

Without thinking, Cassidy climbed in with them. She sat on a fold-down stool and reached for Jasper's hand.

He lay back and closed his eyes. "Tell Dad…hotel…"

When they arrived at the hospital, the nurse stopped her at the doors to the ER. "You can't go in with him, Cassidy. You're not a relative. Rules is rules."

Casting about for something to do, she remembered Jasper's request. *Now where was his father staying? Oh, yes, the hotel in East Penhallow.* She went to the information desk. "Can you get me the Penhallow Harbor Inn on the line, Wanda? I need to notify the patient's father."

"Sure." The nurse dialed and handed the receiver to Cassidy.

"Can I speak to Philip MacEwan? He's a guest there." She waited. "Mr. MacEwan? This is Cassidy Beauvoir. I'm at the Waldo Memorial Hospital. Your son's had a...an accident."

The voice on the other end paused a millisecond before answering briskly. "Serious?"

"I don't know. They're checking him for a possible concussion."

"Address?"

She gave it.

"I'll be there shortly." He hung up.

Okay...

By the time MacEwan arrived, the doctor was in the lobby talking to Cassidy. MacEwan started to shove them apart, but the doctor held up a hand and continued to address Cassidy. "Took a blow to the back of the head. We'll keep him here for the rest of the night just to be sure he's stable." He finally acknowledged the new arrival. "And you are?"

"Philip MacEwan. The boy's father."

Cassidy didn't think a thirty-something-year-old qualified as a boy, but apparently his father did. *That may explain why Jasper's so unsure of himself.* She curled a censorious lip at Philip, which he didn't catch.

The doctor was speaking. "Would you all like to see him?"

"I do."

MacEwan waved Cassidy back, but she followed him in anyway. Jasper lay supine on the bed, tubes snaking from his arm. She felt a rush of fear and affection and elbowed MacEwan out of the way. "Jasper! It's me, Cassidy."

He opened his eyes. "Cass? What are...what are you doing here?" He saw his father behind her. "Hey, Dad. How's tricks?"

Cassidy expected the older man to be, at the least,

impassive—maybe even cold—and was unprepared for his response. He went down on his knees beside the bed. His voice broke. "Oh, my son." He clasped Jasper's free hand and held it to his cheek. "Don't scare me like that."

"Dad—"

Philip raised his head to the nurse. "You gave him an antibiotic, I presume?"

She looked bewildered. "No, sir. We're treating him for concussion."

He pointed at the needle in Jasper's forearm. "He has mitral valve prolapse. You must administer an antibiotic before inserting anything into a vein."

The nurse ran out, returning in seconds with a new pouch. She unhooked the old one and replaced it. "I'm sorry, sir. We had no medical records for him. We didn't know." She flicked at the bag. "He should be okay."

He stood up. "He had better be, or—"

"Dad." Jasper's voice was soft but very firm. "Stop."

The doctor put his head in. "Okay, folks, time's up. You can come back in the morning. If you'll give your contact information to the registrar, she'll get in touch with you should anything change."

MacEwan hesitated, then bent down and kissed his son's forehead. "Take care." He left.

As Cassidy made to go, Jasper called to her. "Cassidy, wait." She returned to the bed. "I didn't want Dad to hear. Cass, someone hit me."

"Hit you! You mean, a person? You didn't knock your head on the window frame?"

"No. I heard noises—a doorknob rattling, and then

footsteps—"

"Just like Digby did?"

"Uh-huh. It seemed to come from the attic. I went to investigate. Did you know that place is a warren of little rooms and halls? It's like a maze. Plus, there aren't any light switches, at least that I could find, and in short order I was lost. I passed a room with a window and thought I'd open the shutters for some light and to orient myself. I don't remember anything after that."

Cassidy was still back on the first sentence. "A person hit you?"

"That's what I've been saying." His hand went to his head. "Digby was right. Someone's been breaking into Mrs. Spinney's house."

"But what on earth for?"

The night nurse came in. "Really, Miss Beauvoir, you have to go."

She reluctantly let go of Jasper's hand. "I'll be back in the morning. We'll talk further."

His eyes pleaded. "Tell the police."

****

Penhallow police station, Monday, June 26

"I understand, Toby, but he was adamant. He was sure someone hit him."

"Waall, you know these Hollywood types—they get all kinds of wacky notions. Not down-to-earth like us Mainers." The sheriff absently rubbed the belly of the laughing Buddha on his desk. "Besides, Graham Rutter says he didn't see anybody."

"No, but the house was dark. He wouldn't have seen anyone behind Jasper...Mr. MacEwan. His assailant probably ran out the back door."

"All right, I'll dispatch Jeff. He can take a look

around."

"I want to go too."

"As long as you don't interfere." He paused. "Are those movie people working at the house?"

"I don't know, but whatever they're doing it will be downstairs. The upstairs should be unoccupied."

"I can chuck them out if necessary. Police take precedence." He didn't seem to be joking.

Cassidy had a thought. "Would it make sense to have Jeff wait till Jasper's released from the hospital? That way we can bring him along."

"You work it out with him. Now get along. Having to shuttle back and forth all day between the police station and the jail is driving me crazy. I've got to get some paperwork done before Edna Mae hits me with another jaywalker video."

Cassidy crossed the street to her store. All was quiet. Doctor Wilberforce had said he'd call her when Jasper was free to go, but that he'd have to inform Philip first. She hoped Jasper's father wouldn't insist on taking him back to the hotel in East Penhallow. *Or worse, back to California.* She'd been caught off guard by the elder MacEwan's display of affection and worry. He had seemed so aloof and dismissive of Jasper before. *Maybe that's his way of keeping it professional.*

She was working on the front window display, replacing the Memorial Day military histories with biographies of the Founding Fathers for the upcoming Fourth of July celebrations, when the phone rang.

"Miss Beauvoir? Mr. MacEwan is ready to go. You can pick him up any time."

"Did you call his father?"

"Yes, but the senior MacEwan said he had some

business to attend to first and wasn't sure how long he would be. He didn't want his son staying here, so he insisted I release the patient to you."

"Thanks, Doc. It'll be okay."

When she arrived at the hospital, Jasper stood out front. Behind him a nurse scowled and muttered. She swung the empty wheelchair back and forth angrily. Cassidy grinned at her. "Hey, Peggy. I'll take it from here."

Peggy twisted a lip. "He's all yours. He'd better not trip over the curb. There will be hell to pay."

Jasper pecked the nurse on the cheek. "Don't worry, Miss Peggy. If I do, I'll blame it on Miss Beauvoir, not you."

Cassidy hustled Jasper into her car.

He said, his voice full of mirth, "Let's get out of here before she calls an ambulance chaser."

She braked at the hospital entrance. "Right or left? Do you want to go to the B&B or to my house?"

"I want to go to Mrs. Spinney's."

She looked him over. "I don't think you should do anything strenuous for a couple of days."

He grinned at her. "Then why did you ask me to come to your place?"

Her cheeks stinging from all the blood rushing to her face, she snapped, "What are you implying?"

He touched her hand. "Cassidy, you came with me in the ambulance. You sat by me last night. You don't think that means something? Like maybe you're beginning to feel a little warmth somewhere around there?" He pointed at her heart. When she continued mute, he said diffidently, "I can't pretend to have all the fine upstanding qualities you require in the Perfect

Boyfriend, but give me a chance."

She gave a mighty sigh. "You're right, but—" She touched his nose. "You'll do for now."

He leaned over and kissed her, then yelped. "Ooh, don't let me do that again."

"Kiss me?"

"No, lean my head down. *Ooph*."

She was about to pull into her carport when she saw a squad car marked Penhallow Sheriff drive by. "That's Jeff. Come on." She took the short cut and beat the deputy to Mrs. Spinney's house by a second. "You stay in the car." She got out. She didn't hear him scramble out the other side.

"Hey, Jeff, didn't Toby tell you I wanted to go with you into the house?"

The deputy took off his hat and ruffled his hair. "Nope. And anyways, not sure that's kosher, Cass."

Cassidy felt her back go up. "Of course it is. I'm an overseer. As a government official, I have the right to…to…oversee." *Take that.*

"Oh. Okay. So, Sheriff says one of those actor guys claims he was bonked by person or persons unknown. He doesn't think much of the charge." He squinted at her. "You order him to investigate?"

"Me? I'm no Edna Mae—just a concerned citizen. And he's not an actor—he's the director of the picture." She felt a hand on her shoulder.

"That's right, officer. I'm Jasper MacEwan, director of *American Waterloo: The Rout of the Penobscot Expedition*. And the victim."

Cassidy pushed Jasper forward. "I brought him along to show us what happened."

She assumed Jeff wouldn't deny her, and she was

right.

"*Hmm*. Well, you'd best come then."

When Jeff got to the door, he stopped. "Uh…"

"Need a key?"

"In Amity? No. Someone's inside."

Chapter Eleven

Mrs. Spinney's House, Monday, June 26

Cassidy took a step back, hand to mouth. "You don't think…but it's broad daylight!"

Just then Philip MacEwan came out, the crewman named Phalen behind him. "Oh, Sheriff, glad you're here. I was asking this grip about last night."

The man stepped forward. "See, Sheriff—"

Cassidy interrupted. "This is Jeff Pierce. He's the deputy."

"Oh. Well, I was telling Mr. MacEwan here that I was taking a walk last night and saw his son leaning out the window swatting at something—"

"A bat?"

"Too dark to see what it was, but probably. Anyway, he must have slipped or something, 'cause he fell forward and was just hangin' there. I'd noticed an adjustable camera stand in the yard, so I ran to get it."

MacEwan gave the man a funny look. "Camera stand? In the yard?"

Phalen's eyes flickered, but he merely shrugged.

Jeff picked up the thread. "Why didn't you go into the house and pull him in?"

Cassidy had the answer. "It would have taken him too long—Jasper was all the way up under the eaves. And he was three-quarters of the way out—it looked like he was hanging by his toes. He would have fallen before the firemen arrived if Mr. Phalen hadn't reached him."

"Let's have a look." Philip turned and headed back inside. "Follow me, Deputy."

Jeff caught Philip's elbow. "Sir, I think I should take the lead."

"Oh? I see." MacEwan frowned but stepped aside.

Jeff climbed the stairs two at a time, the others struggling to keep up. At one point Jasper stopped, hand to his head. Cassidy took his other hand. "Are you okay?"

"Just a little dizzy." He smiled at her. "Maybe I shouldn't have come along."

"After this, we'll get you back to bed."

"As long as you promise to tuck me in."

They broke apart at the sound of Philip's voice. "Son? You coming?"

"Yes, Dad." He started up the stairs.

After a minute, Cassidy followed.

When he reached the third floor, Jeff walked slowly down the hall looking from right to left. Another, narrower corridor led to a wing that projected at right angles to the main house. Several doors opened onto it. Turning to Jasper, Jeff asked, "Can you retrace your steps?"

Jasper shuffled forward. "I'm not sure…I heard a strange rattling and saw a flashing light—"

Phalen said, "That neighbor guy was waving his flashlight around."

"Maybe that was it. So I decided to investigate. I…" He paused at a door. "I think I tried this one." It opened on a small broom closet. "Oops, that can't be it.

Maybe it was this one." The next room held a cot with a bare mattress. A ewer and basin stood on a beautiful French Empire-style walnut dresser. Sitting under the single dormer window was an old leather-bound foot locker. Several brown paper-wrapped pictures were stacked next to the bed. "This couldn't be it either—I would've had to push the chest aside." The third room seemed more promising. It had a dormer window, which was open. The ceiling sloped, so the men had to stoop. Jasper went to the window. "This looks about right."

The grip agreed. Cassidy wasn't sure, but then she had been much farther away. Jeff checked the window sill. "There are scuff marks on the paint—must have been your shoes." He headed to the door. "Yup—I'm guessin' that, like Mr. Toff-Smythe, what you most likely heard was acorns on the roof, mebbe squirrels."

"Or bats," put in Phalen helpfully.

Jeff paused, bent down, and pulled at a loose floor board. "You probably tripped on this." He straightened. "I think that about clears it up, Mr. MacEwan. Mystery solved."

Jasper was surprisingly acquiescent. "Okay, that must have been what happened. I was pretty tired. And"—he glanced at his father—"I've been known to sleepwalk. Thanks for investigating, Deputy. Really appreciate it. Now, if you don't mind, I'm going to rest for a bit. Dad? Didn't you have a meeting with the producer this morning?"

His father leveled a piercing look at his son. "Yes. Are you going to be in any shape for the canvass of Castine tomorrow?"

"Of course." Jasper opened his arms expansively.

"Off you go." He smiled, a little lopsidedly.

As the rest filed out, he caught Cassidy's sleeve. "Stay."

"Oh, Jasper, I'd love to, but you really do need to rest."

"It's not that, although…" He gave her a leer which reminded her more of a kid looking at a lollipop than a man lusting after a woman. He pulled her back inside and whispered, "It's something else. I think someone did break in and hid in one of these rooms. When I appeared, he tried to knock me out."

"How come?"

"Jeff found scuff marks on the windowsill."

"Yes, from your shoes."

"I wasn't wearing shoes."

"You weren't?"

"No. I was in my stockinged feet. Cassidy, someone climbed in that window before I fell out of it."

"Why didn't you tell Jeff?"

He held a finger to his lips. "I want to explore some—see if I can find more evidence. I'd also like to follow up with that grip. A ladder shouldn't have been left outside." He nodded at the police car outside. "The good police of Penhallow will begin to lose interest, and maybe patience, if I don't have something concrete to prove my theory. Are you with me?"

Cassidy heartily wished she could say yes. She shook her head. "I can't. I'm expecting a shipment of leftovers from the First Congregational Church bazaar. I have to be at the store." She laid a hand on Jasper's arm. "Don't do anything without me. Rest. We'll investigate tomorrow."

He pressed his lips together, then let a long breath

out. "All right. First thing tomorrow."

"Absolutely." She gazed around the room. "But just in case someone *is* trying to burgle this place, I really think you'd better stay at my house." At his raised eyebrow, she said firmly, "I have a very comfortable guest room."

She settled Jasper on her couch with a cup of herbal tea and went to town. It was almost six o'clock in the evening when she returned. A lamp was on in the living room, but the rest of the house was dark. She crept up the stairs and peeked around the door of Jasper's room. He was sprawled across the bed, snoring. *He is so cute. I hope he got something to eat.*

She went back downstairs to the kitchen. A plate with two crusts of pizza sat in the sink. An empty beer bottle lay on the floor near, but not in, the recycle bin. *He may be cute, but he's a slob.* She heard a step behind her.

"I know I left a mess, but I was just so tired I thought I'd take a little nap. I didn't realize how late it was. Must have slept for hours." He peered at her from under an unruly thatch of fawn-colored hair. "Sorry."

She turned around. "It's okay. I'll clean up. I need to eat something anyway. Did you finish the leftover pizza?"

"No, there's one piece for you. And I made a salad." He pulled a bowl out of the refrigerator. "Some nice greens." He winked. "Very California."

She settled at the table. "I'd offer you another beer, but Dr. Wilberforce says no alcohol with a concussion."

"S'okay. It was a very mild concussion. Nurse Peggy gave me a waiver. I think she's taken a fancy to me." He got two bottles from the refrigerator and sat across from her, pushing one beer to her side of the table. "So…I've been thinking."

"About the burglar."

"No, about us."

Cassidy swallowed. "Us?"

He leaned across the table. "You made it very clear from the get-go that you couldn't stand me—or rather, what I stand for. I was positive I had no chance with you." His eyes swept the kitchen. "For my part, I envied you. You've got such a cozy life here. Friends, roots, your own business. All the stuff I've never had. I've lived in five of the seven continents, never attended any school for more than two years, and never spent more than forty-eight hours with my parents." He patted the logo on his polo shirt. "Being rich is not all it's cracked up to be, believe me."

And I hurt you. Guilt washed over her. *I've been a closed-minded, pig-headed mule, haven't I?* "I'm sorry, Jasper."

"But then…you were there. When I needed you." His dove gray eyes, eyes that—in this light—reminded her of her comfy old ragg sweater, appealed to her. "Just tell me you've softened a little toward me. Tell me it's not all in my imagination."

The feeling that had been inching into her heart for days blossomed, and a melodious voice murmured something in her ear. It sounded an awful lot like *Kiss the boy.*

She was about to act on it when his phone buzzed. He pressed Talk. "Hi, Dad. Yes. Yes. Okay. Nine tomorrow. Got it. No, I'll drive. Doc says I'm good to go…What was that?" His eyes opened wide. In a strangled voice, he gurgled, "I love you too." He clicked Off, a mystified look on his face. The phone dangled from his hand.

"I take it your father made a rather unusual statement."

He didn't move. Finally he whispered, "He's never said that before. Ever." He looked at Cassidy. "Do you think he's dying?"

She laughed. "No, but he may have thought you were. Be happy. It's a new day."

He seemed to wake up. "Oh, that's the thing. We can't search the Spinney house tomorrow. I forgot—I have to go to Castine."

"To set up for the scenes there?"

"To scope out the town, and to find another house. Sally says there's a lighthouse near the fort. It should provide the elevation we need for filming the battle scenes."

"Yes, there is, and as I recall, it's got a good view of the point and surrounding islands." She chuckled. "With any luck, it's also haunted."

"Oh, dear. Let's not suggest that to the Toff."

Castine. Tomorrow is Tuesday. Cassidy hesitated. *Why not? I should spend some time with him. Work on those prejudices. Try to be a bigger person.* "Do you mind if I tag along?"

He started and gave her a searching look. "Not at all."

"I'll have to be back in Penhallow by two."

"Oh, we won't stay long." He gazed at her questioningly.

"I…I think we should get to know each other." She looked at the floor.

"Me too."

She jumped. He had moved so fast she didn't see him come around behind her. He gently pressed her back in her seat and kissed her forehead. She raised her arms and pulled him down over her shoulder. When it became clear that she couldn't actually reach his lips in this position, she pushed the chair back.

"Ow!"

"What did I do?"

"You dropped the chair leg on my toe." He bent his knee and hopped around the kitchen holding his foot. She tried to catch him, but he hopped into the living room and flopped on the couch. She knelt down and gently took his foot in her hand. "What are you doing, Cass? I'm not Cinderella."

"Role reversal. Didn't they teach you anything in acting school?"

"I didn't go to acting school. I preferred to acquire my theatrical skills through life experience."

"Never mind then." She rocked back on her heels.

He pulled her up onto his lap. "Tell you what, let's start at the top and work our way down to the lower appendages."

"It's a long way down." She giggled.

"We've got plenty of time."

Chapter Twelve

Cassidy's house, Monday, June 26

In fact, it was precisely an hour later that Cassidy languidly flexed her toes while Jasper kissed them. The rest of her deliciously sated body lay on the couch. She considered telling him that his nose was tickling her arch but decided instead to sit up and replace her foot with her mouth. He came around the arm and lay down next to her. She pulled a quilt from among the clothes cast willy-nilly around the living room and drew it over them.

She had just about dozed off when Jasper threw the cover off and heaved himself erect, taking up the conversation as though the recent interlude had only temporarily interrupted his thoughts. "I think I should stay at Mrs. Spinney's tonight, though."

"Huh? What are you talking about?"

"Me. Staying there. Tonight." He touched her breast playfully. "We discussed this. I think perhaps you were distracted." He raised his eyes to the ceiling. "What could it have been?"

Cassidy figured she could play it cool too. *Besides, I need time to get my head around this.* "Not at all. We're going to Castine in the morning and therefore will have to postpone our investigations."

"Right. I figure if the burglar doesn't see anyone

107

there tonight—no lights on or signs of activity, he may try again."

No! "What if he *does* come back? You're still recovering. I don't like it. It's too dangerous, I—"

She knew she was babbling, but the foreboding that something terrible would happen threatened to overwhelm her.

He held up a hand. "My stuff's still there. He won't risk discovery with me in the house, not after the last time." He smiled at her. "Don't worry, Cass. I'll be fine, but…" He bent down and kissed her full on the lips. "I think I'll have some delightful dreams."

****

Castine, Tuesday, June 27

Cassidy and Jasper met the rest of the crew at the Penhallow Harbor Inn the next morning. In a caravan of expensive cars, they drove up Route 1, across the bridge at Bucksport, and down the Blue Hill peninsula to Castine. Cassidy, observing the procession of black Mercedes and Land Rovers from the comfort of the Lamborghini, grumbled, "Maybe they should fly Black Brothers' flags on the front car, so everyone knows someone *special* is passing through."

Jasper laughed. "They usually do—don't know where we stashed those pennants. Should we beep our horns to the tune of 'God Save the Queen' as we roll through the charmingly quaint settlements? Perhaps tender a royal wave or two at the peasants?"

The rest of the trip was spent in stony silence.

On the outskirts of Castine, he stopped behind a long line of idling cars. Ten minutes later, they had gone two blocks. Jasper made a quick right on a side street. They circled around until they found a parking

108

space on an elm-lined lane called—appropriately—
Green Street and backtracked on foot toward the center
of town. As they passed a hotel festooned with bunting,
Jasper called to a man rocking on the wide porch.
"What's going on? What's with all the traffic?"

"It's the maiden voyage for first-yeeah students at
the academy."

"The Maine Maritime Academy?"

"Ayuh. All the families come to see the cadets off.
Most important event of the yeeah."

"Sure looks like it." Cassidy shaded her eyes and
surveyed the solid line of cars in the street. In the
distance, she could make out a large ship. "Is that the
State of Maine?"

"Yup. Trainin' ship for the school."

Jasper grimaced. "We probably won't be able to
explore much today then."

The man apparently thought Jasper's statement was
directed at him. "Sure you can. The ship leaves port at
noon. After that, everyone goes home." He squinted at
the two. "You tourists?"

"No. We're here on business."

"Ayuh?" The man waited, likely assuming his next
question was obvious and there was no reason to strain
his voice.

"We're…considering…making a movie here.
About the Penobscot Expedition."

"You from Hollywood?"

Cassidy could see that Jasper didn't want to
answer. She spoke rapidly. "He is, but his company's
camped down in Penhallow. They probably won't be
too disruptive."

"Ah." The man began to rock again, the

conversation clearly over.

Jasper and Cassidy ambled down the hill. Toward the bottom, shops and restaurants replaced the beautiful white Federal-period and Greek Revival houses. Ahead of them was the harbor, where the enormous ship loomed. Tiny figures roamed the upper deck, yelling and waving at the people on the wharf. "They must be students, saying goodbye to their parents."

"Do you suppose my father's stuck on the road too?" Just then Jasper's phone buzzed. He pulled it from his pocket. "Dad? Oh? Okay. Yeah, we found a spot to park. We'll just walk around until the crowds thin…get a sense of the place…I see. Well, if that's your decision…Okay…Oh, Sally is? Tell her to meet us by the—" He looked around. "—the Castine variety store at the corner of Main and Water Streets. All right." He clicked it off. "They've decided to head back to Penhallow. Sally found parking, and he wants the three of us to reconnoiter."

They waited at the corner until they saw the buxom figure of the PR chief roll into view. She came up to them, exclaiming, "Isn't this an amazing town? It's picture-postcard perfect." She must have caught sight of Cassidy's face, for she added, "Almost perfect, that is. Not quite as perfect as Amity Landing, as I'm sure goes without saying."

Mollified, Cassidy replied, "Well, Castine was primarily a ship-building town. It didn't have the economic diversification we had, so it was spared all the red-brick industrial architecture of the nineteenth century."

Sally looked skeptical. "Industrial architecture? I didn't see any factories in Amity Landing."

"Oh, sorry. I meant Penhallow. Since it's the principal city in the county, we tend to identify with it—at least when it serves our purposes." She grinned. "Penhallow had a fish cannery, and shoe manufacturing, and chickens. At one time, it was the largest distributor of processed chickens in the country." She ignored Jasper's subtle clucking. "We were also on the Penhallow and Moosehead Lake railroad line, at least until a few years ago." She gestured at the bay below them. "Castine, on the other hand, is stuck way out here on a rural peninsula. Visitors used to come by steamship, but when Route 1 was built in the 1920s, it bypassed Blue Hill. If it weren't for the academy, this would be a ghost town." She paused, struck by the frequency with which the word "ghost" seemed to enter every conversation.

"Whew. I guess we'll be welcomed with open arms then—Hollywood bringing a little excitement into their humdrum lives." Jasper put up an arm to deflect the blow.

She was going to surprise him with a kick but decided to save it for a more deserving infraction. "I don't know about that. Castine does have a crazy quilt of a history. *Fake* Hollywood history would make a poor substitute."

"Oh, yeah?" His shoulders straightened. "How so?"

"At one time or another, control of the town passed among the Tarratine Abenaki tribe, the French, the English, the Acadians, even the Dutch—all before the end of the Revolutionary War."

Sally's eyes widened. "The Dutch! And French? What the hell?"

Jasper patted her head. "Not to worry, Sal. We only need to focus on the English and the Americans."

Cassidy explained. "The Penobscot Expedition was mounted to evict English squatters from American territory."

Jasper jumped in. "That's right. As I told Dad, the English had established a fort here to defend Canada. Massachusetts organized a fleet to drive them out. Trouble was, no one—from the commanders on down—had any battle experience. The recruits were mostly boys and old men. While they sat anchored in the harbor arguing over what to do, a British relief force showed up."

When Jasper paused to take a breath, Cassidy saw her chance. *I'll be damned if Sally thinks the guy from away knows more about Maine than a Mainer. So what if I did learn it from him?* "And the Americans fled for their lives, burning or abandoning their ships. They lost all but one of their fleet, and over four hundred lives. The survivors literally walked home to Boston."

Sally had been listening raptly. Now she burst out laughing. "What an embarrassment! I hope those survivors had a doozy of an explanation by the time they reached home."

Jasper said wryly, "I'm sure they had prepared a variety of creative excuses." He stopped. "At least one fellow claimed the sailors stashed a hoard of gold before they left." He looked down the street. "I wonder…could it still be here?"

The other two gaped at him. Sally recovered first. "You know, that might make a good twist to the script."

Jasper slapped his hands together. "By Jove, you may be onto something. We'd originally planned a tale of hardship and perseverance. You know, the stragglers trekking over two hundred miles back to civilization, encountering bears and hostile natives and—um—rushing rivers. Then I came across the account of the cabin boy's adventures in Canada, and we went in that direction. I'm thinking if we mix in a little buried treasure we could have a blockbuster." He took Sally's arm. "Call the writers. Let's get them working on this."

Cassidy cleared her throat. "Don't you…er…want to have more facts before they start rewriting?"

Both film people raised their eyebrows. "Facts?"

"I mean, shouldn't the film have some semblance of a relationship to the actual history?"

"What history? I thought it was made up? A legend?"

"Even so, you want to get the details straight, don't you?"

Sally waved an airy hand. "Oh, the writers will do that. No problem." She picked up her phone. "You guys do some snooping around. That stringer Ahearn's last dispatch was from Camden, so I'm guessing he didn't get up this far north."

"Maybe because he was dead," Cassidy muttered. She added more loudly, "East. This far east."

"Huh?"

Jasper interrupted hastily, "We're on it. Are we looking for anything in particular?"

"A good house for the British commandant. Something near the fort. Oh, and check out Fort George too. It's a historic site, so I don't think it's been built over. Let's see…" Her eyes went down the list on her clipboard. "We'll also need a place—like a storefront or condo—that we can use for staging. I'll look for that and check in at the real estate office."

"Got it." They left her and walked along the waterfront. Jasper found a map of the town that indicated Fort George was a couple of miles away. They walked back to Green Street, retrieved the car, and drove along a winding country lane.

"There's a historical marker. Pull over here." Cassidy got out of the car. She read the sign and turned. "This is Fort George. It says it was begun by the British when they invaded Castine in 1779. It was never finished, but the partial earthworks stood until 1783. The English came back and rebuilt it in the War of 1812, only to demolish it in 1819."

They passed through a break in the grass-covered walls to find a large green field pockmarked by furrows and hummocks. She stepped across a small ditch. "Not much here."

Jasper consulted his guide. "There are a couple more fortifications in the town." He looked up. "Boy, for a little backwater, they sure felt the need to defend themselves." He tapped the map. "If one of the others has a better layout, we can probably use it instead."

"Sure. Let's keep this movie as detached from the truth as possible."

"Come on, Cassidy. Suspension of disbelief only goes so far—we have to have actual battlements if we're going to stage a naval battle."

"I believe you said the fort walls were only waist high by the time the Americans arrived. The attackers could've just hopped over them."

"Yes, I did tell you that, didn't I?" He surveyed the area. "That means that the site hasn't actually changed that much. Okay, maybe we should use it—in the interests of authenticity." He winked at her.

"I'm going to look over there." She had climbed halfway up a slightly larger hill when the ground suddenly gave way beneath her. She fell about four feet. "Jasper! Help!"

His head appeared. "Cassidy? Where are you?"

"Down here! I fell into a sinkhole."

"Are you hurt?"

"No." She scanned the area. A few feet away lay a pile of masonry bricks. *Rubble from the old walls?* She crossed to it. *Maybe one of them is marked.* She bent down to pick up a brick, and her backside banged into something hard. "Ouch!" She turned around. "Hey—Jasper? There's some kind of bunker down here. I see bars."

"Hold on, I'm coming down." A shower of gravel and dirt preceded him.

Cassidy tried to push at the bars, but they wouldn't give.

Jasper shook the gate. "Rusted shut, I imagine."

She peered between them. "It's too dark to see what's inside."

"I've got a penlight." He shone it into what appeared to be a small cave. Rubble filled most of it. "Wait, what's that?"

Cassidy took the light. "Something white. Oh, God, Jasper, it's a bone!"

"Helloooo down there. You folks all right?" A man's shadow crossed the shaft of sunlight.

They both looked up. "We think so."

"I'm the caretaker here. Name's Flint. What happened?"

Jasper answered. "We were walking and broke

through the soil. There's a cave entrance down here, with a gate across it."

"Ayuh. All that's left of the fort. That there was the brig. Sturdiest part of the whole place." He chuckled. "The Brits' top priority was to keep their prisoners from escaping, even when the town was being bombarded."

Cassidy called, "I thought I saw a bone in there."

"Didja now? Mebbe it's the drummer boy. Here, want help climbing out?" He extended a hand.

"But—"

Jasper whispered, "*Shh*. We can ask him when we get topside."

Flint yanked them out of the hole one at a time, and they sat down on a couple of boulders to catch their breath. Their rescuer—clad in faded overalls and a denim shirt—handed Cassidy a bottle of water. Behind him steamed a riding mower, its motor running. He inspected the damage. "With all the rain we've had, soil slid down the hill and covered up the opening. Happens every year. I'll have to clean this up and string some tape around so no one else discovers this the hard way."

Jasper pointed down. "You were saying about a drummer boy?"

"Ayuh." He plucked a stalk of hay off his shoulder and chewed on it. "Name of Horace Catchpole. Kid was conscripted by the Brits when they snuck into Castine and built Fort George. He was in the brig when they left. Died there."

Jasper nodded knowingly. "That's right, now I remember. I read about the boy. Didn't know there was any physical evidence of him."

Cassidy stared into the pit. "So…what did he do to end up in the brig?"

Chapter Thirteen

Fort George, Tuesday, June 27

"The boy had been caught stealing. He'd been tried and sentenced to thirty days in the brig. After the naval battle, General McLean—the British commander—abandoned the fort. Story goes they simply forgot he was there. He yelled and screamed, but no one heard him." Flint waved a hand at the road. "Town was too far away, and this part of the peninsula was uninhabited. He finally fell to drumming." His fingers did a little rat-a-tat in the air. "Not sure if it was to keep himself company or if he was still holding out hope he'd be rescued. Whatever—he never was. Drummed for three days and three nights, they say. Then the drum fell silent. It was full on a year later...on a dark and stormy night"—eyes closed to slits, his tone grew ominous—"the townspeople heard drumming coming from the fort. Some hardy folks followed the sound. When they reached the brig, all they found was a pile of bones."

Cassidy said in a small voice, "The drummer boy? Horace Catchpole?"

"Yes, ma'am. Must've died of starvation. The English rebuilt the fort in 1812, but the site was all overgrown and they never found him." He took off his John Deere cap and wiped his brow. "Ever since, folks say on hot summer nights they can still hear him—a-wailin' and a-drummin'." He leered at the two. "Stick around. Might be you'll hear him this evenin'."

"You mean…he's…it's…a ghost?" Cassidy tried not to shiver.

Jasper squeezed her hand. "So, do the bones down there belong to the boy?"

"Mebbe. Or to a dog. Dunno for sure. I have a key to the gate, but I'd have to clean the rust off. No reason to go in anyway. Besides"—Flint's grin grew wider—"a good ghost story always gives the tourists a bit of a tingle."

Cassidy bent over the sinkhole to look down. "If the brig was covered over, how did you know it was there?"

"We had a crew from University of Maine up here last year. They did some kind of sonar soundings and excavated it."

She noticed for the first time that the walls of the sinkhole were clear of roots and rocks, as though they'd been manually smoothed. "Ah."

He looked them over. "You folks ain't from around here." It was a statement.

Cassidy volunteered, "I'm from near Penhallow. This is Jasper MacEwan. He's making a film about the Penobscot Expedition."

"Is he really." The man looked him up and down. "You get permission from the town, I'll be glad to show you around."

"Thanks, Mr. Flint. We'll definitely call on you."

As the caretaker turned toward his tractor, Jasper whispered excitedly to Cassidy, "This is great! We can weave the drummer boy into the cabin boy's thread."

"How?"

"Remember the pension petition he submitted? In it, he mentions he discovered the drummer boy in the brig but says he couldn't figure out how to release him and had to go on. I'm sure he was wracked with guilt."

"More pathos?"

"Gooey, slushy pathos. Movie-goers'll eat it up."

The caretaker rumbled by on the tractor. Jasper ran over to him. Flint put it in park. "Need somethin' else?"

"Yes, please. We need space for the filming and the staging. We're looking for suitable houses—one for the commandant of the fort, maybe a couple more. Any ideas?"

He pressed his lips together. "Might try down Dyce Head. Keep going west on Battle Avenue till you hit a curve in the road. Driveway'll take you to a lighthouse with an attached house. It's right on the point."

"Is it an inn?"

"No. Family name of Deckers own it, but they spend most of the year in Florida now. They'd prob'ly let you rent it."

"We'll take a look. Thanks for everything."

He didn't bother to answer but started up his tractor and began to mow down the long grass.

Cassidy and Jasper cut across the field to the car. "Mr. Flint said it was this way." Jasper drove slowly down the lane. The houses petered out, until only empty fields lay on either side. At a curve in the road, a gravel drive led off to the left, ending at a house. The roof pitched precipitously from two stories in front to one in the back.

"Odd-looking building."

"It's a saltbox—you know, named after the boxes

the colonists kept salt in." A fence barred the way. "Look, there's a sign." Cassidy read it. "This is it. Dyce Head Lighthouse." The notice underneath told them the house was a private residence. "But it says visitors are welcome to take the path down to the bay. Let's take a look."

They opened a side gate to find a dirt path snaking through the trees. At the end, they had to scramble over some granite boulders and through a thicket of blackberry bushes, finally arriving at a rock-strewn promontory. Water surrounded them on three sides, small islands dotting the bay like a giant's muddy footprints. They turned around to view the comfortable cottage attached by a breezeway to a squat white lighthouse. Jasper made a frame with his fingers. "This would be perfect for the commandant's house. He can stand there with his binoculars—"

"You mean his telescope, don't you?"

"Yes, and watch the American fleet sailing aimlessly back and forth. He'll wonder what the hell they're doing."

"But nonetheless prepare for an attack."

"And send a courier for relief."

Cassidy gazed toward the town a few miles to the east of them, then to the west and the vast bay. "Why did they abandon the post after their victory?"

"Didn't you tell me they never finished building the walls? They probably just moved to a more luxurious fort. There was a French-built one somewhere on the peninsula. Better chow." He bent down to tie his shoelace. "Ready? It's time we found Sally and headed back."

They were climbing the hill when Cassidy halted.

"Look, there's a window open on the second floor of the house." She saw the glint of something metal. "I think someone's watching us."

"I'm sure the Deckers have a property manager. He's keeping an eye out for trespassers."

"But the sign said visitors are allowed."

"On the grounds. Not in the house."

She grudgingly agreed. "I guess."

They continued on to the side gate. A red SUV was parked in the lot next to the Lamborghini. Jasper said, "See? That must belong to the manager."

Something pinged off the Dyce Head sign. Jasper took a step toward his car, and a puff of gravel flew up at his feet. He stopped. Cassidy swung around toward the house and saw a curtain flutter. She screamed, "Run!" Instead Jasper fell flat on his face, his arms covering his head. "I said, run, Jasper!"

Holding a finger to his lips, he scrabbled like a lizard around the trunk of the Lamborghini. He rose on his knees, hoisted himself up to a crouch, and took off after her. They sprinted down the lane till they were out of sight of the house. "Hold on, Cass." Jasper panted. "We're out of range now. Let's walk back to Fort George. Maybe Flint's still there. We need to call the police."

The caretaker was nowhere to be seen. Cassidy slumped down on a rock. Jasper bent over, hands on knees, catching his breath. She indicated his pocket. "Why don't you just call 9-1-1 on your cell?"

"Left it in the car. Where's yours?"

"Left it in my purse. In the car."

"Well, Ollie, here's another fine mess you've gotten us into."

121

Cassidy couldn't help but giggle. "We could sure use Lowry and Hadley now, couldn't we?"

Jasper leaned against a fence. "Shall we knock on doors, or try to flag a driver down?"

Cassidy shaded her eyes. "No houses around. Also no cars. Let's keep moving. We'll need backup to tackle whoever's there."

"You want to go back?" Jasper stopped. "Why? In case you missed it, someone was taking potshots at us."

She gave him a sidelong glance. "Did you bring a spare Lamborghini in your suitcase?"

"Oh. Yeah." They headed back to the lane. "I hear a car coming." Jasper pushed Cassidy gently toward the asphalt. "You stand in the middle of the road, and I'll whistle it to stop."

She pushed back. "Or we could both whistle."

Luckily, before the argument degenerated into fisticuffs, a yellow Volkswagen stopped of its own accord. Sally stuck her head out the window. "Jasper? What are you doing?"

"Looking for you." He jumped in the shotgun seat, leaving Cassidy to climb into the back. "We need to call the police. Someone shot at us."

"Shot you? Where?"

"At the lighthouse."

"I'm on my way there now. The real estate agent got hold of the owners, and they said we could rent it."

"Well, I wouldn't advise approaching the place until we get help."

She pulled out her phone and dialed. "I'll put it on speaker phone."

After one ring, a loud voice said distinctly, "Nine-one-one. What is the nature of your emergency?"

"I want to report someone firing shots."

"What is the address in Burbank, California?"

"I'm not in California. I'm in Castine, Maine. Can't you tell where I am?"

"You have that feature turned off, ma'am. Let me get in touch with the Castine dispatcher. Sit tight. They'll call you."

Ten seconds later, the phone rang. "Nine-one-one. What is the nature of your emergency?"

"We're on the road that goes past Fort George."

Cassidy leaned over the seat. "Battle Avenue."

"Battle Avenue. My friends were at the Dyce Head lighthouse when they were fired upon."

"Dyce Head? No one's there."

"That's what they thought. Can someone please come down here? They had to flee and left their car there."

"Alfie's on his way." The dispatcher hung up.

They could already hear the siren. The squad car pulled in behind them, and a thin, short cop emerged. "You the ones who called Debbie?"

"Yes." Jasper gave a brief description of what happened.

"Okay. I'll go on up. You'd better stay here."

No way was Cassidy going to sit this out. The others seemed in tacit agreement. When the police car had gone around a bend, they proceeded to crawl along the pavement. Sally parked behind a hedge. "We should wait a bit. Make sure he's secured the area."

"You sound like an FBI agent."

"Last job was on the set of *CSI Dallas*." She smirked. "You always pick up a little of the jargon."

Jasper checked his watch. "It's been long enough.

I'm going ahead." They followed him in single file.

When they got to the house, they could see Alfie on the porch. The red SUV was gone. He called, "I'm going to check inside." The three stood out in the parking lot and waited. Finally he came out. "No sign of anyone in there. No forced entry. No spent shells. You sure they were shots?" He pointed up at the trees. "Could've been acorns."

Jasper said in exasperation, "You Mainers claim every unexplained knocking is acorns. For your information, those are elms—really nice elms. Last I checked, they don't have acorns."

Cassidy remarked, "There was another car here."

Alfie gave the lot a cursory glance. "No sign of one. I'm guessing some kids with a BB gun took advantage of an empty house. No one got hurt. Sorry I can't help you folks."

Sally said, "Black Brothers Studios is occupying this house while we make the movie."

The deputy's jaw dropped. "Movie? Here?"

"Yes, yes," she said impatiently. "We have an appointment with the mayor to explain what it entails. You'll be fully briefed." Before he could start asking questions, she said quickly, "Can I count on you to keep an eye on the property? We don't want any more incidents."

"Well, ma'am, I'm only in Castine a couple days a week. Sheriff's office is in Ellsworth."

Sally asked sharply, "You mean there's no full-time police presence in Castine?"

"Sorry, ma'am."

"What's the sheriff's number?" She wrote it down. "Once the crew and talent get here, we'll expect a bit

124

more security. I'll give him a heads-up. He can post a temporary detail."

From the look on Alfie's face, Cassidy didn't think the sheriff would respond positively to demands from strangers. *Especially these guys.*

Sally left, promising to catch up with them back in Penhallow.

Jasper said, "Er…Alfie?"

"What?" The policeman was clearly miffed.

"Would you mind calling us if you learn any more?" Jasper gazed appealingly at him.

"Yeah. All right." Jasper gave him his card. Alfie made sure the house was locked and drove off in his patrol car.

Jasper spent some time examining the Lamborghini. "Seems unscathed."

"The place is safe enough now. Want to look around some more?"

Jasper demurred. "I've had enough near-fatal accidents for one week. I want to go home." He drove out to the lane and turned left.

"Isn't this the wrong way?"

"I figure all roads lead up to the highway. No reason to go all the way back into town." They had only gone half a mile when they came to a barrier. Jasper sat staring at the orange cones and beyond them, a bank of spiky blue lupines. "This is a dead end."

"You noticed that too?"

"But…"

"Remember," said Cassidy patiently, "this area isn't developed. You're going to have to turn around and go back to Castine. There must be only one way out of town."

"But…"

Cassidy kept her annoyance in check. "But what?"

"Then where did the red car go?"

Chapter Fourteen

Castine, Tuesday, June 27

"The red car—? Oh, yeah. It must have followed us back to the fort."

"Then we would have seen it behind us."

Cassidy gestured at the cones. "It obviously didn't go this way either."

"Right. It would have had to turn around, just like we do. So, where is it?" His slate-colored eyes were baffled.

Cassidy suddenly felt tired. "I don't know, and I don't care. It's in the police's hands now. I thought you wanted to go home?"

"I did, but I'm hungry. I didn't get any breakfast." He checked his watch. "It's almost lunch time. Shall we try that little fish place on the pier?"

Cassidy wanted to get out of Castine badly. She didn't like the feeling that she had a big fat bull's-eye painted on her forehead. Beyond the barrier lay a thick wood. *Maybe the sniper's hiding in those trees. Maybe his gun's trained on us as we sit here.* "No. Let's go back to Penhallow."

"But I need sustenance!"

"Chew your nails."

By the time they reached the exit for Route 3, Jasper was muttering under his breath. "Look over

127

there—see that sign? Wasses hot dogs. Lyle—he's our key grip—told me they have the best frankfurters in New England."

"Key grip. I heard your father and Toff-Smythe use that term. Is it like the gaffer?"

"No—the gaffer's the chief lighting technician. Grips help move the cameras and other stuff around. Head honcho is called the key grip. That's Lyle Korn."

"I guess every industry has its terms of art, huh?"

"Yeah, and movie people have some of the most colorful slang. Like an electrician is a 'juicer.' And a 'martini'—"

"Let me guess. It's what the talent drinks?"

Jasper shook his head. "Actually, it's the last shot of the day." He chuckled. "Before the first shot of the evening." He swung the steering wheel right. "Aren't you the least bit hungry?" Before she could reply, he barked, "I'm stopping whether you like it or not." He took the exit and turned right into the parking lot of a small shopping center. A single-wide motor home with a metal awning took up one corner. He parked in front of it. "I'm buying. What do you want on yours? Mustard? Onions? Relish? Ketchup? Cheese? Chili?"

"Ketchup on a hot dog? That's gross. Everything but that."

"Duly noted." He pulled out his wallet and headed to the window.

Cassidy got out to stretch her legs. Across the highway lay a car dealership. The large sign said Low Country Auto—Sales and Rentals. Rows of sedans, pickups, and sports cars filled the big lot. As she watched, a uniformed man with a clipboard came out, went over to a car, and got in. *A red SUV. Huh.*

Couldn't be the same one.

Jasper called. "Let's sit on this picnic bench. A Lamborghini is not designed for proper dining."

She went over. He had two hot dogs in little cardboard shoe boxes piled high with condiments, two bags of chips, and two beers. "Where did you get the beers?"

"From my trunk. You didn't look like a cherry Coke kinda gal."

"Right you are. Haven't had a soda since I was fourteen."

"What was it?"

"Moxie."

He made a face. "Now I understand why you gave it up. I've had Moxie."

"You only have it once." They fell to. Cassidy was half finished with her meal when she paused. "Jasper? When we're done here, we should cross over to that dealership." She pointed.

"How come? You want to trade in your Subaru?"

"Never. No, there was a red car parked at the entrance that looks just like the one in Castine. I want to take a look—just in case."

They wiped their hands on the tiny paper napkins, emptying the dispenser. Jasper licked a splotch of mustard off his Rolex. "Dad says if I ruin another watch, I'll have to settle for a Patek Philippe."

"Oh, boo hoo. Good frank, though."

They crossed Route 3 and drove into the parking lot. Cassidy went round the back of the building. "Here it is."

They both examined it. "I'm pretty sure this is the same SUV. It was a Ford. And didn't it have

Massachusetts plates?"

"Yes."

The man with the clipboard came out to greet them. "Hey there. Dave Higgins, manager of Low Country. Can I interest you in a nice used Honda? Just got one in. Only twenty-five thou—"

Cassidy took the lead. "Thanks, but we were looking at this red car. I noticed you parking it a few minutes ago."

"Oh, sorry, it's not for sale. It's a rental. We have a clearinghouse for Company Rent-a-Car here."

"Was it just returned?"

"Why, yes." He cocked his head at the Lamborghini. "You looking for something a little more practical?"

"No, no. We just have a couple of questions."

"Fire away."

"Who rented it?"

The man hesitated. "I'm not sure I can tell you. Privacy rules."

Jasper towered over the shorter man. His voice rang with authority. "We're acting on behalf of the Castine police. We believe that car was involved in an…incident."

"An accident?"

"No, an incident. A shooting."

The man dropped his clipboard. "What! Was it damaged?"

"No—at least I don't think so. It was parked."

"Someone shot from inside it?"

"No, from a house."

"And hit the car?"

"No, no, no."

Cassidy put a hand on an increasingly flustered Jasper's arm. "Someone shot at us from the house at which this car was parked. When we returned with the police, the car was gone. We need to know who rented it."

"I'll check." They followed him inside. "Here it is. A Rick Ahearn. Address in Boston."

"Ahearn?" She turned to Jasper. "Why is that name familiar?"

Jasper said in a low voice. "Because, Cass, he was the fellow who turned up dead in Kelly's Cove nine days ago."

Cassidy gaped at Jasper. "But that means…"

Jasper addressed the manager. "What did the guy look like?"

Higgins lifted his hands, palms up. "I didn't really pay attention. He dropped the keys on the counter and left."

"How long ago was this?"

He looked at his watch. "Maybe half an hour ago."

Cassidy's spirits dipped. "He's long gone, whoever he is." She went to the door. "Thank you, Mr. Higgins."

Jasper took a card from his wallet and handed it to the manager. "If the guy comes back, could you call me?"

"Sure."

At the door, Cassidy paused and looked over her shoulder in time to see Higgins toss the card onto a desk littered with papers.

Jasper dropped her off at the store. "How am I going to get home?"

"I promise I'll pick you up at closing time. Five, right?"

Sure enough, the flashy sports car parked in front of a fire hydrant just as the last customer left Mindful Books. By the time Cassidy finished locking up, a gang of young boys had gathered. Keeping a discreet distance, they gazed, openmouthed, at the Lamborghini. She came up behind Edna Mae's grandson. "You want me to fetch your grandpa, Clive Quimby? Scram." The boys scattered.

They drove home. Jasper followed her up the outside stairs to the deck. Cassidy toyed with the idea of sending him away but didn't want him in Mrs. Spinney's house after everything that had happened. *I can't ask him to stay here, though. Think what the village would say! And...* She paused to admire the way his gray eyes gleamed as his slender fingers pushed the sliding door open for her...*I don't think I can trust myself.*

"Can we talk?"

Talk? No, no, no. I'm not ready for this. Play it safe, Cassidy Jane. She pushed the door closed again and indicated the picnic chairs on the deck. "Let's sit outside. Er…what do you want to talk about?"

"The sharpshooter."

She sighed. "Well, he was hardly a sharpshooter, or he would have hit something. He missed two easy targets…and two cars."

"Maybe he was just trying to scare us off." He hunched his shoulders. "You sure we can't go inside? It's getting chilly."

Cassidy sighed again. *Face it, it's a done deal.* She opened the screen door. "Come on." She turned on the lamp in the living room and pulled the curtains. Hoping to force him to the easy chair, she plumped down in the middle of the sofa.

He shoved her to one side and sat down next to her. "Where were we? Oh, yes, the sniper. I was speculating that he only wanted to scare us off."

"Maybe. Possibly. But why?"

"Because that's where the treasure is hidden."

"What treasure?"

"So soon they forget." Jasper shook his head in mock disappointment. "Mr. Flint told us about the drummer boy. We saw his bones."

"So?"

"So, what he didn't mention was that the British had a chest of gold bullion which they planned to use to soften up the Indians to come in with them."

"The British! Now I remember…Didn't you tell Sally it belonged to the Americans?"

His tone was wry. "I had it wrong. I've been perusing Azeban Glooscap's *Definitive Study of Buried Treasure in America*, a copy of which rare and valuable book you sold me for the princely sum of a dollar."

Aha. So that *was the book that put him in such a tizzy*.

"It turns out that's a local variant of the legend. Probably Mainers trying to claim ownership should it ever be recovered."

"*Hmm.* So what happened to the gold?"

"Glooscap believes it never made it out of Castine. Like Flint said, the drummer boy was convicted of theft. According to an eyewitness account in Glooscap's book, he stole the gold."

"Eyewitness? Of the crime?"

"No…not exactly. A jury member's journal, in which he described the court martial proceedings. It's

133

the only record of the British occupation of Castine that we have."

"So…not really an eyewitness. This journal—it was found at the fort?"

"Uh…no." Jasper shifted in his seat. "The juror wrote about the Penobscot Expedition years later when he returned to England. He was an enlisted man…" He screwed up his eyes. "Can't recall his name."

"*Hmm*. 'Years later,' you say? His memory could have been faulty. Or he wanted to frame Horace Catchpole."

Jasper clearly did not appreciate the pointed questions and gave her an exasperated look. "That's absurd. Besides, Glooscap claims it would be corroborated by the commandant's log, but that disappeared some time during the Revolutionary War."

"Glooscap read the log?"

Jasper's expression said it all.

Cassidy decided to let him off the hook. "Well, if Catchpole stole the treasure, they must have gotten it back when they arrested him."

Jasper snorted. "He didn't have it with him. Duh. Like the boy would be lugging around a box full of bullion. Of course he stashed it somewhere. That's the mystery. At any rate, it's never been found."

"And you think it might be in the Dyce Head house?"

"Well, someone does. By golly…" He stood up and paced. "We should look for it ourselves."

He is so adorable. "Don't you have your hands full with the movie?"

"What? Oh, yes." He sat back down. "I'm not used to thinking about a job. This is my first director gig.

Dad's taking a big chance on me."

Now he's not so adorable. "Giving Junior his head? I don't know…can you cope with anything more strenuous than signaling for a frozen margarita as you loll by the pool with assorted bikini-clad bimbos?" She zoomed in for the kill. "Or do you only drink Stoli?"

"Yes, I'm pretty sure I can handle it." He glanced at her. "After all, I led an entire platoon in Afghanistan."

Oops. "A platoon?"

"Yes. Did two tours of duty. First Lieutenant Jasper MacEwan, at your service." He saluted smartly.

"Are you still in the army?"

"Reserves. They sent me to graduate school, which took so long I'd fulfilled my active duty obligation and could laze around by the barracks pool with the trunks-clad non-coms."

She peeped at him. "I'm sorry. I've been such a weenie, haven't I?"

"Yes, yes, you have." He kissed her hand. "However, I happen to love weenies." He smacked his lips. "I can still taste that Wasses dog. Now, when can we set out on our treasure hunt?"

She rose. "I have an idea. Let's start the search here. Just to be thorough."

His eyes widened. "Excuse me? I doubt if the little Catchpole made it this far before he was apprehended."

"Agreed."

"Then…oh."

She took his hand and led him to the stairs. "I want to see if you have designer underwear."

"Well, they're not off the rack."

Chapter Fifteen

Cassidy's house, Wednesday, June 28

The doorbell rang. Cassidy sat straight up in bed. "Uh oh." She rolled over the big lump under the covers and landed on the floor. "Jasper," she hissed. "Make no sound."

"Wha'?"

"*Shh.*" She threw on a robe and dashed down the stairs.

As she feared, Nellie stood on the porch, her face dappled by the light shining through the screen door. "You forgot to lock the door, Cass. Not a good idea with all these flaky Hollywood kooks around."

Cassidy giggled.

"It's not funny." Nellie was stern. "I don't want another rash of burglaries. Or murders. Amity will get a reputation."

"Yes, *Mother*. Look, I know I said I'd jog with you this morning, but I had a very long day yesterday—"

"You went to Castine with the movie people."

"How did—? Oh, well…why do I even ask?" *I hope she doesn't know what happened after that.*

Nellie gave her an odd look. "I expect to hear everything. Word on the street was there was some kind of gunfight, but we couldn't pin down whether it was movie-related or not."

Oh dear, was that thump from upstairs loud enough for her to hear? "Later, okay? I've got to open the store early." She started to shut the door.

"Okay." As she left, Nellie threw over her shoulder, "By the way, Mr. Leadfoot MacEwan had better skedaddle on the double. I can't jog with you this morning either. I only dropped by because I have it on good authority that Bobby B. Goode is marching over here to give you a piece of his mind."

Cassidy was too floored to ask what Bobby was upset about. She ran back up the stairs, gathering pieces of clothing scattered the length of the hall. "Jasper! Out!" She ran into the bedroom. "Jasper? Where are you?"

He came out of the bathroom, fully clothed, his hair slicked back and his face glowing. "Was that fast enough?"

"Bravo! Now get out of here."

He stuck his lower lip out and let it tremble oh-so-slightly. "What is this—'wham bam, thank you, Jasper'?"

"Jasper MacEwan, I love you, but you have to leave. By the back door…no, the side door." She leapt down the steps. "Through the kitchen. And don't let anyone see you."

He huffed. "Okay, I'll go, but I expect an apology." He got halfway to the door before spinning around. "Did you just say you loved me?"

Cassidy marched up to him and gave him a push. "Merely an expression. Slip of the tongue."

The doorbell rang.

Cassidy made sure her robe was buttoned and Jasper gone before opening the front door. "Hi, Bobby, what can I do for you?"

"Cassidy Jane Beauvoir." The man's face was bright red, which was not so unusual given his reputation for a quick temper. What *was* unusual was that he had a cowed Digby Toff-Smythe in tow. "Do something about this!" He shook the Toff by the collar like a rag doll.

"Why don't you two come in?" She led them to the kitchen table. "Would you like some coffee?"

Digby began to nod, but Bobby cut in. "Already had m' morning coffee."

"Okay." She sat down, hands folded, not sure what to expect. No way could she have predicted what happened next.

Bobby B.—whose color had slowly been dissipating, allowing his freckles to reappear—flushed again. "Um. I know I voted, against your advice, to allow this bunch to make their movie here. The rest of us thought it would be pretty nifty—not to mention a way to attract summah people. But it's turnin' into a nightmare."

"How so?"

"Have you seen what they've done to Grace Spinney's house? Or to Eunice Merithew's garden?"

"I was away yesterday. I haven't seen anything yet."

"Well…" He took a deep breath and blurted, "They put a fence up all around the house and black curtains on every window. They won't let me walk Susie at the bottom of Beecham Park—my own park, dammit!"

Cassidy opened her mouth to interrupt, hoping she could come up with something—anything—to soothe the savage beast, but Bobby wasn't finished. "And poor

Eunice. She's distraught. They've trampled all her dahlias, not to mention her prize hybrid tea rose. And the dirt road behind the boat house? Mud!"

"Oh, my."

He waved his arms over his head. "They erected this huge tent and set portable stoves up inside that they keep going all day. Makes it as hotter 'n Hades all the way up to Charles Street."

Digby cleared his throat, apparently planning to put up a defense, but Bobby raised his voice. "*And*"—he pointed an accusing finger at Digby, nearly poking his eye out—"they're parkin' their big sound trucks down by the marina, blockin' the path to the dock. No one can get to their boats." He drew in a shaky breath.

"I see." She gestured at Digby. "And Mr. Toff-Smythe is the author of these atrocities?"

"Him? No. It's Tweedledum and Tweedledee—that skinny feller and the fat one. Don't know their names. *This* twerp"—he grabbed the long-suffering actor's shoulder and shook him again—"has been paradin' around Puddleby Park smokin' filthy seegars and a-cacklin' and a-moanin' like some walkin' zombie. Even the kids are complaining. And don't get Velma Puddleby started."

"Well…if it's during the day…"

"Ha!" He glared at Digby. "No, it's in the middle of the night! Wakes the whole village up with his racket."

"You mean after ten?"

"*Yes*." He gave the word a splendid flourish. "Appallin'."

Cassidy turned to Digby. "Cackling? Moaning?"

The Toff stared back at her. "Ten is the middle of

the night?"

Bobby broke the impasse. "He claims he's exercisin' his voice—vocalizin' he calls it. Sounds more like a Pekinese in heat."

Cassidy spared a moment to enjoy the image. "Okay, Bobby B. I'll take it from here. I'm glad you brought this to my attention."

"I'm sure the other overseers'll back you up now they've seen what we're up against. Tell those…those left coasters they're not welcome here. They need to pack up and beat it out of Amity Landing."

Cassidy gasped. "Oh, dear. I'm not sure we can throw them out like that. We did give them permission. And they've probably sunk quite a bit of money into the project already."

Digby nodded vigorously. "Why, my fee alone set them back a tidy sum."

If he thought this would seal the case, he was mistaken. Cassidy put a gentle finger across his lips. "Mr. Toff-Smythe, if you want to avoid further persecution, you will confine your cigar smoking to your hotel. Oh, and could you please try to practice your…er…vocalizations inside and before ten p.m.?"

He nodded mutely.

Bobby B. chortled. "Now that's the spirit. See how long you can keep it up." Digby gave him a wan grin. The other man examined him speculatively. "How about this? You share one of those seegars with me and we'll call it even. We'll go up Hilltop Road. No one there but old Merle Crosby, and he fancies a stogie himself now and then." For answer, the actor drew a cigar from his shirt pocket and handed it to Bobby, who accepted it with delight. "Hey, sir. You're okay."

Cassidy rose. "I have to get to work. I'll give Mr. MacEwan a call later about the parking and other grievances."

"Philip?" Digby shook his head. "He's back in California."

"He is? When did he leave?"

"Last night. Some kind of crisis on another movie set. He left his son in charge."

Bobby scoffed. "He'd better tell Tweedledum and Tweedledee. They treat him like an apprentice."

Digby said, "Well, he is, after all. He's made some documentaries before, but this is his first major motion picture. He's on a big learning curve. They only want to guide him through it."

"Huh." Bobby remained unconvinced. "While he was gone yesterday, they started filming."

"Really?" Cassidy had a feeling that wasn't kosher. *Maybe I should warn Jasper. He's so naïve about these things.* The thought made her heart go all fluttery. *So cute.* She realized the other two were staring at her and shook it off. "I'll have a chat with the younger Mr. MacEwan when I get back. And now, gentlemen, I must let you go."

The two men walked out together. As Cassidy watched, Bobby B. clapped Digby on the back. *They just might become fast friends.* She ate a light breakfast and drove to the store.

Nellie dropped by while Cassidy was tacking up bunting on the bay window. "The Fourth isn't till next week, Cass."

"So? Can't I be patriotic for the heck of it?"

"Of course." They went inside. "Did Prince Charming get away before Bobby saw him?"

141

"Prince…" Cassidy stared at her best friend. "How on earth did you know?"

She grinned. "I had to run down Coast Road to give Fred his CSA box and saw two silhouettes on the shade."

"You sure it was my house?"

"That's a dumb question, considering it was my brother who sold it to you."

"But…but how did you know who it was?"

"It's not rocket science. You've been sashaying around starry-eyed ever since Mr. California arrived. Last time you acted that way was when you had a crush on Mark Eden in the sixth grade." Nellie picked up a book. "*The Five Children and It.* Since when have you been stocking children's books?"

"Oh…" She hoped she sounded blasé. "Connie had a trove of Oz books she wanted to unload. Jasper bought several. It inspired me…to…uh…to offer something for the kids. There are so many visiting families in the summer, and a lot of the parents are trying to wean their progeny off video and television."

"Good idea. So Jasper was with you in Camden?"

"We just happened to cross paths."

"I see." Nellie waited.

"And he let me go to Castine with the crew." *Aha. Here's where I throw her off the scent.* "We were indeed shot at."

"With a camera?"

"No. A gun."

Nellie sat with a plop. "So the scuttlebutt is true. Tell me."

Cassidy told her about the sinkhole and Dyce Head. "And on the way home, we saw the same car. It

142

was a rental, just turned in at the Low Country dealership."

"You didn't see the customer?"

"No, but…Nellie, the car? It was rented by Rick Ahearn."

Nellie raised her eyebrows. "Wasn't that the guy who washed up in Kelly's Cove?"

"He didn't wash up. Newt Slugwater found him on the mussel barge—in a sailor suit."

"Right. Yeah. So we can safely assume that Ahearn did not shoot at you, nor did he return the car."

"So who did?"

"His murderer?"

Cassidy gulped. "That would mean…that would mean…"

"That the same guy who killed Ahearn fired at you?"

"But why?" Cassidy's voice trembled. "I never met the man. He wasn't from here. Black Brothers hired him to find sites for the movie through an agency. Nobody knew him. Not Jasper. Not even Sally Crook."

"Sally Crook?"

"She was his contact. She's the PR person."

"*Hmm*." Nellie rubbed her chin. "It can only be something related to the movie then. Sally Crook's the one connection."

"I…guess." Why did the thought make Cassidy miserable? *Because it means Jasper should leave before the fellow tries again.*

Chapter Sixteen

Mindful Books, Wednesday, June 28

"You'd better inform Toby, you know."

"Inform him of what?" Edna Mae barged in, dropping her wet umbrella on a table displaying cookbooks. "Are you aware, young Cassidy Jane, that it is pouring out, and your lovely bunting is melting?" The other two looked out the bay window. Sure enough, a squall had come up while they were talking and the rain fell in sheets. As they watched, a big chunk of red, white, and blue tissue went flying across the street, papering the police car parked at the station. "I repeat: inform my husband about what?"

They both knew it would be catastrophic if Edna Mae were to learn about Cassidy's near-death experience. "Uh…About the parade. For Independence Day." Cassidy thought desperately. "The movie people want to participate. I told them they have to apply to the sheriff's office."

"As well they should. I've been hearing complaints from many quarters about these Hollywood types usurping our turf. It's a crime, I say. Tobias will have to speak sharply to them. We're not some picturesque backdrop to drug- and sex-infused party animals. Can you imagine the name of our fair city being dragged through the gossip columns?" She nodded to herself.

"And we certainly don't want Maine associated with what I'm sure will be a film glorifying depravity and moral turpitude. Think of the message it sends to our children!"

"Yes. Well." Nellie got up. "I've got to go. I'm supposed to be delivering the kale to Hunter's." She picked up a newspaper and, holding it over her head, tripped out.

Edna Mae shook out her umbrella, unaware of Cassidy's pained expression as the drops rained on the shelves. "You make sure you tell them we don't want their kind sullying our good reputation, Miss Cassidy Jane."

"Yes, ma'am."

Left alone, Cassidy made a cup of tea. The phone rang. "Hello?"

"Cassidy? It's Jasper." He sounded breathless. "We can't find anyone to ask, and I was unconscious when I was last there. How do we get to the hospital?"

Her throat constricted. *Oh, God, someone's tried to kill him again.* "Hospital?"

"Hospital. You know, the place where they fix you up when you're hurt?"

"Are you all right?"

"Who, me? Yes. Oh, I see. No. It's a member of the grip crew. Another grip backed into him with a camera stand. I think he broke his arm, and I want to run him up to the hospital."

She gave him directions. "Let me know how it goes."

"Will do."

****

Cassidy's house, Wednesday, June 28

A few hours later, Cassidy sat on her couch flipping aimlessly through an ancient copy of *Celebs Galore*. She had given up on finding a television show she wanted to watch—*I wish I'd kept those old Love Boat DVDs.* She'd tried and failed to concentrate on the mystery she'd been reading. *Silly premise, finding an old skeleton in a pit and tracing it back to a murder decades old. Who comes up with these plots?* She was about to get herself a stiff drink when she heard a tap at the door.

Jasper—a bit bedraggled—stood on the stoop. "May I come in?"

"You're wet."

"It's raining."

"There are ways to protect yourself from a downpour." She held up her umbrella. "Maybe it's just a Maine thing."

"My convertible top got stuck in the open position, and I gave my umbrella to Sally."

"Well, that was very chivalrous of you."

"She needed it more than I—at least before the roof broke. She was helping Trent back to the hotel."

"Trent? He's one of the grips, right?"

"Right. Got in the way of a Steadicam. Little Bill didn't see him and knocked him right over. Luckily only sprained his wrist. Doc says he might be out of commission for a few days. We'll have to hire a temporary replacement. I sent a text to Ollie."

Cassidy remembered Bobby B.'s nickname for the producer. "You mean Tweedledum?"

"Huh?"

"As in, Tweedledum and Tweedledee. So named by one of our more prominent citizens."

"Does he mean Lowry and Hadley? Not identical enough."

Cassidy agreed. "I propose we continue to refer to them as Laurel and Hardy. Of course Bobby may dispute the decision, in which case it will have to be put to the whole board of overseers for a vote. I…" She trailed off when she noticed the spreading puddle of water under Jasper's feet. "Take your shoes off, please. And your jacket."

"I will if you promise to provide me with an adult beverage."

She retrieved the bourbon and poured him a tot.

He held his glass out until she poured a little more. "Thanks. It's been a trying day."

She led him to a wooden chair in the kitchen and laid a clean towel down before allowing him to sit. "Anything besides the grip's tumble?"

"Well, Dad ran out on me, for starters."

"Oh, yes, Digby told me."

"He did? He was here?"

"Yes—although not voluntarily. He came with Bobby B. Goode."

Jasper straightened. "Bobby…who?"

"Bobby B. Goode. The prominent citizen I mentioned. One of our overseers. You met him at the hotel."

Jasper squinted at her. "Is he ever just 'Bob'?"

She'd never thought of that. "I don't think so. Even his wife Mary Jo has given up and calls him Bobby B."

"And why did Lord Bobby B. conduct our—I presume unwilling—hero to your doorstep?"

"He was exceedingly disturbed about the crew taking over our town. The Toff's behavior elicited particular opprobrium."

"Let me guess. The cigars? Or the incessant chirping sounds he makes when he's exercising his vocal chords?"

"Both."

Jasper sipped his whiskey. "Huh. So the Toff accompanied a member of a hostile tribe into the royal presence? Did they pass the peace pipe?"

Though Cassidy disapproved of American Indian clichés on principle, she let it pass. *Note to self: give the man a lesson on Passamaquoddy culture in the near future.* "On the contrary, they tried to duke it out, but the blows went wide. I think the bungled altercation brought them closer together."

"That's nice." He poured himself another tot, ignoring the menacing glare from the trustee of the bottle. "But I thought you wanted to hear about *my* day?"

"Of course." She squeezed his shirttail. "You've dried out enough. Let's go into the living room." They sat on the couch, and she settled into the crook of his arm.

"Well, Ollie spent the day on the phone, and Stan laid out the staging for the scenes in Mrs. Spinney's house. We should be able to begin shooting tomorrow."

She thought it prudent not to mention his colleagues' unauthorized filming. "Can I come watch?"

He pursed his lips. "I wish you could, but it might set a bad precedent."

"Well, that's not fair!"

"I suppose you could claim you had to be present as the...what are you called anyway? Chairperson? Director?"

"Chair. I'm the chairman of the Amity Landing Board of Overseers."

"Not chairwoman?"

"Too many syllables. Mainers are thrifty even with parts of speech."

"Well, knock me down with a titmouse's tail feather. So, as the queen of Amity Landing, do you while away your days whipping the peons and taxing the tenant farmers?"

"Another bad joke. I suggest you quit trying to be clever."

He sniffed. "You have no sense of humor. You're probably one of those snobs who eschew puns."

"Not at all, when handled by a master."

Jasper evidently decided to surrender gracefully and changed the subject. "So, the Toff-Goode spat is resolved. What else did you do today?"

"Put bunting up on the store. And had a chat with Nellie."

"Nellie is your friend?"

"Nellie Shute. My best friend, God bless her. Who knows all and sees all."

"You mean us?"

"Uh-huh. I've sworn her to silence, which should last until the weekend with any luck."

He kissed her. "I don't mind if people know."

She wiggled away from him, blushing. "You don't know this town." She paused to admire his generous lips as they slurped up an ice cube. "We also talked about the sniper. She thinks he has to be the same person who did Ahearn in."

"Because of the car."

She nodded. "And that means it must somehow be

149

connected to the movie." She sought out Jasper's eyes with her own worried ones.

"Not necessarily. Ahearn was a subcontractor. Nobody at Black Brothers had any contact with him."

"Except for Sally."

"Right. I forgot. Still, the only link to us was through Sally, who hired him. Sight unseen as I understand it."

"As you understand it…Jasper, maybe she *does* know him." She tented the tips of her fingers. "She was in Castine when we were attacked."

"You're suggesting that Sally Crook is guilty of attempted murder? Other than that being totally ridiculous—she's my cousin, for Christ's sake. I've known her since we were children. What on earth would be her motive?"

Cassidy straightened. "Bear with me. Sally is sent east as advance for the movie. She meets Ahearn. Together they hatch a plot to sabotage the project. They plan a series of scary occurrences—hoping you'll pull out."

Jasper went to the kitchen and came back with the whiskey bottle. "There are a number of holes in that scenario. Setting aside the sheer idiocy of the entire hypothesis."

"Oh?" She held her glass out.

"Okay. Number one—why would two employees deliberately put themselves out of a job? Then there are the dangling questions—like, did Ahearn plan to get himself killed before Black Brothers even got here? He was dead at least a week before I fell out the window. That was the first event after all. So either he botched the whole thing or he wasn't involved."

Cassidy fumed. "We're only at the beginning of the investigation. We have to collect the information. Find the pattern. Then we can nail the culprit."

"Who you're postulating is Sally Crook." Jasper drummed his fingers on his glass. "All right. When Ahearn is found dead, Sally decides to carry on without him? Why?"

"Er…maybe she was the brains behind it. He was the muscle."

He put the glass down. "Another thing: Sally was in Castine, yes. But she came along the lane *behind* us, not in front of us. And she was in a yellow VW, not a red Ford."

Cassidy waved his objections off with a lofty air. "Your questions will be answered in good time, my lad."

"Still." He frowned. "These are serious crimes you're accusing my cousin of. She may have a checkered history—"

"Aha."

"Which consisted of stealing a candy bar from the dollar store and selling me a defective bike when we were ten. Neither of which landed her in the clink."

Cassidy plunked her glass down in frustration. "Well, then, *you* tell *me*. What the hell is going on?"

Jasper ticked his fingers off. "I hit my head on a ceiling light and fell out the window. Kids snuck into the lighthouse while the owners were away and used us for target practice with their brand-new BB guns."

"Wait, what about Trent's accident?"

"He ran afoul of a piece of equipment and wrenched his arm. Happens all the time."

"*Hmm*. Could someone want him out of the way?

Who was there at the time of the accident? Perhaps he knows something damaging to the killer." Her eyes gleamed.

"Most of the crew were there. And if Trent knows something, he doesn't know that he knows it."

Cassidy had a comeback. "All right, but you can't deny that Ahearn was murdered."

"True, but he was nowhere near the movie set and in fact had never set eyes on any of us."

Desperate, she threw out, "What about the treasure?"

"What treasure?"

"Oh, for heaven's sake. For someone immersed in the world of make-believe, you're awfully cynical."

"Maybe that's why." He put the drink down. "Do you mind if we talk about something else?"

"Like what?"

"Like how your eyes remind me of the inside of an abalone shell—shifting greens and blues and silvers."

She leaned back on the sofa. "Go on."

He ran a palm down the back of her head. "Your hair glitters like volcanic glass and smells like"—he sniffed—"whiskey…and roses." He sniffed again. "And bacon. Yum."

"You're making me hungry."

"Well, it *is* way past dinner time, but I'm thinking a little *amuse-gueule*—that's French for an appetizer— might be appropriate. Something to get the salivary juices flowing. What do you think?"

"Are you proposing what I think you're proposing?"

His hand drifted down her shirt and parked on a handy ledge. "Yes." It drifted lower and squeezed her waist. "I suspect that there are still more nooks and crannies of your body to explore."

"Indeed."

Chapter Seventeen

Cassidy's house, Wednesday, June 28

An hour later, Cassidy woke to hear a whoop and a crash. "Jasper!" She crossed the hall to the top of the stairs. He lay sprawled in a heap at the bottom. "Did you fall?"

"Me? No, I was in such a giddy mood, I decided to slide down the banisters." He got up, brushing off his seat. "Haven't done that in, oh, two years."

"Truly?"

"Of course." He smiled up at her. "You make me feel young again."

"How old are you anyway? Four?"

"Now, how could I have performed those remarkable feats of sexual prowess if I were only four?"

She saw no reason to continue a losing debate and went back to her bedroom. She drew on a red cotton skirt and a white tunic and braided her long, black hair. By the time she arrived in the kitchen, Jasper had the rotisserie chicken she'd bought earlier that day sizzling in butter. The aroma of fresh tarragon hovered over him. "I noticed you had a good supply of fresh herbs and greens in your garden, so I took the liberty of making a salad and a morsel of *poulet à l'estragon*. Hungry?"

For answer, she poured wine into two glasses, sat down, and started pounding her knife and fork on the table, singing, "Food, glorious food."

Jasper plated the chicken and delivered it to the table, a white napkin draped over his arm. "Mademoiselle."

Conversation lagged.

After sopping up the last of the buttery sauce, she said, "You know, I do believe I'm beginning to take a shine to Californians. Thank you."

He looked modest. "It's the least I could do after your efforts."

"Upstairs? *Hmm*." Cassidy waited for the blush to subside. "So where did you learn to cook?"

"In the army." When she continued skeptical, he admitted, "Okay. Before I joined up, I spent a couple of years at the Culinary Institute of America. Like Sally, I've had a somewhat checkered career."

"You too have hidden crannies, I see." She rose. "I'll do the dishes, but first, would you like to go see which constellations are out?"

"I wish I could." He held the door for her. "I really have to go back to Mrs. Spinney's house tonight."

"Oh, no!"

He paused, his eyes warm. "Will you miss me?"

"It's not that…It's—"

"Look, I think I've put to bed all these overblown notions of yours. I'll be fine. Besides, all my stuff's there. And there's no room at the inn."

"At least take my big flashlight."

He took it. "We'll be starting the setup at six tomorrow morning, so I may not see you."

When he reached the bottom of the steps, she

called, "Oh, I forgot: the Fourth of July parade. You'll have to keep the roads clear for that."

"Parade? You mean the one in Penhallow? I think Black Brothers is participating in that, if Ollie gets the permit."

She leaned over the railing. "No. Amity Landing has its own. Ours is special. Our volunteer firemen drive the fire engine, and kids wear costumes and decorate their bikes." She turned a little pink. "And the overseers march."

"Ooh, we'll definitely put the filming on hold for that. I'll stand in the throng and unfurl a big Amity Rocks banner."

"Won't you be riding with the other Hollywood celebrities?"

"Not me. We have the Toff for that. So…I've lost all track of the days. When is the Fourth?"

"Next Tuesday."

"Will there be fireworks?"

"In Penhallow, yes. They're really pretty good. They send the tugboat out into the harbor and shoot them off from there."

"Sounds great. Do we have a date?"

"As long as you don't make a nuisance of yourself at my parade."

His cell phone buzzed. "MacEwan…Oh, dear. No, we don't want to press charges. No one actually got hurt…What? That's too bad. Yes, thanks." He hung up and looked up at her. "That was the Hancock County police. They have good news and bad news."

She waited.

"Good news is, they nabbed a couple of kids sneaking into the lighthouse. They had BB guns."

"Ah."

"Bad news is Mr. Flint—the Fort George caretaker—was found dead."

"Oh, what a shame." She visualized the grizzled old Mainer. "Run over by his tractor?"

"No. He was inside the dungeon where the drummer boy died."

"What? How—?"

"That's all the detective said. Gotta go."

"But…" *A fresh mystery?* She watched Jasper's flashlight bob as he went down the hill. She said a little prayer for his safety, then went to bed.

****

Amity Landing, Thursday, June 29

The next morning she woke to pandemonium. Heavy trucks rumbled down Charles Street. Shouts and yells came from the marina. She went out on the porch and surveyed the scene. The movie staging was in full swing. In the distance, Jasper pumped his arms up and down. She sighed. *It's not going to get any quieter. Might as well go to the store early and get something done.*

The sun shone and the sky was a perfect blue as she drove down Amity Landing Road toward Route 1. A car passed her. *Wait a minute—isn't that Digby's McLaren?* She checked the rear view mirror as the car turned right into the golf course. *Yup. And Bobby B.'s with him.* They seemed to have become bosom buddies.

It wasn't until she'd made coffee and sat down at her desk that she remembered the phone call of the night before. *Poor Mr. Flint. He seemed so chipper just yesterday.* Even more of an enigma: what was he doing in the dungeon, and how did he get inside it? She and

Jasper had both tried to open the barred gate. It was rusted but solid.

Nellie knocked on the front door. "Open up!"

Cassidy let her friend in.

"Hey, stranger. I saw your lights on. What are you doing here in the morning?"

"They're setting up for the movie in Amity. Couldn't think with all the din."

"You mean your beau was too busy for you."

"Knock it off. What are you doing in town anyway? Who's at the farmer's market?"

"Hank's there. I have to make a run up to Bucksport. Want to come along?"

She started to say no, but then had an idea. "Can I talk you into going all the way to Castine?"

Nellie checked her watch. "That's a bit of a hike. I don't know. Why?"

She told her about Flint and the dungeon. She knew Nellie wouldn't be able to resist the intrigue. "I just want to talk to the police. It won't take long."

"What about the store?"

"We'll be back in time for me to open up."

Nellie brushed her dungarees off. "Lemme check in with Hank. If he's okay at the market, I'm game."

A few minutes later, they were driving up Route 1. Cassidy was quiet until they reached Stockton Springs. "What do you have to do in Bucksport?"

"You know Gertrude Kessler? We share a booth at the Monday market in Freedom. She saved some heirloom tomato seeds for me, but she says if I don't get there today, she's going to donate them to the seed bank in Waldoboro."

They reached the outskirts of the town at the mouth

of the Penobscot River and turned down a dirt road. A shingled farmhouse loomed into view. In the dirt yard, two dogs were playing tag with a flock of chickens, egged on by a child of about seven. Cassidy watched them while Nellie ran inside. She came out holding a paper bag, which she tossed into the back of the pickup. "All right, full speed ahead to Castine."

****

Castine, Thursday, June 29

The sidewalks on Main Street were nearly deserted. Nellie shaded her eyes. "Where are all the people?"

"The training ship is gone. I guess the town must be pretty dead without all the students."

"Oh, right. The midshipmen's maiden voyage. Hank's cousin just matriculated here. The family's so proud."

They couldn't find a police station, but the town hall clerk told them the Hancock County sheriff had an office in the fire station. "That's right. I forgot. Alfie said the police are in Ellsworth."

"Ellsworth!" Nellie was startled. "Don't you have any crime around here, Miss Jones?"

The clerk grinned. "Not much. The school disciplines students who get out of hand. The rest of us all know each other too well to get away with anything. One or two deputies are usually around during the week though. Fire and Rescue's over on Court Street. Try there."

Alfie was lounging in the lobby and greeted Cassidy like an old friend. "All's quiet since you went away, miss. You ready to start making the movie? Need any extras?"

Cassidy shook her head. "I'm afraid it's not my department. I was hoping you could tell us about the murder."

"Murder? What murder?"

"Mr. Flint."

"You mean Jebediah Flint?" He eyed Nellie's overalls and muddy work boots. "She a reporter?"

"No, no." Cassidy spoke. "When I was here a couple of days ago, we stopped at Fort George and talked with Mr. Flint. He was such a nice man. We were distressed to hear about his death. Have you caught the murderer?"

Alfie goggled at her. "Now tell me, where did you come up with the nutty notion that someone killed him?"

"I...uh...I just assumed his death was suspicious, what with all the incidents."

"Incidents?"

"I mean, the shots and..." Cassidy realized the other things would mean nothing to Alfie. "I was hoping you had more information. Like I said, he was a nice old man."

"You'll have to ask Lieutenant Parsons. Fort's on the historic register, so state police have jurisdiction. Here he comes now."

A man of middle height in a wrinkled cotton shirt and stained khakis came through the revolving door. "Hey, Alfie. What's up?"

"Lieutenant, these here lasses were the ones the Baylor boys took a plunket at Tuesday last down to Dyce Head."

Cassidy interrupted. "No, no, Deputy. Nellie wasn't involved. I was with a man—Jasper MacEwan.

You—or somebody from the police—called him last night. I'm Cassidy Beauvoir. This is Nellie Shute. She came along with me today." *For backup.*

Parsons eyed her. "What do you want to know?"

"Well, for starters, I understand he was found in the fort's dungeon—where the drummer boy's bones are. If so, how on earth did he get inside it?"

"What do you mean?"

"When Mr. MacEwan and I were in Castine, we visited Fort George. We were wandering around the grounds, and a sinkhole opened up next to the dungeon. I fell in."

"Were you all right?"

Cassidy could tell by his tone that the question was rhetorical. *Public servant, my eye.* "Yes. Thanks so much for asking." When he didn't respond, she continued. "While I waited to be rescued, I tried to open the gate and it wouldn't budge. So, I repeat: how did Mr. Flint get inside?"

"He's the caretaker. He has—had—a key."

"But why would he go in?"

Parsons just shrugged. Nellie nudged Cassidy. "Maybe the killer used his key and dumped his body in there."

The lieutenant rounded on her. "What the hell are you talking about? He wasn't murdered."

Nellie stood her ground. "How do you know?"

"Forensics found no evidence of a second person." He paused. "Unless you count the drummer boy."

Nellie gaped at him. "You mean the ghost?"

"So they say." Parsons chuckled. "Maybe he scared poor Jebediah to death." At Cassidy's look, he added, "Look, the medical examiner says he died of a heart

161

attack. Case closed."

"Oh." *Maybe my imagination* has *been running away with me. The Hollywood effect?* She wasn't quite ready to concede, though. "If he was having a heart attack, why go into the dungeon? He told us he never opened it."

"Looking for buried treasure?"

For a detective, he sure has a rotten sense of humor. "Yes. Well. Thanks for your time, Lieutenant." She turned and propelled Nellie out the door.

"I must say *that* was unproductive. Home?"

"I guess." But as Nellie turned the car toward Main Street, Cassidy laid a hand on her arm. "No, wait. Let's drive out to the lighthouse. Alfie didn't look all that hard for evidence of the red car, and I'll bet there are at least some tracks."

"Your wish is my command."

They drove slowly down the lane. When they came up on the sign for Fort George, Cassidy woke from her reverie. "Stop!" She jumped out of the car and ran across the rolling hummocks to the dungeon. She slithered down the mud slide left by the sinkhole and tried the gate. Locked. *Not conclusive. The medics could have locked it after they removed the body. However...* She ran back to the car. "Quick! Back to the fire station."

Nellie groaned. "Hank is going to kill me. And you better pay me for the gas."

Cassidy paid her no attention, leaning forward as if urging the car to go faster. She hopped out at the station. The detective was still in the lobby chatting with Alfie. She blurted, "Lieutenant, one question. Was the gate to the dungeon locked when you found Flint?"

"Why, yes. We had to jimmy it open. I've asked the town to put a chain on it. Gotta keep the juvies out of there."

"Was Flint's key in his pocket?"

"Yes….Oh."

"Indeed. If the key was still in his pocket, and he was dead…"

"Who locked it after he died?"

Chapter Eighteen

Mindful Books, Thursday, June 29

Nellie chattered the entire way home, speculating on the murder, asking questions to the thin air, generally making it impossible for Cassidy to think. When they reached Penhallow, her friend wanted to stop for a beer, but Cassidy declined. "Just drop me at the store. Thanks for coming, Nell."

"Ooh, wouldn't have missed it for the world. Wait'll I tell Hank. Do you think the detective will keep you in the loop during the investigation?"

"He said he would. I don't know how fast these things move."

"Well, call him tomorrow if you don't hear anything. I mean, he would have closed the case if you hadn't pointed out that bit about the key. He owes you."

"Okay. See you."

A horde of buyers kept Cassidy busy until closing time. She locked up the store, hoping Amity would have quieted down by now. *I'd love to tell Jasper what we found out, but now that production is in full swing, he'll hardly have time for me.* She drove home in a funk.

****

Amity Landing, Friday, June 30

Unfortunately, the activities had not slowed down

over the hours and kept on into the night. The next day brought the same upheaval and chaos. Inhabitants roamed the streets with increasingly morose faces. A couple of long-time renters accosted Bobby B. Goode and demanded he kick "the blighters" out. Saturday morning found a delegation pounding on Cassidy's door.

"Miss Beauvoir, you're the big cheese around here. You *have* to do something. Our kids can't play on the basketball court when they're filming, and they're not allowed in Nobby Park at all! John here had to put the roofers off until next month. We can't sing outside. Whistling is totally taboo. And that fat man— Hadley?—he keeps shooing us away whenever we get near Grace Spinney's house."

One young girl sniffed. "I only wanted Digby Toff-Smythe's autograph. He was real nice. He said he'd sign my copy of *Celebs Galore* magazine. It's got his picture in it. Can you *imagine* what my friends would say?" She wiped a tear away. "Then that snotty manager guy came over and ripped it out of his hands and tossed it back at me. He was so *mean!*"

A buxom woman in a T-shirt that unfortunately left her substantial midriff open for viewing, whined, "When the director calls, 'Roll 'em,' we all have to stop whatever we're doing and hold our breath until he yells, 'Cut.' I haven't been able to run the washer for days! Been forced to borrow my tweeny daughter's clothes." She plucked at the shirt. "You think I'm wearing this in public on *purpose*?"

The voices rose higher and higher. From a distance, they heard an air horn blast. Then an amplified voice broke in. "Quiet on the set! Will whoever's making that racket please shut up."

The group fell silent, then slowly, the muttering began to build again. Cassidy lowered her hands, palm down. The muttering died away. "Okay, I will speak to the director. I'll ask how long this is going to last and if they can maybe cut back on their work hours."

Bobby B. Goode's voice came from the back. "If they won't accommodate us, throw the bums out."

A chorus rose from the group: "Throw the bums out! Throw the bums out!"

The air horn sounded again.

"*Shh*. Please folks. Let me handle it." *After which I intend to say a few choice words to that coward Bobby B.*

When the mob had broken up, she went upstairs, put on some mascara and her prettiest sundress, and marched down the hill. Jasper was arguing with the producer. She tapped him on the shoulder. He spun around, his face purple. When he saw her, his expression softened and he broke out in a smile. "Cassidy! I missed you. Where have you been?"

"Hiding from the bedlam."

He looked over her shoulder. "Isn't it great? I'm sure the locals are finding it as thrilling as I am."

"Sorry to disabuse you, Jasper, but I have been delegated to order you to cease and desist. If you refuse, I am authorized to—in the immortal words of Bobby B. Goode—'throw the bums out.' "

He took a step back. "You're kidding. They get to see a motion picture being made. They even get to be in it as extras. I can't imagine anyone objecting to this."

"Well, it's true." Cassidy was beginning to feel cross. "It's too noisy and too restrictive. A lot of these people are here on vacation. They don't like having to park miles away from their cottages." She gestured at the fat man. "And they don't like Ollie telling them to shut up."

Jasper seemed totally befuddled. "Huh." He ran his fingers through his hair. "What do you want me to do?"

"What you promised me you'd do when this whole thing started. Limit the hours of production."

He made a wry face. "I did tell you that, didn't I? I'll remind Stan. See, Dad's been on my back about the schedule. He has two other movies in pre-production, and he wants to see substantial progress on *American Waterloo* so he can focus on them."

"Tell him you won't be making *any* progress on it if you keep this up."

"Ulp." Jasper cast an eye at his producer. "You heard the lady."

Cassidy pressed her advantage. "Oh, and move any unnecessary vehicles"—she looked pointedly at the Lamborghini, currently blocking the entrance to Bay Street—"to the golf club parking lot. And stop bossing people around. That goes for Ollie and Stan too. And Digby."

"That's not fair. Digby has been exceedingly gracious."

"Well, the rest of you haven't been. So?"

"Let me confer with my team. How does a nine-to-five schedule sound?"

"I think that will do."

He bent forward as though to kiss her, but she skipped out of the way. "Not here."

He pretended to be dismayed. "I thought everybody knew? Isn't that how small towns work?"

She had yet to formulate a good riposte when her phone rang. "Hello? Lieutenant Parsons? Oh, really. Thank you for the information…No, thank *you.*" She hung up.

"Parsons? Do I have a rival for your affections?"

"He's a detective for the state police."

His brows rose. "I told you you wouldn't get away with it."

"Oh, but I did. I cracked the case."

"What case?"

"Nellie and I went up to Castine yesterday to poke around. I wanted to find out more about Mr. Flint's death. We noticed something anomalous that the police hadn't, so he promised to look into it and call me."

She could hear Ollie muttering angrily from ten feet away. Jasper growled, "It's like pulling teeth. Tell me already."

"Somebody else had to have thrown him into the dungeon, since the gate was locked and his keys were still in his pocket. I postulated murder. Lieutenant Parsons agreed to have the medical examiner take a second look."

"And what did he find?"

"The autopsy showed that Flint was smothered to death."

Jasper wiped a sweating brow. "They seem to be dropping like flies…or locusts. Could this place be cursed?"

Cassidy was reminded of the train incident in Penhallow the year before, and the string of murders her friends Rachel and Griffin had solved. "I hope not." She shivered.

Jasper patted her shoulder. "Don't mind me, Cass.

It's true there have been a series of mishaps, but they're probably just coincidence. Nothing's happened in Penhallow itself so far." He laughed. "Maybe I should move back to the B&B."

"Don't even say that." She crossed her fingers.

"Look, I've got to go back to work. We'll knock off at five today, okay? Maybe stick to quieter activities tomorrow."

"That sounds good. Thanks." She trudged back up the hill.

****

Cassidy's house, Saturday, July 1

As the day wore on, the clouds thickened and turned the color of woodsmoke. About four thirty, the rain came sluicing down, forcing Cassidy out of her garden and inside. *At least this will stop the filming.* She had showered and changed into her puffy pants when Jasper climbed the outdoor steps. She let him in. "I see you have acquired an umbrella."

He hooked it on the door knob and indicated the sky. "As promised."

"You didn't promise to make it rain."

"And yet back in California, they call me a rainmaker."

"Is that from your farming days or your movie-making days?"

"You caught me. Before the advent of my soon-to-be brilliant career as a director—"

"And after your military service?"

"Yes. I was an itinerant rainmaker. I traveled from hamlet to hamlet banging my pots and chanting…er…stuff. Worked like a charm."

"You have a vivid imagination, sir."

"Thank you. Which brings me to the reason for my presence."

"I thought you just wanted to get out of the rain."

"That too, but I came for this." He kissed her, a long, lingering kiss.

As her insides liquefied, she thanked God for her ribcage; otherwise she would have ended up a puddle of warm, syrupy happiness on the floor. Jasper let her go. She slumped onto a chair.

He looked down at her. "I have beer in the car. Want some?"

She only had enough strength to nod.

He came back with a six-pack in each hand. He held them up. "Penhallow stout or Beauvoir IPA? I couldn't resist the latter when I saw the name. Is it as tasty as its namesake?"

She took the ale and set it on the table. "They're both from my dad's brewery."

"Your dad's a microbrewer?" He raised his eyes to heaven. "Am I a lucky stiff or what?"

"Not any more. He's...he's been dead for five years. We sold the business, including the trademarks." She stopped suddenly.

"What is it?"

"Oh...nothing. We just...Well, I've never been sure what happened. It was all a bit...fishy."

"You don't think..." He petered out, his eyes concerned.

She hunched her shoulders. "No, no. I guess my imagination can be just as vivid as yours."

"And without the benefit of my years in the fantasy business. Impressive." He opened a bottle and handed it to her.

For a while, they sat sipping and watching the rain come down. It slowed to a drizzle, then all of a sudden built up steam and poured down in a thick gray curtain. Thunder pounded on the mountain behind them.

"So, tell me, what happened when you went back to Castine?"

She told him about the detective and her doubts about Flint's death. "They'd assumed he went into the dungeon and had a heart attack there. That is, until I asked about the key."

"Why would he go into the dungeon?"

"It seemed strange to me too. Didn't he tell us there was no reason to go inside?"

"As I recall, yes. So how come the police weren't suspicious when they found him there?"

"Maybe Flint just meant there was no reason to go inside while we were there. Maybe his duties included periodic inspections. On the other hand…" She tapped a nail on her bottle.

"What?"

"Remember, the area was so overgrown that I didn't see the dungeon until the ground gave way. You'd think if it was part of the maintenance schedule, he would have kept it cleared."

"To be fair, he did mention a recent landslide. So why *was* he in there?"

"Maybe he was doing his job and cleaning up the mess?" She gave the last word a hopeful ring.

"Fine, but how—or why—did he go inside the brig?"

"He…uh…he…I don't know." She gazed miserably at Jasper.

"Well, we can't ask Flint." His voice was somber.

"No."

Jasper rose. "Rain doesn't look like it's going to let up any time soon. Does anyone deliver pizza around here?"

"Unfortunately not. Are you hungry?"

He leered at her. "Why yes, thank you for asking."

She ignored the hint. "How about we go into town? Fedora's is having a special on lamb from my friend Nellie's farm."

"Nellie's a farmer? Oh, goody, we can talk about fallow fields and heirloom breeds. And tomatoes. I was always good at growing tomatoes. When do I meet her?"

"We're meeting up on the Fourth for lobster before the fireworks. Would you like to join us?"

"I believe we already had a date." He cocked his head.

Her hand flew to her mouth. "Oh, my! We did, didn't we?" How on earth could she forget a rendezvous with the man who made her head spin? *Must have been back when I hated him. Quick, deflect.* "Yes...er...I guess I didn't make it clear it would be a group." She got her umbrella and gave him a vivacious smile. "Shall we go?"

Fedora welcomed Cassidy. "If you want any of Nellie's lamb, order it right away. Bert Weems just came in."

When Jasper nudged Cassidy, she whispered, "Let's just say you don't want to be behind Bert in the line for an all-you-can-eat buffet. Unless you're not hungry."

The waitress informed them that she was in a position to snag the last two orders, if the tip was right.

Jasper reassured her on that point and, to celebrate, ordered the one expensive wine on the list.

Nellie's lamb lived up to its reputation. A perfect slice, rosy pink and glistening, was garnished with roast parsley potatoes and fresh steamed spinach. Jasper pronounced it first-rate. "Definitely worth the price of admission, by which I mean this 2010 Pomerol Clos du Clocher Bordeaux."

Cassidy hadn't seen the wine list but guessed from the raised eyebrows of the waitress that admission was pretty steep.

By the time they'd finished, the rain had stopped, and they strolled around the bustling town. Jasper stepped off the curb to avoid a band of tourists in Birkenstocks and Hawaiian shirts. "This must be high season."

"It's just starting. June is still pretty cool. It gets busier in July and August."

"And then?"

"Winter can be lonely."

He squeezed her arm. She looked up at him, and their lips met in the middle of a busy sidewalk. A bone-chilling voice brimming with outrage made them jump apart. "Well, I never!"

Cassidy was the first to recover. "Oh, hello, Edna Mae. Eunice. Audrey." She surveyed the group of older women, dressed alike in red dresses and hats. "Um...may I introduce Jasper MacEwan? He's the director of the movie they're making in Amity Landing."

Edna Mae looked him over. "*Hmmph*. I believe we've already met. I must say, young man, that kind of deportment is not condoned here in Penhallow. We have an ordinance against PDA."

Cassidy noted Jasper's uncomprehending expression and whispered, "Public display of affection." She faced the Red Hat ladies. "There's no such ordinance, and you know it, Edna Mae Quimby. Now if you'll excuse us." She took Jasper's hand and marched around the group. As they passed, she distinctly heard the old lady muttering, "Sex and drugs. Don't say I didn't warn you."

"I need a drink." Jasper pointed across the street at a bar.

Chapter Nineteen

Penhallow, Saturday, July 1

Two hours later they stumbled out of the bar, giggling and singing. Jasper's lively tenor burbled, "Edna Mae, I'm home again, Mae, without a sweetheart to my name." After a few wrong turns, they found his Lamborghini. He pulled out his key but paused. "I am *not* driving my baby in this condition. Let's get a taxi."

At that moment, a car pulled to the curb. Maude rolled down the window and called, "You two look like you could use a ride."

"Oh, Maude, that would be—*hic*—great." Cassidy got in the back seat. Jasper slid into the shotgun. "Maude, this is—*hic*—Jasper MacEwan. He's the director of the movie."

Jasper lifted a shaky hand. "How do you do?"

Maude laughed. "You two seem quite cozy. Where can I drop you, Jasper?"

"Oh. Uh. At the top of the hill."

She started up Belmont Avenue. Cassidy peered over Maude's shoulder. "Where are you going?"

"Mr. MacEwan said the top of the hill." She pointed. "That's the top of the hill."

"Oh, dear, no. He meant in Amity, not in Penhallow. He's…uh…staying in Mrs. Spinney's house."

"I see." She clicked on her turn signal, took the ramp onto Route 1, and followed it to Amity Landing Road.

As she neared Cassidy's house, Jasper—who had been gently snoring—woke up. "Thank you...er, Maude. I can walk from here."

Cassidy's friend waited long enough for the fidgeting to start before saying, "Sure."

Jasper made a show of marching down the hill, then, when Maude's car was out of sight, made a quick U-turn and came up the back stairs. Cassidy let him in. The rest of the evening played out in a very satisfactory manner.

****

Amity Landing, Sunday, July 2

Cassidy didn't remember much of Sunday. After Jasper left in the morning, she stumbled to the bathroom and swallowed several aspirin. She spent the rest of the day lying on the couch, alternately reading and watching old movies until it was time to go back to bed.

Monday was much better. The clamor didn't start up until nine—*thank you, Jasper.* She restocked the shelves at the store and hiked along the Penhallow Riverwalk. Returning to Amity about four, she made her way down to Mrs. Spinney's house. Jasper was talking to Stan Lowry. She came up to them.

"Oh, hi, Cassidy. We were just discussing logistics. We're about to start work in Castine—background filming, that sort of thing, so we'll have to move some of our equipment up there."

"I think a lot of people here will be grateful for that."

"Of course, we'll be going back and forth for a while."

"You *are* closing down for the Fourth, right?"

"Yes. Dad's coming back to ride in the Penhallow parade with Digby. He wants to bolster relations with the town elders. I'm staying here to cheer you on."

A couple of grips came up to Stan asking for guidance. Cassidy noticed Trent was with them, one arm in a sling. "Are you feeling better, Mr. Trent?"

He pulled the arm out. A thick brace held his hand rigid. "Much. It was only a sprain. I'm using the sling to rest the wrist when I don't need it. Should be right as rain by next week."

Lyle added, "He'll have to come back to work after the Fourth, since the day player I hired has already given his notice." He spat on the ground. "Mainers aren't used to hard work, I reckon."

"Oh, really?" Cassidy's tone was chilly. "I guess it's the year-round balmy weather here. And all the indentured servants. We're not used to having to do anything backbreaking, like hunt for our supper, or plow a field in the snow, or build a wall out of granite boulders—"

Jasper coughed. "I'm sure Lyle gets your drift, Cassidy."

The key grip executed an elaborate bow. "I've learned my lesson, ma'am."

"That's good." She turned to Jasper. "I may come up to Castine when you're working there. I want to get the latest on Flint—and maybe search for treasure." She winked.

Lyle perked up his ears. "Treasure? Did you say treasure?" The others pressed closer.

"What kind of treasure?"

"Is it in Castine? Or here?"

"Gold?"

"Pirate booty?"

Jasper held up his hands and said loudly, "She's joking, guys. It's another one of those Maine legends they tell around the fire during the frigid winter months. There's no *there* there." Out of the corner of his mouth, he said to Cassidy, "Don't get these guys started, okay? They're easily distracted by shiny objects."

"Yes, sir. Sorry, sir." As she left, she heard Lyle whisper to one of the others, "So the rumor's true."

She stopped to talk to Sissy and went home to decorate the house for the holiday. Tomorrow she'd line up with the rest of the overseers at noon. Amity Landing went all out for Independence Day. For years, residents had conducted an unofficial but friendly competition for the most elaborate patriotic displays. Bobby B. Goode's was usually voted best-decorated house, and this year was no exception. Cassidy dropped by to admire his handiwork. "I love the spray of red, white, and blue lights on the roof. It'll look just like fireworks!"

Bobby B. stuck the fifth of ten American flags into a holder attached to his porch railing. "Thanks. Hope we get more of a breeze tomorrow. I want these flags to be visible all the way to Turtle Head Island."

She noted the bunting that fluttered limply in the humid air. "Me too. By the way, the movie people are moving some of their equipment to Castine today. It will be much quieter after this."

"Thanks, Cassie. Great work."

No thanks to you. "So, how did you explain your

palling around with Digby Toff-Smythe to your buddies in the lynch mob?"

"Lynch mob? Oh, you mean the citizens who came to you with perfectly warranted concerns? The ones who asked politely for you to do somethin' about the noise?" He did not meet her eyes.

"You didn't tell them. Okay, then, how did you square your rabble-rousing with your new boon companion?"

Bobby ducked behind his railing and fiddled with a box of streamers. "Uh…See you in the parade then!"

She gave up and walked on.

The movie company packed up several trucks and vans and rolled out of Amity that evening. People came out of their houses like groundhogs seeking the light. Chattering and high-fiving each other, both renters and owners gathered in Puddleby Park. Cassidy didn't have the heart to tell them it wasn't over. *Let them have their hour in the sun.*

****

Amity Landing, Tuesday, July 4

Tuesday morning dawned cool and sunny. It was going to be a perfect day for the parade. Cassidy donned a red dress and twisted a scarf emblazoned with blue stars and white stripes around her neck. She walked up Center Street to the fire station, where the overseers were gathered at the beginning of the parade route. Ahead of them marched a dozen children with painted faces and carrying flags. Behind them rolled a phalanx of bicycles decorated with crepe paper and streamers. Bringing up the rear was the Amity Landing Volunteer Fire Department water truck, its sirens going full blast.

They marched south on Hilltop Road, then down Old Stable Lane to the Coast Road, and back to Puddleby Park. Jasper lounged on the grass in front of the inn. He jumped up when Cassidy came into view and, putting his fingers in his mouth, gave a piercing whistle.

Bobby B. nudged her. "Dabblin' in a bit o' romance with Mr. Hollywood, are we?"

She reddened. "He's…uh…nice."

Bobby B. grinned. "Just so it's clear: I'm not the only one fraternizin' with the enemy."

The parade straggled back up to the fire house, sloughing off participants as it went.

Jasper met Cassidy at her house. "I must say—you all looked impressively public-spirited."

She noted his red shirt and blue slacks. "As do you. How come your father didn't make you ride in the Penhallow parade with him?"

"He said two MacEwans was one too many. Besides, he had the sheriff and the mayor with him. And Digby insisted on standing on the back seat for the whole route." He shook his head. "Dad says he actually waved a cardboard cutout of himself at his adoring fans. So—no room for me. What now?"

"We meet Nellie and Hank at Childe's."

"Childe's?"

"It's the big lobster pound on the other side of the harbor. We always have a picnic there on Independence Day. It's a local tradition."

They took her Subaru across the bridge, turning down a dirt road that ended at a big red boathouse. A sign said Childe's Lobster Pound. Pick Your Own. Jasper studied it. "Pick your own what? Nose? Teeth?"

"Lobster, you ninny. We bring everything else though."

The place was packed. Cassidy noticed some of the movie crew at another table. Trent waved his good arm at them. Sally followed his gaze, pushed away from the bench, and came over. "Mind if I join you?"

"More the merrier." Jasper indicated the grips. "Fancy a more decorous party?"

"They *were* getting a little rowdy." She punched Jasper's shoulder. "I need my beefy cousin to protect me."

Nellie and Hank had grabbed the last picnic table. Cassidy introduced them to Sally and Jasper. Hank—his barrel chest and thick, stumpy legs a stark contrast to Jasper's tall, lean physique—carried a huge cooler in each paw. His muscles rippled through the cotton of his shirt. "Hope you Californians don't expect sushi and tofu. We brought beer and coleslaw. And cake."

"We've got chips and pickles." Cassidy held up a six-pack. "And more beer."

"I hope it's your pa's ale." Hank pulled a bottle from Cassidy's carton. "Ah, yes. Excellent stuff."

A young man with a thatch of red hair came over. "Hi, all."

"Hey, Kenny."

"Laurie says there are too many people here, so we're taking orders instead of letting you pick your own. I've got one- and two-pounders, culls, and a coupla soft shells."

Nellie asked for a soft shell, and the other two Mainers requested culls. Jasper had to shout over the growing din. "Sally and I want big ones. Two-pounders."

Kenny didn't seem surprised. He wrote it down and moved to the next table.

Jasper immediately asked Nellie about her farm, and they yammered away happily while waiting for the lobster. Nellie caught Cassidy's eye and gave a thumbs-up.

The lobsters for Sally and Jasper came, red and steaming. "Two pounds each, special order," said the boy. He stuck a chin out at Nellie and Cassidy. "We had to chase down the little ones you guys ordered. They kept a-yellin', 'We're too young to die!' "

"You need to get some new jokes, Kenny." Cassidy insisted that Jasper wear a bib. "It's required attire for neophytes. Do you need help picking?"

"No, Nanny. I am not a child. We have lobsters in California too, you know."

"Yes. Flown in from Maine."

"Still."

Later, in the parking lot, they parted company with Nellie and Hank, Nellie promising Jasper a tour of their farm. Cassidy said, "You're not staying for the fireworks?"

Nellie shook her head. "I'm awfully tired. It's been a long day. Besides, we're expecting a call—"

Hank nudged her. "Nellie…"

"Oh, yeah. Well, see you tomorrow." They left.

As she pulled her keys out, Cassidy knocked a knee on the bumper. "Those three beers are making me feel a little woozy."

"Good thing I only had one. Why don't I drive?"

"Thanks." She examined his profile. "I wouldn't mind skipping the fireworks either. You?"

"S'okay. I'm a little bushed too." He blinked at

her.

Sally flagged them down. "The grips are going to some biker bar. I've had enough."

Jasper guffawed. "No wonder. I can't believe you ate that entire lobster. You've got to be bursting."

"At least I didn't poop out halfway through. Who knows when I'll get another Maine lobster? You guys going my way?"

"Are you staying at the Harbor Inn with the others?"

"No, I got myself a room in a B&B on Route 1 the other side of Penhallow."

"No problem. Hop in."

As they crossed the bridge, Sally rolled down her window and hung her head out. "Is it just me or is it even hotter than it was at the lobster place?"

Cassidy looked over at Jasper in the driver's seat. Beads of sweat pilled on his forehead. She noticed his shirt was damp. "Are you all right?"

She turned to the back seat. "Sally?" In response, Sally slowly fell over in a dead faint. Jasper grabbed Cassidy's hand. His was shaking. "I don't feel so good." He pulled over onto the verge under the overpass and rolled himself out of the car. He lay panting for a minute before climbing to his knees. "You'd better take the wheel."

"Okay." They traded places. By the time Cassidy had put the car in gear, he was out cold too. "Oh my God, Jasper!" He didn't respond. She looked over her shoulder at Sally. Her face was stark white, and her mouth was slack.

She wished now she were driving the car that clocked a hundred and ten miles per hour instead of her four-cylinder Subaru. Too many minutes later, she pulled up in front of the emergency entrance of Waldo Memorial Hospital, wheels screeching and steam rising from her hood. An orderly rushed out with a wheel chair. "I need two!" she shouted.

The orderly signaled through the glass door and a nurse came out with a second chair. They wrangled the two unconscious bodies into them. As she pushed Jasper into the ER, the nurse asked Cassidy, "Car wreck?"

"No, Peggy. I don't know what happened. One minute they were fine, the next they both keeled over."

A doctor came in. "Car wreck?"

"Hi, Dr. Wilberforce. No. Sudden illness."

"Any signs before they fainted?"

Cassidy tried to think, but her mind raged with worry. "I…uh…wait—they both said it was hot. Jasper was perspiring." She didn't have to add that it was a cool evening. "Sally was clutching her stomach."

The doctor bellowed some orders and said crisply, "Wait here."

Chapter Twenty

Waldo Memorial Hospital, Wednesday, July 5

Cassidy didn't know how much time had gone by, but the pale light coming through the windows of the waiting room had begun to show some pink when the doctor came in. "You still here? I thought I asked Wanda to tell you to go home."

She roused herself. "Wanda did."

"Oh. Well, we've got the results back from the lab. As I suspected, it was food poisoning."

"Food poisoning? From what?"

"You went to Childe's for the Fourth, right? I'm guessing your friends ate bad lobsters."

"There are no bad lobsters."

"Yes, we're all agreed that lobsters are delicious. What not everyone knows is that once they're dead, the bacteria that occur naturally in their flesh rapidly multiply and turn toxic. Ingestion results in severe gastrointestinal distress and sometimes death."

"Even if they're boiled?"

Dr. Wilberforce hesitated, then, his eyes grim, replied, "If the dead lobster is left out for twenty-four hours, the toxins cannot be destroyed by cooking."

Cassidy was at a loss. "But we all had the lobsters at Childe's last night. I'm not sick."

"You each had your own lobster, right?"

"Yes. Oh, I see."

The doctor put a hand on Cassidy's arm. "You should get in touch with the others in your party. And with Childe's."

She rubbed her eyes. "Will do. How are the patients?"

The doctor heaved a heavy sigh. "One didn't make it, I'm afraid. We did what we could."

Cassidy froze. She opened her mouth and closed it. Her eyes asked the question. He answered it. "The woman—Sally Crook—died. The man—Jasper MacEwan, right?—he'll be okay. We pumped his stomach. He's uncomfortable but awake. Would you like to see him?"

She didn't waste time answering.

Peggy pulled aside the curtain for her.

"Jasper?" He groaned. Without warning, her tears began to fall. She hadn't known how frightened she was until she saw him, mouth distorted like the man in Edvard Munch's *The Scream*, curled up in a fetal position, and holding his stomach. She picked up his limp hand. "Jasper? Can you hear me?"

He muttered something. She put her ear next to his mouth. "What?"

"California lobsters are better."

She kissed him. "The doctor told you?"

He nodded and looked up at her, puzzled. "So how come you're okay?"

"I guess Mainers are just tougher."

"Ha." He rolled over. "*Arrgghh*. I have to go…go…"

Cassidy called the nurse. "Peggy, he has to go…"

Peggy brushed her aside. "I'll take care of him.

You go home. Doctor Wilberforce will call you." She gave Cassidy an appraising look. "Be careful, Cassidy."

"Driving home?"

"No. With your heart."

Cassidy backed out of the room. In the lobby, a clutch of movie people milled around. Philip MacEwan strode toward her. "Miss Beauvoir? I returned to my hotel an hour ago and was given a message that Jasper had been admitted here. What's going on? He didn't fall out a window again, did he?"

"No. The doctor says food poisoning."

"Food poisoning!" Cassidy waited for him to start railing against Maine sanitary conditions, but instead he stuttered, "Is he…is he okay?"

She nodded. "The nurse shooed me out. He's recovering but not in any condition for visitors yet."

"Oh, really?" His face tight, he marched to the door of Jasper's room and threw it open. A minute later, he backed out.

Nurse Peggy—a foot shorter and thirty pounds lighter—had one finger on his chest. She pushed him halfway across the room. "No, *you* listen. This is *my* hospital, and I say who goes where."

Philip bowed. "I submit to a higher authority." As he turned around, Cassidy caught flashes of both worry and humor. *He's Jasper's father after all.* He returned to her side. "I understand you were with him at—" He paused and waved Ollie forward.

Ollie looked at the clipboard. "Childe's Lobster Pound."

MacEwan turned to Cassidy. "Do we know what caused the reaction?"

"Doctor Wilberforce thinks some of the lobsters

were bad." Sadness washed over her. "Sally Crook—your public relations person—she...she..."

"She died?" His lips set in an angry line. "Where is the doctor?"

"He said he'd be back in a minute." She regarded the key grip, who lolled near the door. "Some of the crew members were at Childe's too. Were any of them affected?"

Lyle straightened. "No. I checked on everyone who was there. No problems reported."

MacEwan began to pace. The others parted before him and closed ranks behind him. If Cassidy hadn't been so upset, the sight of Laurel on one side and Hardy on the other, with the tall, lanky Clint Eastwood look-alike in the middle, would have made her chuckle. He wheeled around, knocking his aides over like bowling pins. "Did you have lobster as well?"

"Yes, but we each had our own. Mine apparently was fine. I'll check with the others in the party and make sure they're okay. Then I'm going back to Childe's."

"Shouldn't the police be doing that?"

"Police? Why?" Cassidy's chest knotted up. *Does he know something I don't? Could this be linked to all the other events?*

"I assume they're responsible for inspecting restaurants if there's an incident like this. We have a death after all."

"Good point. Let me call Toby."

She had pulled out her phone when the deputy sheriff came through the swinging doors. "Hi, Jeff. I was about to call you guys."

Jeff ran a hand through the tuft of hair at the top of

his mohawk and said, "Hospital notified us when the patients were admitted. Regulations. Sheriff Quimby called in the state consumer food inspection unit. They're on the scene now. We'll let you know what they say."

"Okay. I'll check with Nellie and Hank. They were with us." She dialed Nellie's number. "Hi, it's Cassidy. How are you feeling?"

Nellie's voice was fainter than usual. "Awful. But wait—oh my God, how did you find out so fast?"

Cassidy gasped. "Why aren't you at the hospital? Where's Hank? Call an ambulance! Call 9-1-1 *stat*!"

There was a momentary pause. "No real rush, Cass. I think I have a few months—like seven—to go before I have to do that."

"Huh?" Cassidy's mind began to turn over any number of fearsome possibilities. "Does the bacteria stay active that long?"

"Bacteria? I hope not! Doc says it's progressing normally."

"But…you're sick!"

"Goes with the territory when you're pregnant, Cass."

"Pregnant!"

"Yes. We just got the test result five minutes ago. I'm over two months along." When Cassidy didn't respond, she asked, "Who told you?"

Cassidy dropped the phone. Philip, who had been watching her, picked it up and handed it back. He whispered, "What is it?"

She tried to catch her breath. "It's…it's okay." She hiccupped. "Nellie? Congratulations! So, you're all right?"

"*All right* is a relative term. At least the nausea is beginning to subside."

"Oh, dear. Then maybe you wouldn't have noticed. I was calling because two of the people at our table yesterday got food poisoning from the lobsters. One of them is dead."

"Dead? Not your Jasper?"

"No. Sally Crook."

"That amiable young woman with the big boo— well, oh, dear, that's terrible! No, Hank and I are both fine—except for the morning sickness. Mine, not his. He's fine. He's hunky dory. He thinks chartreuse is a perfectly legitimate color for a complexion." She lapsed into resentful muttering.

"Nellie?"

"Oh, sorry. Are they investigating Childe's?"

"Toby's there now with the food inspector. Doctor Wilberforce's theory is they ate lobsters that had been dead a while. Evidently, toxins that develop after twenty-four hours can be lethal."

"Childe's would never sell dead lobsters."

"I guess we'll find out, won't we?"

Cassidy put her phone away and started to her car.

Philip stopped her. "Are you going to the restaurant?"

The sleepless hours finally caught up with her. "I need to go home first. The sheriff is there. He'll deal with it." She paused. "Did you attend the VIP party after the fireworks in Penhallow?"

"Yes. It went very late. That's why I didn't learn about Jasper earlier." He sighed. "I feel so helpless. Every time I turn around something seems to happen to my son."

She tried to reach his shoulder but gave up and patted his hand. "We'll get to the bottom of it. Are you heading to Castine with the crew?"

"No. I'll stay here till I'm sure Jasper is out of danger."

"Okay. If I hear anything, I'll call you."

"Thanks. And Miss Beauvoir?"

"Cassidy."

"Cassidy. Thanks for being a friend."

As he left, she watched his Zegna-clad back. The shoulders slumped a little, less rigid than usual. *How would he feel if he knew just how much more than friends we are?*

****

Childe's Lobster Pound, Wednesday, July 5

To her surprise, Cassidy fell immediately asleep and slept for ten hours. She awoke just as the sun dipped behind the hills. "Four o'clock! I never opened the store up." She leapt out of bed and went downstairs to check the answering machine. It blinked furiously. The first three messages were solicitations. The next two were from Nellie asking if there was any news. The sixth was from Philip with the same question. No one seemed to have inquired why the store hadn't opened. *Would anyone notice if it stayed shut?* Finally, she heard the welcome voice of Toby Quimby, Penhallow's sheriff.

"Cassidy? Just wanted to let you know Childe's is clean. All lobsters alive and healthy."

That's it? That's the extent of an investigation into a fatal poisoning? Sheesh.

The light on the machine showed one more message. It was from Doctor Wilberforce. "Hello, Miss

Beauvoir. If you'd like to take Mr. MacEwan off our hands, he's ready to go." The call had been at three p.m.

She called the hospital. "Wanda? This is Cassidy Beauvoir. Is Jasper MacEwan still there?"

"MacEwan? Let me check…No, his father claimed him."

"Did they go to the hotel?"

"Which one?"

Oops. Good question. "I think Penhallow Harbor Inn. The one out on Route 1 in East Penhallow."

"I'm not sure. Mr. MacEwan didn't say."

Then why did you ask? "What about Sally Crook?"

"Mr. MacEwan said he'd get in touch with her relatives. He didn't have the information handy, so he said he'd call us back. She's at the morgue in Augusta."

Cassidy sat by the phone. *So what now?* She didn't think she should go see Jasper—not with his father there. *I can't just sit here. I've got to do something. Too many deaths—too many accidents.* She stood. *I'm going to Childe's. There's bound to be some clue that Toby missed.*

Pretending not to hear the sheriff's reproving voice in her head, she dressed and drove across the Passagassawaukeag River to the lobster pound. It was empty except for the kitchen crew. A handwritten sign informed her that the restaurant was closed until Saturday. She found the manager. "Laurie? Can I talk to you?"

"Sure, Cassidy. Is it about your friends? I'm so sorry. Nothing like that has ever happened here before."

"Yes, I know." With the image of Jasper's contorted body still swimming around in her head, it wasn't easy to cut the woman any slack. "I understand Toby was here this morning with the food inspector. They were asking about your operation."

Laurie wiped her hands on her rubber apron. "You know we'd never, ever serve a lobster that was dead before we cooked it. Never."

"I'm sure you wouldn't knowingly, Laurie. So how do you think it happened?"

"No idea. It might not have been the lobster anyway. It was a hot day. Maybe someone left their coleslaw out in the sun."

Cassidy contemplated whether to be diplomatic. *Hey, Sally died, and Jasper barely recovered. Do I really have to worry about Laurie's feelings?* "Bill Wilberforce is positive it was the lobsters. A certain type of bacteria develops in their meat after they die."

Laurie's lips formed a thin line. "You think we don't know that? What are you implying, Cassidy?"

"Nothing, nothing." *Calm yourself, Cassidy*. She said placatingly, "I'm just trying to find answers. If we don't, Toby will let it lie and…and people might think…well, you know."

Laurie stared at her a minute, then nodded. "You're right, but we're at a loss. We chucked all the remaining lobsters, just in case. That's why we're closed. We ordered a new batch from Canada."

"Oh, dear. Canada? If word gets out, it could be even worse for your business than one bad local lobster." Cassidy tapped her chin. "Let's see. You must get dead lobsters in a shipment from time to time though, right?"

"Well, of course. Kenny—you know Kenny Cross?—he's working here for the summer." She indicated the barn. "He's finally picked himself up after six months of therapy. Poor kid."

"That's right. It was Kenny who found the dead body down by the fishing bridge last year. Must have been very traumatic."

"Well, to be honest, there was one filament missing in his light bulb even before that. Anyway, he's supposed to pick through every shipment that comes in and discard any dead or even lethargic ones he finds." She pursed her lips. "It's a good job for him. Not worth much otherwise, but it keeps him away from the drugs."

"Can I talk to him?"

Laurie yelled, "Hey, Kenny, can you come here?"

The red-haired youth jogged over to them. "Yup, Ms. Larson?"

Cassidy smiled at him. "Hi, Kenny. Nice to see you again. How are you doing?"

Skinny as a flagpole and tall as a giraffe, he wore a torn T-shirt with a picture of My Little Pony on it and board shorts. He would have tugged a russet forelock if he were a medieval serf. Since he wasn't, he tipped his Red Sox baseball cap. "Jes' fine, Miss Beauvoir."

"Were you here yesterday, the Fourth?"

"Sure. I brought you your lobsters, remember?"

"Oh, right, so you did. Now, you inspected the lobsters in the tanks before you opened yesterday, right? Did you find any dead ones?"

"No, sir. They was all kickin' and screamin'." He grinned.

Laurie stirred. "How about Monday? Didn't you say you found a couple of dead ones in the order from Kilwan's?"

"Yeah. Tossed 'em in the dumpster out back. Too

bad. They was big ones."

"Kenny! You shouldn't leave 'em in there! It's way too close to the customers." Laurie looked both nervous and upset.

"Ah, but the garbage truck picks 'em up on Tuesdays, Ms. Larson, so I knew they'd be gone afore they really began to stink up the place."

"So"—Cassidy wanted to be clear—"any dead lobsters would have been gone by Tuesday lunchtime."

He nodded.

"*Hmm*." *Dead end?*

Laurie looked at Cassidy. "Maybe it was something your friends had for breakfast. Just took a while to kick in."

"It's an idea. I'll check with Dr. Wilberforce. I'm sure he ordered a toxicology report. That'll settle it. Sorry to take up your time." She considered apologizing for her insinuations. *Nope—not until we have answers.*

"No problem."

Cassidy started to leave, but a thought struck her. "Wait a minute. Tuesday…Yesterday was Tuesday—Independence Day." She turned back to Kenny, her eyes wide. "No trash pickup."

Chapter Twenty-One

Childe's Lobster Pound, Wednesday, July 5

"Oh, yeah." Kenny scratched his head. "Well, they must've been gone when I took out the trash yestiday evenin'."

"Was the dumpster empty?"

"Nope, there was stuff in it, but there wasn't any smell."

"Thanks." Cassidy drove home, pensive. Her cell buzzed. She pulled over to answer it. "Hello?"

"Cassie? It's me, Jasper."

"Oh. Where are you?"

"Shouldn't you ask me how I'm feeling first?"

"Whatever. Are you with your father?"

"Ah, so that's it. You want me all to yourself, and he is standing in the way."

"Not at all. Why are you calling?"

"Since you didn't ask, I'm feeling quite chipper." He paused. "Doc says it's because I only ate part of the lobster." In a choked voice, he rasped, "If only Sally…"

Cassidy said briskly, "There's nothing we can do about it now. If you'll forgive the reiteration, what did you want?"

Jasper pitched his voice low. "Dad's busy arranging for Sally to be transported to LA for the funeral. I thought I could sneak away, and we could…you know."

Cassidy was about to refuse, but then the thought occurred he might be able to offer some insight into the mystery. "Can you drive?"

"I'll be there in two shakes of a lobster's tail."

She was walking up her outside steps when he roared around the corner and pulled in next to her car.

After a vigorous and satisfying interlude, they lay on Cassidy's bed panting. "You're definitely not the worse for wear, my man."

He tickled a nipple. "Nor you. I take it you got some sleep after you deserted me in my hour of need."

"Peggy is much better at dealing with yucky gastric problems."

"She's a very good nurse. Pretty too. Ouch."

Oh good. The noogie hurt. Cassidy gathered her clothes from the floor and began putting them on. He watched, a lazy smile on his face. *Better snap him out of it.* "Are you allowed to eat?"

"Starving. What've you got?"

"I have some lobster salad…no? How about leftover pizza?"

"Perfect. Since they pumped my stomach, I've got room for a whole banquet. After the pizza, let's go to that Chinese buffet over by the Jiffy Lube."

She settled him before a plate and a mug, then told him about Childe's. "So there were dead lobsters on Monday, but not Tuesday. I don't know where to go from there."

He put down the slice of pizza. "Dr. Wilberforce says the bacteria only becomes deadly after twenty-four hours."

"And Kenny said the dead ones were gone from the

dumpster on Tuesday. Twenty—of *course*! Jasper—" She stared at him, her eyes troubled. "Someone took those lobsters and somehow slipped them into a pot—and served them to you and Sally."

He coughed. "Are you saying…Wait a minute. How would the cook know we would be the ones who got them?"

"I don't know. Maybe it was an indiscriminate attack, like terrorism or something." She stopped. "Except…except for all the other attacks. Jasper, I think someone is trying to kill you."

"What about Sally?"

"Collateral damage?"

"She could as easily have been the target." He wiped a splash of tomato sauce from her chin. "Maybe your speculation that she was at the bottom of the incidents wasn't so far off the mark."

"So you're postulating a cohort did her in? Someone who was in on it with her?" Cassidy nibbled on a chunk of crust. "Maybe a third partner who took offense when she dispatched Ahearn?"

"I don't know. The gang seems to be getting a tad unwieldy. Not to mention testy, bumping each other off like that. Eventually you run out of co-conspirators." He drank from the mug. "There's another possibility. Someone discovered the plot and took matters into his own hands."

Ollie? Stan?…Philip? She wished she knew more about the depth of rivalries in the Hollywood establishment. *How far would one of them go to save his film?* Sometimes Ollie and Stan were helpful and sometimes disrespectful of Jasper. *Are they angling for him to be replaced as director?* Or Philip. He loved his son. Would he kill to protect him?

Jasper had another question. "How would the killer know she would be the one who didn't survive?"

Cassidy slapped her palms on the table. "This is all so bizarre. It makes no sense…unless…" She gazed at him. "Could Sally have been jealous?"

"Of me? She's my cousin!"

"First cousin? Kissing cousin?"

"No, no. Her father was my mother's first cousin. We're second cousins. Legally compatible." When she frowned, he hastily said, "But only legally. We were never attracted to each other."

"So, we're simply dealing with a disconnected set of events?"

"That still makes the most sense. Nothing ties them together, and there's no obvious instigator. Look, we only have two verified murders, right? Ahearn and Flint."

"Yeess." She waited.

"And neither of them had a personal link to the movie." He chewed a carrot stick thoughtfully. "Yes. I believe it's just a string of unfortunate mishaps."

"But…you and the window! Trent and his arm! The shots at Dyce Head!" She began to wail. "There's got to be an explanation."

Jasper carried his plate to the sink. "Tell you what. We'll take our suspicions to the sheriff tomorrow."

"Lay out the incidents?"

"Yes. Maybe he can see a pattern. Or it could all be coincidence."

Cassidy tried to calm down and think positively. "Maybe you're just accident-prone?"

Jasper didn't seem to think that was funny.

****

Penhallow police station, Thursday, July 6

"I've got my hands full right now, Cassidy, what with Chief Nichols retiring. Besides the death of an out-of-towner, I have a deluge of movie people and hangers-on"—he nodded at Jasper—"plus I'm dealing with a rash of vandalism. I think the townies are collaborating to scare off summer visitors."

"Vandalism? Like what?"

"Gum on the sidewalks. Bumper stickers appearing on cars with out-of-town plates that say Yankee Go Home and Hands Off Our Lobsters."

Jasper snorted. "Yankee Go Home? Someone's not thinking this through."

Toby ignored him. "To top it off, some juvenile delinquents have been digging holes in all the parks in Amity Landing. Velma Puddleby fell in one and twisted her ankle. I have a hunch it's the Lyndsey twins. They get worse and worse every year."

Jasper sniffed. "Well, we've got more serious issues to discuss than vandalism."

"You mean the lethal crustaceans?"

Cassidy sat down on the chair in front of Toby's desk. "I learned that Childe's did in fact get some dead lobsters on Monday. Kenny Cross threw them in the dumpster, but he claims they were gone by Tuesday."

Jasper put in, "It takes twenty-four hours for the bacteria in a dead lobster to reach toxic levels."

"Yes, Mr. MacEwan. We know." Toby shook his head. "So you're asserting that Childe consciously served poison lobsters to its customers?"

"No, no," Cass said impatiently, "but someone may have taken advantage of the Independence Day chaos to slip them into a pot. Customers weren't picking their own like they usually do."

"How did he know the bad ones would end up on those particular plates?"

"We're still working that out."

Toby said angrily, "If it turns out to be the twins, this time they've gone too far."

"Unless…" Jasper stroked his chin. "How about this? The killer knew that Sally and I would choose larger lobsters."

Toby looked intrigued. "Because tourists always think the bigger ones are better?"

Cassidy mused, "Except for the movie crew, everyone else there was a local. We always get the pounders or the culls 'cause they're cheaper."

"Yes," Jasper said eagerly. "It at least narrows down the number of potential victims."

"Someone from away?"

"Possibly."

"Or…" Cassidy had another thought. "Someone overheard our orders."

"Ah. Now that's a much simpler explanation." Toby nodded with satisfaction.

Cassidy agreed. "Especially since the dead lobsters were big ones. He heard you, Jasper, and Sally, ask for two-pounders—"

"Which he happened to have heating in a pot?" Jasper was increasingly skeptical.

Cassidy stuck her lip out. "You have a better idea?"

The sheriff stood up. He hitched his pants up, failing to lift the waistband over his substantial stomach. "Worth checking. Laurie often hires transient cooks for the holidays. I'll go talk to her."

"Wait, don't you want to hear about the other incidents?"

"Okay."

Cassidy reminded him of Jasper's falling out of the window and told him about getting shot at in Castine, and Flint's death. She looked at Jasper. "Was there anything else?"

"Can't think of anything." He crossed his arms, his expression stubborn.

"The grip's wrist."

"Trent? He wasn't paying attention and got in the way. Common occurrence in the business."

She was not to be swayed. "Did anyone get the Steadicam operator's version? Who was it, anyway?"

Jasper's tone reeked of exasperation. "You're convinced someone has it in for Black Brothers."

"Or maybe just this movie."

"A disgruntled extra?" He rolled his eyes. "A Red Hat lady?"

Cassidy sucked in her breath. "You *do* know who you're talking to, Jasper, don't you?"

Toby said mildly, "Never mind, Cassidy. It could just as well be someone who hates anyone from away."

"Hey!" Jasper looked at the other two. "We're not monsters, you know."

If he expected a response, he didn't get one.

Toby picked up his hat. "I'm heading to Childe's. Thanks for the tips."

Dismissed, Jasper and Cassidy stood uncertainly on the sidewalk. She noticed a crowd at the door of her bookstore. "Oh, no—I forgot. It's two thirty! I should have opened up half an hour ago!" She ran across the street, dodging cars, unlocked the door, and let the stream of customers in. "I'm so sorry—I was delayed."

One teenager glared at her. "You were closed yesterday, too. You weren't supposed to be closed yesterday. And I've been waiting an hour today."

"Sorry, Melvin. I have the Mickey Spillanes you ordered. Meet me at the register, and I'll get them for you." She looked back at Jasper. He started across the road but stopped and pulled out his phone. He listened a minute, then turned back to his car.

Please don't make it more bad news.

****

Amity Landing, Thursday, July 6

Jasper waited for her on her porch as the sun disappeared behind the mountain. "We've halted production until after Sally's funeral."

"Ah." Cassidy's eyes filled with tears. "She was a nice person. It's so unfair."

"Agreed. I just hope it turns out to be a tragic error."

She didn't say anything. *I don't have high hopes. Poor Sally.* She shivered. "Let's go inside."

She got the whiskey and two glasses out, and they sat at the kitchen table, both quiet as the late Sally engaged their thoughts.

Finally Jasper spoke. "Dad's flown back to LA. He feels responsible for her death and wants to make sure her family is taken care of."

"He's a good man."

"I guess so."

"What do you mean, you guess so?"

"Well, lately he's shown a side of him I never saw growing up. I'm not sure what to make of it."

Cassidy remembered a childhood filled with laughter and games—her mother's impish sense of humor, and her father's cheerful tolerance of whatever joke his family visited upon him. *I guess I was lucky.* "Sometimes parents think they have to be super strong and strict to ensure their kids are prepared for the world. Especially fathers."

"That's not what Marcel Proust says."

"Oh?"

"*Remembrance of Things Past.* There's a scene in *Swann's Way.* A formal dinner party. It's the father who is inclined to indulge the children, while the mother is the strict disciplinarian." He beetled his brows at her. "I can see you now, brandishing a bullwhip over our cowering children."

Moving on. "You'll be going back too, then."

"Just for the funeral. We want to keep the crew on standby, so Stan Lowry and Ollie Hadley will remain here until I get back. We've lost a lot of time as it is."

"That reminds me. You've spent the past few days arranging the set and getting equipment in place. I know you've been filming, but where has Digby Toff-Smythe been?"

"We won't need him until we do the scenes in Castine. Right now, he's preparing for his role."

"Which means?"

"Spending his time sitting in a director's chair or hectoring the store owners in Penhallow."

"Ah." She sipped her bourbon. "Come to think of it, he's also the *only* actor I've seen. Where's the rest of the cast?"

"That's how it works. First we do sound and light checks. Then we do a lot of background filming before we bring in the actors. That way we keep their presence—and associated costs—to a minimum."

"So who else is in this major motion picture?"

"We scored a coup on that one—or rather Ollie did. See? He's good for something."

"Well?"

"Have you ever heard of Flavia de Montville?" He waited.

"Flavia de Montville? Really?" Cassidy's eyes were huge. "She's a fantastic actress. Wow. This movie might work after all."

"What do you mean by that? We have a great plot, great scenery, and great actors. The Toff alone could carry it. Now we're over the top."

"Flavia de Montville. *Wow*." Cassidy faded into memories of sitting in the Roxie's balcony, she and Nellie stuffing popcorn into their mouths in time with their heartbeats, as they watched the great Flavia de Montville smiling and waving from her royal coach. "Ooh."

"Are you quite finished?"

Cassidy woke up. "Can I…can I meet her?"

"I doubt it. She's a recluse. Well, not a total recluse, but she's really only comfortable before a camera. Like Greta Garbo."

Cassidy's heart sank. "Does she talk to you?"

"Well, she has to—but she tries to ignore me. You'll see. It's kind of freakish. She talks to the camera as though it were human and to a human as though he were an inanimate object." He held out his glass for more. "But the two boys are fun."

"Boys?"

"Yes. The script calls for two teenagers. Teddy

Bickford plays the thirteen-year-old cabin boy, Israel Trask, who escapes and slogs all the way to Nova Scotia. Teddy's actually nineteen but has one of those eternally youthful faces. Good stick. Plays by the rules and is always on time."

"Who's the other one?"

Jasper curled a lip. "Rory Fiddick. He's Humphrey Catchpole, the drummer boy."

"The one who was left to die? The ghost?"

Jasper choked. "Whatever you do, don't tell him about the ghost. He'll insist on double pay, claiming he's playing two parts."

"Rory Fiddick. Name's not familiar."

"You might remember him from that repulsive sitcom *Who's Your Daddy?* He played the snot-nosed snitch Albert."

"I never watch TV shows that feature snot-nosed snitches. Is he one in real life?"

"Shall we say he was type-cast? At least as the drummer boy, he's only in a few scenes before he's abandoned." He rolled a finger around the top of the glass. It made a humming sound. "Knowing him, he'll insist on a full two minutes of desperate ululation as the camera fades on his prostrate body."

Cassidy got some crackers from the bread box and put them on a plate. "So when do they arrive?"

"Flavia's already here. She's been lurking in the Perry Arms resort in Knightston for weeks, having her meals sent up."

"So no one knows she's in the state?" *I could get her autograph before the rioting begins!* "Jasper, you've *got* to introduce me before anyone else finds out she's here." She gave him her best kittenish look.

He laughed. "I'll try. She's really very personable when she's in a good mood. Do you want to meet the boys? I'll be bringing them back with me after the funeral."

"Well, maybe just Teddy."

He rose. "I'm afraid I have a meeting with Ollie, and then my flight is super early. Will you be all right here without me?"

"Huh?"

For a second, he seemed just as perplexed as she. "Er…Don't know why I said that." His shadowed eyes flickered. "It's just…there have been so many…we don't know who…I'll worry…" He bit his lip. "Cassie…"

"I'll miss you too."

For some reason, Cassidy was buoyantly happy all evening, despite the fact that Jasper had forgotten to kiss her goodbye.

Chapter Twenty-Two

Cassidy's house, Friday, July 7

Cassidy awoke to an empty house. Even though she'd lived alone since moving out of her parents' house after her father's death, she'd quickly become accustomed to Jasper's presence. *Too quickly. Golly, how long have I known him? Not even three weeks. And just exactly when did I go from dislike and disinterest to trust and...and...um...* She had to stop there. No sense in getting her hopes up. *Hollywood types always have flings on their movie sets, don't they? It's probably in the film industry book of etiquette.* There was no reason to think Jasper was different. She sighed. "What day is it? Friday?" She had promised to help Nellie out at the farmer's market in the morning; then, since the store was closed on Fridays, she would have the afternoon free.

Nellie was piling apples in a display bin when she got there. "Hi, hon, how's the new stud?"

"Who? Oh, you mean"—she whispered—"Jasper?"

In response, her best friend shouted, "That's right—Jasper! Your new boyfriend—how's it going with him?" She looked over at the next stall. "Hey, Frances, did you hear Cassidy's finally found a beau?"

The woman she addressed—about four feet tall with thick arms and a braid of pure white hair—looked up from arranging cheeses of various shapes and sizes. " 'Bout time." She went back to her work.

"See?" Nellie nudged Cassidy. "No one cares. Just so long as it doesn't get back to your mom."

Cassidy felt a tremor. Since her father's death, her mother had become quite crotchety and was best avoided. She lived on the family farm in Unity with her horses and dogs, having run off all her family one by one. Still, she had an uncanny ability to nose out activities of which she disapproved. Edna Mae Quimby was a pussycat compared to her. Cassidy made a furtive recon of the vicinity.

"Relax. She never comes to this market." Nellie gave a little burp. "Ugh—I'll be so glad when I feel more myself. Doc Gimpy says in a week or so my hormones will settle down a bit."

Cassidy gave her friend a hug. "I forgot! I haven't really had a chance to congratulate you. This is so great. How is Hank taking it?"

"He sleeps a lot. But he's happy."

Cassidy went around the table to the back of the tent. "What do you want me to do?"

"Set up the cash register—then unpack those carrots."

Cassidy worked until the customers started coming into the big schoolyard where the farmer's market was held twice a week.

Hank strolled in carrying a large wooden crate. "Where do you want the onions?"

"In front. Everyone's asking for scallions today." She patted Cassidy on the back. "Now that Hank's here, you can go if you need to."

"Thanks—I want to check out that new used

bookstore in Castine—see if they have any books on the Penobscot Expedition."

"Castine again? Are you sure you want to go back there? Seems to be turning into a hotbed of crime." Cassidy started to laugh, then stopped at the look of concern on Nellie's face. "I'm not kidding, Cass."

"I'll be fine. I won't go near Dyce Head, okay? I'm going book shopping, that's all." She wiped her hands, got her purse, and left.

The drive up was quiet without Jasper. *Or Nellie, of course.*

She had taken stock of the shelves of Blue Hill Books and given her business card to the proprietor in case any pertinent titles came in, when she saw the deputy sheriff's car go by. "Well, thanks! And good luck here. If you need any advice, just give me a buzz." She ran out. The car turned left on Perkins Street and parked beside the Pentagoet Inn. She tapped on the glass. "Alfie?"

He rolled down the window. "Yes? Oh, aren't you the movie gal?"

"Cassidy Beauvoir, yes. I came by to see if you had any new information on Jebediah Flint's death?"

"Nothing yet. Sent some fingerprints off to the lab but haven't heard back. I'm driving out to Dyce Head— sheriff's making us check it daily for juvies. The Hollywood people had a powwow with the mayor and put the squeeze on him about security." He grinned. "Want to come along?"

"Sure!"

"You'll have to ride in the back."

She hopped into the car. "No problem. Nobody knows me here except you." The deputy laughed. As they drove along the lane, the fort grounds came up on the right. "There seems to be some activity there."

Alfie braked. "Shouldn't be. It's been closed since Flint's death. Town needs to hire a new groundskeeper." He pulled off the road and got out. After a minute, Cassidy followed him.

Four men in jeans and flannel shirts were digging at various spots in the grass-covered battlements. Mounds of dirt were piled next to each hole. Cassidy recognized one of them, the key grip named Lyle Korn. She called to Alfie. "I think these guys are part of the movie crew. They're from away."

"Away, huh? Like, as in Hollywood?"

"Right. California."

"Well, they'd better not be thinkin' they can squat in the park. This here's a historic landmark. See?" He pointed at the sign. He strode over to the key grip, who was standing in a knee-high hole. "Hey you, whatcha think you're doing?"

Lyle looked up and wiped his brow. "Well, hello, Officer." He threw his shovel to the ground.

The other three men came over. Alfie glowered at them. "Who are you people?"

"Us? We're just some regular joes looking for buried treasure." Lyle gave him a broad grin.

Alfie reddened and shouted, "*What the hell*? Who told you you could deface government property? Look at this place! This is vandalism!"

Cassidy put a hand on his arm and spoke to Lyle. "You're Lyle Korn, right?" He nodded. "Did you say buried treasure? What makes you think there's treasure here?"

"Well, ma'am, you said it yourself just the other

day."

"Me!" *Damn. That'll teach me to open my big mouth.* "Like Mr. MacEwan said: I was joking. He told you the truth. It's merely a Maine fable."

"But, ma'am, you weren't the first one to bring it up." Lyle pointed at one of the other grips, an enormous fellow with arms the size of oil drums. "Little Bill here heard it at a bar and told Reggie and Martin. Story goes that the English left a hoard of gold behind when they quit Castine."

"Yes, but did he say it was in Fort George?"

The four men regarded each other before nodding in unison. "Yup."

"Yup."

"Sure did."

Alfie was growing angrier by the minute. He stepped forward until his face was inches from Lyle's. "Even if that were true, you've no right to dig here. It's against the law to desecrate a historic park."

Lyle climbed out of the hole. "Really? That's not what we heard. Reggie says Maine has, like, this scavenging law—anyone who finds stuff has first dibs on it."

"That's for shipwrecks." The deputy waved at the grounds, pockmarked with brown piles of dirt. "Does this look like a beach to you?"

"Okay, okay." He rounded on the others. "Policeman says we can't dig here. Come on, Martin. Bill. Greg."

Greg hefted his shovel. "So, Reggie was wrong? We don't have the right to scavenge?"

"No, you don't. And there's no treasure here. Someone's been pulling your leg." Alfie didn't say it, but Cassidy knew he was thinking, *Dumbass Californians*.

Bill muttered to Greg, "I guess Big Bill was right after all. He said it was a total fantasy and we were wasting our time."

Lyle shrugged. "Well, don't nobody tell him, okay?" He picked up his shovel. "Might as well get some lunch. Lowry wants us to sort through the gear before we start work tomorrow."

They started to head toward a pickup parked on the verge, but Alfie held up a hand. "Hold on a sec. Now, I can arrest you for despoiling public property, or I can give you a warning."

Lyle halted. "Warning sounds good."

"I'm not finished. In exchange for me not running you in, you have to leave this park in the condition you found it. That means all those holes have to be filled in and the sod replaced. We're missing our caretaker at the moment, so I expect you to return for the next couple of days to water the sod."

A chorus of complaints greeted this pronouncement. Alfie yelled over the outcry. "Who's your boss? Who's in charge of this movie thingy?"

Lyle answered. "That would be Stan Lowry—the production manager."

Greg piped up. "I think Ollie Hadley has final say on our time."

"And where can I find them?"

"Well, likely at this hour, Ollie's bellying up to the all-you-can-eat place on Route 1. Stan's likely next to him drinking a Diet Coke."

"All right. You tell them to come by the fire station. Sheriff'll want to explain how things work

213

here." He pointed at Lyle. "You got a card?" Lyle handed him a dog-eared, stained business card. He read it aloud. "Lyle Korn?" He indicated the other men. "Where are you all staying?"

"We have a couple of motor homes hooked up at the campground on Route 166." Before Alfie could ask, he added, "We have a permit."

"All right."

The men turned back to the park. Alfie looked like he was settling in to watch them, but Cassidy tugged his sleeve. "Um, do you mind running me back to town?"

"Oh! Sure." He called to Lyle. "I'll be back in a few to see how you're doing."

Alfie dropped Cassidy off at her car. "Those gits better be working when I get back."

"Who do you imagine told them there was gold at Fort George?"

"Oh, that yarn about buried treasure has been around for as long as I can remember. No one's ever found it. According to my grandpa, the drummer boy—you know, the kid abandoned in the fort brig? The ghost? He stole it and hid it somewhere. Paw-Paw said when the English discovered the gold had disappeared, they left without it. Although—" He shook his head.

"What?"

"My history teacher at Bucksport High claimed the Brits took it with them." He chuckled. "O' course, that didn't stop us kids from huntin' for it."

"Did you dig in Fort George too?"

"Lord, no. Best guess we had was over to Dyce Head or up in Witherle Woods."

"Where's Witherle Woods?"

"West Castine—north of Dyce Head."

Right, that wooded area beyond the cones where the road ended. Cassidy drove home mulling over what she'd just heard. Jasper said he was going to ask the writers to insert the bit about the gold into the script. *Are stage hands required to read the script?* She wasn't sure. Someone *told those grips about the legend. Who did Lyle mention? Reggie? No, Bill...but he'd heard it from someone in a bar.* At any rate, according to Alfie, it was common knowledge that a pile of bullion was buried somewhere in Castine. *Okay, but who—or what—caused them to fix on the fort?*

****

Shute Farm, Saturday, July 8

She didn't have time on Saturday to continue the speculation. First Hank called, hysterical. "Nellie's having an attack! Is she in premature labor? Oh my God, Cassie, is she losing the baby?"

By the time she got to the farm, things had simmered down. She found Nellie lying on an old corduroy sofa. A large Chesapeake Bay retriever lay across her feet, while a scruffy little terrier protected the approach. Nellie looked up at Cassidy. "Gas."

"Ah."

"Hank is sulking. I was inclined to forgive his palpitations, but the midwife—you know Agnes Thorndike?—she gave him a talking-to about frightening me."

"You're going with a midwife? What's wrong with old Doc Gimpy?"

"He's fine. I'm keeping him in the loop, but I want to do it more naturally. Emily used Agnes, and they were very professional and everything went fine." She was silent a minute. "I'm thinking I might give birth

215

here at home. In one of those baby pools."

Cassidy knew her friend was expecting an argument. "Well, we have plenty of time to talk about it. How does Hank feel?"

"Right now he just wants to get through the next six months. I've set him to building a crib."

"That should keep him occupied. He loves carpentry."

"Just so long as he stays calm." Nellie grinned. "So what's with you and Jasper?"

"He's in Los Angeles. They're holding the funeral for Sally Crook there."

"Oh, right—the PR person who sat with us at Childe's. Such a shame. She seemed like a pleasant person. Any more news on how the toxic lobsters got in the pot?"

Cassidy told her about Kenny and the dumpster. "Jasper thinks the person knew that tourists generally pick larger lobsters."

"So…a local?"

"Possibly."

Nellie's eyes clouded. "Doesn't make a lot of sense. For one thing, what would the motive be? Xenophobia? And besides that, how could the killer be sure one of us wouldn't break precedent and order a two-pounder?"

This stopped Cassidy cold. "That I don't know."

"Maybe…maybe he didn't care."

Chapter Twenty-Three

Cassidy's house, Monday, July 10

"I'm baaack!"

"Who is?" Cassidy straightened, her hands full of weeds. As she turned around, Jasper threw his arms around her and squeezed.

Stepping back, he looked down at the front of his Saint-Laurent linen suit and a tie that had to have cost more than Cassidy's house. "*Hmm*. My sartorial splendor has been sullied."

She tried to knock some of the soil off but only succeeded in rubbing it in. "Oh, dear. Sorry." She noted the duffel bag hanging from his shoulder. "Have you just come from the airport?"

"Yes. And"—he crooked a finger—"for your viewing pleasure, I've brought two former Best-in-Show winners of the American Kennel Club registered breed Hollywood Child Actor."

He beckoned two young men who had been hanging back. Cassidy examined them. One was about fifteen, short and stocky with an uncombed mop of hair; the other a little older and a foot taller. She gestured at the latter. "Let me guess: this is the notorious Teddy Bickford."

His gentle smile and modest manner endeared him to her immediately. "Miss Beauvoir, it's a pleasure to meet you."

"And this"—she noted the rather sly expression on the younger boy—"must be Master Rory Fiddick."

"Yes, ma'am." His eyes flicked from her bosom to her legs and back up. "Jasper's description did not do you justice."

"Er…thank you." *He really is a little ick.*

Jasper propelled them back toward the taxi. "I have to get them settled in their hotel rooms at the Penhallow Harbor Inn. You guys have your scripts?" This last to the boys.

They both nodded. Rory whined, "You promised you'd get me something to eat before you stuck us in our rooms. You promised lobster."

"I most definitely did not promise lobster." Jasper looked quite green at the prospect. "But we'll get something for you at the hotel restaurant." He pecked Cassidy on the cheek. "See you later."

The Fiddick boy leered.

It was after one when Cassidy looked up to see Jasper's face plastered against her sliding glass door. Pushing her heart down her throat and back to its normal cavity, she spoke through the door. "What do you want?"

"I wanted to see how long I could stand here before you felt prickles going up your spine and realized you were being surveilled."

"How long?"

"Let me in, and I'll tell you."

She gave it two minutes, then slid the door open. "Are the poster children tucked up?"

"For the time being. I've set a watch on Riddick—no, not by Teddy—by hotel security. The staff have a pool organized on how long it will be before he sneaks out of his room, or gets in trouble, or both."

"Okay, then we have some time."

"Yes, we do." His arms went around her, but she wormed her way out of them.

"I want to tell you what happened while you were in LA."

"You missed me?"

"No." At his crestfallen face, she relented. "Maybe. But there was more excitement."

"Than that provided by me?"

"Yes, and a deal less pleasurable."

Mollified, he sat down. "Give."

"Well, for starters, your crew seems more interested in rooting for stolen doubloons than staging a set."

"Ah, the bullion in Fort George."

"How did you know?"

"Stan Lowry may appear slightly batty, but he rounds up his crew with efficiency. He called me after they were corralled at the fort by our deputy friend." He scratched his chin. "Not sure where they heard about it. It's in the script, but grips don't usually read them."

Ah-hah. "Lyle Korn says they heard about it from a stranger in a bar."

"A bar in Castine?"

"That I don't know. I just assumed…" She cupped her chin with a pensive palm. "Alfie says the gold isn't there."

"Not where?"

"Fort George. He says most locals think it's buried in some woods north of Dyce Head."

"What made the crew zero in on Fort George

219

then?"

"The guy in the bar?"

"Maybe. Ever since we arrived in Maine, tales have been circulating among the crew about a treasure. Stan hired some day players from around here. I'm guessing one of them thought it would be amusing to gull the naive Hollywoodians and send them on the Maine version of a snipe hunt."

"Shouldn't it be Hollywoodites?"

"Not according to Merriam-Webster."

Cassidy had a horrible thought. "You don't think one of them took it a step too far?"

Jasper gaped at her. "You mean killed Flint? That's crazy."

"I just wish we knew more about how he died. *Someone* locked him in there."

"Again, that points to an acquaintance—someone close enough to swipe Flint's keys and have one made."

"Maybe." Cassidy hoped so. She didn't want Jasper or, for that matter, any of his associates mixed up in murder.

Her companion said bracingly, "But enough about the crew. You implied there was more."

"Oh, yes. You know my friend Nellie is pregnant. Well—"

"You don't say?"

"Oh, sorry—with everything else I haven't had a chance to mention it. She only just found out herself. When I called to see if the lobster had made her sick, she said, no, it wasn't the lobster."

"Not the lobster, huh?" He snickered.

"What's so funny? Oh. Anyway, we talked about our picnic at Childe's. I mentioned that you opined the killer assumed the tourist—i.e., you—would order a large one. Well, Nellie asked why he could be so sure I wouldn't. I thought she made a good point."

"*Hmm*. That kind of rotates the finger toward someone targeting you and not me."

"Or both of us."

"Who knows both of us?" They looked at each other. Jasper said slowly, "Precisely no one. At least, no one who could have a grudge against both you *and* me."

"Bobby B. Goode?"

"Toff's buddy? Can't see it."

"Then you're postulating a random attack?"

"Terrorism? Gee, that sounds a bit thick." He closed his eyes, then opened them. "It could have been a prank gone wrong. Not many people know that dead lobsters are that poisonous. Kids may have thought it would just make someone puke in public."

Cassidy flopped down on a chair. "Or it was merely a failure of the system. It wouldn't matter except that…Sally's gone." A tear fell on her collar.

He went behind her and massaged her shoulders. "These things happen, my dear. It's too bad, but we need to let it go." His hands slid down her arms. He kissed the top of her head. "Cassie?"

"*Mm-hmm?*"

"Did you miss me?"

Cassidy decided it was time to show, not tell.

****

Amity Landing, Tuesday, July 11

Jasper was gone when Cassidy woke up. She could hear the beginnings of work down the hill and checked the clock. Nine. *Good—at least I won't have to fend off protests from the natives today.* She rose and made herself a big breakfast before heading to the store. The morning was occupied with accepting donations, checking used book sites, and processing the shipments that had arrived. In the afternoon, a steady stream of customers came through. Edna Mae stuck her head in. Cassidy could see another of the Red Hat ladies, Audrey Carver, peering over her shoulder.

"You can come in, Edna Mae."

"Nope. Just checking that you were finally open." She glared at Cassidy. "You've been closed more often than not these past weeks. What's going on? Are you dilly-dallying with that Hollywood hooligan? You'd better be careful. I warned you about those…those—" Her eyes closed as she groped for the most alarming word in her vocabulary. "—*libertines*."

Behind her, Audrey nodded vigorously. "Wicked bad people, those actors. They *drink*." Audrey had never forgiven President Roosevelt for rescinding Prohibition.

"I'm sorry, ladies. It's been rather a disruptive time—what with three deaths and all."

"Three?" Edna Mae stepped over the threshold, Audrey on her heels. "We know about the sailor, and that poor girl at Childe's. Have there been more?"

Cassidy wasn't sure if she should egg them on, but she'd already said too much. "A man was found dead in Castine. The police"—she crossed her fingers behind her back—"think it was a heart attack."

"Well, what does it have to do with you?"

"I…uh…" Cassidy weighed whether to tell them about the murder attempts or really bring down the house and tell them she was seeing Jasper.

Luck was with her, for at that moment Eunice and Deirdre passed by on the sidewalk and saw their two cohorts inside. "Edna Mae! Audrey! There's a disturbance at the library. Come on."

The women pivoted and trotted out. Over her shoulder, Edna Mae observed darkly, "Mark my words—it's them California people. They brought the troubles with them."

Cassidy, amused, watched the four canter down the street. *Build the gallows! Hang the scoundrels!*

After closing up, she drove to Hannaford's. For some reason, she had a hankering for a lobster. *Death wish?* She asked the fish man to steam one—"Pick out the liveliest one in the tank, if you don't mind, Mikey"—and chose a nice French burgundy. She wondered if she'd see Jasper. *I doubt it.* He said he was going to meet with Flavia today. He'd described her as a recluse, but then also that she was meticulous in her preparation for a role. Her phone rang.

"Cass? It's me."

"Hi, Jasper. How did your day go?"

"Whew. The great diva lives up to her name. I'm still trying to accommodate her with props and background materials."

"Who is she playing?"

"Mercy Spinney. The Canadian woman who takes in the cabin boy after the rout."

"Mercy Spinney." Cassidy was thoughtful. "By any chance, was she related to our Mrs. Spinney?"

"I believe she was an ancestor of her husband's. Anyway, she takes him back to her home in Nova Scotia, but when he insists on returning to Boston, she travels with him. They face some grave perils before she leaves him in Castine to make his way on alone."

"Sounds like a juicy part."

"Well, we can't just do a movie about a battle. There has to be some human interest. The cabin boy's story is based on fact. According to his deposition, Israel Trask escaped the bombardment but became separated from the Americans and, disoriented, marched east instead of south. He was rescued near Mount Desert Island by a Canadian fisherman, who delivered him to Mistress Spinney."

"Deposition?"

"He detailed his journey in the petition for a pension I told you about. I also found a reference to his diary in the Gloucester, Massachusetts, public library, but the librarian said it had been borrowed and never returned."

She cradled the phone on her ear and pulled a corkscrew out of a drawer. "What about the woman, Mercy?"

"He talks about her kind treatment of him, even though it was a dicey time in that part of North America. The Indians, the British, the Acadians…were all embroiled in shifting relationships with the Americans."

"You really have been boning up on Maine history!"

He was quiet a minute. "I was always interested in it—and I knew Flavia would expect me to brief her. Now, however…"

"What?"

"I've recently discovered there are a lot of things about Maine besides history that are of interest to me."

Chapter Twenty-Four

Amity Landing, Tuesday, July 11

Her heart kicked like a feisty pony. *Change the subject.* "I suppose you'll be working all evening then."

He hiccupped. "Almost forgot. That's why I called. Can you do me a big favor?"

"Sure."

"Come down here in five minutes and demand my attention. Use any excuse—town business or something. Otherwise I *will* be dealing with Flavia until the wee hours. Guess what? She's insisting on staying in the Spinney house overnight, so I'll be bunking with you." The phone shook as though he'd just shivered. "I hope she doesn't run into Snookie."

"Or a bat. I'll be glad to extricate you. Does that mean I get to meet her?"

"Sure. Just pull me away before she can object."

Cassidy took a shower and brushed her hair out. She usually wore her mane of ebony locks in a loose braid, but today she thought she'd let it flow down to her hips. When she came up on Jasper, he had his back to her and was speaking earnestly to a diminutive older woman wearing a tailored silk suit and a necklace of large, opalescent pearls. Her gently waved, ivory hair was cut short, revealing a long, patrician neck unscored by wrinkles. As Cassidy neared, the woman turned brilliant hazel eyes on the newcomer. "Why, hello." Her voice—imbued with a cultured British accent—was low and melodious.

Like a deep river running.

Jasper spun around. Cassidy heard a distinct intake of breath. "You let your hair down." He stood there, his mouth slightly open, until his companion touched his elbow.

"Jasper? Who is this?"

"What? Oh. Allow me to introduce you. This is Cassidy Beauvoir—she's the sort of mayor here."

Cassidy nudged him gently. "Chairman of the Board of Overseers."

"Oh, right." He blinked. "Did you need something, Miss Beauvoir?"

"Why, yes, Mr. MacEwan." She kept her mouth from twitching with difficulty. "The overseers have a slight problem with…with…the cook. Could you come with me and see if we can't sort this out?"

"Certainly, certainly." He turned to Flavia. "We try to maintain good relations with the community. Making a movie is such a disruption."

"Yes, indeed." The woman looked at Cassidy. "Jasper has forgotten his manners." She held a tiny hand out. "I'm Flavia de Montville."

Cassidy was enchanted. The woman projected an aura of grace, serenity, and a kind of innate power she'd never encountered before. She floundered, grappling for something to say, and finally babbled, "Yes, you are."

The woman smiled. "You're very kind to confirm my identity. Now, Jasper, will you accompany me into the house? Then you may go with the mayor."

Cassidy stood rooted to the spot. The title

correction seemed to be stuck in the jellied gumbo of her brain, unable to move down to her mouth. *Gulp.*

A few minutes later, when Jasper returned to her, she still hadn't moved. "Well done. She's settled in with her script and a file on the historical background. She'll be good for the evening. Shall we?"

"Ah…um…"

"Did you like her? She's something else, isn't she?"

"Um…ah…"

He took her arm and gently led her back up the hill. When he'd seated her and put a tumbler of whiskey in her hand, he snapped his fingers. "Wake up!"

She jumped, spilling the drink. "What did you do that for?"

"Well, your eyes were glazed, and you were acting like a zombie. I thought a little shock talk would flip the ignition switch."

"Thanks a lot." She wiped up the spill and poured more. "She's a remarkable person, isn't she?"

"Yes. Unfortunately, she is not happy. My father had told her we'd be filming in Canada. It was left to me to explain that, with a limited budget, we were forced to restrict the number of filming venues to two. Castine was pretty much obligatory. Then, when Sally saw Mrs. Spinney's house, she recommended it for the rest."

Cassidy was still on her own track of thought. "She was so calm—like a saint. Or a statue. I can't see her angry."

"She never splutters, if that's what you mean, but she can be firm as the dickens. I may need to bring in the big guns."

"Your father."

He nodded.

"So what else happened today? No accidents, or I'd have heard the sirens."

"No, except for Flavia's tantrum, which consisted of a raised eyebrow and a meaningful pause, it was routine. Once we're finished with her scenes here—"

"Here? So Amity Landing is now in Nova Scotia?"

"Yeah, perhaps you missed it. Maine recently ceded Penobscot Bay to Canada. It was in all the papers."

"By papers, you mean *Variety*? *Entertainment Weekly*?"

"Whatever. You needn't worry. Amity Landing will get named in the credits."

"I'm not sure anyone here wants that."

Jasper painted a hurt expression on his face. "I thought I had succeeded in thawing that icy impression of my native land?"

"No."

"Huh." He grabbed a fistful of almonds from the bowl in front of her. "Want to go eat?"

"Okay. Hang on a minute." She put the wine and lobster back in the refrigerator and got her purse.

They drove into town in a light drizzle and parked at the public landing. The Poseidon fish restaurant sported Christmas lights and plastic sheeting to protect those patrons who insisted on eating outdoors despite the weather. "I can't fault the tourists—they probably only have a few days and they want to enjoy the salt air and harbor lights of a Maine coastal town."

"Oh, sure, you're very indulgent with Ohioans and Pennsylvanians, but you don't have anything nice to say about us West Coasties."

"Actually, you're one from the bottom."

"Who's at the bottom?"

"Mass….well, we have a name for them which I won't say in public."

Jasper opened the car door. "Shall we go inside then?"

"Please."

They ordered mussels *marinière* and baked cod. Cassidy speared a mussel from its shell and slurped it down. "You hadn't finished regaling me with the events of the day."

"Right. More wine?"

She held out her glass.

"I had a sad duty. We can't go without a publicity person—although Sally did so much more than that. So I asked around for recommendations. Mrs. Ketchum gave me the name of an employment agency in Boston, but then one of the day players suggested an acquaintance of his. She's a local—Camden woman, I believe—with pretty good references, although I gather she's fallen on hard times. I'll go interview her tomorrow."

"In Camden?"

"Uh-huh."

Cassidy finished her wine. "I have to go to Food for Thought again—Connie has that Zane Grey western that Toby Quimby's been aching for. Shall we go together?"

He took her hand. "It would be my honor."

****

Camden, Wednesday, July 12

Cassidy insisted they take her car to Camden—"I'll

have a box or two of books and your dinky little Lamborghini won't hold more than a take-out coffee cup." They separated on Bayview Street, Cassidy heading to the bookstore and Jasper to his appointment. An hour later, they met on the corner. Jasper shepherded a vaguely familiar, pretty woman.

"This is Pauline Poliquin. She's our new PR person. Pauline: Cassidy Beauvoir."

Cassidy scanned her face. "You look familiar."

"You might remember me from Nemo's."

Jasper said kindly, "She's the bartender there."

Pauline explained. "Yes, but it was only to pay the bills. I worked in public relations for years. Lately I've had some setbacks." She cast a shy glance at Jasper. "Mr. MacEwan is putting his faith in me. I really appreciate the opportunity."

Something tickled the back of Cassidy's mind, but she shook it off. "It's a pretty long commute from Camden."

She hesitated a minute. "I don't live in Camden. I have an apartment near Knightston. I can be in Amity Landing by eight a.m."

"Nine is fine." Cassidy grinned at Jasper.

He helped Pauline into the back seat. "She's coming up to get acquainted and familiarize herself with her duties. I said you wouldn't mind giving her a ride."

"Not at all." Cassidy took note of the bright spot of color in Pauline's cheeks and the way she stared at the back of Jasper's head. "How will you get home?"

"Mr. MacEwan—"

"I told you to call me Jasper."

She flushed pink. "Jasper said he'd give me a lift."

"Oh. Er. Did you quit your job?"

She nodded happily. "This'll be great!"

Cassidy felt a tiny sting of doubt.

****

Cassidy's house, Wednesday, July 12

Sissy cheerily informed Cassidy that Jasper had spent the rest of the day with Pauline, which Cassidy failed to not care about. *The woman has to be five years older than him. Wait…than he.* She put the binoculars down on her deck's railing. *And from the looks of her, she's spent a lot more time on her back than behind a bar.* She sat, drumming her fingers on the table. *What time is it? Five thirty? I've* got *to come up with a reason to go down there.*

Someone knocked on the front door and a voice called, "Cassidy Jane! You home?"

"Out on the deck, Bobby B. Come on through."

The overseer tromped heavily across the dining room and came through the glass door to the deck. "Glad you're here. I have a favor to ask."

"Coffee?"

"Sure."

She went to the kitchen, filled two mugs, and brought them back outside. "So, what is it?"

"Thanks." Bobby sat fiddling with the cup, picked up the binoculars, gave Cassidy a suspicious look, and put them back down. "See…Mary Jo, well, she's a big fan of that English actress Flavia Dee Montyviller, and she's positive she saw her down by Mizz Spinney's house. I told her to get her head examined, but she won't stop badgerin' me about it. So I promised I'd ask. Is she in this here movie?"

Cassidy laughed. "Mary Jo is right. Flavia de

Montville is playing the lead opposite your new best friend, yes."

"Toff? You know, he's not so bad once you cut him down a peg. We're going out for a sail this evening."

Cassidy's jaw dropped. "Really? Digby Toff-Smythe is going out on your boat? I would have thought he'd insist on a luxury yacht, or at least a three-masted schooner."

"He grew up in Rhode Island. Sailed day-sailers all his life. Says he can't do that on the Pacific Ocean—too cold and too rough." He sipped his coffee. "Might see if he wants to go fishing out to Lake George."

"Uh, Bobby? You said you needed a favor."

"Oh…er…Mary Jo…see, she was wondrin' if you could get Miss Dee Montyviller's autograph." He gave her a pleading look. "Atchly, it's her birthday coming up, and I thought it would make a nice present. What do you think?"

The excuse I needed. "Happy to. Do you have a piece of paper?"

He pushed a small notebook decorated with pink bunnies and purple umbrellas across the table to Cassidy. "This here's her autograph book." She took it gingerly. Before she could ask, he produced a neon-green pen with a feathered troll stuck to the top. "And her special autograph pen."

"Got it." She rose. "I'll go see about it right now."

He gasped and tried to grab the pen back. "Oh, there's no rush. Don't want you botherin' the great lady."

"Don't worry. I happen to know this is the perfect time." She shooed Bobby out the door and turned her steps to the movie set.

Jasper and Pauline stood close together—*way too close*—in front of the Spinney house. The producer was at a slight distance talking into his cell phone. Flavia faced Jasper, her arms stiff at her sides.

Pauline turned to see Cassidy coming toward them. She whispered something to Jasper and went inside. As Cassidy drew near, she heard the actress say, "I'm sorry, Jasper, but I insist. I only gleaned so much from my sojourn in this house. If we cannot film in Nova Scotia, I must go there myself. It's the only way to assimilate the Acadian way of life into my consciousness—to absorb a sense of who the real Mercy Spinney was."

"But we're on such a tight schedule, Miss de Montville! My father—"

"You leave Philip to me. And darling, you know you can call me Flavia." She smiled sweetly at Jasper. "It won't take more than a few days, I assure you. If it will make you more amenable, I shall spend Thursday and Friday working with Teddy and memorizing my part. Then on Saturday I shall travel to"—she checked her notebook—"the town of Westport, returning Monday. I believe there's a ferry that will take me from St. John in New Brunswick to Digby, and from there it's a hop, skip, and a jump to Westport." She permitted herself a genteel titter. "Be sure to tell the Toff I shall be visiting a town named in his honor."

Jasper shook his head. "I'm betting the town predates him by a couple of centuries."

"Yes, and won't it be fun when, upon my return, I am forced to disabuse him." She gave Jasper a fond pat. "The crew won't be working on the weekend anyway, and then, when I am back and fully primed, we can dive right in."

Lyle and a couple of grips had been standing by, listening with interest to the discussion. As she spoke the last words, one of them stepped forward. Cassidy recognized Bill Phalen, the man who had rescued Jasper. "I can drive her up there, Mr. MacEwan." He smiled obsequiously at the actress. "Happy to."

Jasper turned relieved eyes on the man. "That sounds good. We—"

Just then Bill Trent joined them. He took hold of Phalen's arm and moved him aside. "Did I hear you say Miss de Montville wants to go to Nova Scotia? I'll take her."

The first grip glared at him. "I already offered, Trent. She don't need you."

Cassidy was surprised at his obvious displeasure. *Is he one of those suck-ups to the stars? Or a stalker?* She took stock of him. Over six feet, with a massive chest and thick arms. *Hopefully just a suck-up.*

"How's about we leave it up to the boss?" Trent gave the man a hard look, then turned to Jasper. "I've been there before. I can give her a tour. Might make it go quicker."

Phalen growled, "What about his wrist? Shouldn't be driving, tha's all I'm sayin'."

In response, Trent flexed both arms and wiggled his fingers. "Doc pronounced me healed three days ago."

Jasper threw up his hands. "Fine. Fine. Trent, you take her. We can finalize staging in Castine while you're gone. That way we'll be ready to roll on Monday."

Flavia bestowed a benevolent smile on Jasper. "There, see? I knew we could work it out. You can find me at the Perry Arms until we leave." She addressed the producer. "Ollie, will you make hotel reservations for us?" Ollie raised an affirmative thumb. "You know what I like." She turned to Trent. Her distinctive mezzo-soprano soared. "Let us set off Saturday at first light. Oh, we shall have *such* an adventure!" She waltzed down the steps to the house and disappeared.

Chapter Twenty-Five

Amity Landing, Wednesday, July 12

Trent produced a dubious smile and took off up the hill. The other grips followed him. Cassidy tugged Jasper's sleeve. "Before Miss de Montville goes, I promised Bobby B. to get her autograph. Can you do that for me?"

Pauline appeared, clipboard in hand, and slipped back into place by Jasper's side. Cassidy handed him the autograph book and gave Jasper a little shove. "I need to talk to Pauline."

He raised a quizzical eyebrow. "Uh…okay." He followed the actress, holding the pink book and troll pen out before him as though they were covered in mold.

As Pauline started after him, Cassidy caught her elbow. "If you have time, I'd like to show you the real Amity Landing. Since you'll be acting as go-between, you should meet some of the residents. Get a feel for the place."

Pauline shook her hand off. "Thanks, but like I told you, I'm a native. Born and bred in Swanville. And I do have experience in PR." She started to march off, but Cassidy kept up with her.

"Still, we like to accompany all members of the crew when they're off the set, just in case." She left the insinuation hanging. "So tell me: what mishaps or misadventures landed you at Nemo's?"

"It would take too long to go into it now," she replied in a curt tone. "Let's just say I had some setbacks." She stopped. Cassidy could see she was struggling to keep her temper. "Look, I'm sorry. It's not something I like to talk about. I told Jasper—Mr. MacEwan—because I had to explain my circumstances. Hopefully, my luck has changed."

Before Cassidy could reply, Jasper emerged from Mrs. Spinney's house carrying the autograph book. Desperate to keep the newcomer from horning in on her man, Cassidy blurted, "You should probably know that some of the grips got in trouble in Castine. They claimed to have heard about a treasure at Fort George in a bar. That bar wouldn't by any chance have been in Camden?"

The woman's jaw dropped. "I…uh…" She gulped. "I…uh…I've heard that story too, but I don't know any of the grips here."

Lyle came by toting a duffel bag. Cables were looped around it, and microphones and other sound equipment bristled in the many pockets. He stopped. "Hey, Miss Beauvoir, isn't it? You seen Greg? He needs this here sound kit." He doffed an imaginary cap at Pauline. "I heard we got us a new PR gal. They didn't say she was so young and pretty, pretty and young." He winked at her. "I'm Lyle Korn, key grip. And you are?"

She simpered. "Pauline Poliquin."

Cassidy said sharply, "This is one of the crew that heard the story."

Lyle raised his eyebrows. "Story." He gave her a

flirty nudge. "So, what's this story of yours, sweetheart?"

"I *mean*," Cassidy said a bit more sharply, "the one about the Castine treasure."

"Oh." He looked back at Pauline. "You the person Reggie got it from? You didn't make it up to scam us out-of-towners, did you, honey?"

"Oh, no." Her eyelashes fluttered so violently Cassidy was afraid they'd fall off. "It's a real legend around here. If it isn't in your script, it should be."

"Well now," he drawled, "maybe we should get together and you can fill me in. I can maybe take it to the writers."

Cassidy didn't think even Pauline would buy that line, but she moved a little closer to the man. "Sure. Meanwhile, why don't you show me around?"

Jasper's voice came from behind Cassidy. "Korn, you want to get a move on?"

The key grip grinned, and he and Pauline tripped on down the street. Jasper looked nettled. *He's not jealous, is he?* It occurred to Cassidy that her feelings had been racing down a highway on their own without adult supervision. Had she lost control? *What if he is what Edna Mae calls flighty? A Hollywood dilettante who tires of the girl on the casting couch before she's even put her bra back on.* She heard a painful cracking sound. *Is that my witless heart?*

"Watch it, Cass—you're stepping on the power cable!"

"Oh, sorry." *He sounds awfully impatient. Probably dying to get rid of me.* "Did Miss De Montville give you the autograph?"

He handed her the book. "Yes, but she ripped into

me for asking. She hates autographs. She believes her name is part of her soul, and when she writes it down and gives it to a person, a bit of her goes with it." He frowned. "I think she picked up the superstition when she was doing that movie in Jamaica—*The White Witch of Rose Hall*. Came back with all sorts of superstitions. She kept muttering about voodoo and something called Santería."

A baby-blue Prius made its way from Water Street along Bay Street and stopped in front of Mrs. Spinney's house. Trent got out. Flavia appeared and handed him a satchel. As she walked toward Trent's car, Jasper intercepted her. "You're not leaving until Saturday, right?"

"Yes. Mr. Trent has kindly offered to take me back to Knightston now and will pick me up there."

"You'll be back by Monday at the latest?"

"Yes, Jasper." Ollie came up beside her. "Ah, Mr. Hadley. Did you make hotel reservations for us?"

"Yes." He hesitated. "It's called the Dock and Doze Motel, but"—his voice rose to drown out the gasp—"they assured me it's a five-star establishment."

"I cannot abide motels, you know that. I must be on an upper floor. And if this…this…Dock and Doze is a"—she shivered—"bed and breakfast…" She left the horror of such an institution to her listeners' imaginations.

"You insisted on staying in Westport, after all. There are only two places offering lodging on Brier Island. I secured a corner room at the end of the hall for you. It's under your usual alias—Helena d'Artagnan. The staff will bring you your meals. Trent will bunk with the proprietor."

She sucked in a quivering breath. "I will make do, I assure you. Thank you, Mr. Hadley." She settled into the car, and Trent drove off. Jasper, Ollie, and Cassidy stood in an uncomfortable clump, unsure what to do next.

Pauline returned, Lyle at her side. "Jasper, if you don't need me for anything, I'll go get these photos copied and then head home." She didn't look at Cassidy.

The latter was about to reiterate her request to introduce Pauline to Amity locals, but thought better of it. *The less time spent with her the better.*

Jasper seemed oblivious to the waves of feminine tension undulating around him. "That's fine. See you tomorrow. Be ready to go up to Castine. We might as well get started there while Flavia's gone."

"Okay." She went off, flipping through the file in her hand, Lyle in hot pursuit.

Jasper watched her go. "She'll do fine."

"I'm sure she will."

He swung around on her. "That's an interesting tone."

"What?"

He sized her up. A corner of his mouth lifted. "She seems quite competent. Willing to work hard." He raised his eyes to the sky. "Of course, she'll need some coaching. I'll have to take her in hand—be attentive, but not condescending. She tells me it's been awhile since she was on a shoot. She—*ooph*!"

"Oh, I'm sorry. Was your knee in the way? I guess I had one of those spasms. Leg kicks out unexpectedly."

He rubbed his knee. "Sheesh, Cassidy. I was just

teasing you. You don't do jealous well."

"Jealous? Me? Of what?"

"You mean of 'whom,' don't you?"

"You pick your pronoun, I'll pick mine."

The gaffer came up to them. "We're all locked up, Mr. MacEwan. Can I send the troops back to the barracks?"

"Sure. Thanks, Martin." He held out a hand to Cassidy. "Come on, I'll buy you dinner. Peace?"

Take that, Pauline. "Depends on where."

"Ollie mentioned a nice place in Camden? Pen Fifty. How does that sound?"

Cassidy had never actually been to the restaurant rated among the top ten in the state, but that didn't mean she didn't like the sound of it. She said, in a carefully modulated voice, "That would be acceptable. I'd better change though. It's pretty fancy."

"It is? Oh. Good thing I made a reservation then. And brought a tie. Pick you up in half an hour?"

Frantically going through her closet in her mind, Cassidy could only nod and walk away briskly.

She was still discarding dresses and pushing hangers aside when the doorbell rang. "Let yourself in!" She gazed desperately into her closet. "Oh, wait. That's the one." She pulled a light aqua sheath out. She knew—because Nellie and Hank had both commented on it—that it matched her eyes and set off her slim figure beautifully. *Yes!* She slipped into it and tripped down the stairs.

The whistle was enough to make her evening. "You look smashing, Cassidy."

She gave him a dazzling smile and her hand. "Shall we?"

He took it and squeezed. "Say, do you have a middle name?"

Her good spirits flagged. "Why do you ask?"

"Everyone else around here seems to have one, even if it's only an initial. So?" He smiled at her reassuringly. She mumbled something. "What's that?"

"Jane. It's…Jane."

Instead of the expected jeer, she felt his lips on her cheek. "A beautiful name. In fact, it's my mother's name. Cassidy Jane Beauvoir. Slips off the tongue nicely." He stopped. "I'm guessing you were Calamity Jane in middle school. Am I right?"

She didn't answer. *I refuse to revisit that painful time.*

He led her to the Lamborghini. As he turned left on Route 1, a dilapidated brown Nissan cut them off, speeding down the road in front of them. "That's Pauline's car."

"She said she has an apartment in Knightston."

"Must be going home then."

But for some reason the car kept on through Knightston without stopping. No one else was on the road, and they stayed behind her until Camden. "Maybe she's meeting someone."

They forgot about Pauline once they were seated at a table commanding a panoramic view of Camden harbor. A fabulous meal followed. Jasper ordered the wines and barred Cassidy from seeing the wine list, which was just as well. The price of the Bollinger champagne, followed by a 2002 Puligny-Montrachet, would probably have been enough to cover her property taxes, and she didn't want to have to decline.

Afterward, as they strolled along Elm Street, Jasper

looked up at a sign. "Nemo's. Isn't that where we had a drink with Sally?"

"Yes. It's the bar where Pauline used to work."

"Ah. Now I remember. Fancy a nightcap?"

Cassidy made a concerted effort to quell the slight wobble in her step. *I'm not ready to let this evening end.* "Why not?"

They climbed the stairs to the dark tavern. Few patrons were there at that late hour. Nautical paraphernalia from carved bowsprits to rusty anchors covered the walls, and the windows were smudged from decades of unfiltered cigarette smoke. "Why, that's Pauline behind the bar!" Jasper went over to her. "What are you doing here? I thought you quit?"

"Hi, Jasper." She nodded at Cassidy. "Miss Beauvoir. I'm just filling in here. I wasn't sure if you'd only hired me until you found a replacement for Sally, or if it was long-term, so I decided not to burn my bridges."

"Ah." Jasper leaned over the bar, inducing a painful itching sensation in Cassidy's right fist. "It's true it's only for this movie, but from what I've seen so far, you'll be a shoe-in for a permanent gig at Black Brothers." He frowned. "In that case, you'd have to move to LA. Would that be okay? You said you had an apartment in Knightston. Maybe you wouldn't want to give that up."

Cassidy was saved from having to kick him again when Pauline was called away to the other end of the bar. Seeping through the green haze was the impression that Pauline didn't want to answer Jasper's question any more than Cassidy wanted her to. *Maybe she's got a boyfriend.* This cheered her, and she drank off the Irish coffee with gusto. "Shall we go?"

"What? Oh. Yeah." Jasper left a pile of bills on the bar, and they walked down the narrow stairs to the street.

It took an hour to find the car. Cassidy was muttering about conspicuous cars and towaway zones when Jasper yelled, "It's over here. Dang, I was sure we left it on Chestnut. Hop in."

As they turned onto Elm Street, they saw a familiar car ahead of them. "Isn't that Pauline's Nissan?"

Cassidy glanced at it. "I think so. Bar must have closed. Tells you how long it took to find your car." She lapsed into resentful grumbles. The car stayed ahead of them again along the highway. Again they passed through Knightston, the Nissan never slowing. They were only a mile from Amity when Pauline took a right on a small lane and disappeared. "That road goes to Sunday Cove."

"Oh? Where's that?"

"A little bay. The road parallels Route 1, leading eventually to Amity Landing through South Harbor and Shaman Heights." She said thoughtfully, "It's awfully late to be meeting someone. *Hmm…*"

Jasper chuckled. "Not so late if it's a boyfriend."

"Why would she say she lives in Knightston then?"

"She doesn't want to dash my amorous hopes?"

Chapter Twenty-Six

Cassidy's house, Thursday, July 13

Somehow Cassidy was able to brush off Jasper's continued jokes at her expense, and they bumbled through another night of fantastic sex. She had almost forgiven him when the staccato sounds of Beethoven's *Rage Over a Lost Penny* woke them up.

Jasper scrabbled around for his cell phone. The music had stopped by the time he found it. He clicked the screen on. "Oh, lookee, it was Pauline calling."

A jab in the ribs left him gasping for breath. When the wheezing went on just a tad too long, Cassidy jabbed him again. "What does she want?"

To his credit, Jasper caught the look on her face and said merely, "It went to voicemail." He clicked on another screen. "Here it is. She says she's heading up to Castine with Ollie Hadley and wants to know what equipment and crew should go with them." He dialed. "Pauline? I want Stan Lowry to go, too. And maybe the key grip and gaffer…What? Sure—take Big Bill with you. He can handle the heavy stuff…Oh, right. Then you'd better take Little Bill. You need to scout locations and hire extras. I have some stuff to do here today, but I'll be there tomorrow. Sally spoke to the real estate agent about renting Dyce Head for the scenes with Toff-Smythe, but I'm not sure she finished the paperwork for the lease." He clicked Off, rolled over, and kissed Cassidy. "Good morning, sunshine."

"So, you're going back to Castine?"

"Uh-huh, but this time I'm taking my bullet-proof vest."

"I want to come."

He smirked. "I promise to keep the ogling of Mizz Poliquin to a minimum, if that's what you're worried about."

She got up and pulled a ratty pink bathrobe off the hook. "No, it's not that."

He eyed the frayed sleeves and missing buttons. "Right. She could never hold a candle to your understated elegance."

Cassidy chose to overlook his remark. "I want to get inside the Dyce Head buildings. I don't care what the police think—it wasn't kids who shot at us. Someone drove that Ford SUV there, and someone drove it away. And it wasn't Rick Ahearn."

****

Castine, Friday, July 14

Cassidy spent Thursday at the store, making up for all the time spent in other activities. She didn't see Jasper until the next morning when he picked her up in a Land Rover. The two child actors lolled in the back. Teddy greeted her politely. Jasper explained. "We're taking the boys to Castine. They want to acquaint themselves with the town."

Cassidy settled on the fine Italian leather seat and admired the sleek, black SUV. "Still no bumper flags?"

"Rory has his own, but his mother forgot to pack them."

"Ah."

The trip was uneventful, and the four of them met the key grip and Pauline in the center of town by the Hotel Pentagoet.

Lyle shouldered a backpack. "I'm meeting Ollie, Stan, and the others down at the waterfront, then the crew will bunk down in the RVs until Sunday."

Jasper said, "Pauline? Did you drive up in your own car?"

She pointed at the brown Nissan. "Yes. I'm going back to Penhallow tonight. Is there anything else you need me to do here?"

"One more thing. Please book the cast into this hotel starting Monday." He gestured at Rory and Teddy. "You two stay together. Rendezvous with us back at this hotel"—he checked his watch—"in an hour." Rory had started to edge away, but Jasper caught his arm. "I want Teddy with you at all times, Rory. No arguments."

The younger boy wrinkled his nose. "Does he have to go in the bathroom stall with me too?" His infuriated expression was definitely not faked.

My guess is he's not used to being thwarted.

"Don't be a smartass. I signed an agreement with your mother that you would always be chaperoned. You've never been to Maine before, so while you're based in Castine and I'm shuttling between here and Amity Landing, Teddy is in charge."

"Why don't you put a homing device on me? Surgically implant a beeper? Or I could swallow it." Rory continued to fume.

"Good idea. Pauline, you find a suitable device, and I'll make an appointment at the hospital."

The boy's jaw dropped. "You wouldn't."

247

Teddy shook Rory's shoulder. "He's yanking your chain, nitwit. Come on. Let's explore the town." He smiled at Pauline. "We'll be back in an hour." The two went off down the street, the younger boy struggling to keep up with Teddy's long strides.

Jasper watched them until they turned a corner and were out of sight. "Clever. Keep the kid out of breath so he can't whine."

Pauline stroked Jasper's arm, evidently unaffected by the Kryptonite death rays shooting from Cassidy's eyes. "Did you mean that? Should I look for a dollar store?"

Jasper's eyes widened. "No, of course not. I just wanted to stick a pin in his bubble, Pauline."

Cassidy holstered her cosmic weapons and got back in the car.

Jasper put his head in the passenger side. "Were you going somewhere?"

"I thought we were going to Dyce Head?"

"Oh, right. First we have to stop at the real estate office—I want to see if they've drawn up the lease agreement for the house." He straightened and turned to Pauline. "You can head on back to Penhallow once you've reserved the hotel rooms."

"What about Mr. Lowry? He drove up with me."

"Don't worry about the crew—they're set up at that campground up the road. Ollie will drive everyone back to Amity on Sunday." He indicated the hotel. "Make it three rooms."

Pauline counted on her fingers. "Toff-Smythe. De Montville. Teddy. Rory. Shouldn't it be four?"

"The boys can rough it. Oh, and make sure their room doesn't adjoin Flavia's." He grimaced. "We don't want a repeat of the last episode."

"Episode."

"All I'll say is it involved Rory and a camera."

They left Pauline heading into the hotel and went to the real estate office. A nice young woman named Alice helped them sign the lease papers. "Now this is only for the use of the house, you understand. The town owns the lighthouse, which is closed to the public."

"Oh, no! Didn't Sally Crook explain? We planned to film the battle scenes from the lighthouse. The British commandant has to be up there to survey the American fleet."

Alice shuffled through some papers. "Oh, sorry. Yes, here it is. She got a permit from the town to use the building." She looked up. "You can only film during the day, though. It's actually a working light now. They reactivated it in 2008 when a storm knocked the skeleton tower over."

"Not a problem—we don't work after five p.m." He glanced at Cassidy and grinned.

"Good." Alice handed them a set of keys.

They drove down the lane past Fort George to Dyce Head. This time the parking lot was empty. Jasper fit one of the keys in the lighthouse door, and they climbed the winding stairs to the top. A large lamp took up the center of the circular space.

Jasper read from the flyer Alice had given them. "The original tower was built in 1829 on land acquired from the Dyce family. The forty-two-foot structure boasted a wrought iron lantern with ten lamps in fourteen-inch reflectors. It was electrified and automated by 1935, but decommissioned in 1937 and its lamp moved to a new building." He looked up. "That must be the tower Alice talked about."

"But she also said this is a working light now. What happened?"

He read further. "It sat abandoned until 2007 when the citizenry asked the Coast Guard to reactivate it."

"That's rather romantic, isn't it?" Cassidy edged around the lantern. Below her lay a panorama of forested islands and gray water intersecting like the pieces of a jigsaw puzzle. A lone sailboat plowed through the choppy seas toward the harbor. A splash of sunlight hit its mast, sparking bolts of silver light. "It's so beautiful."

Jasper came up behind her. "It truly is. The California coast is very different."

"Is it? How?"

"The Pacific can be very forbidding—vast and cold—especially in the northern part of the state. Makes a person feel puny." He waved a hand at a lobsterman chugging along close to shore. "I get the sense here that it's possible to work with nature rather than in the face of it."

"You haven't been here in a nor'easter. Mother Nature doesn't spare the rod or spoil the child. We had three blizzards totaling eight feet of snow last winter."

He moved slowly around the light taking pictures of the landscape. "We'll have General McLean—he's the commandant—standing here gazing into the distance, waiting for relief while the American ships mill around below."

"Um. I just thought of something. You said the lighthouse was built in 1829. So—"

"Oops." Jasper covered his open mouth. "That means it wasn't here in 1779, was it?"

"Right." She cast an eye over the area. "However, Castine was a continual battleground from its founding in 1613 until well into the nineteenth century. I wouldn't be surprised if there were always some kind of defensive structure here. And anyway, the hill was here, and the British were building fortifications. The view would have been the same."

Jasper rubbed his jaw. "Yeah, so we don't show the actual lighthouse on the screen, just Digby standing."

"Then you'll have to film him out there." Cassidy indicated a narrow walkway that girdled the outside of the lantern room.

"That would be fine, if Digby didn't have severe vertigo. We'd have to string a safety net all the way around the tower." He snickered. "Or how about a trampoline? Can you just see the Toff bouncing wildly, perfect hair streaming out, mouth opened wide in a terrified scream? We could make it a publicity photo. Why—"

Cassidy figured he'd had enough fun at the actor's expense. "So Digby gets to play the British commandant after all?"

"Yes. As he is fond of declaiming, 'Toff-Smythe only plays heroes.' "

"But wouldn't it make more sense for him to play Nathaniel West, captain of the *Black Prince*? After all, that's the ship the cabin boy came from."

"That was the casting director's original choice, but Dad wanted him to play General McLean. After the encounter with Snookie the ghost dog, there was a bit of back-and-forth among the three, until Digby learned that West was court-martialed for scuttling his ship and abandoning his crew. He decided the role was beneath him and put his foot down." He sniffed. "He maintains his change of heart had nothing to do with Snookie."

"Wait a minute. West couldn't have been court-martialed—the *Black Prince* was a privately-owned ship, wasn't it?"

"Yes, but since the ship was conscripted into military service, military law would apply." He started back down. "Anyway, McLean gets to defeat the disreputable Americans and pilot his forces to a glorious victory."

"I don't know about 'victory.' Didn't the Brits leave soon after?"

"Only the fort. A contingent remained, which occupied the town until the end of the war. The general led the rest of his troops back to Canada for a hero's welcome."

"But he left the drummer boy behind! That was cruel."

Jasper had an answer for that too. "He did—by mistake—and the final scene shows him racked with guilt, standing on the widow's walk of his home, staring south to Castine."

"I hope that's in his mind, not in the actual script."

"I don't know. I haven't read that far."

"What?"

"Kidding. Yes, it's in the script. If it wasn't, he'd write it in."

Cassidy opened the hatch to the stairs. "So who plays West?"

"Well, now it's become a bit part. Dad's hoping to find some over-the-hill actor looking to put an Oscar for a supporting role on his mantel shelf."

Cassidy had a fleeting image of Bobby B. Goode in

a Continental navy uniform. She blinked rapidly.

Jasper took her hand. "Let's explore the house. I want to see if we need any extra props."

"And I want to see if there are any bullet holes in the wall."

"You play your games; I'll play mine."

They separated at the end of the breezeway. Jasper went into the living room and Cassidy to the kitchen. The back door faced the parking lot. She opened it and stepped out to check the tiny back porch. As she turned around to go back in, her shoe caught on something. In the center of the threshold, a penny nail stuck up about an inch. *Someone could trip on that and take a header.* She poked around looking for something to pound it back in. The second drawer produced a hammer. *Perfect.*

When she knelt down next to the threshold, she noticed a gap about half an inch wide between the floor boards. She felt along it until she found a corner. *Must be the coal cellar, but how do I open it?* Using the claw end of the hammer, she pried it up. The door opened on blackness. In the gloom, she could make out a set of wooden stairs going down. A long string dangled from a light bulb. Standing on tiptoe, she yanked on it. It only illuminated the first few steps. "Jasper? Where are you?"

No answer. *I'm not waiting.* Leaving the hammer on the floor, she carefully climbed down. The third step broke, and she nearly tumbled all the way to the bottom before catching hold of a beam above her. She stood, panting, pondering whether to call Jasper again or explore on her own. *Where did he go? He was in the living room. He should have heard me.* Just then, a footfall sounded over her head. *There he is.* "Jasper? I'm down here." She continued on, stepping carefully on the outside of each step.

In the faint light, she found another string hanging from another bulb in the center of the room. She switched it on. The bobbling glow revealed a cellar that seemed to span the entire house. The fixture didn't cast enough light to see into the corners, so she started feeling her way around the walls. About halfway along one side, she bumped into a wooden bin. Lifting the lid, she sniffed. "Potatoes." A little farther along she felt the rounded corners and cold metal of the oil furnace and next to it a trough filled with logs. She took a step forward and tripped over a pile of rocks, landing on her knees. When she put a hand out to brace herself against the wall, she met only air. *Huh. A storage niche?* She couldn't feel a back wall. *No. A cave maybe?* She ducked and went in.

Chapter Twenty-Seven

Dyce Head, Friday, July 14

She found herself in a passageway. When she tried to stand up, she hit her head, so she stooped and crept along, hoping it would widen or come to a quick end. *But if the room behind me is as big as the house, where does this lead?* To the lighthouse? *Ah.* It must be a way for the keeper to go back and forth when the weather is too severe for the breezeway. But then why not light it better? Or make it wider? She was lost in speculation when the tunnel veered sharply to the left. She wasn't entirely sure in which direction she'd been walking, but fancied it was now heading away from the lighthouse rather than toward it. *I think I want Jasper with me before I go any farther.*

It took some effort to turn around in the tight space. She scrambled back, eventually arriving at the cellar. She had raised a hand to yank the string on the bulb above her head when she realized that the other light—the one at the top of the stairs—was no longer on. *Bulb must've burned out. Who knows when someone last changed it?*

Her eyes had adjusted enough by now to see her way, so she turned off the center light and padded across the room. She should have seen daylight through the open trapdoor, but all was dark. She climbed the steps. Her head touched wood. *It must have fallen shut.* She pushed on it. *Stuck.* She pushed harder. It gave, but only a little. Claustrophobia threatened. *I've got to get out of here!* Her voice rose to a shriek. "Jasper! Jasper! Are you there?"

For answer she heard running footsteps. "Cassidy? Where are you?"

"Here! Under the hatch."

The feet stopped above her. "I can't see you."

"I'm right underneath you, dummy. Get your big stompers off me."

There was some shuffling, then a thump as he knelt on the floor. She heard scratching. "How do I open this?"

"You have to pry it up."

More shuffling, then some squeaking and a loud *scree* as the hatch was slowly raised. Jasper got a hand under it and lifted it all the way. He reached in and turned on the light. "You look like a mouse caught raiding the larder."

She clambered out. "Thanks a lot." She brushed her pants off. "Where have you been?"

"The question is: where were *you*? I've been looking all over the grounds for you. The kitchen was empty. I figured you'd gone out the back door. I even went down the hill to the water."

"Didn't you see the trapdoor?"

He shook his head. "Wind must've blown it shut."

She sat on the only kitchen chair. "Jasper, I found a tunnel."

"A tunnel! Where does it go?"

"I don't know. I went along it a ways, but then it took a turn. I decided to come fetch you, and we'd explore it together."

He checked his watch. "We'll have to save it for next time. The boys are due back in Penhallow."

"But—"

He dropped the door back into place and held up the hammer. "Where did this come from?"

"That drawer." She pointed.

He returned it and closed the drawer. "Come on, we're late. I don't want Rory to have something to hang over my head."

They retrieved Rory and Teddy down by the docks. As they approached, Rory flicked something into the water. When he saw them, a guilty look washed over his cherubic features, mutating immediately into a sunny smile. Cassidy could understand how he became a child star, with his angelic face and tousled hair. *The audience doesn't have to know what a pill he is in reality.*

Jasper crooked a finger. Teddy ran up to them, Rory trailing him more slowly. As they walked back to the car, Jasper said over his shoulder, "I don't want to know what you just threw in the water, but if the police call, I'm turning you in. We can always get another actor to play the drummer boy."

"Hey!"

****

Cassidy's house, Friday, July 14

Later that night, they lay together on the chaise on Cassidy's deck and gazed at the Milky Way. "This has been an interesting day."

Cassidy snuggled under Jasper's arm. "More for me than you, I think."

"How so? I saw a snake in the grass. And rescued a

257

damsel in distress."

"Was the snake human-shaped?"

"No. Just a normal snake shape. Why?"

"Well, I've been thinking. What made the trapdoor close?"

"The wind?"

She sat up. "The back door and all the windows were shut. Where would a breeze come from?"

"Good point. *Hmm.* Maybe it just fell back into place of its own weight."

"Possibly."

"What I want to know is, why were you down there in the dark? Afraid you'd be caught? According to Alice, the owners are in Boca Raton."

"Down in the…I wasn't down in the dark. There was a light bulb. I assumed it had burnt out, but…" She turned frightened eyes on Jasper. "You switched it back on."

"But that means…that means…"

She said through gritted teeth, "Someone turned it off."

He jumped up. "And closed the hatch on you."

"But what on earth for?"

****

Amity Landing, Saturday, July 15

They had no time to speculate on the mystery over the weekend. Nellie asked Cassidy to meet the midwife, which meant the rest of the day was consumed with arguing over the wisdom of giving birth under water. Hank refused to participate in the debate except to mumble about tadpoles and fingerlings. After an hour he left, carrying a fishing rod and a creel. Having resolved nothing, the two women went to the consignment store to shop for baby clothes.

Jasper spent the weekend conferring by telephone with his father and the investors in Los Angeles. He proudly told a less-than-enthused Cassidy that his father was leaving control of the production solely to him. "He's got his hands full with the other two movies."

"*Hmmph.*"

He had deposited Digby in the Penhallow hotel with the two boys, in the vain hope that they would work on their scenes together.

Monday found him heading downhill to set up the daily shoot just as Flavia and the grip returned. Cassidy saw them from her deck and decided to run after Jasper. She arrived in time to see Flavia jump out of the car in front of the Spinney house. The normally elegant, reserved actress was practically bouncing with enthusiasm. "Jasper! Jasper! There you are. Hurry!"

The grip put the car in reverse and headed back up the street. Jasper, apparently as surprised as Cassidy to see a disheveled Flavia, said "I'm here, I'm here. What's the matter?"

"We found it!" She took a large gulp of air.

"Found what?"

She crooked a finger at them. "Let's talk inside. Is there a chair for me?"

Jasper leapt to the door, and the three of them trooped in. Flavia halted on the threshold, forcing the other two to gyrate to either side. "Where's William?"

"William? You mean your driver? He left in the car."

"Is he coming back? I need him beside me, the better to tell the tale." Before they could respond, she closed her eyes and touched a finger to her lips. "Never mind. Give me a moment."

Cassidy was astonished to see the actress visibly falling into her role. The messy hair disappeared under an imaginary mob cap; her Michael Kors peplum dress magically transformed into a rough-woven wool skirt and apron. Her face became care-worn and tired, her clear skin free of makeup. She curtsied.

"Welcome to my house, Master MacEwan, Mistress…what is thy name, child?" She smiled guilelessly at Cassidy.

Cassidy almost curtsied in return. She stopped in time, confining herself to a slight bob of the head. "Cassidy Jane Beauvoir, Mistress."

"Beauvoir?" She raised an eyebrow. "You are Acadian?"

"Yes. My father's family was from the County."

She scanned the younger woman with a critical eye. "And I infer from your coloring that an ancestor may have engaged in intimate relations with an individual of one of the indigenous races."

"Yes. I am part Passamaquoddy on my mother's side."

"Ah." Flavia sat in a chair and arranged her skirts around her. It being the only chair, the other two remained standing. Jasper leaned against the wall. He was about to speak when the actress resumed. "We Acadians are for the most part on good terms with our Indian neighbors." She scowled. "Not so the Americans. I did hear from my young friend Israel Trask of many a dustup between the settlers and those who came before them. 'Tis a wretched shame and a deplorable reflection on man's inhumanity." She frowned. "As the good Reverend Le Loutre said, 'We are all God's children. We must never forget the Golden Rule.' "

Jasper pushed off from the wall. "Flavia? Can we have you back for a moment?"

The woman closed her eyes. When she opened them, her gaze was clear and present. "Yes, Jasper?"

"What did you do in Nova Scotia?"

She folded her hands. "We found Mercy Spinney's house."

"I see."

Cassidy wracked her brain. "Mercy Spinney. Our Mrs. Spinney's ancestor, right?"

"Yes. She was the lady who took in the cabin boy Israel Trask. He had been wandering for weeks after the battle. A fisherman picked him up on the shore and brought him to her. She nursed him back to health." Flavia smiled. "Wasn't it fortuitous that William accompanied me? It turns out he has kin in Westport who were acquainted with the Spinneys. That's how we located the house."

Jasper leaned forward. "He didn't mention this to you before you arrived?"

"He only knew his family was originally from Nova Scotia—if that's what you're asking. When we reached the town, he recalled that he still had cousins living there. I imagine grips don't bother to read scripts or he might have recognized the Spinney name. I told him the story. He was very interested." She grew thoughtful. "I can't imagine what it's like to know so little about your origins. My grandmother compiled a three-volume genealogy of my mother's side of the family. My father's family was spared the trouble— *Debrett's* chronicled the history of the de Montvilles for us." She smiled serenely.

The royal house of Montville?

Cassidy would have laughed except Jasper asked fretfully, "The house, Flavia. Did you see it?"

She nodded vigorously. "We were taking a leisurely stroll about town when William ran into his cousin. We had a lovely tea together and told him—I believe his name was Donald—about the movie. He directed us to the house." She straightened her skirt. "The current owner, a Mrs. Grace Spinney, was about to put it on the market, and the real estate agent allowed us to accompany him on a tour." Her eyes sparkled. "It was quite enthralling to stand by the enormous fireplace where Mercy did her morning ablutions and boiled her coffee. And in one of the bedchambers, we found a chest with her clothes and a silver brush set, and—"

"Yes, yes." Jasper's impatience was growing. "Did Trent's cousin mention any stories about the cabin boy? We really need some added color."

"No, more's the pity." She gazed sadly at Jasper. "I suppose the battle will dominate the film anyway. Your father prefers an action picture—lots of explosions and bloodletting. Not much room for a heartwarming tale of friendship and survival." She sighed.

"On the contrary, I intend to make you and the cabin boy the principal plot line." Jasper grew animated. "We'll follow the boy's treacherous trek over miles of wild land, portray his desperate clinging to life, and then at last deliver him unto his savior—a courageous woman unhindered by suspicion of strangers and unaffected by wartime rivalries. Why—"

Flavia interrupted him, to Cassidy's relief. "What about the battle? That's not center stage? Digby will be in a towering snit if he's not on Camera One the entire two hours."

"Oh, no," Jasper replied hastily. "He'll have almost as much screen time as you will, my dear. He'll not only oversee the battle, but he will hunt the cabin boy down in Canada and try to arrest him as a war criminal."

"Good—so he gets to be John Wayne *and* Henry Fonda?" She gave a delicate yawn. "I do hope you don't need me this afternoon, Jasper. I really must get some rest after our long journey. Do you have the script handy? I'd like to reconsider how to handle my part now that I have a better feel for the woman Mercy."

"Yes." Jasper took a manila envelope from his briefcase. "Here you go."

The grip stuck his head in. "Miss de Montville? I can run you back to your hotel if you like."

She rose gracefully. "Thank you, William. If you don't mind waiting, I'd like to first confer with young Teddy on our upcoming scenes." She sailed out.

The two left behind gazed at each other before saying in unison, "What now?"

Jasper's phone rang. He clicked Talk. "Hey, Dad. What? You hired *who* to play West? Hoo boy. When are you coming back? Of course I can handle it…Okay." He hung up.

"Sounds as though there's more trouble on the way."

"Right. The only one he could get on short notice was Digby's arch enemy. As if I needed more problems." He wiped his brow.

"Who is it?"

"Artemus North."

"I've heard of him. Are they acting rivals?"

"Oh, yes. They've been cadging each other's limelight since high school. But it gets worse."

"How?"

"Digby was responsible for North's near demise."

"Premeditated?"

"No one's sure. I don't have all the details, but apparently Artemus had been getting under his skin and Digby decked him. He fell off the boat they were on and had to swim to shore."

"Oh, my! Then why would Mr. North want to join the cast?"

"Revenge. Ever since the incident, Artemus follows Digby to whatever location he's filming in. Even if he can't snag a role, he hangs around the set making Digby nervous. He claims his mother told him to."

"Mother?"

"Well, actually, *their* mother."

"Oh, no! You mean—"

"Yes, Digby and Artemus are brothers."

Chapter Twenty-Eight

Amity Landing, Monday, July 17

Cassidy recollected what she'd read about Artemus North, a versatile actor known for stealing the show with his fanciful interpretations of secondary characters. Then she considered Digby Toff-Smythe. "I'm astounded their parents could spawn two such…unique characters."

Jasper held the door for Cassidy. "Well, to be precise, they are half brothers. They share the same mother."

They walked up the hill. "Is it your job to break the news to the Toff?"

"Technically, but I intend to stick Ollie with it. After all, he's the producer."

Cassidy yawned. "I think I'll take a nap too." She raised an eyebrow at Jasper. "I didn't get much sleep last night."

Jasper checked his watch. "That's fine. I'm going to find the two boys. I want them to go back up to Castine with Stan and some of the crew this afternoon to work on staging for the scene between the drummer boy and the cabin boy. I'll probably go up first thing tomorrow." He turned and loped toward his car.

A little disappointed, Cassidy trudged up her steps. *What did you expect, Cass? He does have a job after all. Do you want him to drop everything and cater to your every whim?* She blew out her cheeks. *I assume he's got his hands full doing that for Flavia. And Digby. And Pauline?*

****

Castine, Tuesday, July 18

"Cassidy? Are you busy?"

Cassidy pulled her sweatpants up with one hand and held the phone to her ear with the other. "Actually—"

"Can you come up to Castine now?"

"What?" She checked the alarm clock. "Nellie will be here in fifteen minutes to go jogging, and I have to be at the store at two."

"Put off Nellie. It's only eight now. Ollie's already there—he says there's no traffic. It won't take more than forty minutes. You'll be home long before two."

Cassidy let go her pants, which promptly fell down around her ankles. "I don't recall you telling me why you need me?"

"Oh! Oh. See, Rory's missing."

"Rory?" Cassidy's brain was still fuzzy with sleep. "Is he the one playing the cabin boy or the drummer boy?"

"The drummer boy. Rory Fiddick. You met him. The pill."

"Ah. Would it be so bad if he were missing?"

Jasper made a sound that mixed frustration with a little hysteria—sort of a combination *aargh* and hiccup. "Yes, if you want me to keep both my job and the Lamborghini."

Sigh. "Okay, I'm on my way. Where are you?"

"Actually I'm outside your front door. I can drive

266

you."

Luckily, Cassidy forgot to ask how he expected her to get back to Penhallow. She pulled on her pants, checked her face in the mirror, wrote a note to Nellie begging off their run, and trotted out the door. The Lamborghini steamed in the morning sunshine.

"Hop in." He stomped on the accelerator and roared down the street, narrowly missing Bobby B. Goode and his wife Mary Jo walking their Great Dane Susie.

"You are aware of the speed limit, right?"

"I'm betting it's lower than what I'm doing." He didn't slow down. Route 1 was devoid of traffic, so they made good time all the way to Bucksport. A small jam held them up at the turnoff for Fort Knox. Jasper shaded his eyes. "Looks like a school bus is stuck."

Once past, they sailed across the bridge and down the Blue Hill Peninsula. For once, there was plenty of parking in front of the fire station. They found Alfie in the sheriff's office. "One of my actors—Teddy Bickford—telephoned me. Rory Fiddick has disappeared. He said he had notified you."

"Ah yes." Alfie consulted a clipboard. "Rory Fiddick. White. Brown hair, brown eyes. Fifteen years old. Last seen at the Hotel Pentagoet wearing shorts and a T-shirt that reads Hollywood is for Hams."

"Have you found him?"

"Nope. We've got deputies at the waterfront and combing the streets. Any haunts? Favorite hidey-holes?"

At that moment, Teddy came rushing in. "Oh, Mr. MacEwan, am I glad to see you!"

Jasper didn't bother to chastise the young man.

One look at his ashen face told them how badly he felt. "Where is Mr. Lowry?"

"He went to the campground."

"Is the crew there?"

"Some of them."

"The deputy wants to know where you think Rory might have gone."

He shook his head. "I said goodnight to him at the hotel at ten o'clock. He was yawning, so I thought he was telling the truth that he was going straight to bed." A small smile lit his worried features. "I made sure he got lots of exercise yesterday. We climbed Blue Hill and had a sailing lesson and swam laps in the hotel pool."

"You didn't go back to the room with him?"

"No. I stayed in the lobby reading for another hour."

"Was he in bed when you went up?"

The boy wrung his hands, his expression contrite. "I didn't check closely. There was a lump in his bed. I just assumed…The light was out, so I slipped under the covers and went to sleep."

"And when you woke up this morning, he was gone?"

"His bed hadn't been slept in. The lump was his pillow." Teddy's voice rose. "He's been out all night. He could be hurt, or lost, or…or kidnapped." He buried his face in his hands.

"Kidnapped!" Alfie looked from one frightened face to another. "Is that a possibility? Should I ask the sheriff to put out an APB?"

Jasper took charge. "Not yet. The boy has a history of taking off. That's the most likely scenario. Let's give the police a little more time."

Cassidy hugged Teddy. "Don't panic. It's not your fault. I get the feeling that Rory can never be trusted."

Jasper said heavily, "You got that right." He turned to Alfie. "Do you have my cell number?"

Alfie took it down. "We'll call you when we know anything."

They walked outside. Teddy said, "So what do we do now?"

Cassidy went to the car. "I think we should search too. Any ideas? Did he mention any particular place? Assuming he wasn't kidnapped, that is."

She immediately regretted her words when Teddy started keening. "Oh God, oh God, oh God, oh—"

Jasper shook him gently. "Teddy!" When the boy had calmed, he asked, "Did you ever read O. Henry's 'The Ransom of Red Chief'?"

Teddy paused. "What? Oh, yeah. Required reading in middle school. About a little terror who gets abducted and—"

"He's so horrible that the gangsters pay the parents to take him back. I'm pretty sure Rory would be a match for Red Chief. Now think—where should we start looking?"

"A bar?"

"No fake ID. I confiscated his wallet for the duration."

"So no fake ID. No money either."

They stood in a tight circle. Finally Cassidy remembered something. "Wait a minute…a bar." She faced Teddy. "Lyle Korn and the other grips were at Fort George the other day digging for treasure. He said they'd heard it from someone in a bar. Did he by any chance tell you and Rory about it?"

Teddy's eyes lit up. "Yes, he did. Rory was all excited at first, but then"—he frowned—"he suddenly went very quiet. I should have known."

"Let's go."

They drove down the now familiar lane to the fort. The place was empty. As they spread out, exploring the hummocks that hid old fortifications, Cassidy heard whimpering. She called to Jasper. "Over there."

Together they headed toward the old dungeon. As they neared it, Jasper held a hand up. "Someone's crying. Rory? Rory!" They leaned over the edge of the sinkhole. Stubby white fingers could be seen sticking out between the bars. Jasper scrabbled down the bank and reached the barred gate in one stride. "Rory! Are you okay?"

The boy moaned, "Mr. MacEwan. I'm ss-ss-sooo c-c-cold." Cassidy could hear his teeth chatter even from ground level.

Jasper shook the bars. "Locked. How did you get in there?"

"I c-c-came down the t-t-t-tunnel."

"The tunnel!" Cassidy had a flash of understanding. *It can wait.* She straightened and cupped her hands. "Teddy!"

The young man waved. "The police are on their way!"

A few minutes later, the state police car pulled up behind the Lamborghini. Detective Parsons and Alfie got out and ran across the field. "You found him?"

"He's in the brig."

"But how—?"

"Never mind that." *I want to confer with Jasper*

before we mention anything. "Do you have Mr. Flint's key?"

"Uh-huh. I grabbed it when we got the call. Had a feeling that's where he was." Parsons produced a large, heavy skeleton key. He slid down the embankment and, elbowing Jasper aside, fit it in the lock. Parsons tugged on the gate, but it wouldn't budge. Jasper stepped up, and the two of them heaved. It opened with a loud creak, and Rory fell into Parsons' arms. He yelled, "Alfie, the emergency blankets!"

****

Castine, Tuesday, July 18

Jasper, Teddy, and Cassidy followed the squad car to the maritime academy's clinic—"Closest hospital is in Blue Hill, but these guys know how to deal with exposure"—and sat in the waiting room.

Jasper took out his phone. "I'll call Ollie and Stan and tell them to head back to Amity Landing." When he'd finished, he stood staring out the window. "How on earth did he get inside the brig? It was locked."

Teddy said, "Maybe the door was open when he went in, and it automatically locked behind him."

"Doors with skeleton keys don't usually have automatic locks."

Cassidy had been quiet during the ride and while the doctor was checking Rory in. Now she spoke. "I know how."

"How?"

"Rory said he came down the tunnel. I only know one tunnel around here."

Jasper opened his mouth and closed it again. "The one under the Dyce Head house." He stared at Cassidy. "But we figured that led to the lighthouse."

"Right. That was my first guess, but just at the point where I turned back, it hooked a sharp left in the opposite direction. I think"—she put her hands on her knees—"that our Rory found the trapdoor and walked the whole way to the other end of the passage."

"Which is the Fort George brig?"

She nodded.

"But then—" Teddy was puzzled. "Why didn't he just go back out the same way?"

Chapter Twenty-Nine

Castine, Tuesday, July 18

"We need to go back to Dyce Head."

Cassidy caught Jasper's wrist. "What about Rory?"

"Oops." Jasper went to the reception desk. "How is our patient doing?"

The nurse checked a chart. "If you'll wait a minute, I'll ask the doctor to come out and report on his progress."

"Of course."

Teddy stood so close to the swinging doors that he had to jump away when a man in a white coat pushed through them. "Are any of you Mr. Riddick's next of kin?"

Jasper spoke. "No. Rory is a star in the movie we're making about the Penobscot Expedition. I'm Jasper MacEwan, the director. He is my responsibility."

"I see." He began to write something on his clipboard but glanced up quickly, eyes eager. "Did you say the Penobscot Expedition? You mean, the ignominious rout of the American armada by the British in 1779?" He rose to his toes, his voice squeaky. "And you're making a movie about it? Here in Castine?"

"Yes, we are. We're only in the preproduction phase now, but we will start shooting soon. I take it you know something of the battle?"

The doctor blushed. "American maritime history is a recent hobby of mine." He gestured behind him. "Finding myself here at the Maritime Academy, it was an easy call. So, have you cast Nathaniel West? The commander of the American fleet, Saltonstall? How about General McLean? Who is—"

"Dr. Harris?" The nurse nudged him from behind. "You were going to tell them about Mr. Fiddick's diagnosis?"

"What? Oh, yes. Sorry." He checked his clipboard. "The patient is suffering from exposure. I have administered an antibiotic, but bronchitis can't be ruled out. Normally we aren't allowed to admit nonstudents, but since the school is on summer break, I think we can bend the rules a bit. I recommend leaving him overnight so we can observe him. Are you staying in town?"

"No. We're from Penhallow."

"Oh." He seemed disappointed.

Probably wants to talk Maine history with Jasper…or maybe wangle a bit part.

"In that case, you can take him to Waldo Memorial. It's on South Harbor Avenue down in Penhallow."

"Thanks," Jasper said dryly. "We know where it is."

Cassidy pushed Jasper aside and spoke to the doctor. "We have some…er…errands still to do here in Castine. Do you mind if we leave Rory with you for an hour or so, and transport him back to Penhallow when we're done for the day?"

"That would be satisfactory. I'll call the hospital and alert them you'll be bringing him."

"Perfect."

Cassidy grabbed Jasper, crooked a finger at Teddy, and rushed out the door. "Come on—I want to get to the lighthouse before he's gone."

"Before who's gone?"

"The guy behind all this."

"Wait a minute!" Too late Cassidy realized that Teddy knew nothing of recent events. She turned to see him standing, shock paling his features, on the sidewalk. "Someone is after Rory?"

Jasper glared at Cassidy. "Certainly not. It's more likely that a person or persons is trying to scare us off. Perhaps a squatter in the house. Or those boys with the BB guns. Nobody's actually been hurt."

"You're forgetting Mr. Flint."

That shut him up, and they drove fast down the lane, Teddy wedged into the tiny back seat of the Lamborghini.

They pulled into the parking lot next to a familiar red car. "That's the same rental car Ahearn was driving!" Cassidy felt a prick of fear. She kept her seat.

"Come on, Cass. No one's going to shoot at us in broad daylight."

"What do you mean? They did before."

"Well, what do you propose we do? Stay here like sitting ducks?"

Teddy scrunched down in the back and wrapped his arms around his head. Cassidy realized that Jasper was right. "Okay, but let's go single file."

"Right, that'll make us harder to hit."

Laugh if you want. "Come on."

The door was open. "Hello! Anybody in the house?"

One of the grips came out of the kitchen. "Oh, it's

you, Mr. MacEwan. What are you guys doing here?"

"The real question, Phalen, is what are *you* doing here? I thought I told Stan to take you all back to Penhallow."

"Penhallow?" The man scratched his head. "No, see, he left me and Trent here to keep an eye on the equipment at the campground."

"Lyle didn't stay with you?"

"No. Why?"

Jasper hesitated. "I…um…just like the crew to be supervised at all times."

Phalen shrugged. "He had enough on his hands. We're okay with it."

Cassidy had been wandering around the room. She sidled casually into the kitchen. Everything seemed in order. The trapdoor was closed. She moved to the back door. *Someone's pounded the nail back in.* She swung around. "Did you fix this threshold?"

"You mean the nail? Yeah. I tripped on it. Found a hammer on the counter, so I pounded it back in." He held up the tool Cassidy had used to pry up the trapdoor.

"Oh." She tried again. "You haven't seen anyone else around? Couple of boys with BB guns?"

He started to shake his head, then stopped. "BB guns? Someone taking potshots at us? Boy, locals must really hate strangers."

Jasper said mildly, "I wouldn't necessarily jump to that conclusion. Kids could've just been messing around."

"So *you* were shot at? When?"

"Three weeks ago. And"—Cassidy gestured out to the parking lot—"that car was parked here then, too."

She looked meaningfully at the grip.

He followed her gaze. "It's a rental. Trent picked it up at the dealership in Penhallow on the way here. His old rattletrap doesn't have enough cargo space."

"So you never rented it before?"

"Not me. Ask Trent."

At that moment, Trent walked through the door. "Ask me what?"

"Have you rented this car before?"

"Nah. We just needed it for the day."

Jasper said, "A man named Ahearn had it last. A man who was found murdered."

Trent's jaw dropped. "Murdered! Well, I'll be snookered." He chuckled. "I hope they cleaned up the mess before they rented it to me."

"Making jokes about murder is hardly appropriate."

"Why not? I didn't know the guy." He shivered. "If I let it bother me, I wouldn't be able to drive the damned car, now would I? And it was the only one available that would do."

Cassidy felt as though something were slipping away but wasn't sure what it was. She walked over to the trapdoor. "Did you notice this?"

He hesitated. "Yeah. I figured it went to the root cellar."

"It does. It also leads to Fort George."

"Really? You mean, like a secret passage?" Trent pulled at his beard. "What on earth would it be used for?"

Jasper answered. "The British probably dug it out as an escape route for the commander."

The other grip whistled. "Huh. Cool. You should

use it in the movie. You know, Toff-Smythe could sneak down to rally his troops at the fort. He'd love that." He stopped, pretending concern. "Aw, but then he'd have to get all mussed and dirty, wouldn't he?"

Trent's phone buzzed. "Gotta go. Lyle wants me back by five."

Phalen dropped a heavy hand on his shoulder. "Drop me off at the campground?"

"Sure." The two men left. The three remaining were silent. Finally Cassidy muttered, "It's all a muddle, isn't it? We don't seem any closer to finding out who's behind these attacks—"

"Pranks. Merely pranks."

"Again—Mr. Flint." Cassidy wished she didn't have to remind him.

Jasper was obstinate. "That could've been a fluke too."

"What, he brought a pillow into the dungeon with him so he could suffocate himself?"

"Well…maybe he had an asthma attack."

"Or maybe the killer took the pillow back to the house with him."

"You, my dear, are clutching at straws."

Teddy had been listening to the conversation, his mouth opening and closing like a frog on a hot plate. He blurted, "So you *do* think there's someone out there killing people?"

Both Jasper and Cassidy stopped. "Oh, Teddy. I'd forgotten you were there."

"So much for celebrity." He gave a wry smile.

"I'm sorry…wait a minute! Back at the clinic, you asked why Rory didn't just come back the way he came. I say we go down and see." Cassidy opened the drawer.

"Looking for this?" Jasper handed her the hammer.

"Yes. Huh. I thought you put it back in the drawer."

Teddy cleared his throat. "I believe the grip said he found it on the counter."

Jasper and Cassidy exchanged glances. She breathed, "The killer must have taken it out."

"You mean, the prankster."

Cassidy was in no mood to argue. "Open it."

Jasper pulled the trapdoor open and bent down to grab the string, illuminating the stairs. He stepped gingerly down them.

"Watch that third step. It's broken." Cassidy started after him. Teddy trailed her, but she held up a hand. "Teddy, you'd better stay up here and keep watch."

He gave her a relieved smile. " 'They also serve who only stand and wait.' "

Cassidy quickly lost sight of Jasper in the gloom. "Where are you?"

His voice was muffled. "I found your tunnel. Stay there. I'll see how far it goes."

She waited, trying not to dwell on the many things that could go wrong. *Or things we didn't do—like bring a flashlight.*

"Ow!"

"Jasper? Are you all right?" She felt around the walls till she came to the opening. "I'm coming!"

"No! Stay where you are. There isn't room for the two of us." A minute later, he emerged. The light from the single bulb revealed a man covered in dust, the knee of his trousers torn.

She coughed as he shook cobwebs from his hair.

"What happened?"

"First, let's get out of here." He limped to the stairs and climbed back up.

Teddy rushed to help him. "What did you find?"

"A big pile of rocks. The passageway's blocked."

Cassidy said firmly, "We have to talk to the police."

Jasper brushed off his pants. "Later. I have work to do. This speculation is a waste of time. I am scheduled to meet Flavia this afternoon for a script review. We have to drive back to Amity Landing *now*."

"What about Rory?"

Jasper slid to a stop. "Damn. I almost left him here. That's it: no more conspiracy theories." He headed to the car. The others followed.

"But—"

"No, Cassidy. We're done here."

****

Castine, Tuesday, July 18

They had reclaimed Rory, who for once was silent except for an occasional sniffle. He didn't even grumble about the uncivilized seating arrangement in the sports car. Cassidy said over her shoulder, "Rory, what were you doing in the brig?"

"Looking for gold. Duh."

He must be feeling better. He's almost back to his unpleasant self. "You said you came down the tunnel?"

"Uh-huh."

Teddy prodded his seatmate. "We went back to the lighthouse, Rory. The way is cut off."

"I know."

"Then how—?"

"It was clear when I crawled through, but the gate

was stuck, so I turned around. I hadn't gone far when I heard a rumbling sound. I think part of the roof fell in. I was trapped."

"So that's what happened." Cassidy sat forward. "We have to go back, Jasper. Take a flashlight. Find out what caused the rock fall."

Jasper shook his head. "Not now. We don't have time." He checked his watch. "I believe you have a store to open."

"But—"

"It sounds as though another sinkhole opened up— with that terrain, plus all the rain we've had, it's not surprising. Just Rory's bad luck he was on the wrong side when it happened."

They dropped the boy at the hospital in Penhallow. "Will you call Mr. MacEwan when he's ready to be released, Dr. Wilberforce?"

"Sure, Cassidy. We already have his number." The doctor grinned at Jasper. "Long time no see."

Jasper didn't laugh.

They left Teddy with Rory. "Ollie said he'd pick me up and take me to dinner." He yawned. "It's been a long day."

"That it has. You get to bed early, Teddy. We'll do some background work in Amity Landing tomorrow, now that Miss de Montville has returned." Jasper left a still fuming Cassidy in front of her store, stating merely, "I'll come get you when the store closes."

She opened her mouth to haughtily reject his offer, then remembered that her car was in her carport at home. She closed it with a snap, shrugged indifferently, and turned on her heel.

Chapter Thirty

Penhallow, Tuesday, July 18

Jasper picked Cassidy up on the dot at five, leaving only two disgruntled patrons to be packed off. They arrived at Mrs. Spinney's house just as a taxi pulled up. Flavia got out and wiggled a delicate hand at Jasper, clearly expecting him to pay the man. "I can only spare you half an hour, Jasper. Digby has offered to squire me to supper at my hotel." She went down the steps into the house.

Cassidy tugged on his sleeve and whispered, "Can I stay and listen?"

"Listen to what?" Jasper's eyes turned to Flavia. "We're not going to rehearse, if that's what you're thinking. This will be no more than a general dialogue on the elements of the play."

"Still…I love to watch her transform into Mercy Spinney. It's amazing." Her plea worked.

"All right. Come on."

As they were about to enter, Flavia came out holding two scripts. "Oh, is Miss Beauvoir going to join us?"

"If you don't mind."

"Not at all. She can play all the parts but mine." She gave a tinkling laugh. "It's such a beautiful evening. Let's go out to that little picnic shelter next to the house." She led the way.

The bench in the tiny pavilion only accommodated two, so Cassidy and Flavia sat while Jasper stood. They gazed out over the darkling bay. Sailboats bobbed at their moorings. Graham Rutter, his yellow slicker a bright spot on the water, rowed toward his sloop. A couple of kayakers paddled among the boats. An air horn blast rent the air. "Sailing school must be holding a sunset race." Off in the distance the Penhallow-Knightston ferry chugged south.

Flavia opened her script. "I see Mercy Spinney doesn't make an appearance until Act Two."

"Ah, but from then on, she's in the bulk of the picture. Digby is left behind in Castine while the boy slogs his way to you in Canada."

She read on. "Yes. Until Digby makes a second entrance in Act Three."

"This time as the villain."

"Digby hates being the villain unless he can tug at the audience's heartstrings somehow. What's his motivation?"

"He is distraught about abandoning Rory in the brig and seeks to recoup by arresting Teddy."

"I see." She read a few pages. "So Digby arrives in Nova Scotia with a cohort of British soldiers and pounds on my door. I cleverly disguise the boy, and we evade the evil Toff. I suppose I then see Teddy safely on his way, having packed some hard tack and cider in a small rucksack."

Cassidy felt she had to interrupt. She said timidly, "I thought you accompanied the cabin boy to Castine?"

Flavia stared at her, then riffled through the script. "Oh, my, yes." She addressed Jasper. "I have a scene in

Castine as well?"

Jasper looked uncertain and read a few pages ahead. "Er, yes. Here it is. Page ninety-eight. You accompany Teddy as far as Castine."

She skimmed the words. "After escaping the British soldiers, we make our way to my cousin's house in Castine, which the garrison has abandoned. It's there that I provision him for the long journey home, while I return to Westport." She smiled in satisfaction. "All right, it could work."

"Good. Of course, we'll have to convince Digby that he's doing the proper thing by arresting the cabin boy. As you say, he doesn't like playing the bad guy."

"He's not the bad guy," said Flavia with conviction. "The cabin boy is the bad guy. He's an American sailor—the enemy."

Jasper said hastily, "Technically, yes, but he's also a young boy and you feel sorry for him."

Cassidy watched the two wrestle with the manufactured moral dilemma. *It's so much easier in the real world.*

Flavia frowned. "So who will the action follow: me back to Canada, or Teddy on his trek to Boston?"

"It has to be Teddy. That's where the lone survivor-in-the-wilderness motif comes in."

"He goes alone? Wouldn't that make the action kind of drag?"

"He can have a few run-ins with bellicose natives. Maybe a bear."

She was thoughtful. "I can't see Mercy abandoning him like that."

"Well, it doesn't make sense to have you go all the way to Massachusetts. You'd be captured—maybe treated as a spy."

"Ooh, how perfect. I could act the martyr. Completely upstage Digby." She grinned. "I *like* it."

"You won't like it so much when you're executed."

"*Hmm*." Cassidy could almost see the synapses clicking in Flavia's brain. "Come to think of it, a woman traveling alone could be construed as an anachronism." They were quiet, mulling over the potential tripwires. Flavia sat up. "Or wait. Digby follows us *back* to Castine and tries *again* to arrest my protégé. That will spark things up. I help Israel escape the clutches of the general a second time and send him on his way."

"O…kay." Jasper appeared dubious. "Too repetitive?"

"Perhaps." She rubbed her lip with a pensive thumb. "How about this? We have Captain Nathaniel West come out of hiding, beat back the British, and when they're sent packing, offer to escort the boy back to Boston." She gave Jasper a totally inauthentic innocent look. "Who, may I ask, have you found to play West?"

Jasper glared at her. "You know full well it's Artemus North."

"So the buzz is true." Her little chin wobbled. "This is going to be fun. Yes, I think you should add a scene where Artemus snatches the boy from Digby's clutches. Too, too amusing."

"Yes, Flavia. Now, can we go back to Act Two?"

She flipped some pages. "So, the battle lines are drawn, and the drummer boy is caught stealing. That's Rory's role, right?"

"Yes."

"He's imprisoned in the brig."

"Yes."

"The two forces finally engage. As the Americans flee, burning their ships behind them, the cabin boy from the *Black Prince*—"

"That's Teddy—the character named Israel Trask."

"Yes. He swims to shore and finds the drummer boy in the brig. He can't free him, so he goes on."

"Leaving Catchpole to starve to death."

"Well, to be fair, no one else remembered him." She studied the scene. "That's the version the boy initially told Mercy Spinney in Westport?"

"I don't know. It's the one he told to the authorities when he returned to Boston."

She looked at him. "But I'm not sure that's the truth. Jasper, I—we—discovered something in Nova Scotia." Her expression hinted at puckishness. "But before I tell you, I heard through the grapevine that you discovered a tunnel."

They told her about Rory and Dyce Head. "We think it was a secret passage between the fort and the commandant's quarters."

She nodded. "Perhaps at first, but they must have blocked it—else why imprison the drummer boy there? He would have been able to make his way out the other end."

Jasper said slowly, "Blocked, then unblocked."

Cassidy added, "Then blocked again." She stared out at the water. "Rory went all the way through, so someone in the last two hundred years cleared the rubble. But when?"

Here Flavia closed her script and leaned toward Jasper. "I know when. And I think I know why the drummer boy stayed in the brig."

"You do?"

"I do." She put a hand in her bag and drew out two creased and folded envelopes. "We found these in Mercy Spinney's bedroom. They were stuck behind a drawer in her escritoire."

Jasper held his hand out. "Can I—"

Just then Flavia clapped a hand to her shoulder, dropping the envelopes, and emitted a little scream. "What the—?" She took the hand away. Blood dribbled down her arm.

Cassidy screamed.

Jasper swept the actress into his arms and ran toward the house, yelling, "Call 9-1-1! Miss de Montville has been shot!"

****

Amity Landing, Tuesday, July 18

By the time the ambulance arrived, a crowd had gathered. Chick happily agreed to direct the traffic. "Whatever I can do to help."

Jasper had disappeared into Mrs. Spinney's house with Flavia. Cassidy didn't know what he was doing but hoped it involved first aid.

Two EMTs jumped out of the back of the ambulance. One ran inside, the other stopped beside her. "Hey, Cassidy. The dispatcher said we have a gunshot victim."

She pointed to the house. "She's in there. Felix, it's Flavia de Montville."

"Flavia de Montville…the famous actress?" Felix groused, "This had better not be the Hollywood folks drumming up publicity. There isn't a Mainer on the midcoast who isn't sick and tired of this stupid movie."

287

"No, it really happened! I was there. We were sitting in the pavilion"—she turned her gaze toward the park—"and suddenly she was bleeding."

"Did you hear a shot?"

The question caught her off guard. "Now I think of it, no, I didn't." She had a frightening thought. "Do you suppose he used a silencer?"

"A silencer? Jeezus, Cassidy, it's not like Amity's in the middle of a gang war!" He spat. "So it looks like you don't know for sure if someone fired at her." He peered up at the trees overhead. "Mebbe an acorn hit her."

"But she was bleeding!"

Felix didn't respond. He followed his colleague into the house, Cassidy in his wake.

They found Flavia lying on a couch covered in a sheet as white as her face. Jasper knelt before her, holding her hand. The other EMT was working on her arm. He looked up. "It's just a graze. She'll be okay."

"Definitely from a bullet, Howie?" Felix didn't look at Cassidy.

Howie shrugged. "Can't think of anything else that would leave a wound like that." At that moment, a siren sounded from the street. "That'll be the sheriff."

Toby Quimby bustled in. "What's this about shots fired?" He saw the woman on the couch. "You're the actress, Miss de Montville, right?" Her lips moved silently. He turned to Felix. "Is she badly hurt?"

"No. Just a flesh wound."

"Was she alone?"

"No." Jasper stood. "Cassidy and I were with her."

"Did either of you hear the shot?"

Cassidy shook her head. Just then the air horn

sounded from the dock. "I forgot. There's a race going on. If the gun went off at the same time as the air horn…"

"*Hmm*. Any idea where the bullet came from?" He looked from face to blank face. "No?"

Felix offered, "Bullet—if that's what it was—went through the fleshy part of her upper left arm at a slight angle."

Cassidy indicated Flavia. "She was sitting on the bench facing the bay."

Toby pulled one of the darkening curtains aside and looked out at the bay. "Must have come from one of the boats then."

"You don't think it could have come from the water? Or down on the rocks?" Jasper gestured at the expanse of rocky shore, now exposed at low tide.

Toby turned to the EMT. "You say it exited at an angle. Can you tell if it came from below or above?"

"Like I said, it only grazed her. If she was moving, it'd be hard to tell. You'll have to ask a doctor. Or better yet, the medical examiner."

"She's not dead, Felix."

"Well, I'm not qualified in forensics."

"All right. Miss de Montville, are you steady enough to walk?"

She raised a languid hand. "I feel…I feel rather…" Her voice faded.

Jasper said angrily, "Can't you see she's in shock? Take her to the hospital. *Now*."

Toby rounded on him. "Who the hell do you think you are anyway?"

"I'm Jasper MacEwan, the director of the movie. I'm responsible for the cast members."

"Ah. Well, Mr. MacEwan, we know how to take care of gunshot wounds here in Maine. Not like in La La Land where I'm guessing you've never touched a real firearm. It's all special effects out there, ain't it?"

Cassidy bristled. "I'll have you know, Toby Quimby, Jasper is a lieutenant in the Army reserves. He probably knows more about weapons than you do."

Jasper said mildly, "I did qualify for a sharpshooter weapons badge while on that last tour in Afghanistan. I've seen a few gunshot wounds in my time."

Cassidy was still irritated. "Of course, Toby might've seen more. I hear he's one of those hunters who unloads on anything that moves."

Luckily, the sheriff's legendary even temper kicked in before the conversation degenerated into actual combat. "Tell you what. We'll all go to the hospital. We can continue the discussion there. Jeff, you stay here and secure the area—including the house."

Toby hustled them outside while Felix and Howie lifted Flavia onto a gurney. They followed the ambulance up Route 1, turning on South Harbor Road and right into the Emergency portico. Dr. Wilberforce greeted them like old friends. "Hey there, Mr. MacEwan, what's on the menu today?"

The sheriff stepped between them. "Gunshot victim."

The doctor yelled for an orderly and a nurse. Along with Flavia and Felix, they disappeared through the swinging double doors.

The rest stood—some with hands stuffed in pockets, others with arms folded—in the waiting room. Toby spoke first. "All right, Mr. Smarty Sharpshooter, where do *you* suggest the bullet came from?"

Jasper didn't speak for a minute. Then he said, "It couldn't have come from the house or it would have hit Cassidy or at least whistled past her. Also it would have entered Flavia's arm from the back. I'm betting someone stood on the rocky shore and fired."

Toby considered. "It's low tide, so the shooter could have been down at the edge of the water...but he could just as easily have been in a boat."

"Depending on the type of firearm. If it was a small pistol, the boats might be too far away."

Toby nodded. "Let's leave that for now. How about you set the scene for me."

"Okay, the three of us walked from the house to the pavilion. Flavia sat on the bench with Cassidy on her left. I stood on her right."

Cassidy pulled out a chair and sat, knees together, hands in lap. "She was like this at first." She faced straight ahead.

"Then what did she do?"

Jasper thought a minute. "Remember, she reached into her bag and brought out those envelopes. She was handing them to me—"

"And at that precise minute, she screamed and grabbed her arm with her hand."

"I scooped her up and ran to the house."

"And I called 9-1-1."

"Okay. Cassidy, go through the motions." Toby sat down to watch.

She obediently bent down, rustled in her purse, then straightened slightly and turned with her hand out to Jasper.

"Freeze!"

The two men considered. "What's wrong with this

picture?"

Jasper took her shoulders and gently moved her back to her original position. "Okay, try it again."

Cassidy went through the motions again. Jasper stared at her. "You should be dead."

"Why?"

"Because as you're handing me the envelopes, your left side is exposed. The bullet would have gone through your heart."

Toby moved around to face Cassidy. "Which of Miss de Montville's arms was hit?"

"The left."

"I think I see our problem."

Chapter Thirty-One

Waldo Memorial Hospital, Tuesday, July 18

Cassidy figured it out at the same time. "Miss de Montville is *left*-handed."

Jasper slapped his forehead. "Of course! She handed me the letters with her left hand—"

"Which would mean her arm protected her."

"Yes. If she'd been still facing the bay, the bullet would have gone in closer to her heart." Jasper wiped a wet forehead. "Someone tried to kill her, not scare her."

"Whew. Okay. We need to get back to Amity."

"What are we doing?"

"Hunting for a bullet. And a gun. And a killer."

****

Amity Landing, Tuesday, July 18

The sheriff called for support while they drove back to Amity Landing. It was nearly dark when another squad car and a forensics van parked behind them. Jeff met them at the house. "I strung tape around the area, Sheriff. All secure."

"That's great." Toby untied one end of the yellow police tape and let it fall to one side. "I want you to get the forensics crew set up, then go to the hospital and take Miss de Montville's statement."

"Sure thing." He stumped down the bank to the pavilion.

Two men set up floodlights around the perimeter. This drew the usual audience. Eunice Merithew marched down the street from her house, a line of red hats bobbing behind her. She pulled Cassidy away from the policemen. The rest stood in a tight circle around her. Before Cassidy could break free, Edna Mae arrived, puffing heavily. Like a mob boss, she confronted the hapless prisoner. "Well, Cassidy Jane Beauvoir, what did we tell you! Just *look* at this." She threw her arms out dramatically.

Eunice piped up in her reedy soprano. "It's time we told these Hollywood ruffians to clear out. They should go back where this kind of rowdiness is the norm. Maine doesn't want them." All the ladies nodded vigorously.

The worry and recent fright hit Cassidy like a splash of cold water, and she lashed out impatiently. "For your information, Flavia de Montville was shot— by somebody from here, not away." She didn't care whether it was the truth or not. *These biddies need a dose of their own medicine.* "Where were *you* half an hour ago, Audrey? Eunice? After all, you're the ones spewing innuendo and gossip. How far would you go to stop the movie? Eh? Edna Mae?"

Edna Mae gasped. "I'm going to find Tobias." The others milled around, unsure of their role. Audrey and Eunice shot guarded looks at Cassidy. She didn't notice—her eyes had picked out a familiar blond head wading through the press of people. Digby emerged, his face red, his lips dotted with spittle.

"Miss Beauvoir! Where is Flavia? I have just heard the news. Is she badly hurt? Incapacitated? Is she here? I must go to her!"

"She's fine. She's at the hospital getting patched up."

He whirled and tore back through the mob. When he got to the center, he stopped and whirled around again. His booming voice quieted the throng. "And where is this hospital?"

Several people offered advice, contradicting each other. The debate grew heated. Digby's arms flailed like an octopus being swallowed by a giant anemone. Jeff came up behind the actor. "Mr. Toff-Smythe? I'm heading there. I can give you a lift."

"Bless you, my good man." Digby hopped into the squad car, fanning himself. Cassidy could see him through the window haranguing the poor deputy. She turned back to the investigation.

While the detectives examined the pavilion, the patrolmen scoured the area for the bullet. Toby found it lodged in an overgrown hawthorn hedge below the road. He sucked on his hand. "Gosh, that stings. Hate these brambles." He handed the bullet to the forensics man while dabbing at the cut with a handkerchief. "What is it, Squiggy?"

The criminologist held up the bullet. "Remington three-inch 260-grain sabot slug. We're looking for a twenty-gauge shotgun."

"Not a twelve-gauge?"

"Nope. See the yellow hull? Only twenty-gauge shells have that color."

"Where do you think it came from?"

"Well, I didn't see the wound."

"I did." Jasper slipped in front of Toby. "Considering the victim's position when she was hit, it had to have come from that direction." He pointed at a cottage on the other side of the park. Cassidy wondered if he were testing the investigator's expertise.

Squiggy surveyed the area. "That house is too far away."

Jasper nodded his head toward the shore. "Then could it have come from down there?"

"Likely not. Angle would have been tough. Shooter would have had to sight through that bank of *Rosa rugosa*." He looked out at the water. "Those boats are probably forty, fifty yards out. Pretty easy shot. Especially with that gun."

"The twenty-gauge?"

"Yes. Twenty-gauge usually use shot but can be configured to take slugs. This slug has a 1900 FPS velocity rating. Maximum range of a hundred yards."

Toby gently elbowed Jasper out of the way. "Okay." He looked up at the sky and beckoned a couple of cops. "We'll have to check the boats tomorrow, guys. Who's the commodore this year, Cassidy? Chick?"

"No. Bobby B. I'll call him. You need permission, right?"

"Right. Give him a heads-up, will you? I'll try to catch him at his house."

While Cassidy was on the phone, Jasper wandered around getting in the way of the officers. He stopped in the pavilion by Flavia's chair and stared down. Cassidy clicked off her phone and came over. "Toby's going back to town after he finishes with Bobby. He says for you to stop interfering with the crime scene investigation."

"Huh." Jasper had a vacant look in his eyes.

"What's the matter?"

"*Hmm*." He muttered, "Strange. Very strange."

"What's strange?"

"Remember what Flavia was doing when she was shot?"

"She was about to…wait! She was going to hand the envelopes to you. She said—didn't she say she'd found them in Nova Scotia? Now what were they…"

"She didn't get a chance to tell us."

"Well, we can just take a look ourselves."

"How?"

"They should still be in her bag. She didn't take it with her. See? Here it is." She held it up.

"Unfortunately, they wouldn't be in the bag. Remember? She dropped them."

"Oh, okay."

"So…where are they?"

Sure enough, the concrete floor of the pavilion was bare. Cassidy stopped one of the agents. "Fred, did you find some envelopes here?"

He shook his head. "Only the bag. Wish you hadn't picked it up, Cassidy. It's still evidence."

"Sorry." She stared at Jasper. "The killer?"

"Had plenty of time to sneak in and pick up the letters while we were all at the hospital."

"What about Jeff? Toby left him here to set up a perimeter." Jasper was flagging down a deputy when Cassidy remembered. "No—wait. He's not here. Toby sent him back to the hospital to take Flavia's statement. Uh, Jasper?"

"What?"

"Digby went with him."

"Oh, dear. Digby will be in hysterics. I don't want him upsetting Flavia."

"I didn't know he cared that much about her."

"Oh, they've been friends for years, but the hysterics will be due to the lack of attention. Digby hates being upstaged on or off the set. He'll find some way to redirect the spotlight to himself." Jasper sniffed. "I remember on the set of *Tarzan Takes Manhattan,* a stuntman broke his leg. Digby ran to him, ostensibly to help, and fell over the poor guy. Made a huge scene, complete with staging and props. It took two hours for the medics to wade through the crush around him to get to the poor stuntman."

A siren beeped twice, and Jeff's squad car rolled slowly down the gravel road, dividing the gawkers, and parked on the verge. Jeff got out. Jasper strode over. "Where's Toff-Smythe?"

"Him? He's hosting an impromptu press conference at the hospital. I left him to it."

Jasper glanced at Cassidy. "See?"

Cassidy grinned. "Jeff, we have a question. You stayed here while we took Miss de Montville to the hospital. Did you see anything unusual before the forensics team got here? Anybody near the pavilion?"

Jeff hadn't noticed anyone. "After everyone left, I strung police line tape across the road and around the house and pavilion. Kept an eye on things from there." He pointed to the top of the road. "I figured that would keep anyone out."

"Anyone coming from the village, yes."

"Well, isn't that where the shooter must have been? Sheriff Quimby told me to secure the area."

Jasper growled, "That area should have included the bay."

Jeff took off his hat and scratched the crown of his

head. "Gee, Mr. MacEwan, maybe they can walk on water in your movies, but so far as I know, we Mainers ain't gifted in that direction."

Cassidy put a hand on his arm. "You weren't here for the conversation, I guess. CSI says the shot most likely came from someone on one of the boats."

"Oh." He didn't seem impressed.

Jasper was less patient than Cassidy. "If the gunman was in a boat, he'd either have to row ashore or swim ashore. You didn't see anyone in a dinghy?"

"Oh, yeah." He pointed at the dock. "Saw that guy Rutter coming back. Tied up at the float."

"Was he carrying anything?"

"Duffel bag."

Cassidy said, "Graham Rutter lives across the street."

Another policeman passed them. Jeff stopped him. "Go on over to that brown house, would you? Ask Mr. Rutter what he was doing on the water about five thirty."

"And if he heard anything out of the ordinary. Like a shot." Cassidy's phone rang. "Oh, good, it's you, Toby. Did Bobby B. give permission to inspect the boats? What? Not until tomorrow? But the evidence!...I see...yes, I know the tide's coming in...Well, maybe you could post Jeff here overnight...Oh." Jeff flashed his union card and grinned. Piqued, Cassidy persevered. "Darkness shouldn't be an impediment to police work, Toby. How about the floodlights—can you keep them on?...But you *can't* just leave the crime scene unattended!" She listened for awhile, her expression glum. "Okay." She hung up.

Jasper's hand fell heavily on her shoulder. "I take it the pavilion is available for evidence tampering?"

"They're postponing the investigation until tomorrow except for forensics. Toby says the CSI folks should finish up by seven, so there won't be anything to disturb. He can't spare a deputy to just sit here."

"Well, then, we have to assume the agents will have recovered all the evidence that's here. The boat and weapon can wait. Besides"—he hazarded a smile—"the killer has already taken the important stuff."

"But…"

He checked his watch. "Five minutes to seven. Come on, I'm starving. I didn't get any lunch."

"Lunch! I didn't get any breakfast."

"Durkee's?"

"Durkee's."

Chapter Thirty-Two

Durkee's, Tuesday, July 18

Katie had brought them two beers plus a plate of cheese fries before either spoke again. "So where do we stand?"

Jasper pulled a small notebook out. "Lessee…" He pretended to lick the end of the pencil.

"Don't do that. You'll get lead poisoning."

"There's no lead in pencils. Urban myth. Now, where was I? Oh, yes: accidents."

"I think we should call them incidents."

He cocked his head. "All right—I guess that's more accurate. First: Digby frightened by the ghost dog, but…*but*—it could have been a burglar. Second, my close encounter with the window. Assault?"

"Or graceless bumbling?"

"I told you. Someone pushed me."

"Okay. Moving on. Mr. Flint. A genuine murder. Medical examiner determined someone smothered him and then dumped him in the dungeon. Write that down."

Jasper scribbled on the paper, then stopped. "Or the other way around."

"What? Oh, you mean, the killer didn't toss him into the brig?"

"Yes. How about this? The murder took place

inside the brig, then the perpetrator crawled back through the tunnel and escaped through the Dyce Head house."

Cassidy stared at him. "Which would mean the passage was clear then."

"As I surmised. Sometime in the two centuries since the drummer boy died, the obstruction was cleared."

"Are you also surmising both killer and victim used it?"

"Not at all. Flint didn't mention a tunnel—it's possible he didn't know about it. He said he never went into the cave."

"Maybe he heard something. Maybe he unlocked the gate and went in to investigate."

"And came upon the murderer. But when they found Flint's body, the gate was locked and the key was in Flint's pocket. Either the killer had his own key, or…what?"

"I don't know what." Cassidy's hunger was interfering with her brain function. "Where's Katie?"

Jasper pushed his mug aside. "Okay, let's forget Mr. Flint for a moment. We'll assume the path was clear until a cave-in occurred while Rory was underground." He put his elbows on the table. "When was Flint killed? It wasn't the same day we were shot at, was it? Was it before or after?"

"I'll have to check my diary. I think it was after. So it couldn't have been the same person…Ah, *there* you are." The waitress dropped a plate of eggs and sausage in front of Cassidy. "Oh, and Katie, after breakfast, I'd like a hamburger. For lunch. Thanks." She buttered her toast. "Wait. Remember? Last week, when we were exploring the Dyce Head house, someone turned out the light and closed the trapdoor on me. I still don't think that was an accident."

"No breeze. Right."

"And then Rory too. Just this morning."

"Was it just this morning?" He mopped his brow with his napkin, leaving a swath of cheese across his nose. "My God, this has been a helluva day."

Cassidy wiped the cheese off with a finger and smeared it on her share of the fries. "Indeed. Moving on."

"Okay, so we have some minor occurrences in Amity…thank you, Katie." He accepted a cup of chowder.

"I don't think what happened to Miss de Montville could be deemed minor."

He swallowed a spoonful of the chowder. "*Mmm*." Putting the spoon down, he said deliberately, "I'm going to play devil's advocate here. I know I said the shot could have been fatal if her arm weren't in the way, but it still could have been unintentional. Say a guy's in his boat, and a wave rocks it, and his firearm goes off inadvertently. That ferry went by about then. It left a wake."

"You'd think once he heard about Miss de Montville, he would have come forward."

"Maybe he didn't know he hit anyone."

She thought about that. "Graham Rutter might be able to clear it up. Do you know if that deputy talked to him?"

"We can find out tomorrow. Okay, to recap: could there be any connection between the Amity incidents and the Castine events?" Jasper contemplated his soup.

"Only thing in common is…us. The movie crew. And more specifically, the principals: me, Flavia, Rory."

"Don't forget Sally."

"Like you say, it's possible she was collateral damage. Remember, she wasn't supposed to be with us at Childe's."

"True." Cassidy handed her empty plate to Katie and accepted a new one. "Another Geary's, please." She poured hot sauce on her burger.

Jasper recoiled. "You're really going to eat that?"

She took a big bite and chewed noisily.

He sighed and ordered a draft beer "to keep you company while you eat the horse." He licked the froth off the rim of his mug. "On the other hand—"

Cassidy put down her burger. "No…whatever it is, don't go there."

He was dogged. "We keep ginning up these happenings as though they were all tied together, but…" He held up a hand. "*But* the only confirmed murders are that guy on the mussel farm and Flint. Neither of whom were associated with the movie."

"But these happenings *do* keep piling up, Jasper. At some point, there must be some kind of discernible pattern."

Jasper, lost in his own thoughts, mused, "Could it be those letters Flavia found in Canada? Could they be significant?"

"I can't imagine how. They've been in a desk in Nova Scotia since the eighteenth century."

"Yet there may be something in Flavia's past— someone who is out to get her and seizes his chance while she's out of her element."

"I thought you'd determined it was an accident?"

"Not at all."

Cassidy rolled her eyes. "We're not getting anywhere."

"Too many loose threads. The only person nothing's happened to is Digby."

"Unless you count Snookie and the acorns."

"I don't. However...*Hmm*. Hold on a sec." He pulled out his phone. "Ollie? Jasper here. Oh, you heard? Yes, she'll be fine. Stan took her to her hotel. Ollie, has Artemus North been in touch? He did? Where? Okay, thanks."

"Artemus? Digby's brother?"

"And bitter foe. Who arrived day before yesterday without telling anyone. He called Ollie a minute ago and said he was holed up in a motel on Route 1 and wanted his script brought to him. He asked him not to tell Digby he's in Maine."

Cassidy had another bite and a thought. "You told me he tries to sabotage Digby's movies. Are you suggesting *he's* behind all this?"

"I have no proof, but I do know that he's perfectly capable of constructing an elaborate hoax that would leave Digby with his pants down."

"But would he go so far as to murder someone? Sounds rather implausible." Cassidy signaled Katie and held up her empty glass.

"Really? If so, what's he been doing for the last forty-eight hours?"

****

Amity Landing, Wednesday, July 19

As the sun rose over a distant Cadillac Mountain, Cassidy found Jasper on the dock looking out at the marina. Two police skiffs were shuttling among the moored boats. She could make out one CSI tech in the stern of Graham's little sloop. A few feet away, the agent named Squiggy was hanging over the side of Bobby B. Goode's cabin cruiser. Bobby stood on the float yelling at him. "Those are brand new cushions, mister! I'm suing the police department if you so much as sit on one!"

Squiggy waved an indifferent hand. Jasper put an arm around Cassidy's waist. "And Toby thought *I* was interfering with the investigation."

"Oh, those two go way back. They've been quarreling since they were fifth graders at Edna Drinkwater elementary school."

"Ah. I keep forgetting what a small town this is." He nodded at the boats. "Do you think they'll find anything?"

She shrugged. "I'm no forensic specialist. I suppose they could find fingerprints or a shell casing."

"It's hard to believe no one noticed a man with a gun."

"I don't know. We left right after she was shot, and the CSI team didn't arrive for another fifteen minutes after that. If the shooter rowed ashore, it was probably in that interval."

"Rutter told Jeff he was the only one on the water that late. The race was over, and the kayakers had beached their boats."

"Unless he's the perp, he's wrong." Cassidy sighed. "I wish he—or Jeff—had been more observant."

"Jeff was busy doing what Toby ordered him to do."

She nudged Jasper. "I have to get to the store.

What are your plans?"

He shook himself. "Well, I could stand here all day projecting hopeful thinking but better not. I'll go see Flavia, then round up the crew and see if we can't get some work done. I want to be nearby in case they find anything."

"What about Artemus North?"

"Ah. Now that he's officially on the payroll, he says he's going to move out of the Motel Seven in Searsport and into the Duke of York Inn in Camden. Ollie and I are meeting him for lunch."

"Does Digby know he's here yet?"

"Digby doesn't even know Dad hired him."

The sheriff joined them. "Nothing so far."

"How many boats have you examined?"

"Six. We still have those two over there. Belong to summer people. They've been off camping in the Rangeleys. When I get permission, I'll go aboard."

"They might be the likeliest since the killer would know he wouldn't be disturbed."

Toby turned to Cassidy, surprised. "Are you assuming our villain is a local boy?"

Rattled, she stepped back. "Uh…no…"

Jasper jumped in. "Actually, we were speculating that it had something to do with our cast members—some vendetta from the past that's caught up with us."

Toby nodded. "Makes sense. It's only you Hollywood types who have been affected. I hear one of your child stars found himself in a bit of a pickle up in Castine as well."

"Yes."

"So…" He lowered his brows. "Cassidy? You still think it was one of us?"

"I'm just saying I think we should reserve judgment until we find some evidence."

"Gee, that's exactly what I was going to say." He gave her a meaningful look. "And on that note, I'll leave you two. I have to do my job."

"What about the beach?" Jasper had evidently not given up on his theory. "You're going to search that too, right?"

"We'll have to wait for low tide. It'll take the rest of the day." He slapped on his hat and went down to the float. They watched him hustle Bobby B. back up the stairs before heading uphill.

They parted at Jasper's Lamborghini. "See you later?"

"I close at five."

"I know. We'll regroup then. Drinks on me."

Chapter Thirty-Three

Shark's Tooth Pub, Wednesday, July 19

"So what's new at the bookstore?"

Cassidy put down her gin and tonic. "Well, Edna Mae is continuing her crusade against the barbarians of the West—by which she means you guys—who are roiling the formerly pastoral streets of Penhallow. She asked me to put a poster in the store window depicting Digby with horns and a tail and the headline: The Anti-Christ is Coming. Hide your tweenies!"

"Tweenies?"

"You know, ten- to thirteen-year-olds. Voted most likely to come under the evil spell of the silver screen."

"I knew that. I'm just awed that Mrs. Quimby does."

"She teaches Sunday School."

"She seems to only have it in for the men—no words of reprobation for the ineffable Miss de Montville?"

"Oh, dear, no. To Edna Mae and the Red Hats, she's more exalted than Queen Elizabeth. 'The essence of graceful femininity,' in Audrey Carver's immortal words."

Jasper clinked her glass. "She'll be glad to hear that."

"How is she?"

"Resting. She says she'll be ready to rehearse the first scene with Teddy tomorrow."

"Which one is that?"

"The one in which they meet. Teddy has escaped the battle but is disoriented and ends up on the southeastern shore of Mount Desert island. A fisherman finds him and takes the spent and sodden child across the Gulf of Maine to Mercy Spinney's house in Westport."

"Who's playing the fisherman?"

"Funny you should ask. Bobby B. Goode begged to do it, but he insisted on using his own boat. When Stan pointed out that his Boston Whaler was hardly an authentic replica of an eighteenth-century fishing bye-boat, he went off in a huff. Pauline ferreted out someone from the Penhallow repertory theatre. Her ex-husband used to be in the company, and she had gotten to know several of the players."

"Did you talk to Rory?"

"Also resting. I think his flirtation with disaster really sobered him up. He's been going over lines with Teddy."

Cassidy gazed out at the mud flats that stretched several hundred feet to Penobscot Bay from where they sat on the porch of the Shark's Tooth Pub in the little town of Knightston. In the near distance, the Turtle Head ferry inched toward the dock. "So I guess Toby and his men are beating the shoreline as we speak."

"Indeed. The forensics van was parked at the Amity dock."

"I hope they find something. Edna Mae said they came up empty on all the boats."

"No spent shells labeled 'Property of John Doe'?

No puddle of DNA with a little identification card attached?"

"Nothing."

He sipped. "I'll bet the shooter just dropped everything in the water. Tide would have carried it out."

"Tide would have carried it *in,* if anything, but I think a gun is too heavy to float."

"Okay, so where are we?"

"Artemus North. You were going to find out what the heck he's been doing these last few days."

"Ah. That man would make a boa constrictor seem like your fat Aunt Hattie who hugs everyone."

"Slimy?"

"Snakes aren't slimy. He's more—" He paused in thought. "—suffocatingly oily. Ollie and I met him at his hotel in Camden. Since he moved to the Duke of York, he's been having them send his bills to Black Brothers Studios in Los Angeles."

"He must be a hell of an actor."

"Isn't charlatan just another word for actor?"

"You said it, not me." Cassidy thought they should move on. "So what did he tell you?"

"Nothing. He wanted to know if Digby had been made aware that Dad hired him. We said no. That seemed to make him happy. Which worries me."

"You think he's planning mischief?"

"I think he may have already executed it."

"But what did he *do*? We haven't heard a peep out of Digby since yesterday. He's still exhausted from his performance at Flavia's hospital bed. If something had happened to him, you'd have been informed."

"Well, not all North's jokes succeed. Last year,

when Black Brothers was working on the sequel to *Tarzan Takes Manhattan*—"

"*Tarzan Builds His Dream House*?"

"The very one. They were onsite in the jungle in Peru and had to camp out in this very primitive lodge. No indoor plumbing, just a latrine out back. So one night Artemus lays a net in the path to the john and covers it with leaves. He was going to wait till Digby walked across, then jerk the net up, leaving Digby dangling midair in his jammies."

Cassidy held up an index finger. "Quick question. Does Digby always wear pajamas appropriate for the time and setting of whatever movie he's filming?"

"Why, yes. I presume you noticed the ruffled nightshirt."

"I did indeed. And so did Edna Mae and Eunice. It's probably the reason they're so antagonistic to him. So what did he choose to wear in Peru?"

He snickered. "A loincloth. Which would have made it even funnier, except the plan went awry."

"What happened? Did the net break under his weight?"

"No, no, the net worked, only it didn't catch Digby. It caught a howler monkey. Big fellow. Mean as sin. Bit Artemus in several places, including one very sensitive to men."

Cassidy snorted out some of her drink. "What did Digby do?"

"He forced the director to send Artemus home, claiming the man would infect them all with some exotic monkey virus. Artemus was not pleased. It didn't help future relations."

"So what nefarious act do you think he had cooked

up this time?"

"No idea. From his expression, I got the feeling it didn't succeed either. He's ready to come to the set."

Her phone rang. "Hi, Toby. Really? That's fantastic! Can we come see now? Oh, of course. All right. Tomorrow morning, first thing. Sheriff's office or police station? Okay." She hung up. "They dredged the marina and found the gun."

****

Penhallow police station, Thursday, July 20

"Okay, so this is an eighteenth-century flintlock musket called a blunderbuss. Precursor of the modern shotgun. See its flared muzzle? It was generally used for close-quarters fighting." The state weapons expert sighted through it. "Privateers and pirates loved it." He laid it on the table.

The other people who were gathered in the office contemplated it. Toby finally asked, "Is it functional?"

"It shows evidence of recent firing, so it must be a working model. The lengthy exposure to water makes it harder to determine an exact point in time."

"We know when it was last fired. About five thirty p.m. Tuesday evening."

"Assuming this is the weapon that was used."

Toby looked like he wanted to spit. "You may think this is unusual, Mr. Abbott, but here in Penhallow, citizens don't make a habit of casually tossing their firearms into the drink when they're bored with them. For one thing, it costs an arm and a leg—due to *state* overregulation—to even acquire a gun."

Abbott let the dig pass. "Any idea who it belongs to yet?"

"He does." Toby indicated one half of the Laurel

and Hardy duo.

Stan introduced himself. "Stan Lowry, line manager for *American Waterloo*." He stepped aside and gestured at an old man, so frail Cassidy wondered if his muttonchop whiskers were the only things holding him up. "This is my props master, Duffy."

Duffy shambled forward and studied the blunderbuss. "Yup, it's one of ours. Found one missing from storage. Like the man said"—he nodded at Abbott—"it's the type of gun the old-time pirates liked to swash their buckles with." He swung his arm back and forth in case they didn't understand what he meant. "They used 'em in *Pirates of the Spanish Main*."

Abbott added, "It's said Errol Flynn had a large collection." His eyes went dreamy. "Pistols too."

Toby bore down on Duffy. "Why didn't you report it missing?"

The man looked at Toby as though he were one splinter short of a tree. "Ain't started shootin' yet. No reason to unpack the props till sets are built. Only opened the box 'cause Stan asked me to."

"Where are the props stored?"

"Lockers out on Route 1."

"Do you have the only key?"

He blinked. "Key?"

"Doesn't the locker have a key?"

"No. It's got a combination lock. Twenty-three. Fourteen—"

Stan put a hand over Duffy's mouth. "Duffy, these nice people don't need to know the combination."

The old man peeled Stan's fingers off. "Why not? Everyone else has it."

Cassidy and Jasper exchanged glances. "What do

you mean by everyone?"

"All the crew. I cain't be goin' back and forth all the time. Director calls for some prop, one of the grips goes and gets it. I'm the *manager*, not a gofer."

Toby sighed. "I guess we'll have to question the crew. Are they all here in Penhallow?"

Stan said, "They're in Amity Landing. We were going to try to shoot some scenes with Miss de Montville."

"Okay, can you round them up? We'll conduct interviews here in the station."

Jasper spoke for the first time. "It would be hard to schlep them all into town. Could we instead have them assemble at our canteen in Amity Landing?"

"You mean that tent you erected on top of Eunice Merithew's garden, decimating her dahlias?"

The barb unfortunately shot wide of its mark. "Yes, that one. Look, Stan here will set you up and give you a list of the crew members. We can send them over one by one if you like."

"Fine."

As the props manager started to leave, the sheriff stopped him. "You say the crew has the combination to the locker. Do any of the actors? Or the staff—the producer?" He nodded at Jasper. "The director?"

Duffy looked flabbergasted. "Oh, dear, no! I'd never trust one a *them* with such a precious secret." He limped off.

Toby dismissed the others. "I'll be in touch."

Cassidy took Jasper's hand. "Want to stop at my house for coffee? It's still early."

"Sure."

They were sitting on the deck when a crimson

Bugatti roared by. Jasper slammed his mug down. "Oh, shit. That's Artemus."

"Seriously, do *any* of you drive, like, a Mini Cooper or something?"

"No, although we usually keep a modest sedan for the maid to take the dogs out in." He stood up. "I think he's going to the canteen."

"Where's Digby?"

"I give you one guess."

They arrived to find Digby and Artemus squaring off in Eunice's garden. Toby and Jeff were inside the tent looking out. Several crew members stood around the two antagonists. Cassidy punched Jasper. "Are they rooting them on?"

"Wouldn't be surprised. Let's hope Stan shows up and disperses them before they start taking bets."

Artemus proved to be a dead ringer for someone who didn't look remotely like Digby Toff-Smythe. Where Digby's blond hair fell over his collar in glowing waves, his brother sported a buzz cut. Where Digby's faceted emerald eyes were legendary, Artemus's were a muddy brown hidden behind thick glasses. He was short, with broad shoulders and a stocky build—in stark contrast to the tall, rangy Toff.

The two men circled each other. Digby slipped on the wet grass and threw a hand out to catch himself on a rose bush. "Ouch."

"Whassa matta Diggy-Piggy, you get a boo-boo?"

His opponent sucked his thumb. "Not as big a boo-boo as I'm gonna give you, Artie."

"Oh, yeah? Show me."

They continued to circle cautiously. Cassidy was beginning to think that would be the extent of the show.

A couple of the cameramen wandered over to the coffee urn.

"What are you doing here anyway?"

Artemus paused, one foot in the air. "Oh, nobody told you?" His voice was silky. "Philip MacEwan hired me. They wanted the best for the juiciest part in the picture. Aside from those of the boy wonders, of course."

"You can't mean…No…" Digby reared back and pounded his concave chest. "*I'm* the British commandant. He's top of the bill." When Artemus didn't answer, his swagger returned. "All the talent's set, Artie. Nothing left to cast but extras." He sneered. "I'll bet that's what you're reduced to after the fiasco at *Tarzan Builds His Dream House.*"

"Give it a rest, Digs. Who else would they lay the big bucks out for to play the mighty American hero, Captain Nathaniel West?"

Digby's eyes widened. "Over my dead body!" He lunged at his brother, who deftly sidestepped. Unfortunately, Artemus's legs slid out from under him and he landed on a deposit left by Bobby B.'s Great Dane Susie. From the looks of the pile, she had had a big breakfast.

The crew—who by now had all entered the canteen—turned and stared at Artemus's churning arms and legs. Cassidy was reminded of a turtle flipped on his back. No one made any move to help the poor fellow. Finally, Jasper climbed down the bank and grabbed his hand, pulling him up. Digby took his other arm and together they hauled him to the road. He looked down at his soiled pants—pants Cassidy guessed were thousand-dollar Versace chinos—and his

Ferragamo loafers. "What do I do now?"

Chapter Thirty-Four

Cassidy's house, Thursday, July 20

Cassidy took charge. "I have an outdoor shower at my place. Why don't you come and wash it off there, Mr. North."

He seemed to take notice of her for the first time. "Thank you. And you are?"

Jasper barked, "Save it till you're cleaned up, Artemus."

Cassidy said mildly, "I'll see if I can dredge up another pair of pants for you."

"You're very kind, but I have a change of clothes in my suitcase. It's in the car." Artemus retrieved his case, and they trudged up the hill to Cassidy's cottage, three of them attempting to stay upwind of their odoriferous associate. Artemus peeled off at the little shower enclosure built into the carport. "I'll see you upstairs."

Digby was grilling Jasper on "this casting catastrophe" as he called it when Artemus climbed the stairs to the deck wearing an artfully ripped T-shirt and a pair of crackling new jeans. He held out the soiled pants. "I washed them off as best I could." He seemed to expect Cassidy to take them.

Instead, she handed him a plastic garbage bag. "You'll find a dry cleaner in Penhallow on Waldo

Avenue."

Holding the bag at arm's length, he carried it back down to the Bugatti. Cassidy—watching out the window—saw him carefully lay it on the ground next to the car before plodding back up the hill. Jasper, Cassidy, and Digby sat at the picnic table. Digby acknowledged his brother with a curt nod. "Artemus."

"Digby."

Cassidy jumped in. "Is it noon already? Glory be. Anybody here ready for a beer? I know I am."

Before they could reply, she skipped to the kitchen and pulled out a six-pack. Back on the deck, she handed each man a bottle. "These are from my father's brewery—Pickytoe Crab Lager. It won the blue ribbon at the Union Fair."

Caught off guard, no one refused. They sat quietly sipping beer for a refreshing five minutes. Jasper said, "Not half bad. Almost as good as his Beauvoir IPA. Thanks, Cass."

Artemus stood and bowed. "I believe the time has come for us to be properly introduced. To whom should I direct my undying gratitude for rescuing me in my hour of distress?" He leered, presumably unconscious of the effect this had on his target.

Jasper said, "Cool it, North. May I present Cassidy Jane Beauvoir. She is the head overseer of Amity Landing, in whose jurisdiction you are at present located."

"I know where I am, Jasper." He held out a hand. "How do you do?"

"Never mind that, Artie." Digby's temper hadn't cooled. "You must have angled for this job. Why are you still hounding me?"

"I most certainly did not angle. This was one of hundreds of offers I've fielded since the jungle pic." He smirked. "When I saw my big brother was headlining the cast of a new Black Brothers Studio presentation, I had to enlist."

Jasper interrupted the staring contest. "So tell your brother why you arrived early unannounced, and what you've been doing for the last five days."

Artemus held a palm to his breast, stunned. "Why, Jasper, we had this conversation yesterday. As I said then, I wanted to read up on the story and the script before I confronted…er…met with the star."

Jasper gave him a hard look. "You had a prank in mind. Don't deny it."

Artemus drew back. "*Moi*? The very idea. You know I worship the ground my *older* brother walks on. I wouldn't dream of pulling a number on him. Why, he might be embarrassed. How would that look for the man who has graced the cover of *Celebs Galore four whole times*?" He contemplated his brother with an impudent eye. "Although I maintain the shot of you in the Viagra ad is probably your finest."

Digby grabbed a wad of Artemus's shirt. "What did you do?"

He pushed him away. "Nothing. I did nothing." After a minute he muttered, "Not because I didn't want to."

"What do you mean?"

His gaze shifted from Digby to Cassidy. "May I have another beer?" She indicated the nearly empty six-pack. He took a bottle out and twisted the cap off. "Okay. You know how Diggums loves to be the generalissimo who stands far above the fray directing the battle? Give him a horse and a fancy uniform, and he'll be your lapdog for life."

The Toff made an angry movement. Cassidy held up a hand for peace. "Go on."

"Well, I knew this picture would have a battle scene just made for him—all the action would be down below. He would be visible, high and mighty up on the hill, without ever getting close to any cannon fire." He stopped. "Oh, by the way, did you know Digs is petrified of loud noises? Thunder. Lightning. Gunshots." He grinned maliciously.

Also of acorns hitting a roof and imaginary dogs barking.

"I'm getting the picture here." Jasper took the last beer. "You thought you'd sneak up behind him and set off an explosion. Scare the shit out of him."

"Something like that."

Digby sat like a stone.

Jasper continued. "I knew it. I could tell you had some trick up your sleeve when you accepted the role." He shot a triumphant glance at Cassidy. He turned back to Artemus. "You…" He stopped and blanched. "Oh my God. The gun."

Artemus looked surprised. "Oh, you knew about the gun? How?"

Cassidy leaned in. "A shotgun was used to shoot Flavia de Montville yesterday evening."

"So that's what all the commotion was about. Is the *grande dame* okay?"

"She'll recover. A little shaken up. The bullet grazed her arm."

Jasper leaned in. "The slug came from *your* gun. Why did you shoot Flavia, Artemus?"

"Me? I didn't shoot her."

"You so much as admitted you were going to pop Digby. And that you had a shotgun."

"A blunderbuss. I did. I don't have it now."

"No, of course you don't. It's in police custody."

"No, no. What I mean is…I haven't seen it since Monday night. Someone stole it from my hotel room."

Digby spoke. "Where did you get it?"

"One of the grips took it out of the props storage for me. I wanted something that wouldn't be noticed on the set, so he—"

"Which one?"

"Which grip? Can't remember his name offhand. He's been on a couple of on-location shoots with me. Big guy."

"So how'd he do it?"

"Well, he has the combination. Duffy—he's the property master—hates actors, loves the union guys. Gives 'em all the combination and refuses to let us have it. Pain in the butt. Anyway, so the grip goes and gets this blunderbuss and brings it to me."

"With ammunition?"

"Yeah." At the look on Digby's face, he scoffed, "Blanks, you dummy. You don't think they use real bullets, do you? Not that I wouldn't mind peppering you in the ass with a potato gun."

"Ha. That's about the only gun you know how to shoot," Digby sneered.

Cassidy snatched the beer out of Jasper's hand. When she'd taken a long pull on it, she said quietly, "A real bullet shot Flavia."

"Huh. Some bloke must have figured out how to get the thing to work. I sure couldn't."

Digby raised his eyes to heaven. "Why am I not surprised?"

Jasper stirred. "You couldn't get the gun to fire?"

Cassidy gave the bottle back to Jasper and bore down on Artemus. "You said just now you did nothing, but not because you didn't want to."

"Right. The musket seemed to be in working order. Took it over to that state park across the highway to try it out." He beamed. "Followed the online instructions to the letter, but the darn thing refused to blow. I gave it up as a bad job and left it in my hotel room."

"Well, somebody fixed it. And shot Flavia."

Artemus seemed altogether too unmoved for Cassidy's taste. He swigged his beer. "Yeah, so what happened?"

Jasper opened his mouth, but Digby raised a quavering voice. "Oh my God, Artie. It was *awful*. I had to fight my way through the hordes of ghoulish onlookers in order to lift poor Flavia in my arms and carry her to safety. Once at the hospital—"

Jasper interrupted him. "He made such a fuss that he was removed from the lobby by a nurse. He proceeded to hold court in the parking lot until the security guard stuck him in a taxi and sent him home." When Digby had finished huffing, he added, "Flavia will be all right."

"Good to hear. She's a nice old broad." He looked down the neck of the empty bottle. "You don't really think I had anything to do with it, do you?"

"We don't know. Do you have any idea who stole the weapon from you?"

He shook his head. "To tell you the truth, I'd forgotten all about it until you mentioned it. I was out all day Tuesday, then checked out of the motel on Wednesday. Could've been the maid. Or the desk clerk. After all, it was kind of conspicuous." He rubbed his ear. "Hope that grip isn't liable for its disappearance." From his serene expression, Cassidy assumed the thought of compensating the man never entered his mind.

Jasper rose. "I think we need to take this to the sheriff."

Artemus rose too. "You go ahead. I want to get back to my hotel and get a real shower and swankier clothes."

Cassidy sniffed. "You're right. I think some of the fragrance from Susie's offal may have seeped through the material to your skin."

Digby took Artemus's arm. "I'll go with you."

"Diggums! You do care!"

"I don't want you disappearing until we have this mess straightened out. You're checking out of whatever hole you're staying in and bunking with me."

Jasper cackled. "He's *bunking* at the five-star Duke of York in Camden, Digby. A rollaway bed in the B&B will be just revenge."

The whites of Artemus's eyes showed. "You wouldn't."

"Never fear. We'll get you your own room, Artie. With any luck"—he shook his brother lightly—"the police will toss you into the slammer, and I'll finally be rid of you."

The trio of luxury sports cars paraded through Amity and on to Penhallow. Jasper left Cassidy opening her store and crossed the street to the police station.

****

Mindful Books, Thursday, July 20

There was a line out the door when Jasper squeezed into Mindful Books just before five—getting a few jabs in the ribs for his efforts. He spied Cassidy waiting on Hank and strode toward them. When he was within shouting distance, he bellowed, "Hank Shute—nice to see you again! And whoa! If it isn't Cassidy Jane Beauvoir, the owner herself! As I live and breathe." She glanced at him but kept talking to the farmer. "Cassidy!"

She ignored him. "Here you go, Hank." She handed her friend a pile of books. "These should keep Nellie busy and off your back for at least a week."

"But what do I do after that?" The man sounded frazzled. "She's driving me bananas. I haven't gotten more than an hour's sleep since the test came back positive. I think that old myth about…what's it called? Sympathetic pregnancy? It isn't a myth at all. I'm worn out, Cass."

"And it's only the first trimester!" Cassidy's cheerful attitude did nothing for the poor father-to-be.

He handed her a wad of cash. "So you think *What to Expect While You're Expecting* is the first one she should read?"

"Absolutely. Now get along. I have customers." Cassidy turned with a bright smile to Jasper. "I can't talk now."

"That's fine. I'm in no rush to give you my news."

"News?"

"Hey, it's okay." He swept a hand over the slowly dwindling crowd. "I certainly don't want to interfere with business. I'll just head out and find Digby and Artemus. I'm sure they can't wait to hear the latest." He turned toward the door.

Cassidy picked up a silver bell and started ringing it. "Store's closing! Sorry, folks."

"But it's still five to five! Hey!"

"Sorry. You, Maude, you're the last in line. The rest of you, put one of these sticky notes on your purchases and leave them on the table on your way out. I promise I'll take care of them first thing tomorrow."

A voice in the back yelled, "You're closed tomorrow."

Cassidy checked the calendar. "Oh my God, you're right. Tomorrow's Friday. How the week has flown!" She raised her voice. "Everyone, I'll have special open hours on Saturday from ten to twelve. How's that?"

Amid some pungent grumbling and threats to post bad reviews online, Cassidy managed to finish with most of the customers and bundle the last stragglers out the door. She turned the Open sign to Closed and swung on Jasper. "Well, that little stunt probably cost me fifty bucks in sales, mister. What've you got to offer?"

For answer, he took her in his arms and swept her into a dramatic dip à la Rudolf Valentino, depositing a smacking kiss on her lips.

She stumbled up, panting. "Not bad. Now what else ya got?"

"I just gave you a wet kiss. Now, how about a wetsuit?"

"Wetsuit?"

"As in, they found one."

"Okay, I'll bite…oh!"

He nodded with satisfaction. "Now we know how the guy got away."

Cassidy smiled. "So Graham Rutter wasn't wrong after all. He *was* the only one on the water that evening."

"Right. The killer wasn't *on* the water; he was *in* it."

"Where did they find the suit?"

"A mile down the beach in some prickly bushes. Poor Jeff—he doesn't have a finger left that isn't pasted with a Band-Aid."

"Did any of the grips confess to borrowing the gun for Artemus?"

"Not a one, but I can't imagine he would. It's not as though he knew it would be used to shoot Flavia. He wouldn't risk his job by admitting he was an accomplice."

She started to ring out the cash register. "Have they learned who the wetsuit belongs to?"

Just then the bell on the door started ringing madly. Digby and Artemus stood outside on the sidewalk. Apparently it had just started raining, for they were bickering over who could use their one newspaper as an umbrella. Cassidy opened the door. "Come in, come in."

Artemus shook himself like a dog. "Just my damned luck—this is my last ensemble and it's soaked." He fixed Digby with a beseeching eye. His brother stared silently back at him. "May have to give the mater a call—she's always good for a fiver." He winked at Cassidy. "She'll naturally ask me why my big brother won't help. Whatever shall I tell her?"

Digby snorted.

"Did you get moved into the B&B, Artemus?"

"Yes, yes, all taken care of. Digs generously gave

up his room for me and took the housekeeping closet down the hall." He gave his brother a playful punch in the arm.

Digby snorted again.

Artemus turned to Jasper. "We were ambling along the cobblestones of this bucolic metropolis, bestowing kindly looks and fatherly blessings on the populace, when Diggles saw you coming out of the police station. Any news?"

"Ah." Jasper directed a beady eye at Artemus. "Do you own a wetsuit?"

"Huh?"

Digby answered. "He does. So do I. We used to dive off Catalina Island."

" 'We'? Since when do you two hang out together?"

Digby gave his brother a sidelong glance. "Believe it or not, there was a time when we were inseparable. Then Artie…"

Cassidy put a hand to her mouth. "What did Artie do? I heard about the jungle trap. Was that it?"

"Oh, no, that was only the latest of myriad puerile antics aimed at humiliating me."

"Unless you count the shotgun." Cassidy didn't like mentioning it, but it didn't seem to faze the Toff.

"Oh, yeah. That too." He fixed his eyes on his brother. "It was…it was…" He stopped. "God help me if I can remember what it was that started the feud. Artie?"

Chapter Thirty-Five

Mindful Books, Thursday, July 20

Artemus held his hands up in mock surrender. "If you don't recall, I sure as hell am not going to remind you."

"But you were as angry as I—what set us off?" Artemus just shook his head. Digby studied him. "I know you too well, Artie. You don't remember either."

His brother dropped his hands. "It's true. Whatever pissed me off whisked itself out of the dusty attic of my memory years ago."

Didn't Jasper say something about a boating episode? Cassidy opened her mouth to enlighten them, but Jasper pinched her hard.

He spoke out of the side of his mouth. "Don't rock the reconciliation boat."

Digby hadn't noticed the exchange and addressed his brother. "So why do you keep following me around playing tricks on me? I assumed it was for revenge."

Artemus shuffled his feet. "I wanted you to forgive me. It was the only way I could think of to get your attention. You wouldn't speak to me otherwise." He raised an anguished face. "You're my brother, Digs. I wanted to be friends again. Like we were before…before…"

"Before whatever the hell happened."

Cassidy murmured, "Which couldn't have been very significant if neither of you has a clue what it was."

Jasper said heartily, "I propose we go flush our bad memories down the drain with some adult beverages. It's on me."

This was met with unbridled enthusiasm. *They have at least one thing in common. They're both cheap as baby chickens.*

Cassidy unhooked two umbrellas from the coat rack, and they proceeded to Fedora's in her Subaru. A few martinis later, the two brothers were regaling each other with stories and guffawing over the various tricks Artemus had played on Digby over the years. "At least it kept me employed. I could always wangle a character role in one of your big-screen disaster films. The anticipation of what I was planning usually made what would have been a tedious project bearable to all the stage minions."

"Yes, you always swung a bit part…because my agent knew it would ensure tons of media coverage. You know—the filmgoing public breathlessly awaiting what you would do to me this time."

"Your agent? I figured it was the studio."

"Them too. They went along with it after my agent explained there's no such thing as bad publicity—especially when it's free."

"You mean, you didn't hate me?" Artemus seemed rather put out at the news. "You were using me?" He got off his stool. "You bastard. I knew you were ruthless. I didn't think you'd stoop so low as to exploit your own sibling for press exposure." He put up his fists. "Come on, bro. Fight like a man. For once, your agent isn't here to protect you." He rose up on his toes. "Or do you want to take it outside?"

"Hell, no! It's pouring, Artie." When his brother took a step toward him, Digby jumped behind Jasper. "Hit *him*, Artie! He's only the director. He'll be behind the camera. We can't afford to muck up this beautiful face." He peeked over Jasper's shoulder.

Artemus stood there, facing them, face red, fists still clenched. A stillness fell over the bar. All of a sudden, the two men broke out in uproarious laughter. When they finally calmed down, Digby wiped his eyes. "Ah, that was a good one."

"Like old times."

Jasper and Cassidy looked from one to the other. Cassidy signaled the bartender. "Jack Daniels. Make it a double."

Jasper said, "Same for me."

She didn't remember much after that.

****

Cassidy's house, Friday, July 21

"Oh, my head."

"I *told* you: two aspirin before you go to bed. Try popping a couple now—it couldn't hurt." Jasper sniffed. "And while you're up, you might brush your teeth."

"Get off me."

"That's not what you said last night."

"Please…please get off me." Cassidy rubbed her temples. "What time is it?"

"Almost noon. I've already been to the set. We did a first take on the scene where the fisherman delivers the cabin boy to Mercy Spinney. We're shooting the next scene—where she welcomes him into her home—

an hour from now. Want to come?"

She jumped out of bed. "Coffee. Now."

"I take it that means yes." When she raised a fist, he backed out of the room. "Yes, bwana. Coffee, bwana. Right away. Your wish is my command, bwana."

She didn't bother to point out that bwana was a male term of address. A long, hot shower later, she emerged, feeling slightly better. The coffee helped. "Okay, let's go."

They walked down the hill. Surrounding the Spinney house were camera cranes, sound carts spewing microphones on long extension rods, lighting and electrical carts, and piles of equipment Cassidy couldn't hope to identify. Grips, juicers, and cameramen swarmed the area. Jasper called to Stan. "We'll start filming where we left off. The fisherman has dropped Teddy off, and Mercy takes the shivering boy into her house." He took Cassidy's arm. "Why don't you go on inside. That's where most of the action takes place."

Cassidy found an empty captain's chair in a corner of the big living room. One wall had been transformed into a Colonial-era open fireplace. She had barely settled down when she heard a rumpus outside. The door flew open, and a cameraman backed in. In front of him, Flavia helped a near-prostrate Teddy through what had been Mrs. Spinney's kitchen—now transformed into a larder—and into the living room. She sat him down next to the fire, all the while exclaiming at how cold he must be. She took off his wet jacket and wrapped a blanket around him.

"There, there. Poor wee lad. How did you come to

be so lost? You're American, aren't you? What are you doing so far from home?"

Before he could answer, she took a kettle from its hook above the fire and poured the contents into a ceramic teapot. She opened a cabinet and pulled a jug marked WHISKEY from the shelf. Glancing over her shoulder at Teddy, she poured a dram into the mug, then filled it with tea before offering it to him.

Cassidy watched while the scene unfolded. Teddy was exceptional as the frightened, exhausted boy, pathetically grateful for the widow's help. He gradually came out with the tale of his escape. "I had reached the British headquarters and hid in the bushes. When some soldiers came into the yard, I panicked and snuck into the house. A trapdoor stood open, and I clambered down to the cellar. There was…there was an opening. I thought to hide there till the soldiers left, but it went on and on." He looked up at Flavia. "It was a tunnel, Mistress Spinney."

A crash came from behind the cameraman. Two grips righted a C stand that had fallen over. Flavia waited for quiet, then went on. "And you followed it."

"Yes. At the end was this gate, and a boy in chains."

"Oh, my. More tea?"

Teddy held out his mug for a refill.

"The boy. Was he alive or dead?"

"Dead. I tried to revive him, but he was lost. The gate was barred, so I made my way back to the house."

Cassidy hadn't read the script, but Jasper had told her that Trask found the drummer boy alive in the brig and, unable to open the gate, left him there. *Now he's dead? And when did the tunnel get added?* Flavia, on the other hand, didn't seem shocked at all. She listened, nodding.

Teddy went on. "When I climbed the stairs back into the house, it was empty. I…I think the British commandant had gone down to the harbor to see to the destruction of any American ships that were left. No one was in the yard, so I escaped into the woods."

"And none of the crew from your ship came with you? Did Captain West not send a search party for you?"

The boy hid his face in his hands. "No. The smoke, the fires, the screams. I was terrified. I started walking, but I became disoriented. I must have been heading away from the water, for the sounds of battle receded. I tripped on a tree root and fell, hitting my head on a rock." He gazed at her, his eyes wide. "When I came to, I had no idea where I was."

Flavia bustled into the larder. The cameraman stationed there filmed while she extracted a tin from the cupboard. She put cookies on a plate and brought them back to Teddy. As he picked one up, a thunderous voice rent the air. "Cut!"

Jasper came in, looking more flustered than angry. Ollie and a woman Cassidy didn't recognize followed him in. Ollie was whispering frantically in Jasper's ear. "Teddy? Miss de Montville? A word?"

They huddled by the fake fire. Cassidy knew they were asking about the change in dialogue and wanted to hear what the two actors had to say. She inched closer as quietly as she could.

"Teddy, I had stepped away from the set for a moment, and Ollie tells me you unilaterally revised the script. You know you can't just amend it on your own.

Miss Klaxton here"—Jasper indicated the woman—
"should be consulted before any changes are made."

"But—"

"No buts, Teddy. I—"

"Teddy didn't make the change. I did."

Everyone pivoted to Flavia. Jasper said sternly,
"The underground corridor isn't mentioned in any
official records. We can't just add it in—it distorts the
whole plot."

Flavia was undeterred. "Remember the day after I
returned from Nova Scotia—when I was so rudely
interrupted?" Jasper nodded reluctantly. "I was about to
show you the two letters I found in Mercy Spinney's
house."

"You mean, her real house, not the movie one."

"Correct. The house in Canada. The letters were
written by Sarah Spinney, a cousin of Mercy's living in
Castine. In one, she asks after the cabin boy Mercy
rescued. Well, I showed them to Teddy Monday
afternoon. We studied them to see if there were more
clues about his exploits. Miss Klaxton's original lines
didn't entirely match the boy's version as Sarah
described it." She blinked. "There were certain
anomalies. Then, when you told me about Rory and the
tunnel, we hatched this plot twist. I thought it would
add some pizzazz to his role."

"Even though the official line is that he couldn't
free Catchpole and had to leave him there."

"Right." She shook her head sadly. "Of course,
once we'd made the alterations, it didn't make sense to
have the drummer boy stay behind. So we knocked him
off." She smiled brightly. "He was going to die anyway,
so we didn't think it mattered."

Jasper seemed totally nonplussed by Flavia's casual transformation of the plot line. "You do realize that that cuts Rory's role in half, don't you? He'd only have the scene where he's sent to the brig for stealing."

Teddy whistled. "I hadn't thought of that." He regarded Flavia. "I don't think that would be fair, do you?"

Flavia wrinkled her nose. "Oh, I suppose. We can't have little Rory make a scene that's not in the script, now can we?"

"Besides, if he's already dead, he won't be drumming the nights away, desperate to be heard."

Cassidy spoke up. "What did the other letter say?"

"It's funny. The second letter was clearly in response to one Mercy had written much later. Sarah mentions a trunk, says she'll send it back with the papers Mercy asked for, and promises not to divulge Mercy's secret."

"She doesn't say what that secret was?"

"No."

Jasper tried unsuccessfully to be offhand. "Might it have referred to a treasure?"

She frowned. "It's possible. The bottom of the sheet was torn off. It said something about what a shame it was, then just the letters t-r-e-a."

"T-r-e-a? That was it?"

She nodded. "You think the word could have been 'treasure'?"

Cassidy mused. "Could be…or how about 'treatment'? As in the drummer boy's?"

"Or 'treason'? 'Treachery'? There was a lot of that going around. Makes more sense than treasure." Jasper clapped his hands. "The word could have been anything. There's nothing in the record to show that the cabin boy knew why the drummer boy was in the brig."

"So, like I told 'em, the guys have been wasting their time looking for treasure. It's just an old wive's tale."

Cassidy looked up. Trent stood at the side door, grinning. The key grip, Lyle, slid around him. "Just because the cabin boy didn't know about it, doesn't mean the story ain't true—the drummer boy hid it somewhere before he died. I say we keep digging."

Ollie bellied up to him. "And I say, we get back to work."

The crew reluctantly withdrew. Jasper checked his watch. "I think we've done enough for today. Teddy— get with Miss Klaxton. I want the new bits deleted and the old script back by tomorrow. Flavia? Do you want to go back to your hotel?"

"Yes. William will take me."

Jasper frowned. "He's not your personal driver, you know, Flavia."

"I know, but he's so sweet, and it's really not that far. I'll send him right back." She gave Jasper the look they all recognized. It was her Fanny, her Camille, her Agnes of God. It worked.

"All right, but he's not to do any errands for you. Looks like we'll need another day of filming here before we can move up to Castine." He glowered at his star. She did not squirm.

Cassidy rose and was heading out through the kitchen door when her phone rang. "Hi, Toby. What's up?" She listened. "Hoo boy. The mystery thickens." She hung up.

Jasper came in. "Who was that?"

"The sheriff. They've discovered where the wetsuit came from."

"Oh? Where?"

"A scuba dive center in Camden."

"And who bought it?"

"No one. It was rented. By a man named Ahearn."

Chapter Thirty-Six

Mrs. Spinney's house, Friday, July 21

"Ahearn! Wasn't he—"

"Yes. He was our first murder victim."

"The subcontractor. In the sailor suit."

"Who also rented a red Ford SUV."

Jasper slammed a hand down on the kitchen counter. "What the hell is going on? Does it all go back to Ahearn somehow?"

"I don't know, but I'm tired. I'm going to go watch a dumb TV movie and go to bed." He started to follow her. Cassidy barred his way. "I really need to rest. And think."

His eyebrows went up. "About me?"

"No, about all this. Is it a jumble of random occurrences or somehow interrelated? Are we confusing history and legend with present-day crimes? Or maybe fiction and fact? Movie magic and reality?"

Ollie yelled from the living room. "Jasper, can you come in here?"

"Give me a sec!" He caught Cassidy's hand and gazed deeply into her eyes. "I gotta go. Sleep well. Solve the mystery. Maybe we can make a movie out of it someday." He kissed her and bent his steps toward the living room.

****

Cassidy's house, Saturday, July 22

"Oh, what a beautiful morning!" Cassidy warbled in the shower. She'd fallen asleep on the couch at eight o'clock and slept straight through to nine in the morning. She felt clear-headed for the first time in ages. *Maybe because I didn't think about our mystery—or mysteries—once.* An image popped into her head. *Jasper.* Her mood plummeted.

Was he simply part of the chaos wandering around in her brain? Or did she only like him because he represented the glamor and intrigue of a stranger? *Maybe when the circus leaves town, any feelings I have for him will dissipate.* At the moment, that sounded like a good thing.

Nellie called. "Thanks for the books, Cass. Hank has read all of them. It didn't help. Now he's gone completely bonkers and announced he's going to our camp at China Lake until it's over."

"Why? What's he got to do with the murders?"

There was a pause. "Murders?"

"Well, to be precise, attempted murders. Most of them misfired." She paused to count. "All right, two murders for sure. Or…"

"Cassidy?" Nellie's voice was faint. "I was talking about my pregnancy. What are *you* talking about?"

Dear sweet Jesus, I completely forgot she's expecting! "Oh, the *books*! I'm…uh…impressed that Hank read *any* of them. You should be…er…proud of him."

"But he's deserting me!" her friend wailed. "I can't go through this alone, Cassidy!"

Now you've done it. "He's just stressed, Nellie.

341

You know he won't leave the farm in high season." When the wailing increased in volume, she added, "And anyway, he loves you dearly. He just doesn't like seeing you suffer. You know men—they feel helpless when they can't fix the problem."

"Oh, so now pregnancy is a problem?" Before Cassidy could recoup, Nellie went on. "I'm not suffering. The nausea's gone, and I'm hungry all the time."

"How about lunch, then? I have to open the store this morning, but I close at twelve. I'll spring for it if you're game."

"Thanks, but Maude and I are going shopping in Camden. You're welcome to come along. I just ate a huge breakfast, so it's a sure bet I'll be hungry again in a couple of hours."

"Um. Okay."

"We'll pick you up at the store. You can tell both of us all about your murders."

Great. Maude. The human pony express.

****

Camden, Saturday, July 22

Camden was as packed as ever. Nellie took her time in the baby store, and Maude did the same in the toy store. "I love all the old-fashioned gag gifts they have here. These will be perfect for my niece Charity and her Rancor in Florida." She held up a simulated vomit puddle and a magic eight-ball. "They can put them away until little Spike is old enough."

"From what you've told me about Rancor, I doubt he'd be willing to share."

By the time they were finished, every restaurant was packed. Maude sat down on a bench. "How I hate the season! Camden is getting overrun by foreigners. Look at the plates—Ohio, Tennessee, Ontario. And way too many from Massachusetts. Let's just go home."

Nellie paced. "That'd take too long. I'm starved. How about Nemo's? The tourist crowd doesn't know about it. I'll bet they at least have peanuts."

"Okay."

They climbed the stairs to the cluttered tavern. The tables were occupied, so they settled on stools at the bar. Cassidy was surprised to see Pauline behind the counter. "Hey, Pauline. You're still working here?"

The woman looked up. "Oh, hi, Cassidy. Not full time, no. Ollie didn't need me on the set today, so I'm filling in for a girl with the flu. What can I get you?"

Nellie said, "Seltzer, please. And do you have any food?"

"Sure." She slid a bar menu across. "And for you two?"

They opted for a couple of beers and a plate of sliders. Nellie ordered nachos and fried pickles and Buffalo wings.

Cassidy looked askance at the pile of chicken parts bathed in red dye number two. "You sure you can handle that?"

Nellie picked up the Tabasco sauce. "Having survived the first trimester, I seem to be able to eat anything." She gazed longingly at the beer. "I only wish I were allowed to wash it down with something stronger than seltzer."

They settled on their food. A few minutes later, Maude put down a half-eaten slider and turned to Cassidy. "So what's the latest on the Castine caper? I don't think I've heard anything since that young woman died of a bad lobster at Childe's."

"You mean Sally Crook, the public relations officer." Cassidy indicated Pauline, who had gone to the other end of the bar to wait on a customer. "Pauline was hired to replace her. She has a background in PR."

"Pauline Peach?"

"She goes by Poliquin."

"Must be her married name. She's a local girl. I taught her math. Taught her two younger brothers too." Her brow creased in the effort to remember. "Brick and Butch. Troublemakers, all three—always being picked up for petty theft or vandalism or something." She took another bite out of the slider. "As I recall, Pauline dropped out her last year of high school and went off to Florida with some salesman."

"Yup. She told Jasper she lost a son and the salesman dumped her. Bad luck." *If it's true, that is.* "Haven't seen her around lately." *Thank God.*

The bartender returned. "So, Ollie's been sending me around to do advance publicity. What's going on at the set?"

"You haven't heard?" Maude told her about the shooting, adding as much gore and hyperbole as Cassidy would allow. "Got the exclusive from Eunice Merithew." She gave Cassidy a reproachful look.

Pauline's eyes grew round. "Gee, I've been missing a lot. Is Miss de Montville all right?"

Cassidy answered. "She's fine. It was just a graze. Mr. North is sticking to his statement that the gun was stolen from his hotel room, so we're still looking for the culprit. The police found a wetsuit south of Amity. They think the shooter wore it to swim to shore."

"Really? Where did they find it?"

"It had been stuffed in the hawthorn bushes below Bobby B.'s place. Just up from Kelly's Cove."

"Huh." She refilled their glasses.

Cassidy continued. "The owner of Camden Scuba Duba—you know, the one over on Dillingham Point? He identified the suit. It's a rental."

"Oh, yeah? Do they know who rented it?"

"Guy named Ahearn."

Cassidy wasn't prepared for Pauline's reaction. She dropped a mug, scattering beer and broken glass all over the bar. Her hand flew to her mouth. "Oh, God. I…I…"

Maude gave her a hard look. "Did you know him?"

"I…I…" She pulled herself together. "No…no, not really. I served him a drink here before…before…I read in the paper…He's the one they found dead, isn't he?"

"Yes."

She cleaned up the mess with a shaky hand. "I'll be right back." She headed toward the ladies' room.

Cassidy kept an eye on the bathroom door. She was not surprised to see Pauline slip out and down the stairs a minute later. "I don't think she's coming back."

Nellie observed, her mouth full of nacho, "She seemed kind of freaked out by the mention of Ahearn, didn't she?"

"I don't doubt it." Maude shook her head. "She lives on Kelly's Cove. How would you feel if the man you'd just served a beer to washed up dead at your feet?"

****

Cassidy's house, Saturday, July 22

Cassidy had almost finished relating their excursion to Camden when Jasper interrupted. "So,

Pauline took a powder. A bit out of character for her."

How do you know? "Did she come back here?"

"No." Jasper put down the latest issue of *Celebs Galore.* "Poor girl. You must have scared the daylights out of her. You may be a cold fish when it comes to attempted murder, but she's a more delicate flower."

"Oh, really." Cassidy didn't think Pauline was delicate at all. In fact she thought she was hard as nails. *So what scared her? Wait. What did Maude say?* The answer eluded her, and the telephone ringing didn't help. It was Nellie.

"I thought you'd like to know the latest. I got it from Eunice, who got it from Audrey, who got it—"

"This isn't Genesis, chapter one, Nellie. What's the news?"

"Well, she heard it from Edna Mae—"

"Nellie."

"That that dead man—"

"Which dead man?"

"Oh, I forgot. We've got a passel of 'em, don't we? No, the guy we were talking about yesterday—Ahearn. They're still trying to figure out how he got to the mussel platform. He wasn't in his wetsuit—"

"No. He was in a sailor suit."

"Weird, huh? So he must not have swum."

"And ruin his beautiful bell bottoms? Not likely." Cassidy wished—not for the first time—that her best friend could get to the point in less than a Maine minute. "Do they think he was killed somewhere else and dumped there?"

Nellie paused. "I'm not sure. But Toby did find a rowboat with his fingerprints. And blood."

"Ha. Blood."

Jasper looked up from his magazine. "Blood?"

"Look, Nellie, I gotta go. Thanks for the news."

She was about to hang up when Nellie said, "Wait. I haven't told you the rest. Guess who owns the rowboat?"

"Who?"

"That bartender—Pauline Poliquin."

Kelly's Cove. That's it. Maude said she lives on Kelly's Cove, not in Knightston. She lied to Jasper…but why?

****

Cassidy's house, Sunday, July 23

They heard nothing more that day. The movie crew spent Sunday moving materials to Castine. Jasper and Cassidy sat on her deck, Jasper working and Cassidy watching his long fingers caress the pages.

"We've got to finish up the scenes here by the end of next week. We're way behind schedule, and Dad's getting antsy. With Lyle out of commission, I have to figure out how to redistribute the workload."

"What happened to Lyle?"

"Fell into one of the holes those idiots are digging in Castine and broke a toe."

"They're still looking for treasure? I thought Alfie had run them off."

"Well, they're back—like locusts or whatever returns to destroy the earth." He cast a furtive glance at the sky. "Anyway, Stan put Trent in charge of the grips. He's only got about a year's worth of experience—"

"More than you, at any rate."

"So if he messes up, Dad'll have my head."

"Well, you won't miss it." She topped up her coffee cup. "If people would stop dying or getting shot at or trapped in tunnels, you could get on with things."

"I told him that. Apparently this did not pass muster as an excuse."

"How about the altercations between the leading men? Diminishing at all?"

"Naw. That's a constant. It never really interferes with the filming."

"When is your father coming back?"

"He's busy with a couple of other projects. He'll come back when we're further along." He rose. "Flavia's ready to finish her scene. I'll see you later."

Cassidy didn't ask if she could come watch this time. *Who knows? I could be the jinx...or the target.*

****

Cassidy's house, Monday, July 24

They were awakened at eight a.m. the next morning by Ollie. Jasper put his phone on speaker.

"Jasper? Where the f-word is that PR girl? She was supposed to arrange accommodations for the talent in Castine. She's not answering her cell."

"You mean Pauline. I don't know where she is. Didn't she take care of that a couple of weeks ago?"

"She reserved the rooms, yes, but not the welcome committee. You know the Toff."

"Right. Damn."

Cassidy raised herself up on one elbow. "Welcome committee?"

"You know, banners, bands, blondes in skimpy outfits. It's part of Digby's ongoing campaign to get a star on Hollywood Boulevard."

Ollie chimed in. "Except he expects them to continue even after the star is cemented in."

Just then Cassidy's phone rang. Jasper muted the

speaker on his cell. She clicked hers on. "Hello. Who? Pauline? Where are you? Oh. Yes, I can come down. But don't you have someone—? I see. Sure." She got up and began scrambling into some clothes.

Jasper watched her. "Shall I tell Ollie where he can find the elusive Pauline?"

"He may have to assign the welcome party to someone else. Toby just arrested her for the murder of Rick Ahearn."

Chapter Thirty-Seven

Cassidy's house, Monday, July 24

"Pauline? That's crazy." He put his ear to his phone. "Ollie, you'll have to hire the band yourself. Pauline is…temporarily indisposed. Yes. I'll explain later." He hung up. "You said Toby has arrested her for Ahearn's death? Again, nonsense. What reason would she have to kill a contractor from Boston who was just passing through? The only connection he had to us was with Sally Crook. Pauline wasn't even hired until long after they found his body."

"He had a drink at Nemo's."

"So? So did we."

Cassidy said impatiently, "She served him the night before he died. And Nellie said they found a rowboat that belongs to Pauline with his fingerprints and blood in it. They must be going on the theory that she killed him and then rowed him out to the barge."

Jasper went toward the bathroom. "Give me ten minutes."

"What for?"

"I want to be presentable when we descend upon the good sheriff."

Fifteen minutes later, they pulled into the parking lot of the county jail. Toby didn't seem surprised to see them. "So, you want the down and dirty? Rumor mill not enough for you?"

Jasper said testily, "I understand you've arrested an employee of mine. I'd like to negotiate bond. Where do I find the judge?"

Cassidy glared at him. "How about we find out what Sheriff Quimby has to say before we change the subject?"

"Sure, leave the poor girl to rot in stir while you sate your macabre appetite for details."

Toby huffed. "You won't be able to bail her out, Mr. MacEwan. At this point, we're planning to charge her with first-degree murder. And I'll have you know we have two state-of-the-art holding cells right here in the building. As we speak, Miss Poliquin is partaking of a delicious meal provided by Mrs. Quimby."

Cassidy grabbed Jasper's arm. "Oh, dear, you're right. Let's get her out of jail ASAP."

The sheriff was not amused. "I'd pit Edna Mae's succotash against yours any day, Miss Cassidy Jane."

"I wouldn't take that bet, Toby. You know I can't cook, but surely even you—her fond husband—will admit that succotash is the *only* thing she makes that's good—or even edible."

Jasper muttered something.

"What was that?"

"Is succotash that inglorious concoction of lima beans and corn?" He shuddered. "My nanny from Connecticut used to make that. I still have nightmares."

"All right, all right." Toby couldn't hide the smile. "She picked up a breakfast from Hunter's Daily, okay?"

"Whew." Cassidy sat down. "So what made you fix on Pauline? I warn you, I heard it from Nellie, who heard it from Eunice, who heard it—"

"Yes, yes. Like the game of telephone, I wouldn't put all my eggs in that basket." He sighed and sat down at his desk, indicating the two wooden chairs across from him. "Let me summarize." He steepled his fingers. "A man was found dead on the mussel farm on Monday, June 19. Cause of death: a stab wound to the heart."

Cassidy lurched, startled. "I thought his throat was slit."

"You've been listening to Edna Mae again."

"Does that mean he didn't drown either?"

"Yes. Although his clothes were wet, Squiggy says he was probably stabbed on the platform—most of the blood pooled there. We identified him as Richard Ahearn, of Newton, Massachusetts. During our search for evidence, we came upon a rowboat tethered to a log at Kelly's Cove. In it we found a blood smear and fingerprints belonging to Ahearn, as well as the prints of Ms. Pauline Poliquin."

"But she owns the boat—that's not dispositive."

Jasper said slowly, "If, as you say, the boat was tied up on a public beach, anyone could have borrowed it."

"Right, but Ms. Poliquin was with Ahearn the Saturday before his body was discovered. That was the last time anyone saw him."

"Oh."

"That's not dispositive either, Toby!" Cassidy wasn't sure why she was defending Pauline, but somehow she had to. "She was working at Nemo's when he came in. She told us she'd served him a drink. She didn't try to hide that."

"We spoke to her manager at Nemo's. Turns out

Pauline has herself a record. She's on probation for shoplifting. Her boss had reported her a couple of times for violating it. She stated Pauline left with Ahearn."

Probation. Maude said she was always in trouble. Still... "But—" Cassidy was about to bring up another objection when Jeff came in.

"The prisoner would like to confess."

"Confess!"

Cassidy bit her lip, "But…why?"

Toby shot up, then sat back down. "Does she want to call a lawyer?"

"She says no."

"You read her her rights when you brought her in?"

"Of course."

"Well, then, escort her into the interrogation room. Is the tape recorder set up?"

Jeff tipped his hat. "What about the state police? Should we contact them?"

"Not yet. If she's ready to talk, we should take advantage of it. She might change her mind if we let her simmer too long."

Cassidy didn't wait to be invited into the observation room. Neither did Jasper. Luckily, Toby didn't stop them. Through the window they saw Jeff shepherd the prisoner inside and sit her down at an old wooden table. Cassidy noted a tear-stained face before Pauline dropped her head into her hands. *She looks her age.* Cassidy was surprised that she felt only sympathy for the woman. *How could I ever have imagined her as a rival?* She sidled closer to Jasper. He put an arm around her shoulders and squeezed. Cassidy relaxed into him.

Jeff turned on the recorder and said gently, "Ms.

Poliquin?"

She raised her head. "I did it."

Jeff pressed the pause button. "Hold that thought. I have to set up the interview first." He clicked the machine on and spoke into the microphone. "This is Jeff Pierce, Deputy Sheriff, Waldo County. I am interviewing Ms. Pauline Poliquin. Poliquin spelled P-o-l-i-q-u-i-n. Date: Monday, July 24. Time—" He checked the clock on the wall. "Nine thirty a.m. Now, Miss Poliquin, you are waiving your right to counsel, is that correct?"

"Yes." Her voice was barely audible.

"And your rights regarding self-incrimination?"

"Yes, yes. Can we get on with this?" She sighed heavily.

"Sorry. You stated that 'you did it.' Could you be more specific?"

"I killed Rick Ahearn."

Jeff looked toward the window and shrugged. "Okay, so tell me in your own words what happened."

She took a deep breath. "I was working in Nemo's that night. See, I lost my baby—my son Noah—two years ago, and then my husband Jerry was fired. We came back to Maine, but he—Jerry—he…er…couldn't take the winters and left."

Let her have her fib. Toby seemed to agree with Cassidy's unspoken wish and nodded at Jeff to resume.

"Go on."

"I was down to my last dollar when I got the bartending job. A friend of my mom's rented me a room in a house on Coast Road near Kelly's Cove."

"If you were so broke, how'd you come by the rowboat?"

She almost laughed. "Cap'n Swift—the guy who lives in that little shack across from the golf course? Anyway, he had dumped it in the drainage ditch in front of his house. It had a big ol' hole in the bottom, and he said I could have it if I hauled it away. He helped me tie it on the top of my car. When I reached Kelly's Cove, I just let it slide off the roof and down the bank to the shore. Then—you know that stuff they advertise on TV where you paint the bottom and it's waterproof? I gotta tell you, it works!"

"Huh. Let me write that down." Jeff made a show of jotting a few words in his notebook. "Please continue. You were describing the night Mr. Ahearn died."

Her face tightened. "So, I'm on the bar at Nemo's and this guy—Ahearn—starts chatting. Says he's a traveling salesman. We hit it off. When I got off work, we went to my house for a few drinks."

Cassidy had a feeling that meant a *lot* of drinks.

"We…uh…fooled around a bit. I've been awful lonely since Jerry left." She gave Jeff an arch look, which he totally missed. "Then, we thought we'd take a walk outside."

"This was what time?"

"No idea—probably around midnight, one a.m."

"Okay."

"There's a set of steps across the road from my house that go down to the beach. We were…we were halfway down when he…fell."

"Fell. You didn't push him?"

"I swear to God I didn't! He tripped on a loose board." She gulped. "He went tumbling down to the bottom. When I got there he was lying on his back, his head on a rock. The rock felt wet, and he…he…wasn't breathing."

"Did you check his pulse?"

She looked guilty. "You know, I've never learned how to do that…but he *acted* dead."

Standing next to Cassidy, Toby snorted. "Really? *Acted*?"

Cassidy put a hand on his arm. "*Shh.*"

Inside the room, Jeff stared at Pauline. "Acted?"

"Um, I guess I mean 'looked dead.' You know, floppy." She lolled on the chair, arms and legs akimbo.

"So what did you do then?"

"What would you do?" She fluttered her lashes at Jeff.

Old habits die hard.

Jeff said heavily, "I'd call the cops."

"Really?" Her eyes widened. "Honestly, that never occurred to me. I panicked."

Jeff was clearly itching to scold her, but, with a glance at the one-way glass, closed his mouth. "Go on."

"The tide was coming in. At first I thought I'd just roll him into the water, but I was afraid he wouldn't float far enough. So I dragged him to the dinghy and rowed out to the mouth of the cove."

"Not to the mussel barge?"

"I didn't see the barge. It's not stationary, you know. It floats up and down the bay. Besides, it was pretty dark."

"Okay, you're out in the bay. Then what?"

"I heaved him out of the boat, rowed back, and went home. And finished the whiskey."

Jeff stood. "Thank you. Would you please wait here?"

She gave him a look that said plainly, Do I have a choice?

Jeff appeared a moment later in the observation room. "Cut and dried?"

Toby shook his head. "I have a couple more questions for her."

"So do I."

"Last I looked, you're not a sworn officer of the law, Cassidy."

"I can still have questions."

"Oh, all right. MacEwan better come too."

They trooped into the room. "Ms. Poliquin? I'm going to need a bit more information, if that's all right."

She didn't seem surprised to see Jasper and Cassidy, but merely nodded wearily. "Get it over with."

"We know you left Nemo's with Ahearn, because your manager saw you. She also described him as wearing business attire. So, how did he end up in a sailor suit?"

She cracked a smile. "I said we were fooling around. Well, we were a little drunk—"

No kidding.

"And we got to talking about the theatre and how my husband had played with the Maskers in their production of H.M.S. Pinafore. He was in the chorus. So Rick says, 'I'd love to hear some of the music.' And I says, 'I have a DVD they made of the show. In fact,' I says, 'I think I still have his old costume.' And Rick says, 'Let's have a look at it.' So I got out the sailor suit, and Rick put it on." She smiled reminiscently. "It fit him perfectly. He looked real glamorous. We played the DVD and danced. He wasn't bad. We had…fun." A tear dropped in her lap.

There was silence. To Cassidy, it seemed such a pathetic, even tragic story. *And now she's going to jail. Wait.* "Pauline, you said you couldn't see the mussel platform because it was dark."

"Right. It was kind of overcast, and there weren't many stars."

"There's a streetlight there on Coast Road."

"Yeah, but it didn't shine as far as the bottom of the steps."

"So how were you so sure Ahearn was dead?"

"Huh?"

"You said you don't know how to check a pulse and that he just 'looked' dead. So what made you so sure?"

"I…uh."

Toby leaned forward. "Could it be you weren't positive he'd died in the fall, and that's why you stabbed him?"

"St…stabbed?" Pauline went white. Her eyes rolled up in her head, and she slid off the chair in a dead faint.

Chapter Thirty-Eight

Waldo County jail, Monday, July 24

Jeff called the paramedics, and Pauline was taken to the hospital for evaluation. As he watched the ambulance leave, Toby said, "I know why she fainted."

"Edna Mae's cooking?"

"No, and since I like you, I won't pass that remark on to my beloved wife. No, see, she'd just been confronted with the truth. Confession, my eye. She thought she'd get out of it with some tall tale about a fall."

Cassidy shook that off. "That makes no sense. She must have known the medical examiner would find the stab wound. I imagine it was hard to miss."

Jasper observed, "I thought she seemed very sincere."

Cassidy eyed him. "You would."

He apparently missed her jab, for his ardor increased. "Plus, she said she'd only rowed him out halfway, not all the way to the mussel platform, which she says she didn't see."

Toby rounded on him. "She's lying. How else would he get to the barge?"

Jasper held his ground. "You know what I think? I don't think he was dead. Just unconscious."

"Huh." Cassidy didn't hide her skepticism.

"She obviously doesn't know any first aid. It was dark. She just assumed." He sat back, satisfied.

"But she chucked him overboard! Maybe she didn't succeed in breaking his neck, but that didn't stop her from trying to drown him."

"If she thought he was already dead, she wouldn't be drowning him." He looked positively exultant. She longed to poke him.

Toby cleared his throat. "I repeat. How did he get to the mussel platform if she didn't take him?"

"A friendly dolphin?"

Cassidy rolled her eyes. "In which case he'd be alive. Unless you're implying the dolphin wasn't so friendly? And had opposable thumbs so he could wield a knife?"

Before Jasper could retort, Toby held up a calming hand. "Are you both quite finished? The fact is, Ahearn was stabbed through the heart, resulting in his death. He did not drown, nor did he die from a close encounter with a rock. The medical examiner noted a large cut on the back of his head in his autopsy report. Said it wasn't serious enough to be fatal."

"But—"

"However, I will concede that what we do have is a confession with a lot of holes. I think we might hold off on the first-degree murder charge for now, but I don't want to let her go yet. We need some reason to hold her."

Jeff said brightly, "Improper disposal of a body? Manslaughter?"

"Maybe, although it won't work for long if it turns out he wasn't dead when she dumped him in the water."

Toby picked up the phone. "I think I'll have forensics go over the rowboat one more time."

"And the mussel platform. There may be some hint of whether he died there or elsewhere."

"CSI is positive it was on the barge, but I'll ask 'em again. I'll call the courthouse and postpone the arraignment."

"Will you let her go?"

"Don't see how I can refuse."

They scattered. Cassidy went to the store and spent the rest of the day alternating between speculation and shelving books. She got a call from Jasper at five. "We finished the scene with Flavia, but I have to go up to Castine tomorrow. Problems with the crew."

"Are they still digging for treasure?"

"As a matter of fact, yes. The police have asked me to confine them to their camp during off-work hours."

"A curfew?"

"Yup. Just like the maritime academy students. Any word on Pauline?"

"She's okay. Toby didn't want her to go home— flight risk—so she's staying with them."

Jasper gasped. "Does that mean succotash for every meal? I don't think she deserves that kind of punishment."

"Perhaps Edna Mae can threaten her with it until she spills her guts."

"Literally."

Cassidy was thoughtful. "Hard as it is to admit, I have to agree with you. I think Pauline is telling the truth."

"Which means?"

"Which means someone else killed Rick Ahearn.

Now we just have to find out who."

"And how."

****

Cassidy's house, Tuesday, July 25

"I have good news and bad news."

"Take it away, Toby." Cassidy held the phone to her ear with one hand while she poured coffee into a mug with her other.

"First the good news. CSI found more DNA in the rowboat and another set of fingerprints."

"How about blood?"

"No blood from anyone other than Ahearn."

"Okay, the DNA?"

"That's also the bad news. We identified some as Pauline's and some as Ahearn's, corroborating her story. However, we also found DNA from a third person, a person for whom we don't have a match in our data banks."

"Could it have belonged to Captain Swift?"

"Nope—he checked out."

"Then someone else used the boat after Pauline dumped Ahearn in the water."

"Not necessarily. The DNA could've been deposited any time."

"Did you ask her if anyone borrowed it later?"

"We asked if anyone else *ever* used it."

"But—"

Toby cut Cassidy off. "Look, for one thing, who would ask to borrow a boat at two in the morning?" When she started to object, he raised his voice. "And why would a potential killer bother? For all intents and purposes, Ahearn was already dead."

Cassidy sat back. It was hard to argue with Toby's

deductions. Still, she wasn't satisfied. *I know Pauline is innocent.* "What was her answer? Did anyone else take it out?"

"She said no one—not even her landlady—would get in it. They didn't trust the thing to stay afloat. Anyway, we confiscated it the morning we found the body, so any traces would have to have been left before seven a.m. Monday."

"What about the days between the murder and the corpse showing up?"

"Not days. Only a little more than twenty-four hours. Ahearn died in the wee hours of June 18, and his body was discovered the morning of the nineteenth."

"So he lay on the barge all through Sunday. *Someone* must have seen him."

"That would certainly have aided the investigation, but no. All the houses overlooking Kelly's Cove were empty that weekend, except for Ms. Poliquin's. We had heavy rain that Sunday, so the usual picnickers weren't at the cove. Even without that, the barge had floated out farther into the channel, away from the shore. Newt Slugwater found the corpse when he went to check the mussel nets at six a.m. on Monday."

"What about Pauline's boat?"

"It was on the shore when he hauled his inflatable dinghy up beside it. I talked with a couple of early-morning dog walkers, but they hadn't seen anything. Audrey Carver says she was so spooked by the sight of Newt carrying the body, she picked up her dog and raced back to her house without looking back."

"So why did you confiscate Pauline's rowboat?"

"Normal police procedure. It was the only boat at Kelly's Cove, and since we weren't sure how Ahearn had arrived at the mussel barge, we kept everything that might contain evidence."

"You must have talked to Pauline then."

"Nope. Mrs. Roybal—her landlady—said she worked all weekend. That more or less eliminated her as a suspect until we interrogated the manager at Nemo's."

Cassidy sat in thought. "A third person...Time frame...Okay, for the sake of argument, let's suppose the DNA was deposited *after* she dumped Ahearn in the water. It had to be somebody close by. What about Mrs. Roybal? Did you interview her?"

"Of course. You do know she's in a wheelchair, right?"

"Damn."

"Well, that's not very nice."

"You know what I mean."

Toby's tone was final. "Cassidy, your imagination is running away with you. Pauline Poliquin stabbed Richard Ahearn and left his body on the barge. The third DNA probably belongs to some kid who took the dinghy out for a joy ride."

Cassidy wasn't listening. "Look, is Pauline at your house? Can I go over and talk to her?"

"I don't want you blabbing about our new evidence."

"You mean the DNA? No, of course I won't. I just have a couple of questions."

Toby considered. "Okay, as long as you stick to the publicly known facts. She should be out front. Edna Mae is teaching her to crochet."

"I'll be there in a trice."

She found the two women on the porch sitting on

uncomfortable-looking straight-back chairs. Edna Mae clutched a roll of yarn in her lap, her lips set in a thin line. Pauline seemed subdued.

"Hello, Edna Mae. Pauline."

"Good morning, Cassidy Jane. Did you need something?"

"I'd like to ask Pauline a couple of questions, if you don't mind."

Edna Mae squinted at Cassidy. "Did my husband send you?"

"No, but…*but*"—as the old lady's hackles rose— "he knows I'm here."

Pauline raised a weary hand. "Fire away." She gave Edna Mae a meaningful look. "I'll be fine."

Her hostess rose. "I'll leave you two alone then." She went inside.

Cassidy was astonished that Edna Mae would leave so willingly until she saw the living room curtain move. A second later, the window rose an inch. *The Red Hats will have the full scoop before I even get home.* She came up on the porch and sat down on the empty chair next to Pauline. "So, Pauline, how are you doing?"

The woman's eyes bugged out. "You're kidding, right?"

Cassidy had a sinking feeling. *Was this such a good idea?* She steeled herself. "I've just been discussing your case with the sheriff, and there seem to be a few loose ends. You say no one else ever used the rowboat, right?"

"Right. Old Mrs. Roybal—who I rent from—well, she can't walk anymore, and the neighbors didn't believe me when I claimed it was watertight."

"The next morning—after the…your…er…date

with Ahearn. Did you notice if the dinghy had been moved?"

She paused. "Funny you should ask. Normally I wouldn't have gone down to the water, but I decided to check in case…in case…"

"In case you'd left something incriminating in it?"

"Yes, that too." She blushed. "Actually, I'd been pretty blotto and I was afraid I'd forgotten to tie it up, but it was there at the usual spot. Then I went to work."

"What time was that?"

"I had the noon shift, so about eleven thirty."

Hmm. Maybe Toby's right. Cassidy tried to let her mind wander. *Think outside the box. Dinghy's not in the picture. Or…wait a minute! Their date. They left together…* "Pauline?"

The woman jerked as though she'd drifted off. "What?"

"You met Ahearn in the bar, right? And when you got off work, he came home with you."

"Right."

"How did you get from Nemo's to your house that night?"

"I drove. Rick followed me in his rental car."

"Was it a red Ford?"

She thought a minute. "It was an SUV. Not sure what make. Yeah, it was red."

"Where is it now?"

"What?"

"I said, where is it now? What happened to it? It didn't drive itself away."

A hand flew to her mouth. "I was so upset I forgot all about it. There's no room in my driveway, so he had parked it down the hill."

"By the path to the beach?"

"Yes."

We may be getting somewhere. "After Ahearn took the tumble, you followed him down the stairs to the shore. You told us you couldn't see the streetlight from there. Did you by any chance see headlights?"

Pauline pressed her lips together. Cassidy was about to ask another question when she said slowly, "You know, maybe I did. As I was rowing back to shore, I saw an arc of lights go over my head. You know"—she swung her arm—"as though a car were turning around. Didn't think much about it."

Cassidy patted her knee. "Pauline, I think you may have seen the murderer."

"You mean…you mean…" Her eyes glinted with hope.

"Yes. I think you're wrong. You didn't kill Rick Ahearn."

She goggled. "Well, if I didn't, who did?"

"Sixty-four-thousand-dollar question. Is there anything else Ahearn told you? Anything you remember about him that could give us a clue about who'd want to kill him?"

She thought. "No. The bar was super busy that night—lotta customers. He came in pretty late—said he'd had a tough day. Ordered martinis. He talked about his job—how he scouted sites for Hollywood. He was real proud of that. I didn't get the impression he made a lot of money." She sighed. "If only I'd meet a nice rich guy. Like yours." She grinned. "By the way, you don't have to worry about me and Jasper. He's nuts about you."

Cassidy didn't know what to say. "Anything else?"

She scrunched up her face. "Not much. He bought some guys he knew a beer. Then after it quieted down a little, he let me vent about Jerry and Noah." A spasm of grief clouded her eyes. "He was a good listener."

"That's it?"

"Oh, yeah, we talked about the movie—*American Waterloo*—and he asked about the Penobscot Expedition. Funny how much I remember from elementary school."

Way to make me feel inadequate, Pauline. "Okay." Cassidy rose. "I'll leave you in the capable hands of Mrs. Quimby."

The latter bustled out to the porch. Cassidy didn't doubt she'd heard every word. "Bye now. You go back and tell that husband of mine that I can't be sitting around the house all day. I have a Red Hat Society meeting tonight, and I have to pick up the vodka. He'd better be home by six."

"Will do."

Toby was getting off the phone when Cassidy walked in. "Let me guess: Edna Mae has discovered she has a meeting tonight, and I have to go home and babysit."

"You know her well."

He leaned his elbows on his desk. "So?"

"Pauline remembered something that could be important. Ahearn's car—the red SUV? He'd parked it down the hill while he and Pauline had their tryst. She doesn't know what happened to it."

"It's not still there, is it?"

"No, but if no one else moved it, it would have been towed by now anyway, wouldn't it?"

"Yeah. Merle Crosby's more'n happy to impound

abandoned cars. Keeps 'em for parts. You need something for your Subaru—ask him." He rubbed two fingers together in the universal sign for money. "I'll give him a ring." A minute later he hung up. "No red SUVs recently. Says his only decent find this season was a perfectly good Jeep ditched on the fire road up past the Pardoe place. Nah, some juvie must have seen the Ford and decided to add it to his collection."

"Except that it wasn't stolen. Someone turned it in at the Low Country car dealership."

"It was a rental?"

"Yup. And a few weeks later one of the movie crew leased it."

"So it's likely been rented and cleaned several times since then. Damn." Toby slammed a notebook on his desk. "We can't get a break."

"I don't know—we've learned a lot."

"Yeah. What and where, but not who and why. Fat lot of good that does." He looked glum. "Before you got here, I made a call to the manager of the Scuba Duba in Camden."

"Aha. Did he have a description of whoever rented the wetsuit?"

"No. Clerk is this scruffy kid who works afternoons. Pea brain. But we did learn something significant."

"What?"

"It was rented exactly a month *after* Ahearn was killed."

Chapter Thirty-Nine

Cassidy's house, Tuesday, July 25

"Is it time for another recap?"

"Well, it's definitely time for a refill." Cassidy held her glass out to Jasper.

He poured. "All right, you've told me what you found out from Pauline. I'm pretty sure Ahearn's murderer rented the wetsuit."

"Only if you assume the fellow who shot Flavia also killed Ahearn."

Jasper scowled. "Why must you throw up these ridiculous roadblocks? There isn't some detachment of hit men wandering around midcoast Maine. Besides, the guy used Ahearn's ID." He shook his head. "Look, everyone who's been affected by these incidents has something to do with the movie—however distant. We need to stick with the script."

"Everyone except for Flint."

Jasper whistled. "Sheesh, Cass. He came in contact with us. That appears to be enough."

Cassidy gazed out at the bay. The last drops of rain dappled the graying water. A man in a bulky life vest was tying an inflatable dinghy to the float. Two boys were doing cannonballs from the dock. She could hear their screams of fear and delight wafting up to her. In the far distance a freighter chugged toward the oil terminals of Searsport. "Wetsuit."

"Yes," he said impatiently, "we were talking about the wetsuit. I'm glad to see you're keeping up."

"You never got an answer from the Toff and Artemus."

Jasper pressed his lips together. "Oh, yeah. Digby did say they owned wetsuits, didn't he?"

"Uh huh, but you didn't ask if they had them here. It's unlikely they would lug them all the way from California. We know they like to dive. If they planned to do some here, one or the other might rent a suit."

"Surely you don't suspect our top billers of murder?"

If she were honest, she'd admit she couldn't, but…"When did Artemus arrive in Maine?"

"Well, he's a little vague about the exact date, but he checked into the motel on July 16."

"July 16? Huh." She thought back to her conversation with Toby. "The fake Mr. Ahearn rented the wetsuit on July 18."

Jasper caught his breath. "Okay, you win. What do you want to do?"

"I presume you have publicity shots of both of them." She put her glass down. "Why don't I take them down to the scuba shop tomorrow and see if the clerk recognizes either one."

"If it will make you happy."

****

Camden Scuba Duba, Wednesday, July 26

"How about this guy?" Cassidy held up a glamour shot of Artemus North.

The young man pulled at one of the five steel rings in his ear. "Yeah, he looks familiar. Could've been him."

"You're certain you saw him in person? He was a customer?"

He screwed up his eyes. "Uh…Mebbe."

Inconclusive. She whipped out a copy of the latest *Celebs Galore* magazine and opened it to the inside back page. "Okay…"—she read his name tag—"Elmer. Or this man? Ever see him?"

Elmer glanced at the advertisement. "Hoo, isn't that that old fart in the ED commercial?" He shook his head. "Poor flack. Used to be in pictures I think. Now he's flogging 'purple pills to pick your pecker up.' " He sniggered.

"That, young man, is one of the finest dramatic actors of his age. It's Digby Toff-Smythe."

The kid whistled. "Now there's a moniker!" He took a second look. "Yeah, that's him all right."

"The one who rented the wetsuit?"

"Nah. The actor. That's where I seen him before. In those commercials."

Sigh. "Can you remember anything about the person who rented the suit the police brought in yesterday?"

"Look, lady, this time of year we rent mebbe a hunnerd suits a week. I couldn't tell you who came in last week, let alone a month ago." He started grumbling. "Manager said he was going to dock my pay when the suit wasn't returned. Now it's back, he's *still* going to charge me."

"Why?"

"Well, the guy who rented it isn't around anymore, is he? Cops said he bought the farm." He seemed to think this would be news to Cassidy.

Cassidy wasn't sure reminding Elmer that Ahearn didn't actually rent the suit would help, so she held up the photo of Artemus again. "Okay, but you're sure you saw this person?"

He peered at it. "Nope. Never saw him before."

Cassidy gave up. "Thanks." *So many dead ends. Something's gotta give.* She drove back to Penhallow. Pauline stood on the sidewalk by the door to the police station. She saw Cassidy park in front of the bookstore and crossed the street.

"Hi. Can I come in?"

Cassidy unlocked the door and ushered her in. "Edna Mae let you out of her sight? She must be losing her grip."

"The sheriff dropped the charges against me." Pauline didn't seem particularly happy.

"That's good, isn't it? What's wrong?"

"Well, since we don't know who's committing these crimes, I'm afraid maybe I'm a target."

"Because you work for the production company?"

"Huh? No. Because—like you say—I may have seen the killer. What if he thinks he has to snuff me now?"

Snuff you? You've been watching too much HBO, my girl. She looked Pauline up and down. *But given what's happened, I can't dismiss it out of hand.* "Don't worry. We'll take care of you. Maybe Edna Mae will let you stay on there until we solve the case."

She drew back in horror. "I knew you didn't like me; I didn't think you *hated* me!"

"I don't hate you, Pauline." *Now that I know you're not after Jasper.* "But just in case, maybe you shouldn't go back to your apartment."

She threw up her arms. "Easy for you to say. Where *can* I go? I can't afford a hotel." She looked over her shoulder at the police station. "Maybe the sheriff will let me bunk in the jail."

Oh, for heaven's sake. Enough with the histrionics. Cassidy weighed her options. "All right, why don't you"—*I can't believe I'm saying this*—"stay with me in Amity? We can get some clothes at your place, and you can park in the guest room."

Her face wreathed in relief, Pauline didn't give Cassidy a chance to retract it. "Done. Oh, I feel so much better! Thank you, thank you." She pulled out her phone. "I'd better let Jasper know I'm free and can go back to work."

Cassidy put a restraining hand on her arm. "I think Ollie's the one you should inform."

"But—oh, okay." When she got off the phone, her face had reverted to pessimism. "Ollie says they don't need me until tomorrow." She looked about to cry. "I need the money—they only pay me for the days I work."

"What about Nemo's?"

"I don't want to drive to Camden." She glanced furtively around her.

I know I'm going to regret this. "Tell you what, I'll put you to work here this afternoon. Ten bucks an hour."

"That would be swell!" Pauline leaned forward as though she were about to kiss Cassidy, who scooted out of the way just in time. "What do you need me to do?"

It turned out that the alphabet was not one of Pauline's strong suits, so shelving books was out of the question. Cassidy had her emptying boxes and breaking them down for the few hours left. Then they drove to Pauline's apartment to pack some stuff, returning to Amity as the sun set behind the hill.

They were sitting on the deck sipping wine when Cassidy had a flash of intuition. "You remember when Jasper offered you the job?"

She nodded vigorously. "Bless him!"

"He had seen you before—at Nemo's. He and I were there a couple of weeks earlier. Sally Crook—the woman you replaced—was with us. We were talking about Ahearn's death, and I noticed you seemed nervous. I chalked it up to the normal discomfort when people talk about murder. But then, when he hired you, you told us you lived in Knightston." She watched Pauline carefully. "A couple of nights later we were driving back to Amity from Camden and saw your car. You passed right through Knightston and took the turn at Saturday Cove. You were going to your apartment on Coast Road, weren't you?"

"Yes."

"Why did you lie? Were you afraid we'd connect you to the murder?"

"Uh-huh. After all, I thought I'd killed him. Since the house is right across from Kelly's Cove, I didn't want anyone placing me so close to the scene of the crime."

"You must have been even more worried when Mrs. Roybal told you the police had confiscated the rowboat."

"I was petrified, but then no one came back or said anything, so I began to relax."

Cassidy refilled her glass. "That is, until I came into Nemo's with my friends last week. I saw you sneak out. Was it the talk about the shooting that freaked you out?"

"At first. I'd been doing PR work up the coast and hadn't heard anything about Miss de Montville, but then you mentioned Rick and the wetsuit. I knew he couldn't have rented it. That meant someone else had figured out what I'd done. You know, like maybe Rick had a brother or something. Maybe he was going after other people—like Miss de Montville—so when he offed me no one would notice."

"You mean, the police would be flummoxed by the string of murders and you—the real victim—would get lost in the shuffle?"

"Yeah, something like that."

Definitely way too much HBO. "You know, it could merely have been someone who found his wallet and used the credit card."

She looked relieved. "You think so?"

Cassidy didn't, actually, but refrained from replying. "So Ollie said he needed you tomorrow. What for?"

A new voice intruded. "We're holding an all-cast and crew meeting tomorrow morning in the canteen. I want everyone there."

"Is that you, Jasper?"

As his head came up over the stairs to behold the two women, he held a hand to his open mouth in feigned shock. "Ollie told me Pauline was seeking refuge under your sympathetic wing. If you're considering a ménage à trois, I must state that I have reservations."

"We're not. Are you here for dinner?"

"Yes."

"Did you bring something?"

"No. Should I have?"

"Well, I've nothing in the larder. Perhaps…" She looked at him through her lashes.

He didn't miss a beat. "I would be honored to escort you both to dinner. Poseidon's?"

They had a congenial dinner, and Jasper left the women at Cassidy's front door with only a few backward glances. "I trust I shall see you both tomorrow? Nine a.m."

****

Eunice Merithew's garden, Thursday, July 27

The clan had gathered by the time Jasper arrived. Cassidy and Pauline had settled on stools behind the principal actors. Flavia, Digby, Artemus, and the two boys, Rory and Teddy, were seated in a semicircle in the center. The crew—gaffers, juicers, cameramen, and grips—hovered on either side, flanked by Stan Lowry and Ollie Hadley. Lyle Korn, the key grip, leaned against the fence, an open-toed boot on one foot.

"You okay to work, Lyle?" Jasper indicated the boot.

"I can get around fine as long as I don't have to stand for a long time." He pointed at the grips huddled together by the coffee urn. "The other guys can do the heavy lifting."

"So nuthin's changed," muttered the grip named Greg.

Stan ran through the schedule for the next week. Then Jasper said, "If the cast will please pull their scripts out, we're going to do a full reading."

Rory started to whine. "Ah, come on. It'll take hours. I'm hungry. It's cold. You're—"

"That's enough, Rory. It'll only take longer if you complain."

Lyle spoke up. "Do you need the whole crew here, Jasper?"

Cassidy knew Jasper wasn't quite sure. Stan gave a slight shake of his head. "I think we only need you here, Lyle, plus props, best boy, and head gaffer. The rest can go start breaking down the Spinney house set."

When they'd gone, Jasper started the session with some stage directions. The actors read their lines with little emotion. Cassidy was getting bored when Flavia spoke up. "Jasper? I have a question."

He rubbed his face to hide the grimace. "Yes, Flavia?"

"I see you deleted the bit about Teddy escaping through the tunnel, but I'd like to make a plea to put it back in. We should be attempting to keep the script as authentic as possible."

"Flavia, you know the official record states that he couldn't free the drummer boy and set out on foot. There's no mention of a tunnel."

Cassidy added, "He also said the drummer boy was alive when he found him."

"Yes, but I maintain that the cabin boy covered up the truth. If, instead of a conventional ending, we blew the audience away with a sensational denouement, it would create great box office appeal." Flavia tapped a beringed finger on the chair's arm. "I so wish we still had those letters."

"Even *with* them, there's no proof that the cabin boy's testimony is false." Jasper's voice sounded firm, but his eyes were doubtful.

Cassidy remembered something else. "Miss de

378

Montville—"

"Please, child. Flavia."

"Flavia." Cassidy fought back the blush. "Didn't one of the notes say something about 'Mercy's secret?' Could that have anything to do with the cabin boy?"

"I'd forgotten about that. Maybe." Flavia rose. "It also said she would ship a chest back to Westport. I wonder…"

"You wonder if Mercy's secret is inside it."

Chapter Forty

Canteen, Thursday, July 27

The actress picked up her bag. "We must go back to Westport. I—"

"Hey!" Artemus was standing in the middle of the circle. "What the hell is going on?"

Cassidy gasped. "Oh, my. Mr. North hasn't heard about any of this?"

Flavia took a step toward the road. "It doesn't matter. We don't have time to explain now. Where's that grip? He can drive us—"

"Wait a minute." Jasper cut her off. "Mrs. Spinney's house. Remember the night I went to check on a noise in the garret and someone hit me on the head?"

"Or you knocked your unnaturally large head on the window frame." Cassidy couldn't help it.

"Never mind that," he said impatiently. "The point is—there was a chest in one of the rooms."

Cassidy's hand flew to her mouth. "Chest! Of course! Mrs. Spinney told me she'd shipped some things here from her house in Canada. Books, pictures, some lamps. And a chest."

In a body, Cassidy, Jasper, and Flavia started down the hill, leaving Artemus with his mouth hanging open.

Digby called, "Shall we continue the reading?

380

We're coming to my big prebattle warm-up speech."

"Sure. We'll be right back."

The three passed the crews working in the darkened living room and climbed the narrow stairs to the third floor. They moved single-file down the hall looking in doorways.

"Here it is." Jasper led the way into a low-ceilinged room. A large wooden chest, leather straps encircling it, stood under the dormer window.

"See there?" Flavia sounded awed. On the lid of the chest was a tarnished brass monogram. "The initials M and S." She gazed at Cassidy. "Mercy Spinney."

"Let me see if I can open it." Jasper unhooked the leather belts and pried the top up with some effort. He stood back, hands on hips, panting. "Empty."

Cassidy bent over and examined the interior. "No, it's not. There's a scrap of paper stuck in the bottom." She wiggled it loose.

Flavia took it from her. "I think it's the same stationery as the letters we found in Westport. I remember the light blue color. Unusual for the period." She read. "This must be the part that was torn off." She looked up. "But how on earth did it get *here*?"

"Where exactly did you find them in the Nova Scotia house?"

Flavia thought. "They were in the back of a rolltop desk…but they were in envelopes."

"Were the envelopes new or old?"

"Old…ish. Yellowed."

"*Hmm*." Cassidy thought. "They must have been in the chest, and Mercy removed them at one point—"

Jasper stopped her. "The envelopes weren't torn, though. This fragment must belong to a different letter."

Flavia pouted. "Is it important? The two women probably had a copious correspondence."

"But—"

Cassidy interrupted. "In one of Flavia's letters, Mercy's cousin Sarah said she was going to send a chest on to Mercy in Nova Scotia."

"This chest?"

"It's got her initials. This must be the one she meant."

"That's right." Flavia agreed. "I remember she said she was 'sending it back.' That means it belonged to Mercy."

"Sarah lived somewhere in Castine."

"Dyce Head."

The others turned to Flavia, jaws slack. "What did you say?"

She seemed puzzled. "Dyce Head. The house Mercy's cousin lived in."

"Dyce Head belonged to the *Spinney family*?"

"Yes. I'm sorry, I assumed you knew. It was commandeered by the British when they were building Fort George, but after General McLean was recalled, the Spinneys reoccupied it."

Jasper looked stricken. "When…how…did you learn this?"

Flavia pressed her lips together. "When we were in Nova Scotia. Isn't that why you rented the house?"

He shook his head. "Serendipity. We only knew Mercy and the cabin boy had parted in Castine. Sally chose the Dyce Head house because it was available for rent and well situated for the commandant's headquarters."

Cassidy pointed at the paper in Flavia's hand.

"What does the fragment say?"

Flavia flattened it on top of the chest. "-s-u-r-e—that must be the rest of the word 'treasure.' " She looked up, triumph in her eyes. "This is part of the same letter, Jasper."

"Okay, Okay. We'll operate on that theory for now. Is there any more?"

She read. "There's a smudged bit, then 'Safely arrived in Westport. No one need know about the boy.' "

"Know what about the boy?"

"That she had saved him?"

"Or sent him home?"

Jasper mulled it over. "*Or*…that he knew where the treasure was."

"If he knew, why didn't he have it?" Cassidy felt oddly cross. *There doesn't seem to be a clear path through this murk.*

By contrast, Jasper grew steadily more assured. "He had no chance to retrieve it. When he escaped, the battle was still raging. If he tried to dig it up, he would have been caught. Then he got lost."

"What about when Mercy accompanied him back to Castine? They would have stayed in the Dyce Head house, wouldn't they?" Flavia gazed hopefully at Jasper.

"Depends. Had the British decamped yet?" Cassidy wished she had spent more time studying her local history. It galled her to depend on a California native to elaborate.

"Yes. At least from the fort. British soldiers were still billeted in town, but the contingent from the fort had returned to Canada. In the movie, Digby—General

McLean—had failed to arrest the boy in Canada and is on his way back to Castine to try again."

"But that's fiction. What really happened?"

There was a short silence, then Flavia spoke. "Mercy would have immediately bundled him off to Boston to escape the clutches of the English soldiers." Her tone was unequivocal. "He never had time."

Cassidy examined Jasper's expression. "You think the treasure's still in Castine?"

"In Dyce Head. Yes. Where it's been all along."

"Shall we?"

"I think so, yes."

They trooped down the stairs and up the hill to the canteen. They could hear the Toff's resonant baritone droning on.

"Director, stage left. Cut, Diggs." Artemus seemed relieved to have an excuse to force his brother to desist. He spread his legs and, palms up, held the little group at bay. "I insist you give us an explanation. What is going on?"

Jasper gulped. He looked from Flavia to Cassidy. Both women shook their heads. "Later. Why don't you all carry on? We'll be back anon."

"Anon?" Digby's voice trembled. "But I need you to hear my lines. It's important that I capture the commandant's worldview—his…er…*Weltanschauung*. As it were."

"Really, Digby?" Artemus sniffed. "This is a read-through. Save your theatrics for the camera."

Flavia plumped down on a camp chair. "I'd better stay here and chaperone. Let me know what happens."

"Are you sure?" Cassidy couldn't believe it. *How could she possibly miss out on what could be an extraordinary discovery?* "This is your adventure too."

The actress folded her hands in her lap. "I'm too old to be gallivanting around like some female buccaneer. I shall keep the troops in reserve in case you need backup."

Cassidy refrained from pointing out that she had been gung ho to drive all the way to Canada only a few minutes ago. Jasper took her hand. "I know better than to argue with a diva. We'll keep in touch."

Flavia gave a regal nod and turned to the actors. "Now, Digby, you were giving the commandant's exhortation to the troops as they prepared for battle, I believe."

"No, he wasn't. He was whining about the upstart American captain who was lobbing insults at the Brits." Artemus held up his script and began to shout. "Friends, Romans, Redcoats—lend me your ears!"

"Artie, will you shut up?"

"Now, Digby…"

Jasper and Cassidy left Flavia to soothe the ruffled feathers and headed to Cassidy's car. Pauline caught up to them. "Hey, if Miss de Montville isn't coming, do you have room for me?"

"You don't know where we're going."

"Doesn't matter." She looked over her shoulder. "I can't take five more minutes of that."

"We're going to Castine."

"Really? Why?"

"To look for treasure."

She jumped in the back seat. "I'm in."

Jasper shrugged. "Okay by me."

They took off, Jasper driving fast enough to earn a glare and a shout from Bobby B. Goode, who was walking his Great Dane. No one spoke on the way to Castine.

When they reached the town, Jasper said, "Should we notify the police?"

"Of what?"

"Er…that we may have found a clue to a hoard of treasure?"

"Are you crazy?"

Pauline chirped from the back seat. "Uh, guys? Anyone want to tell me which treasure we're talking about?"

Jasper began to explain. "The British had imported a load of gold bullion with which they intended to bribe the Indians. No one knows what happened to it, but the legend persists that it was stolen by the drummer boy."

Cassidy added, "Who hid it somewhere before he was caught and court-martialed."

"Whew." Pauline's voice thrummed like the wings of a jittery bird. "So the old stories are true? I've been hearing about the gold since I was a little girl, but I don't remember a drummer boy." She bounced on the seat. "And you have a clue where it's buried?"

"Well, we think so." Cassidy hesitated to state out loud what they'd guessed. "Let's just go straight to Dyce Head. At the very least, I want to see if the tunnel is still closed."

"Why?"

"Because if it's clear, someone has been using it regularly."

"And that someone is looking for—"

"Treasure," said Pauline with satisfaction.

Chapter Forty-One

Dyce Head, Thursday, July 27

The gravel parking lot was empty. Cassidy felt a twinge of relief. The last thing she wanted to see was another car. *Especially a red SUV.*

"So…where do we start looking?"

"Let's leave the tunnel till last." She suppressed the shiver. *Not a pleasant memory.*

"All right, we'll start with the house. I'll take the living room. Pauline, you take the kitchen—and watch out for the trapdoor. Cassidy, you search upstairs."

They met in the living room half an hour later. Jasper wiped a perspiring forehead. "Hot as the dickens in here." He plopped down on an armchair. "This is nuts. We don't even know what we're looking for."

"A million dollars' worth of gold?" Pauline said brightly.

"Ha-ha."

Cassidy fanned her face. "It *is* in the historical record, is it not?"

Pauline answered. "Has to be. I've heard the tale all my life."

"A million dollars' worth of gold bars would make a pretty big pile."

"Then it's not in the house. We've checked every room."

Jasper went to the front window and looked out. "We're forgetting something. The Deckers."

"The owners? They're in Florida."

He turned around. "Maybe they already found the gold and it's resting comfortably in their mansion in Boca Raton as we speak."

Cassidy thought this over. "No. For one thing, the leasing office said they owned a double-wide in Sun City. For another, they wouldn't still be living in a dinky house like this."

"All right." Pauline got up. "Let's keep looking. How about the lighthouse?"

"Not enough space there either, but..." Jasper furrowed his brow. "Maybe we should be looking for a clue instead of the actual bullion."

"Wait—the letters in Nova Scotia. If they were in the trunk, and it went from Castine to Westport to Amity, maybe there's some evidence of its sojourn here."

"Like what? Dust motes? A faded square on the floorboards?"

Cassidy had not quite formulated her snarky retort when Pauline took Jasper's place at the window. "We could see the entire surrounding country from the top of the lighthouse."

Jasper perked up. "That's right, we can. It could be buried on the grounds."

Cassidy was enthusiastic. "That whole area in front and to the west is empty. Worth a try."

They followed the breezeway to the lighthouse and climbed the circular stairs. A hatch led to the lantern fixture proper. Circling the tower on the outside was a small catwalk protected by an iron railing, presumably to allow repairs. The great lamp took up most of the room. They shouldered into the narrow open area and spread out. Pauline shaded her eyes. "There's a barn over in that field. No house nearby. Maybe it's abandoned."

"A good prospect."

"And over there—a big mound covered with weeds." She turned to the others. "Could be a cave."

"Or the septic pond." Pauline frowned at Jasper's frivolous tone.

Cassidy put her elbows on the windowsill and surveyed the bay. She said slowly, "You know what I'm beginning to think? We've been wrong all along. None of the incidents has anything to do with the movie."

"That's crazy." Jasper paused. "But for the sake of argument, let's hear your proposition."

"Well, first off, in Amity, there were the events at the Spinney house, and then the attack on Flavia. And here at Dyce Head—the shots, locking me in the cellar, Flint's murder. Someone could be trying to scare us off." She looked at Jasper beside her. "Someone else is after the treasure. We should be careful."

"Indeed you should." They spun around. Bill Trent stood on top of the trapdoor, a gun pointed at Jasper's head. "At least I got to the letters before you bozos did. But why the hell you insisted on hanging around I'll never know."

Jasper grabbed Cassidy and pushed her behind him. "What do you want?"

"Want? I want to know where the treasure is. Duh."

"But we—" Cassidy felt a sharp elbow in her ribs.

Jasper said, his voice tense, "What makes you think we know?"

"I saw you roaring out of Amity, the three of you. You must have found something in the house. Something I missed." He pointed at Jasper. "You slipped a scrap of paper in your pocket just now. Is it a map? Where did you find it?"

"In the bottom of the chest."

"Bottom of the—? Oh, so *that's* what happened. The envelope wasn't torn, so when Flavia told me part of the letter was missing, I was stumped."

Jasper drew in his breath. "That's because they weren't originally in envelopes, were they?"

Trent cocked his head. "Bingo."

Jasper explained to the women. "The envelopes didn't match the stationery."

Yellow. Not yellowed. Cassidy said, "We assumed the cousin had put the letters in envelopes to protect them."

"Wrong. I did. I'd found them the night Mr. Toff-Smythe arrived. When I heard him screeching, I tossed them back in and split. Once he left the house, I thought I'd be free to go back and remove them. But no…"

"It was you! You were the one in the attic."

"I thought the coast was clear after I got rid of the Toff, and then *you* showed up. Had to do something a little more drastic than the groans and pinging sounds that worked on him."

"So you hit me."

"A mere tap. You went over like a bowling pin. It wasn't my fault you almost fell out the window."

Jasper shook his head. "Now I think about it, the fact that the rolling ladder was right by the house should have been a giveaway. The other crew members were in Penhallow, and most of the equipment was stored. You probably used it to climb up to the third story."

He wrinkled his nose. "When that prick Phalen showed up and trundled the ladder around the side of the house, I was sure someone would pick up on that."

"Prick? You mean the grip who saved Jasper?" Cassidy had a horrible thought. "Is he in it with you?"

"Nah. He was skulking around. Has a rep for sticky fingers. Should've reported him to Stan."

The conversation seemed to be drifting into irrelevant waters. Jasper brought it back. "You were still in the house when all hell broke loose, weren't you?"

"You're smarter than you look."

Cassidy restrained Jasper. "You grabbed the letters, but you were in a hurry and didn't realize that part of one had caught on a splinter in the bottom of the chest."

"Right." He spat. "Ruined everything."

"How?" Pauline was staring intently at Trent. "What was your plan?"

"To take them with me to Westport and pretend to find them."

"Ah, I see." Jasper nodded expansively. "The wording made it sound as though the treasure was in Westport. It would direct everyone's attention to Nova Scotia and away from Castine."

Trent closed his mouth with a snap. "Doesn't matter now. Letters are moot. You're trying to get me off track, aren't you?" When no one answered, he continued to speculate. "It's here in Castine. Has to be. I searched the house and grounds in Westport. I searched the Amity house—everywhere mentioned in the letters."

"Letters? Flavia's letter only mentioned the treasure in passing."

"Yeah, that one did, but there was a whole slew of 'em between Mercy and her cousin in the chest, talking about the cabin boy and the British occupation. I kept most of them and took the two I could use as a decoy to Westport."

Jasper said, his tone a bit too impertinent for Cassidy's comfort, "It must have really aggravated you to have us constantly underfoot."

"Too right. The last thing I wanted was for you to find the trapdoor. At least I made sure you didn't get far."

"You turned the light off and closed the hatch."

"And when none of you said anything about a tunnel, I concluded that you hadn't found it. Bad luck you saved that Fiddick kid. If he'd died from exposure, I could've kept it a secret." He didn't seem to notice the general shiver of revulsion that filled the room. "Boy, did it give me a turn when you told me you knew the passage went to Fort George. And then Flavia adds it to the script, so everyone and his brother now knows about the tunnel."

"But I had it taken out."

"Doesn't matter. The damage was done. That damned Lyle and his cronies had the bit in their teeth. The tunnel would've been scraped clean by the next day."

Cassidy was curious. "How did *you* find out about the tunnel, anyway?"

"From the letters. The cabin boy used it to hide

from his pursuers."

"That wasn't the account Israel Trask gave the Massachusetts pension board."

"No, but he told the truth to Mercy Spinney."

Jasper prodded. "So what did the boy tell her?"

"When the *Black Prince* caught fire, he jumped off and swam to shore. He had reached the battlements when he heard Catchpole—that's the drummer boy— calling from the brig. The boy told him about the tunnel." Trent stopped and shook his head in admiration. "Evidently the kid had been using it to steal stuff from the house. My kinda Charlie."

"So, he hears the drummer boy calling. What happened then?" Cassidy guessed Jasper was trying to keep Trent talking while he scouted for a means of escape. Her eyes drifted to the outside railing.

"Brits were all stationed at the fort by then, so the house was deserted. Trask found the trapdoor and the tunnel, went down it and cleared the rubble away. Little Catchpole was shackled to the floor. The boy confided in him about the gold, hoping that Trask would help him escape. Trask said he had to go back to get something to break the shackles off. Instead, he walled him up again."

"Leaving Horace Catchpole to die." A lump rose in Cassidy's throat. *Poor little mite.* For an instant she pictured Rory, shivering and scared, behind the same bars. *If we get out of here alive, I'm going to make it up to him—buy him, what? A copy of* Penthouse*?*

Pauline had been studying Trent during the conversation. "Wait a minute...The cabin boy. What did you say his name was, Jasper?"

"Trask. Israel Trask. Why?"

She held her hands up to frame the gunman's face. Trent bared his teeth in a malignant smile. "Took you long enough."

"It's *you*. You're Rick's friend. That's why you look familiar. You're Izzy—his high school buddy—aren't you? You were in the bar with that other grip that…that night." She dropped her hands, her eyes like saucers. "*You* murdered him, didn't you?"

"Right on all counts. You're smarter than you look, too." He sneered at Jasper.

Cassidy was getting muddled. "If I've got the timeline right, you killed Ahearn *before* you discovered the chest and letters. What for?"

Pauline had the answer. "Because Rick was going to recommend Mrs. Spinney's house to Black Brothers. Izzy didn't want the movie people crawling all over it until he had a chance to scope it out."

Trent shook the gun at her. "Who's telling this story? Shut up." When she shrank back, he resumed more calmly. "When I was growing up, my father loved to tell the tale of our ancestor, the brave cabin boy, and his savior Mercy Spinney. He even named me after him. He used to drop heavy hints about a buried treasure that the boy had left behind. When I finally got the chance, I did some homework. Followed the Spinney wagon trail from Westport to Castine to Amity Landing. I'd gone to Camden to Spinney's rental agency, hoping to lease the house so I could search it at my leisure. And what happens but I run across my old high school buddy Rick in Nemo's. Turns out he was going to recommend her house for the movie. Fool hadn't contacted Sally yet, but I knew I only had a tiny sliver of time to stop him."

Cassidy said suddenly, "He *had* contacted her though. She knew about the house when she got here. I showed it to her."

Pauline nodded. "He made a call while we were at my house."

"Well, that explains why I couldn't persuade her to look in Camden. Damn."

Pauline stirred. "You followed us, didn't you? From Nemo's. You must have seen Rick fall."

"Yeah. Couldn't believe my luck. Watched you row him out and dump him. Figured you'd taken care of my problem for me, and I'd have free rein to pursue my goal."

"I don't understand." Cassidy spoke over Pauline's intake of breath. "Why didn't you just drive away then?"

"Because Pauline didn't finish the job, the dumb bitch. I saw Ahearn surface while she was rowing to shore. Had to make sure he didn't make it back to land, so I waited till she'd gone in her house, then went down and took the dinghy out." He shook an admonitory finger at Pauline. "You're lucky I happened by—you'd forgotten to tie it up and the tide was coming in. Would've floated off to sea if I hadn't secured it when I got back."

That's right. Pauline checked the next morning to make sure the boat was still there. "So then what happened?"

"I intended to hold his head under water until he drowned, but he'd already managed to swim to that floating dock."

"Mussel farm."

"Whatever." Trent ground his teeth. "Just like in

high school—Ahearn always cramping my style."

"You rowed to the barge and stabbed him."

"He was lying there, only semiconscious. Never saw it coming." He smiled in satisfaction. "Took care of business, I did."

Jasper spoke for the first time. "And then you drove his SUV off."

"What did you do with your own car?"

"I hadn't wanted to risk someone seeing me in the area, so I left the Prius in a garage in Camden. Hot-wired an old Jeep parked in some hick's front yard. Stashed it in the woods before I"—he snickered— "*acquired* Ahearn's Ford. Jeep was gone the next day…who says Maine isn't full of thieves?"

Jasper harrumphed. "I don't understand. Why not leave the SUV there? Wouldn't that have led the police directly to Pauline?"

Trent leveled a sympathetic gaze at Cassidy. "Your boyfriend's one stripe short of a barber pole, isn't he? Good thing he's not trying to commit a crime. No, you moron, the longer Ahearn remained unidentified, the better, and I knew Pauline was sure not going to tell anybody about her little tête-à-tête with him."

Cassidy nudged Pauline. "How come you didn't recognize him before?"

Trent answered for her. "She never saw me. I avoided her when she was on the set. Wasn't difficult— she was hardly ever there. Slacker."

Jasper had been mumbling to himself. Cassidy was about to shush him when he raised his voice. "Did you say the cabin boy was your ancestor?"

Trent grinned. "Ayuh, as they say Downeast."

Jasper pointed a finger at him. "Pauline called you

Izzy. As in Israel."

"Israel William Trask, at your service." The man had the effrontery to preen. "He was a phenomenal kid—found his way alone over two hundred miles." He frowned. "Unfortunately, without the treasure. Probably shouldn't have abandoned the other boy."

"But…the public record says Trask couldn't free him. How did you learn the truth?"

"His diary. He wrote down everything he'd confessed to Mercy Spinney in it."

Jasper nodded. "When I was doing research for the movie, I found the petition for pension, but there was also mention of a diary." He glared at Trask. "It was stolen from the Gloucester public library."

Trask was unfazed. "Hey! It's a family heirloom. The *library* stole it from *me*."

"Did the diary contain the whole story?"

"Most of it. He wrote about the drummer boy and Izzy's failed attempt to find the loot. Mercy's letters told the rest."

Cassidy was almost afraid to ask. "Why did you kill Mr. Flint?"

Trask reddened. "Gawd, what an interfering old goat! I was digging along the tunnel wall, and he heard me. Came in through the gate. Had a real fit. Said he was going to call the police."

Jasper was baffled. "If he came in through the gate, how did the key end up in his pocket?"

"Easy. He left the key in the lock. I closed the door and gave it a turn, then stuck the key back in his pocket."

Pauline stifled a sob. "I don't see why you had to kill him. If he'd reported you, all the police would have done is charge you with vandalism."

His lip curled in disgust. "I take it back. You're not much in the brains department after all, are you, sweet pea? Even if they didn't arrest me, everyone would learn of the tunnel. Those grips would have ransacked the place, and I hadn't finished with it. I had to get him out of the way."

"Mr. Flint was an innocent, nice man. And you— you're a monster!" Cassidy's voice shook.

"Aw, thanks. Nice to know the family genes are intact." Trask trained the gun on her. "Now, you three. Move closer together." When they had shuffled toward each other, Jasper pushed the two women slightly in front of him.

"If you think the ladies will shield you, think again," Trask jeered. "Lily-livered coward. Typical West Coastie."

Jasper didn't answer.

Cassidy said timidly, "Now what?"

"I gotta hand it to you. You were so predictable. Knew you'd start with the house before you tackled the lighthouse." His eyes swept the tight space. "This is a perfect spot to hold people hostage. Too narrow for more than one of you to come around the light at a time. It'll be like shooting fish in a barrel. I'm sure clever, aren't I?"

Jasper said, "If you shoot us, you'll never find the gold."

Chapter Forty-Two

Dyce Head, Thursday, July 27

Cassidy opened her mouth, but quickly closed it again. *Jasper wants Trask to believe we know where the treasure is. To give us time? What for? No one knows we're here. We're walking dead.* She tried to shut off the paralyzing thoughts. *Jasper's taking the wrong tack. We need something else…Questions…Yes, questions will keep Trask off balance.* "And what about Sally? She wasn't involved in any of this. Why kill her?"

For the first time, Trask seemed rattled. "Bad luck there. Kid I hired was an imbecile. It was his fault. He was *supposed* to give one of the lobsters to Jasper, and one to someone at another table. You know, so the illnesses would be chalked up to bad restaurant practices. Since the victims were random, there'd be no incentive to tie them to the movie."

"Are you saying you wanted to kill *Jasper*? Why? He wasn't interfering, was he?"

He shook his head. "No. I only meant to incapacitate him for awhile. I didn't realize dead lobsters could be lethal. Just thought it'd give him a touch of food poisoning. With him out of commission, work on the movie would be suspended, and I'd have more time to sniff around."

Cassidy asked, "Was it you who pulled the lobsters

from the dumpster?"

"Yup. Fished 'em out Monday night and plopped 'em in a big pot of water. Told the kid they were special orders. All he had to do was carry the pot into the kitchen and heat it up, then bring the lobsters out—one to MacEwan and one to some other customer." He frowned. "How was I to know he and Sally were the only ones who would order two-pounders?"

Behind Cassidy, Jasper whispered, "You were right. She was collateral damage after all."

We can't dwell on that now. "I presume you were the one who sent the other grips off on that wild goose chase to the fort as well."

"Too easy. What's that called? Reverse psychology. Just told them there was no way the gold would be there." He rolled his eyes. "Kept 'em focused on the fort so they never even thought of the house."

Hmm. "So...you'd successfully distracted the treasure hunters, leaving the most promising site unattended. What made you move on from Castine to Nova Scotia?"

"Good question." He gave Cassidy a little thumbs-up. "Lucky I happened along when I did—heard the duchess making her demands and snatched the gig. Obviously I wasn't finished here, but I couldn't pass up the opportunity to go with Flavia. There was bound to be more correspondence there, or at least some hint of where Catchpole stashed the gold."

"That's when you planted the two letters in Westport." Cassidy was beginning to see the picture. *Every move he made was intended to clear the field for his quest.*

"Of course. It's what they call a 'red herring.'

Those damned grips were sniffing around. Only a matter of time before they turned to the house. Tried to put them off, but that Lyle has a nose for gold. Bill too."

Pauline burst out, "Lyle's toe. He broke it in one of the holes the grips were leaving around Castine." She glared at him accusingly. "He had to break off our date."

"Oh, sorry, lady. Didn't know you two were an item."

Neither did I. Cassidy entertained a brief splash of euphoria before the sight of the revolver reminded her of their predicament.

"Yeah, he tripped over his own dirt pile, the schmuck. Should've been looking where he was going. Of course, it didn't help that his flashlight had somehow been knocked out of his hand." Trask smirked. "I figured the letters would imply the bullion was in Nova Scotia and they'd lay off."

Jasper's voice was muffled. "I don't understand. If you wanted to use the letters as a decoy, why shoot Flavia when she was just about to show them to us?"

He grunted. "When I found out the part about Westport was torn off, I knew the ploy wouldn't work. I had to get those letters back. Saw her nip them when she thought I wasn't looking. Knew she wouldn't be able to resist showing 'em to Jasper. Started to panic, but then I thought to myself, "Izzy, my lad, is there a way to turn her dirty trick to your advantage?" And there it was. Just when I needed it, Li'l Artie North hops along asking for help with his usual antics. Gave me the perfect setup."

"The gun."

Trask snorted. "I told the little reptile the prop gun wouldn't work, but he kept stuffing powder and balls down the muzzle and pulling the trigger. Dumb git. Wouldn't know a twelve-gauge from a water pistol. The clerk had seen me bring it to him, so he didn't blink an eye when I walked out with it. Then, after I shot Flavia, I dropped the blunderbuss in the water and swam around the point."

Jasper muttered, "I thought you just said the gun didn't work?"

His eyes lit up. "That one didn't."

He thinks he's cute. My God. Mad as a meatball.

"I knew the police would find the blunderbuss and all eyes would focus on the slime bucket who's always stealing Mr. Toff-Smythe's thunder." He spat. "North doesn't deserve to be on the same planet as the greatest living actor in the world." He broke off, panting slightly.

Oh my God—who'da thunk it? He actually idolizes the Toff!

Trask made a visible effort to pull himself together. His gaze moved from Cassidy to Pauline. "And now it's time to tell me."

"Tell you what?"

"What you discovered. You guys were all excited. You've gotta have an inkling where the treasure is." He shifted the gun to Cassidy. "So give."

Cassidy stepped back to put whatever distance she could between herself and the shiny black barrel and discovered that Jasper was no longer behind her. She kept her eyes on Trask, hoping—irrationally she knew—that he wouldn't notice Jasper's absence. A creak sounded in the stillness. Trask shoved the women aside. Cassidy followed his gaze. Jasper had managed to open the door to the tiny catwalk and scramble out on it.

Trask guffawed. "Idiot. What's he going to do now? Jump? It's a thirty-foot drop. Might as well leave him there." He grabbed Cassidy's arm and swung her around, pressing the gun to the small of her back. "You, Pauline, start down the stairs first, and no funny business or this one gets it."

"What about Jasper?"

"Good point. Hang on." Clutching Cassidy's arm, he turned the lock on the door. "He can sit out there till the cows come home. No one to hear him for miles. Come on."

When they were halfway through the breezeway to the house, they heard what sounded to Cassidy like a bull horn. "Did someone just call your name?"

Trask hesitated. "I—"

"Israel Trask, this is the police. Come out with your hands up."

This time Trask heard it. He began to push the two women ahead of him. "Quick. Quick. If we hurry, we can beat them to the cellar."

"But…" Cassidy hated to interrupt. She sensed Trask was desperate. *He might just shoot us and get on with it.* On the other hand, if they were trapped underground, he'd shoot them anyway. "The passage is closed. We'll have to find another way out."

"Not anymore."

They had reached the house when Pauline halted. "Wait a minute. The police yelled the name Israel Trask. Everyone knows you as Bill Trent. As far as they're concerned, isn't Israel Trask just a character in the movie?"

"You're insinuating they're not actual cops? Like, they're just some extras rehearsing?" Trask scratched his chin. "Might be worth a try...Nah. Too much of a risk." He held up the pistol. "How would I explain this?"

He opened the door to the kitchen. As the two women halted, he grabbed Cassidy with his left hand, raised the gun with his right, and struck Pauline a sharp blow to the temple with the butt. She toppled over. Cassidy gasped. "You killed her too! What are you thinking? The police are right outside. You'll never get away with this."

For answer, he shoved her across the floor toward the trapdoor. He dropped a sinewy hand on her shoulder, forcing her to her knees. "Open it."

She scrabbled along the edge, finally slipping her fingers under the lid and raising it. Trask pushed her down a step. She reached for the light, but he batted her hand away. "No reason for them to know we're down here." He closed the trapdoor over their heads.

She stumbled down the stairs, Trent's hot breath on her neck. Feeling her way around the walls, she found the entrance to the tunnel. When she hesitated, he growled, "Keep moving."

She ducked and began to worm her way through. "How are you going to escape? The gate at the other end is locked."

"Never you mind."

Is he going to shoot me here and jam the entrance with my body? Ulp. They kept going. "The police are aware of the tunnel, you know. They're probably waiting for us at the fort."

"We're not going to the end."

"Huh? Where are we going then?"

"Not far. There's an adit we can wiggle through."

"Adit?"

"Secondary mine shaft. For drainage. Opens on the other side of the road."

A side entrance? Suddenly an idea came to her—a wonderful, marvelous, miraculous idea. "Why, that must be where…" She paused.

She heard him catch his breath. "Where *what*?"

When she didn't answer, he shook her. She heard something skitter away in the dark. *A rat?* She shuddered.

"The treasure. It's there, isn't it? I knew it! I knew you were on the right track." He pushed her aside and turned on a flashlight. "I only just found this passage and haven't had a chance to explore it yet. You take that side, and I'll take this one. It must be in a niche or something."

The adit was larger than the tunnel, and she could stand upright. She dutifully pretended to search, all the while dropping behind little by little. Trask was so absorbed in his task he didn't notice. She stumbled over something. Bending down, she felt around on the dirt floor. Her hand touched cold, hard metal. *The gun. That's what the skittering noise was.* Trask must have dropped it when he shook her. She picked it up and pointed it in his general direction. He still didn't turn around. *Maybe I can just steal out and he won't even know I'm gone.* There were advantages to mania. She backed up another step, and another, but when she tried to turn and run she was hindered by something— something soft and warm. She let out a screech.

Trask turned and shone the flashlight on her. "Shut the hell up. I…"

"She can screech all she wants. She has your gun."

Cassidy nearly fainted with relief at the beloved voice. "Jasper! How did you—"

He interrupted her. "Oh, and these fellows have guns too." He stepped aside. Lights flipped on, revealing several large, effective policemen, each with his very own standard issue .45. Currently pointing at Trask.

"Mr. Israel Trask? You're under arrest. Read him his rights, Alfie."

****

Waldo Memorial Hospital, Thursday, July 27

"Will she be all right?"

"Just a bruise. She'll be fine."

"Thank you, Dr. Wilberforce. May we take her home?"

"Sure. Let me sign the papers."

Jasper brought the Lamborghini around, and Cassidy helped Pauline from the wheelchair to the car. Pauline gave her a shy smile. "I get the front seat?"

"Just this once."

They retrieved her clothes from Cassidy's, then drove her to her apartment and got her settled. Jasper said, "Shall we hie to the police station?"

"Not now, Jasper." The exhaustion had just hit and Cassidy couldn't keep her eyes from closing. "Tomorrow."

"As you wish." He took her home, put her to bed, and kissed her forehead. "I'll be in Mrs. Spinney's house. See you in the morning."

She mumbled, "Watch out for Snookie."

"Snookie?

"The ghost dog."

"Ah yes. I shall keep a leash handy."

Chapter Forty-Three

Waldo County jail, Friday, July 28

"So, Toby, why don't you start?" Cassidy, Jasper, and Flavia were gathered in front of the sheriff's desk, with Pauline reclining on a couch in the corner.

Toby said shortly, "Why, thank you, Cassidy. Most gracious of you."

Cassidy looked flustered, but Jasper chuckled. "Could you hold off a minute? I can't hear anything with that racket going on."

Trask was yelling from the cell block next door. "No! I told you, lady, I don't want oatmeal. Or chicken soup. And take this lima bean glop away. It's gross...No! If you're not going to bring me a bottle of whiskey, get the hell out of my face."

There came a furious squeak from Edna Mae. "You watch your language, young man. You're in no position to make demands. Alcohol, indeed." She scuttled past Toby's glass door, the feather in her red cap vibrating angrily.

Jasper leaned across the desk and poured another tot of bourbon into Toby's mug. "You were saying?"

"We were at a dead end with the first murder, so I opted to concentrate on the rash of pranks and incidents we'd been having. They all seemed to start when the movie people came to town."

"Hey!"

"What?" Toby gave Jasper a severe look. "I don't just mean the tattooed gangsters wandering our streets unnerving my wife. There was the haunting of Mr. Toff in Mrs. Spinney's house, and then"—he indicated Jasper—"the attack on you. When the crew member appeared out of nowhere carrying a ladder, it struck me as a touch fortuitous. So we gave the guy a second look."

"It wasn't him," Cassidy put in. "Trask had left the ladder on the other side of the house. His first mistake. All the other equipment had been stored. It shouldn't have been there."

"Right. We learned that later when we interviewed the stage manager, Mr. Lowry. The grip had no good answer to the question—just said he found it sitting there. He remained on the list of suspects."

Jasper raised an eyebrow. "You never considered Trent? I mean, Trask?"

"No, but as the number of events accumulated, we focused more and more on the production staff."

"And Trask had an accident too. Remember?" Cassidy turned to Jasper. "He injured his wrist."

"True." Jasper flicked a doughnut crumb off the desk. "I'll bet he did that to deflect attention."

Toby took another whack at taking charge. "It was the episode with the poisoned lobsters that changed things into a full-fledged investigation. A second person associated with the movie had now died. What had been an uncomfortable feeling grew legs."

"Actually, Trask claims he only meant to make me sick—to slow down work on the movie. He didn't know that dead lobsters can be fatal."

"Really?" Toby pursed his lips. "I assumed, what with everything else he'd done, that it was another murder attempt."

"Due process, due process." Jasper's hearty bellow was not received with the appreciation he probably expected.

Cassidy explained, "He may not have meant to kill anyone, but you should bring in the kid he hired to deliver the lobsters. It can't be Kenny Cross. Kenny would never have gone along with serving spoiled lobsters."

"Oh, I forgot to tell you. You're wrong: it was indeed Kenny. He says a man gave him twenty dollars to heat up a pot with two two-pound lobsters and take it out to the customers. He says the man told him they were special orders. When you asked for two-pounders, he naturally assumed you and Miss Crook were the special orders. He had no idea they weren't fresh."

"Does he know now?"

"No." Toby sighed. "Kenny's never gotten over finding that dead body last year. I didn't want to send him back to the sanitarium so soon. He's only now settling back into his comfort zone."

Cassidy rewarded the sheriff with an understanding smile. "You're a good man, Toby."

"Thanks, Cassidy. So, to continue. Then came the Castine incidents—the shooting at Dyce Head, the boy trapped in the brig, Mr. Flint's murder…"

Cassidy whispered, "Poor Mr. Flint. Trask told us he had threatened to report him to the police."

Jasper added, "There was one more. Trask closed the trapdoor on Cassidy and turned out the light." He looked at her. "He thought he'd kept us from discovering the tunnel but didn't reckon on Rory."

"And don't forget me!" Flavia's face shone. "I must say it was thrilling to be shot with an actual bullet."

Toby acknowledged her with a gruff nod. "I hadn't forgotten about you. That's another mystery we have yet to account for. We know Trask shot Miss de Montville, but what was his motive?"

Cassidy thought she had the answer. "She was about to give us the letters. Trask found them in the chest here and planted them in Nova Scotia. When he learned that the crucial part had been torn off, the part that finished the word 'treasure' and said 'safely arrived in Westport,' he changed his plans."

"What was so crucial about those words?"

"They would have sent all the treasure seekers haring off to Nova Scotia, leading them away from Castine." Jasper nodded sagely.

Toby put his pencil down. "Thus giving him a clear path to hunt for the gold. I see."

Flavia broke the silence. "Yes, that was his original plan, but when I told him the page was missing the last bit, he knew the diversion wouldn't work."

"You told him?" Toby was intrigued.

"Uh-huh. That morning, while we were driving back. He was very angry. It…uh…" She clutched the perfectly matched Akoya pearls at her throat. "It was most disquieting."

"What did he do?"

"He snatched them out of my hand."

"I don't understand. How did you come to have them in your bag the next day, then?"

Flavia glanced quickly at Jasper and then at

Cassidy. She said primly, "I pinched them."

Cassidy nodded. "Trask told us he saw you take them."

Toby picked his pencil up again and tapped it on the desk. "Okay, so Trask now wants the letters back. You're telling me he decided the easiest way was to bump you off?"

Jasper gave a little squeak. "Yes! He'd already killed or tried to kill at least three people—what was one death more? When the ambulance took you away, he swept in and snagged the envelopes from the pavilion."

Cassidy frowned. "Hold on a minute. It's not as though Flavia couldn't tell us what was in them. We didn't actually need the text."

Flavia fidgeted. "He might have"—she blushed—"might have believed I hadn't read them. When he discovered them in the desk, he kept them to himself. He said he wanted to inform the Gloucester museum of our find first."

"Didn't that strike you as odd?"

"Well, a bit. So, as we were starting on the return journey, I finally asked him if I could take a look. He rather grudgingly gave them to me—"

Jasper interjected, "That was for show, I'm sure. At that point he *wanted* everyone to know about the letters."

Flavia took a minute to fasten Jasper with a penetrating glare before resuming. "*But* when I unfolded the paper I saw that the last part had been torn off. I pointed it out, whereupon he grabbed them, scrunched them up, and threw them on the floorboard. He made me promise not to touch them."

"A promise you broke?"

"Of course." The blush faded and a new, determined look washed over her face. "When we stopped for gas, I…er…appropriated the envelopes and hid them in my bag." She tossed her head. "I do not take orders from stagehands."

"Trask would expect you to read them when you got home, and therefore you were marked for death."

"So the little lady from London foiled not just Trask's *original* plot to have the letter divert attention to Nova Scotia, but also his effort to hide it from said attention."

"Well put." Flavia's benevolent smile indicated that Jasper had returned to her good graces. "Although…" She paused, and her pale cheeks flushed again. "I hesitated to disclose this before, but I do indeed fear that William considered me a danger for another reason."

"Besides the letters?"

"Yes."

"Why?"

"Because he thought I knew his true identity."

Jasper rose from his chair. "You *knew* he was Israel Trask?"

"No, I didn't. Well, not right away. I didn't put two and two together until it was too late."

In the hubbub, Toby raised a hand. "Please, Miss de Montville. Explain."

She settled back. "You see, I saw him with the first victim."

"Ahearn? The scout?"

"Yes. I—"

A low sound jerked their attention to the couch.

"Oh my God, that was you! I don't know why I didn't recognize you!" Pauline giggled nervously.

Cassidy turned bewildered eyes on the young woman. "What are you talking about?"

"Miss de Montville. She was in the bar the night I met Rick. Remember, I told you he was drinking with an old friend. He called him 'Izzy'—as in, Israel Trask. Lots of people were gathered around the bar, including a woman who was alone. She—"

"I was enjoying an evening escape from my confinement in the hotel. I hoped to remain incognito, and so I did." This last seemed to vex her slightly. "I overheard the men talking about the Penobscot Expedition and listened in, hoping to garner some insights. Alas, they were not helpful."

Jasper rubbed his chin. "But Trask recognized you. He knew you'd heard Ahearn call him Izzy. He couldn't take the risk that you would connect the dots once you found the letters."

"And so he shot me." The conclusion seemed to buoy her. "After my experience, I do believe I shall be much more convincing in any future suspense roles. Perhaps I should give Helen Mirren a call. She knows about guns…" She trailed off.

Toby broke into the general mood of contentment. "Unfortunately, the aggregation of events made it imperative to remove you entirely."

This didn't seem to frighten Flavia. "I don't believe you've described how he came by the weapon?"

"He went to Artemus North's motel in Searsport and retrieved the blunderbuss he'd brought to him the day before."

Jasper woke up from his reverie. "How did you

know that?"

"The hotel clerk saw a man bring a long, thin package to Mr. North's room Monday, July 17. When he saw him return the next day, he didn't think much of it. That is, until we inquired. Then he remembered: North wasn't in his room for the second visit."

"Yes, but I meant—how did you know it was Trask?"

"The clerk identified him in a photo of the crew." Toby broke off. "I must say, I expected him to choose Bill Phalen, the crew member we were focused on. It kind of blew a hole in my theory."

Flavia stirred. "Phalen?"

"The grip who saved Jasper when he fell through the window."

Cassidy straightened. "He was also with Trask in the Dyce Head house. He fixed the nail."

"Even if he wasn't the ringleader, do you think he was in on it?" Flavia looked at Toby.

Jasper answered for him. "Trask said no."

Pauline spoke up. "Anyway, if he were conspiring with Trask, don't you think Trask would have fingered him when he was arrested?"

"Huh. You're right." Jasper lapsed back into thought.

Cassidy soldiered on. "When was the second visit?"

"Tuesday, July 18."

"The day Flavia was shot."

"So I was pinked by the prop blunderbuss?" Flavia gave a little nervous hiccup.

"No. Turns out the prop is a nonworking replica."

"We knew that." Jasper and Cassidy nodded

sagely.

Toby shifted in his seat. "Ahem. Er…due to a failure to communicate, it took the police a while to winnow out the truth. The State firearms expert had correctly identified the weapon we pulled from the bay, but since he called it a shotgun, I assumed the sabot slug I found at the crime scene would have worked. I recently learned that a blunderbuss takes black powder and minié balls. Not slugs." He gulped down the bourbon. "I should have listened to Squiggy."

Pauline stirred. "Squiggy? Who's he?"

"County crime scene detective."

Flavia had grown even more confused. "If not the blunderbuss, then what did Trask shoot me with?"

"A Remington twenty-gauge semi-automatic shotgun, just as Squiggy stated."

Jasper jumped up. "Wait. Could he have used the same gun on us at Dyce Head?"

"Whoa!" Toby held up a hand. "I'll get to that in a minute. Once we realized our mistake, we expanded the area of interest. Found the real weapon in the dumpster behind the Motel Seven on Route 1."

"You mean behind the motel Artemus had been staying in?"

"Yes. Let me back up. After Trask had nicked the blunderbuss from North on Tuesday, he went to the dive shop and, using the ID he'd stolen from Ahearn, rented the wetsuit."

Rented. Hang on. "Wait. Ahearn was killed June 18, correct?"

"Right."

"And the wetsuit was rented July 18."

"Yes. What's your point, Cassidy?"

"Wouldn't his credit card have been cancelled by then?"

Toby grinned at her. "Might have been. However, the store keeps the card on hold until the renter brings the gear back. No reason to run it through until then."

Jasper gave Cassidy a kindly squeeze as if to say, "It's okay, dear. Financial stuff." Cassidy kicked him. "Ouch!"

Toby huffed. "May I continue?"

"Please do." Cassidy used her most supportive voice.

"Okay. So Trask left his car on Coast Road, took the stairs to the beach in front of Bobby B. Goode's house, swam up to the marina—"

"Shot Flavia and dropped the blunderbuss in the water…Then what?" Jasper bounced up and down on his toes like a beagle hot on the scent.

Toby repossessed the floor with a growl. "Who's telling this anyway? As far as we can tell, after he shot Miss de Montville, he ran up and seized the letters, then swam back the way he'd come."

"I see. But why go all the way back up to Searsport to dump the twenty-gauge?"

Cassidy sucked in a breath. "I know why. When he was holding us hostage, Trask told us he had thrown the blunderbuss into the marina—knowing it would be found—in order to point the finger at Artemus. But say someone realized it didn't work…"

"You think he left the functional firearm in Artemus's vicinity to cement his guilt?"

"Something like that."

Toby clucked his tongue. "Not sure it wasn't overkill—if you'll pardon the expression."

"Why? I mean, what do you mean?"

"At that point, the blunderbuss was our only clue. Mr. North confessed his connection to it the same day we discovered the wetsuit. We might have stopped there, assuming we had the culprit. Since North had actually tried to fire the replica, the ballistics expert found powder residue and assumed it was a working model." He glared at Jasper. "Maybe if *someone* had had the courtesy to mention that the gun was a replica, we would have been spared a lot of confusion."

"Hey, Duffy didn't tell *me* it was a fake either." Jasper looked offended. Cassidy wasn't sure if Toby's reprimand bothered him, or if he were ashamed of his lack of expertise.

"Wait a minute." Pauline sat up. "Like Jasper said, Trask was at Dyce Head on Tuesday. How could he have had time to get all this stuff together and be in the water when Flavia came outside?"

"Ah," Jasper held up an index finger. "Recall, he said he had to get back to Penhallow by five. But when he left it was still early—not even noon."

"Which gave him plenty of time."

Cassidy opened her mouth, but Jasper jumped in. "How did Trask know Flavia would be outside?"

Flavia's blush returned. "It was he who suggested it. He had brought me back from the hotel, and I remarked on how cozy the little pavilion looked. He said, "Why don't you sit out there to go over your script? No sense staying inside in the dark." It seemed such a sweet gesture." She broke off. "He didn't really want to murder me, did he?" She fanned her face. "It seems a trifle extreme."

Jasper started to laugh, but the look on Toby's face

stopped him. "He isn't exactly sane, Flavia."

"I've been thinking." Cassidy wasn't finished with the letter. "The rest of the fragment said, 'No one need know about the boy.' We assumed that meant that the British shouldn't be alerted to Trask, the cabin boy...but it could have meant the drummer boy. Catchpole."

"Mercy's secret?"

Cassidy nodded. "The main part of the letter mentioned a 'shame.' Perhaps she meant it was a shame that Trask had left him to die." Her eyes filled with tears. "It must have been a terrible burden to be forced to keep silent about what the boy had done."

Her statement dropped like wet burlap on the group. To break the mournful silence, Flavia turned to the sheriff. "So it all began to converge on William."

Chapter Forty-Four

Waldo County jail, Friday, July 28

"On William Trask. Yes. I had the lab take swabs of the crew and check them against the third DNA we found in the rowboat. Matched his. Then we revisited the first death and Pauline's statement. The medical examiner said that, while Ahearn didn't die from the fall, he *had* aspirated some seawater."

"He could only have done that if he were unconscious when he hit the water."

Cassidy looked over her shoulder at Pauline. "Meaning he woke up after Pauline dumped him and swam to the platform on his own."

"Correct. The most likely scenario was that someone else saw him out there, rowed out, and finished him off."

"Which is exactly what Trask told us he did."

Pauline made a noise like a cross between a snicker and a cough. "You know, if Trask hadn't been such a neatnik and tied up the rowboat, he might have gotten away with the murder."

Cassidy held a hand to her mouth. "Oh my God, she's right. Pauline forgot to secure it after she'd dumped Ahearn in the water."

"What difference would that have made?"

"The boat would have floated away."

"Along with the DNA evidence."

"So…not so clever after all." Jasper smirked.

Still smarting after Trask insulted you? "But what about the blood in the boat? That was Ahearn's. How did it get there if Trask killed him on the barge?"

Toby patted the back of his head. "From the cut he sustained in the fall. Nothing to do with the stab wound."

"Ooookay." Jasper looked uncomfortable. "We still don't have a convincing motive, though."

"Deterring Black Brothers from utilizing the house in Amity Landing?"

"But Sally already had the information. It was too late to change venues."

"He didn't know that."

"I might have the answer." Pauline stood up but quickly sat down again. "Ooh, my ears are still ringing." She closed her eyes.

Cassidy waited for her to recover. "You were going to say?"

"Rick knew him by his real name. If he came to the set, he would have blown his cover. You would have connected him to the cabin boy and questions would be asked. That's why Trask had to kill him."

"Right. When we took the DNA samples, we got full names of the crew from the employment records. His legal name is—"

"Israel William Trask. He told us."

"A direct descendent of the cabin boy."

Cassidy snorted. "And he probably thinks he's the rightful heir to the treasure."

Flavia said, "Well, actually, doesn't the treasure belong to the drummer boy's family? He's the one who found it."

Cassidy had a fleeting vision of Rory Fiddick's squirrely face and her heart sank, but then she remembered her vow not to judge him harshly. *He only needs a strong hand to guide him. I wonder if Nanny McPhee is available?*

Toby harrumphed. "From what I understand, Catchpole stole it. Therefore it was ill-gotten gains. If it's ever found, it would belong to the State of Maine."

Jasper got up and paced. "You haven't explained how you linked Trent—or rather, Trask—to the Castine incidents."

Cassidy interrupted. "I just thought of something. Remember when we went back to Dyce Head after we rescued Rory? He claimed he'd seen the trapdoor and that he didn't know about the tunnel, but—"

"The hammer." Jasper slapped his knee. "The other grip said he found the hammer on the counter, but I had returned it to the drawer the Friday before. Trask must have been there Monday night."

"I'll bet he was searching for the treasure both that day and the day he shut me in the cellar."

"He hid when Rory came in, then trapped him in the tunnel."

"About that." Toby looked pleased. "Lieutenant Parsons of the Castine police asked an engineer to check for sinkholes along the route of the tunnel. Except for the one where the gate is, there hadn't been any subsidence in the last six months. The blockage was man-made."

Cassidy's stomach reminded her it was past lunchtime, but she wanted to clear up as many details as possible before breaking up the meeting. "Back to the shotgun. Did Trask take the potshots at us too?"

"Parsons doubts it. When they caught the Baker boys with their BB guns on the property, they broke down and admitted they were shooting out the upstairs window. They ran away when they realized someone was in the line of fire."

"What about Trask's red SUV? That was parked at the house when we were chased off. He must have been there."

Toby clucked his tongue. "Maybe so, but he was gone before you came back, right? He saw the boys and took off."

Cassidy wasn't satisfied. "He would have had to drive by us."

"Depends. Did you get off the road at any time?"

She thought back. "We did stop at Fort George and look for Mr. Flint."

"There you are."

"Now I think about it, the BB boys' guilt is more plausible." Jasper was thoughtful. "Trask didn't want us traipsing all over Dyce Head. Shooting at us would only have drawn more attention."

"Which it did. Alfie was ordered to keep an eye on the place after that."

Jeff stuck his head in the door. "There's a bunch of those movie guys outside, Sheriff. They want to talk to you."

"What about?"

"Dunno. But the skinny one seems real upset."

Toby leaned back in his chair. "Show 'em in, then."

Lyle, Stan, and Greg crowded into the already crowded room. Lyle shouldered his way forward, to the obvious displeasure of Stan. "What the hell are you doing, Sheriff? My boy's done nothin' wrong. I demand you release him!" The other two nodded vigorously.

Toby said quietly, "Your boy?"

"Bill! We just heard you'd arrested him for murder. He may be a little on the sneaky side, but he's no killer."

Cassidy hissed, "You might have missed the part where he shot at Miss de Montville. And knocked your director out a window. And smothered the caretaker of Fort George. And stabbed a subcontractor to death. And—"

Jasper laid a hand on her arm. "What makes you think he's innocent, Lyle?"

"I've been working beside him every day. When would he have time to get up to this kind of...of hijinks?"

"Working with you! Don't tell me you and he were partners?"

Cassidy thought of the holes Lyle had dug everywhere. *And he was back and forth between here and Castine as much as any of the crew. Could he actually have been the one in cahoots with Trask?*

"Partners? No. I'm his boss." Lyle gave Jasper a funny look. "I know you're new at this, but you have to know the key grip is in charge of all the grips."

"Of course I do," replied Jasper angrily. "I—"

Toby broke in. "Would you like to see the prisoner?"

Lyle's mouth snapped shut. For a minute he looked like he would refuse, but then Stan spoke up. "Yes, of course."

Flavia stayed in her seat. "You all go along. I've

seen enough of William to last a lifetime."

Pauline said from her couch, "I'll keep her company."

Jeff led the way to the cell. Trask sat glumly on the cot, a tray of uneaten food next to him. He looked up. "What the hell do *you* want?"

Lyle, Stan, and Greg stared at him silently for a long minute. Finally Lyle said, "This isn't him."

Jasper, still annoyed, barked, "Of course it's him. We didn't just pick up a stranger on the street and arrest him."

"It's not Bill."

Trask knit his brows. "Am too."

"Are not."

The conversation threatened to descend into one worthy of Artemus and Digby, when Trask's face cleared. "You thought they'd arrested Little Bill, didn't you?"

Lyle sat back on his heels, his eyes blinking rapidly. "Uh…"

Toby seemed dazed. "Little Bill?"

Stan explained. "Bill Phalen. We have three Bills on the crew—Cartwright, Phalen, and Trent. So one became Billy, one Little Bill, and one Big Bill." He gestured at the prisoner. "That's Big Bill."

Big Bill? He's half the size of Little Bill!

"Who said irony was dead?" An undercurrent of mirth rippling in his voice, Jasper asked, "So where is Little Bill Phalen?"

Greg slapped his forehead. "Damn, I totally forgot. He went to the Walmart in Rockland. Left this morning."

There was a short pause. Finally, Lyle cocked his

head and said, "Um…well. Never mind." They shuffled out. Toby, Cassidy, and Jasper returned to Toby's office.

"*Hmm*." Cassidy's stomach, which all this time had been murmuring hungrily in the background, took matters into its own hands and gave a loud gurgle, which everyone but Jasper politely ignored. Over his snigger, she said, "That brings me to my final question. We didn't tell anyone where we were going when we left Amity Landing to go up to Castine. How did the police know we were there?"

Toby bowed to the actress. "Miss de Montville."

Flavia almost simpered. "I was worried. I mean, after all…" She touched her arm gingerly with a trace of remembered pain. "Someone was out there with a gun. So I called Sheriff Quimby." She bestowed a regal smile upon him. "He did me the honor of taking my concerns seriously."

"We were on our way to Amity to arrest Trask, but when Miss de Montville informed us of your movements, I called the Castine police and alerted them."

Cassidy added, "And when you realized Trask was gone, you hightailed it up to Castine."

Jasper took up the tale. "They arrived in a brigade of squad cars and flashing lights and saw me hanging on to the railing of the lighthouse."

Toby grinned. "A sure sign something was up."

Jasper clapped him on the back. "I was waving my shirt and yelling at the top of my lungs."

Chapter Forty-Five

Cassidy's house, Monday, July 31

"Well, Dad offered Pauline a permanent job. She's moving to LA after we finish the movie."

"That's nice." *The farther away from Jasper the better.* "What about Lyle Korn? I thought they were dating."

"They were…until Lyle heard about her promotion. The horrified look on his face was priceless." At Cassidy's bemused expression, Jasper said mildly, "She can do much better than Korn. For one thing, he's addicted to gambling."

"Why doesn't that surprise me?"

"In fact, she may have already improved on him. I was downtown and noticed Pauline and Little Bill chatting on the sidewalk. They were standing awfully close together."

"I'm glad we're finally down to one Bill."

"Yes. Billy goes by Ralph now. We are much relieved."

Cassidy stole the last bite of Danish from Jasper's plate. "Artemus and Digby seem to be getting along famously. I hear from Maude that they're planning to produce a new movie together right here in Maine."

"Maude?"

"You remember my friend Maude Jewett. She's the

427

one who gave us a lift home the night we tied one on. She's enticed Artemus into a doing a cameo in the Maskers' production of *The Mousetrap*."

"I know." Jasper grinned. "For once, he's more in demand than his brother. It's killing Digby."

Cassidy put down her coffee mug. "You'll be finishing up soon, I suppose."

"Yes." His voice was deliberately casual. "Yes, we will be wrapping in a week or so. Then it's on to post-production."

"And you do that in Los Angeles." *Please God, don't let him hear my voice crack*.

"Yes, but—"

"Halloo there! Cassidy Jane Beauvoir, is that you?"

Cassidy leaned over the railing. "Why, Mrs. Spinney, you're back a day early! Come up and have some coffee."

"Don't mind if I do." The old lady clumped up the stairs and accepted a mug. "I hear there have been some goings on while I was bored to tears at my sister's in Winnipeg. Tell me, should I regret having rented my home to the horde from Hollywood?"

"No, no." Cassidy patted Jasper's hand. "It turned out just fine. This is Jasper MacEwan, director of *American Waterloo*. Jasper? Mrs. Grace Spinney."

"How do you do." Mrs. Spinney gave them each a quick look. "It appears at least one good thing came out of all this." When Cassidy blushed, she turned to Jasper. "I understand a member of your crew was attacking and terrorizing people, all in pursuit of a treasure?"

"Yes. According to my research, General McLean—he was in charge of the Castine incursion—"

"Yes, son. I know all about Fort George and the Penobscot Expedition. After all, McLean commandeered my family's house."

"Oh, right. Anyway, the British brought with them a million gold pounds to enlist the Indians in their cause, but it had disappeared."

Mrs. Spinney coughed delicately. "You've been reading Azeban Glooscap, I take it."

"Why, yes." Jasper waited for her to comment, but she just sat there, a small smile on her lips. After a minute, he went on warily, "It was alleged that a drummer boy purloined the gold and stashed it somewhere. He was caught and imprisoned in the Fort George brig. During the final battle—"

"Rout."

Jasper hesitated. *I bet he can't tell if Mrs. Spinney's humoring him or ragging him.*

"If you insist, rout. Anyway, in the midst of the fracas, one Israel Trask—cabin boy of the privateer the *Black Prince*—escaped. He came upon the drummer boy, who told him about the treasure. Trask then made his way to Canada, where your ancestor, Mercy Spinney, took him in."

Cassidy interrupted. "I've been thinking. If, as the original Trask claimed in his petition to the state of Massachusetts, he couldn't free Horace Catchpole—"

"No, you forget. He confessed to Mercy Spinney that he'd purposely left the boy behind."

"That's true," said Mrs. Spinney comfortably. "The cabin boy had found the trapdoor and cleared the passage. Catchpole was chained to the floor. The drummer boy begged Trask to unshackle him, and to sweeten the deal, told him about the treasure, intimating he would show Trask where it was."

"Exactly what his descendent—William Trask—told us." Jasper peered at the old lady. "How did you know all this?"

Cassidy answered for her. "Remember, the letters that Trask found had been in Mrs. Spinney's house in Westport for generations. I'm sure she read them."

"Oh. Right." He looked to Mrs. Spinney, who gave him an encouraging nod. "But Trask decided not to share."

Cassidy hated to say it out loud. "When he couldn't free Catchpole, did he perhaps do more than simply leave him behind? Did he in fact murder him?"

"No." Mrs. Spinney shook her head in sorrow. "That would have been more humane. Trask told the boy he had to go gather supplies and would come back for him. Instead, he went on his merry way. The boy starved to death."

Jasper clucked his tongue. "But little Horace had the last word."

Mrs. Spinney perked up. "He did? How?"

"He hadn't told him where he buried the treasure. That's why Trask didn't go with the other Americans, but instead wandered the countryside. He was looking for it."

Cassidy added, "He got lost."

"And Mercy took him in."

"Yes, and he confessed to her he'd left Catchpole to die."

In their excitement, they forgot Mrs. Spinney. Jasper faced Cassidy, his silvery eyes alight. "Wait—the letter from the cousin—Sarah? Mercy's secret. We figured it was that he left Horace to die. Could it have been the whereabouts of the treasure instead?"

A piping voice made them pause. "The secret referred to the murder. There was no treasure."

Both Cassidy and Jasper chorused, "Whaaat?"

Mrs. Spinney held out her mug. "May I have some more coffee?"

Cassidy, huffing a little, went inside and brought the pot out. "Cream and sugar?"

"Well, I usually take it black, but for this second cup—yes, I believe I shall indulge. Thank you. There's a dear."

When Cassidy had provided the requested items, and Mrs. Spinney had taken her sweet time adding them, Jasper, teeth gritted, ground out, "Comfortable? Coffee sufficiently blended?"

"Yes, thank you so much, Mr. MacEwan." She took a tentative sip. "It's just right." She fluttered spindly fingers at him. "Now, let's see. Where was I?"

"There was no treasure."

"Ah, yes. Actually, that's not entirely accurate. General McLean had indeed brought a thousand pounds' worth of gold bars from Canada, with which he was instructed to buy the loyalty of the local Indians— the Micmac, the Penobscot, and the Passamaquoddy." She nodded at Cassidy. "His superiors in London were convinced the tribes could be won over, but he was unsuccessful. In fact, a few Penobscots actually fought with the Americans at the battle."

Cassidy felt increasingly restless. *Why doesn't she get to the point?* "Okay, so he couldn't sway the Indians. What happened to the gold then?"

"When he learned of the planned offensive, the general sent it north...in July, before the American armada even arrived. It was safely ensconced in Port Royal when Saltonstall and Lovell—the two commanders of the American forces—were still at sea."

"Well, I never. It wasn't hidden in Dyce Head?"

"Or buried in Witherle Woods?"

She shook her head. "Horace Catchpole was aware the treasure was gone. He gave the cabin boy a song and dance about burying it in order to get Trask to take him along."

"Except his ploy didn't work."

Mrs. Spinney daintily wiped her mouth with a napkin. "So tragic. By all accounts, Master Horace was a decent lad. Just a little mischievous."

" 'Just a little mischievous,' you say. Yet he *was* court-martialed and thrown in the brig. If not for stealing gold, what for?"

"For stealing meat."

This news was greeted with embarrassed silence.

Mrs. Spinney put the napkin on the table and prepared to rise. "I must go. I have a luncheon date with Edna Mae Quimby." Her faded eyes twinkled. "She wants to bring me up to date on local events."

"But Mrs. Spinney! You can't go yet. You have to tell us about the drummer boy!"

She stood but swayed slightly and grabbed the chair back. Cassidy held a hand out to steady her. "Thank you, child. I shouldn't have had that second dose of caffeine. My doctor says it'll be the death of me." She grinned at Jasper and Cassidy. "Anyway, my heart surely doesn't need an *artificial* jolt when there is so much natural stimulation occurring in this little village."

"Are you all right? Do you need some water?"

"No, dear. Just give me a minute to catch my breath. I may as well finish the tale." She sat down again. "As you know, Horace Catchpole was sent to the brig. According to the cook, he was caught with a whole side of bacon in his rucksack."

"Bacon!" Jasper leaned forward. "Was that in the letters?"

"Certainly not. Sarah and Mercy had more important things to discuss than petty misdemeanors in the British ranks."

"Then how do you know all this?"

"From the register, of course."

"What register?"

Mrs. Spinney blinked. "It wasn't in the chest? Oh, my. I guess I forgot to put it back before I shipped it. It must still be up in the Westport house attic. Or no…" Her brow furrowed.

Cassidy tried to mask her impatience. "Mrs. Spinney, what are you talking about?"

"The register—the general's official log. A daily record detailing the activities of the British encampment."

Jasper whistled. "There was only the excerpt from the juror's journal—the eyewitness at Catchpole's court-martial—to go by for our script. I had no idea there was an extant official record. How did you end up with it?"

"Mercy's cousin Sarah found it when she returned to the house after the British left. She put it in the chest for safekeeping, and it went to Mercy along with their correspondence about the cabin boy."

Jasper closed his eyes. "If the court-martial of the drummer boy as recounted in the register only mentioned meat, why did the eyewitness claim he stole the gold?"

"I haven't seen the witness's journal, but what was detailed in Glooscap's book was made up out of whole cloth."

"Glooscap!" Jasper's voice resonated with both curiosity and trepidation. "What's wrong with Azeban Glooscap's work? He's a well-known expert in treasure lore."

Mrs. Spinney said firmly, "On the contrary, Azeban Glooscap is a well-known *humbug* in academic circles. Why, even his name is fictional—it was taken from the Passamaquoddy word for liar."

That's why it sounded so familiar!

"In fact, both Azeban and Glooscap are tricksters in the lore of the Wabenaki tribes of Maine."

Cassidy's attention was momentarily diverted by the gargling sound coming from Jasper. She decided to leave him to his misery. *I guess a dollar was a fair price for the book after all.*

Mrs. Spinney went on. "Glooscap would consider the jailing of a small boy for stealing from the kitchen too dull for his readers. Since he sees boodle under every bush, he, shall we say, massaged the account to render it a bit more dramatic."

Silence followed this revelation, punctuated by snorts and whinnies coming from Jasper's corner. Cassidy finally spluttered, "You say the log is still in the house in Westport. It's strange that Trask didn't find it there. He says he searched it thoroughly."

"Not that thoroughly, I'll wager." Jasper heaved himself out of his chair and his chagrin. He leaned his back against the deck railing. "With both the real estate agent and Flavia in constant attendance, Trask wasn't in a position to turn the house upside down. I doubt they would have let him rummage in the attic. The letters he claimed to find in the desk he had taken from the chest here and planted there."

Cassidy nodded. "That's right. Trask said he'd recovered a pile of letters from the trunk. If the log had also been there—"

Mrs. Spinney apparently hadn't been listening to the conversation, for she started in mid-sentence. "No, I'm wrong. Now it's coming back to me. I didn't leave it in Westport. I brought it down last year with some other papers."

"Well, where is it?"

She chuckled. "Right here in Amity."

"Amity!"

"Yes. In my bedroom."

Jasper stared at her. "Trask combed through every inch of that house. He may have been constrained in Westport, but not here. How could he not have found it?"

Mrs. Spinney blushed. "I feel so silly. I'm not sure I should tell you."

"But Mrs. Spinney! We need that register. We need to know what really happened for the movie!" Jasper was breathing heavily.

"Do you?" The old lady regarded him with an indulgent expression.

Cassidy thought she understood where Mrs. Spinney was going. "Jasper, the movie's in post-production now. It would be very expensive to alter the script—let alone the footage."

"No. That's not it." The old lady laid a wrinkled

435

hand on Jasper's arm. "I hate to say it, but Glooscap's version is so much more cinematic, don't you think? Much better suited to the big screen and modern audiences. I'm sure your father would agree. Philip always likes to *stupendify* things, doesn't he?"

Jasper's mouth snapped shut. "You know my father?"

"Why, yes." The old lady didn't seem to notice his shock. "Didn't he mention it? When he was young, his parents sent him to the summer camp in Nova Scotia where I was director. Such a sweet little boy. Loved to act in the camp skits. I was more than happy to accommodate him when he called this past June about renting my house." She gazed out over the bay. "He once told me his father was not an approachable man. Displays of affection were rare in his family. Very sad."

Cassidy risked a glimpse of Jasper's face. His eyes were damp. He gave a slight sigh. She said quickly, "You must have hidden the log well if Trask couldn't find it."

"Hidden in plain sight." She chortled.

"All right, we give up. Where?"

"You see, that old house has settled over the years, and the upstairs floors aren't exactly level. My bed used to rock badly whenever someone walked down the hall. Quite unsettling. That is, until I stuffed a book under one leg." She folded her hands in her lap. "It was the perfect thickness."

The young couple sat in dumbfounded silence. Mrs. Spinney rose. "Now I really must be going. Thank you so much for the coffee." She descended the stairs carefully and walked down the hill.

Jasper watched her out of sight. "You know, if

436

Trask had found the log, it would have proved the drummer boy was lying to the cabin boy. Trask would have realized his whole enterprise was for naught."

"As were his murders."

Epilogue

Durkee's, Tuesday, August 1

"Wow, what a denouement!" Nellie finished a second plate of eggs. "Golly, I'm starving. This second trimester is worse than the first. I've gained ten pounds, and it's all from healthy food, not what I crave." She pointed out the window. "Everywhere I go, I see beer trucks." She sighed. "I could kill for a Pickytoe Crab Lager."

"Don't use that word, Nell. I've heard it too often this past month." Cassidy sat across from her in a corner booth.

Her friend shrugged. "So, is your beau clearing out with the rest of the crew?"

Thanks a lot. The other subject I don't care to touch. She closed her eyes to hide the sudden glistening of tears. "He has to. They're doing post-production in Burbank. He…he says he'll write."

Nellie scoffed. "That's what Hank said when he joined the Marines. I got a postcard from London and a box of chocolates from Vienna. Filled with marzipan. Currently in the running for the most disgustingly vile foodstuff in the universe."

"Worse than kale?" Cassidy grinned.

"Worse than cottage cheese. And you know I love kale. I'm sick of comedians using it as a punch line. It's delicious." She lapsed into exasperated mumbling.

A UPS van trundled by, going up the hill. "I'll bet he's going to the store. I'd better intercept it." Cassidy ran out of Durkee's and up Main Street, turning left on Church Street. The van was idling in front of Mindful Books. She started to call out but caught sight of the person talking to the delivery man. *Jasper.*

The man handed him a clipboard. Jasper signed it, then turned and saw Cassidy. "Hey there, Cass, my shipment's in. Want to come look?"

"*Your* shipment? I'm expecting a box of remainders from Wild Columbine Publishing. What did you order?"

"You said you've been wanting to expand your Maine history section. The Penhallow *Republican* reported that this professor fellow at Bowdoin College had died and his widow was selling his library, so I bought it."

"Dr. Crenshaw's books? You're kidding! I've been badgering his poor wife for six months. However did you succeed in prying them loose?"

He looked abashed. "I paid an arm and a leg for them, is what I did. Or rather, a steering wheel and a set of fancy tires, along with what goes in-between."

She looked over his shoulder. A beaten-up brown Nissan was parked next to hers. "Isn't that Pauline's car?"

"Well, she doesn't want it now that she's heading to LA, and I needed wheels."

"Miss Beauvoir?" The UPS man had been shuffling his feet, his arms holding a large cardboard box. A dolly piled high with more boxes sat next to him on the sidewalk. "Where do you want these?"

"Oh! Sorry." She unlocked the door. "All the way in the back, please." The man trundled the boxes down the narrow aisle between the book displays. He came back with the empty dolly. "Your package from Columbine was delayed. It should get to Bangor tomorrow. I'll try to have it here by Thursday."

"That's okay. I have Crenshaw's collection to unpack." She licked her lips at the prospect.

Cassidy was heading toward the rear of the shop at a trot when Jasper clasped her arm, holding her back. "Sit." She sat reluctantly. He circled her, cocking his head this way and that.

"Jasper? What are you doing?"

He stopped before her. "Cassidy Jane Beauvoir, do you remember the day we met?"

Every single bob and whistle. "Maybe."

"I told you then that I would do anything to chuck the Hollywood torture mill someday and own a bookstore. Well."

"You're going to buy a bookstore?" Her mouth puckered. "Do they even *read* books in California? I thought they just surfed and watched movies and…and drank dirty martinis."

He rolled his eyes. "Cassidy. I'm not going back to California. I want to stay here in Maine."

"Well, you've picked the right place. With our winters, everyone reads *a lot*. Why, even here in Penhallow we have two bustling bookstores. And in Bangor—"

He placed a firm finger on her lips. "I'd like—if you're agreeable—to buy half of your bookstore. What do you say?"

"You're going to cart it all away? No! I love my

store. You can't..." She gulped. "Just because you're rich doesn't mean you can walk all over people like that. I—" She finally caught sight of his face. *Disgruntled? Peeved? Why should* he *be peeved?*

"Cassidy, do you have an inkling of what I'm asking?"

"You want to take my books away."

"No, I want to give you more books. To wit: Professor Crenshaw's remarkable collection."

"Well, that's okay. But what do you want in return?"

"My name on the front door?"

"How's that going to work?" She got up and, opening the door, scanned the glass. "There's not much room left after Mindful Books and Cassidy Jane Beauvoir, Prop."

He blew out his cheeks. "Well, there's one way I can think of."

Cassidy wracked her brain. "What's that?"

"How about if our names were the same?"

She contemplated a face she had lately been daydreaming about way too much. "You just don't strike me as a Cassidy Jane."

"I meant last name." He held out his hand. "The widow Crenshaw also sold me her grandmother's ring. I know you like emeralds. They go with your eyes."

In the open box on his palm lay a beautiful antique gold ring, set with three square-cut emeralds surrounded by diamonds. She stared at it. He pushed it toward her. "Well?"

"Uh. What about Hollywood?"

"Oh, did I forget to mention it? Dad fired me. He said I was the worst director he'd ever seen. Won't

441

even let me work on post-production. Said I hadn't concentrated enough on the job at hand."

"That's not fair! It's not as though you asked to have a murderer mucking up the film schedule."

"That's what I said, but he was adamant. 'Son,' he said. 'Get thee to a bookstore. No argument.' Oh, and because he took a shine to you, he gave me a small nest egg to get me—us—started. If you'll have me."

"Oh, Jasper."

That was all she said for a while.

A word about the author...

Librarian, anthropologist, research assistant, Congressional aide, speechwriter, nonprofit director— M. S. Spencer has lived or traveled in five of the seven continents. She holds a BA from Vassar College, a diploma in Arabic Studies from the American University in Cairo, and Masters in Anthropology and in Library Science from the University of Chicago. All of this tends to insinuate itself into her works.

Ms. Spencer has published fourteen romantic suspense and mystery novels. She has two fabulous grown children and an exuberant granddaughter and currently divides her time between the Gulf Coast of Florida and a tiny village in Maine.

http://msspencertalespinner.blogspot.com